# PUBLIC RE

**Also by Katie Heaney**

*Never Have I Ever*

*Dear Emma*

# PUBLIC RELATIONS

Katie Heaney &
Arianna Rebolini

GRAND CENTRAL
PUBLISHING

New York Boston Nashville

This book is a work of fiction. Names, characters, places, and incidents are the product of the authors' imagination or are used fictitiously. Any resemblance to actual events, locales, or persons, living or dead, is coincidental.



Grand Central Publishing
Hachette Book Group
1290 Avenue of the Americas, New York, NY 10104
grandcentralpublishing.com
twitter.com/grandcentralpub

First Edition: May 2017

Grand Central Publishing is a division of Hachette Book Group, Inc. The Grand Central Publishing name and logo is a trademark of Hachette Book Group, Inc.

The publisher is not responsible for websites (or their content) that are not owned by the publisher.

Library of Congress Cataloging-in-Publication Data is available upon request.

ISBN 978-1-4555-9568-6 (trade paperback edition)
ISBN 978-1-4555-9567-9 (ebook edition)

Printed in the United States of America

LSC-C

10 9 8 7 6 5 4 3 2 1

*To One Direction, whose music gave us so much,*
*including the idea for this novel.*

# PUBLIC RELATIONS

# 1.

*JOANNA IS GOING TO KILL* ME.

I was already fifteen minutes late getting off the R train, and despite a masterful sprint through Union Square—dodging old men playing chess, and shoppers comparing artisan cheeses at the farmers market, all while wearing a black shift dress and heeled sandals that smacked loudly against the street with each step—I still didn't walk through the door of Weaver-Girard Public Relations until 9:13. Joanna (the Girard of Weaver-Girard, and the head of the firm's music division) likes me to be in the office, her coffee in hand (black, no milk and *obviously* no sugar) by 8:55. As I came to a screeching stop outside her massive, glass-windowed office, a spray of hot coffee leapt from the cup onto the back of my hand. "*Shit*," I hissed, wiping my hand on my dress. When I looked up, ready to receive the scolding of a lifetime, I finally realized that Joanna's office was dark, and she was nowhere to be seen.

"Where have you *been*?"

Harper, my best friend, cubicle mate, and ally in perpetual fear of Joanna, was at my side, taking the now-soggy cup from my hand and throwing it into the garbage bin next to reception.

"Hey," I said. "*I* could have had that."

"Oh my God, you're right," she said. "I don't know what I was thinking, I just panicked."

"What's going on?" I asked. "Where's Joanna?"

"She flew to Dubai," she whispered. "Left an hour ago. Trevor sent for her."

"Oh my *God*," I said. Trevor James was Weaver-Girard's biggest client, on both sides. He was twenty-seven years old, had three platinum rap albums and an always-intricate blond undercut, and was a complete and total drama queen. He was the only client big enough to have Joanna herself on call, and the only one for whom she'd do just about anything. Even, apparently, flying to Dubai last-minute on the morning of the firm's first meeting with its *second*-biggest client, who'd broken up with his previous publicity team after a major dip in sales. "What about Archie Fox?" I asked.

"Have you not been checking your email?" hissed Harper. "What's wrong with you?"

"I was underground!"

Instead of giving me an explanation, Harper rolled her eyes and walked off in the direction of our desks. Because Harper was about seven feet tall, I practically had to jog to keep up.

"She's sending you in," said Harper, once we were safe within the (relative) privacy of our cube.

"What do you mean, 'sending me in'?" Surely she wouldn't ask *me* to take coffee orders in the Archie Fox meeting. *That's supposed to be the administrative assistant's job*, I thought, tightening my jaw in annoyance. It was bad enough I had to bring hers every day. I might have been, at twenty-six, one of the younger people on staff, but I certainly wasn't green. I'd been promoted to media relations associate more quickly than anyone in company history, or so I'd been told.

"To the meeting," said Harper, the *duh* implied. "In her place."

"What?" I was sure I'd heard her wrong. "Like. On her behalf?"

"Yeah," said Harper. "Read your email for once."

She folded her hands on top of her desk and raised her eyebrows at me, clearly planning to watch me while I logged into my account. Even though I'd been warned, my heart still started racing when I opened my inbox and saw four separate emails from Joanna at the top. Each of the subject lines began with URGENT.

I opened the most recent first, and read aloud:

> Seriously, Rose, I almost hope you actually *are* dead, because at least then I'd know I hadn't been completely insane when I promoted you last month, and it's not that you're suddenly and inexplicably UNREACHABLE, but that you've been run over by a bus.

I looked back at Harper, who was doing a very bad job pretending not to laugh.

I continued to read:

> If you ARE still alive, and want any hope of redeeming yourself for falling so maddeningly silent these past sixty minutes, you will go to my 10:00 a.m. As you have, no doubt, already heard, we're working on putting together a rebrand package for Archie Fox. Weaver, Daniels, and Fitz will all be there, so your job is more or less to be

the music person in the room. Do not mistake me—this does not mean that you should speak. Don't look at anyone more than necessary, and *especially* not Archie. Take detailed notes, and email them to me immediately afterward. You are ONLY there to keep them accountable. Do you understand? Please, for the love of God, email me before 10:00 to tell me you understand.

Joanna.

I got to the end of the email and shook my head, feeling both terrified and incredibly flattered that Joanna Girard had referred to *me* as a "music person." I looked back over to Harper.

"You are so lucky," she said.

"How do you figure?" I asked, but of course I knew what she meant. Joanna was terrifying, and the other three were even worse. I was about to be in way, way over my head.

But I was also about to meet Archie Fox—effortlessly charming, famously flirty, boyishly handsome Archie Fox, international pop star and the number one crush of, oh, about a billion or two women worldwide. I typed up a quick reply to Joanna's email (`I'm sorry for my delayed response. I understand, and I'll be there.`), and before I could back out of the whole thing altogether, I pressed SEND.

---

What I knew about Archie Fox before walking into the meeting was as follows: He was twenty-four years old, British, and blew up about five years ago when an amateur video of one of his open-mike-night performances got a million views on

YouTube within thirty-six hours. Unlike many YouTube sensations, however, he actually had the goods to support a career, and before the world even had time to process what was happening, his dimpled smile and shaggy hair were everywhere. Not that I could complain about that; he had one or two songs that I really liked—maybe not the kind of tracks I'd ever put on a party playlist (not if I was trying to impress people with my eclectic tastes, anyway), but the kind of thing I'd happily sing along to in the car. He seemed charming in person, speaking in a slow, deep drawl—though there was less of that now that he was ducking out of interviews, avoiding paparazzi, and blowing off red carpets. And that was kind of the problem.

"Okay, wait, remind me where he is in the tour right now," I said.

Harper sized me up with her arms crossed, and then reached over to unravel the black velvet ribbon she had just wrapped around my neck.

"He just finished up in Europe. Oh my God, you didn't see that Vine from his last night in Madrid? With the hip thrust?" She tossed her head back in feigned ecstasy. "It probably killed about ten thousand girls in that stadium."

"No, somehow I missed that one," I said while she held her leather jacket up against my chest. "I need you to stop transferring your entire outfit onto me before you're naked, okay?"

"Listen, don't blame me when Archie's like, *Oy, right, I'd quite fancy the brunette if it weren't for that totally shapeless dress, mate.*"

"Did he just become a pirate? Is *that* what the meeting is about?"

"Shut up." She shoved me, laughing. "Just put on the jacket. It'll look cool."

"I don't need to look cool, Harp. Fancying me isn't exactly the goal here." I put the jacket back in her hand. "Wait—what's the name of that song of his that everyone likes, off the last album?" While I was obviously familiar with Archie Fox's debut—there couldn't be many people left worldwide who weren't—I wasn't exactly a fangirl.

"You think he's gonna quiz you?"

"You never know."

"You're not even supposed to talk!"

I looked at my watch—9:47. I ran back to my computer and quickly scanned the other emails from Joanna. When I found the song, I choked on a laugh.

"'Kiss Me, Kill Me,'" I told Harper, miming a knife to the chest.

"Be nice!" she shouted to me as I dashed down the hall.

## 2.

My journey to PR was indirect, slightly arbitrary, and catalyzed almost entirely by Joanna, though I'd never told her as much. I grew up in the Bay Area, certain I'd be a music journalist, I guess because no one thought to warn me the industry was dead. In the defense of my parents, teachers, childhood friends—anyone whose proximity to me meant listening to my tales of future rock journalism stardom, really—the industry was putting up a decent fight back then. People were still reading (and writing about) Joel Selvin's column in the *Chronicle*, and you could find copies of music monthlies and biweeklies (real, tangible zines!) stacked at coffeehouses and record shops. I passed summer afternoons cycling through my parents' records (Jackson 5, Blondie, and Hall & Oates were on heavy rotation) and, as soon as I started getting one, I spent my allowance on my own growing collection, sourced mostly from Amoeba. (My first: Fiona Apple's *When the Pawn...*, whose lyrics sailed way over my nine-year-old head, but which nevertheless stirred in me a confused but steadfast and righteous sense of angst.)

While most of my classmates were figuring out how to

pronounce *Hermione*, I was asking the Internet what *seminal* meant, or when shoegaze started. When they began cryptically blogging on their LiveJournals about secret crushes, I was mimicking all of my favorite critics at heartofglass777.xanga.com. When I started dating Dave, my first (and, honestly, only real) boyfriend, at the end of ninth grade, we spent our first of six summers together dragging each other to any and every gig that would let under-eighteen kids in, as well as any basement show that didn't pretend to care. *How lucky am I?* I'd think as we got closer to graduation, whenever my classmates and friends agonized over what the rest of their lives would be, and how they were going to get there. I knew exactly where I was going.

Here's what the plan looked like: NYU, with a double major in music and journalism. First year dorm (Hayden Hall, ideally) to get the full college experience, until sophomore year, when Dave—who would be studying comparative literature at the New School—and I could get a sweet little studio in Greenwich Village. Or Soho. Honestly (I'd tell anyone who'd listen), I would happily live anywhere that would place us within walking distance of the Bowery. I'd get internships at any and every music publication: *Village Voice*, to start, then maybe *Spin* or something super indie like *Paper*, until I was ready for my holy grail, *Rolling Stone*. There I would prove myself so capable, and so precocious, that I'd be offered a position in my final semester. This would, of course, lead to bestselling anthologies of critical essays, not that I was getting ahead of myself or anything. And in any free time throughout these years, Dave and I would gallivant around every musical landmark in the big city and drink it all up, having already sucked our home scene dry.

Only about a quarter of the plan came to fruition, and that's probably me being generous. I did get into NYU (early decision) and arrived at Weinstein Hall with two suitcases, no fewer than thirty magazine cutouts and CD covers to plaster over the prison-like cinder-block walls, and a canned answer ready for anyone who asked: Rose Reed from California, already declared, journalism major with a concentration in music. Of course, the last part hardly mattered. I hadn't yet learned that unless a person was pre-med or pre-law, first-year curricula were pretty much indistinguishable among the students. Still, my conviction seemed important. Yes, I'd sit through the generic natural science class and statistics for beginners, but at least I knew what was coming after they were out of the way. I had the rest of my years blocked out in my head, and even went so far as to introduce myself to the professors I wanted to recognize me. I studied hard my freshman year; I did well. I made a few friends. I developed a friendship-esque concord with my roommate, which I took as pretty lucky, considering the horror stories of passive aggression (or outright aggression) I'd heard from other incoming freshmen. Life didn't seem all that different from how it'd been in years prior; it was just unfolding in front of a different backdrop. I went to shows, I trawled through discount bins at record stores, and I did most of my socializing with Dave and his friends.

The first crack to weaken my plan came in the form of a sparse email from Pitchfork, which arrived in my inbox in mid-March of my freshman year. The letter informed me that despite my "obvious talents," I hadn't been accepted into their summer fellowship program, but I was urged to please try again next year. Soon after came similarly phrased rejections from *Spin*, the *Village Voice*, *New York Magazine*, and *Rolling*

*Stone*. Each time, Dave arrived at my door with a pick-me-up in hand—flowers the first time around, then the boxed set of the third season (the best) of *The X-Files*, and then, eventually, just cartons of ice cream. He patted me on the back, assuring me this wasn't the end of the world, while I wished I hadn't broadcasted every aspect of my plan so widely. After the fourth rejection, he gingerly asked if I was pursuing other options, adopting that tone people use when they've decided your dream is a bust, but they're trying to gauge whether or not you've figured that out yourself. Our favorite coffee shop was hiring baristas for the summer, he reminded me, and didn't I make a mean cup of coffee? And, honestly, he said, he'd always thought waiting tables seemed kind of fun. All of this was easy for him to consider, because for him it was a distant hypothetical—he'd gotten his dream job on the first try, an editorial internship at Macmillan.

For my part, I wasn't keen on giving up quite yet. By late April, I was back into the job listings, scouring the Internet for any outlets or publications that still had summer positions open. I applied for anything that would land me in the same room as working writers—internships or fellowships in social media, marketing, communications, copywriting, something called "social storytelling"—which, to be honest, I was hoping to get just so I could find out what the position entailed. Finally I was offered a position as an editorial intern at The Dish, a gossipy pop-culture site with a sizable following. It was technically unpaid but came with a stipend, and the man who would be my boss assured me it wasn't like *other* internships where I'd ended up ordering lunches and doing grunt work. I'd be learning. I'd fact-check, take notes, and sit in on brainstorms. I wasn't on the music team per se, but nightlife was within my purview—and what did people do in cities at night if not see live shows? I fantasized about casually dropping details regarding the concerts I was planning to attend that summer in the vicinity of some editor I hadn't yet met, who would of course immediately suggest I write up a review. It was as if the offer wiped my mind clear of the rejections that led to it. I was thrilled.

About three weeks after my first day on the job, the thrill had worn off. My boss was true to his word, and I did work closely with writers, but it turned out I didn't like many of them. I was certain the feeling was mutual. Most were in their early twenties—usually no more than five years older than me—but this didn't stop them from posturing as old pros, seasoned cultural critics already disillusioned by the entire entertainment industry.

In simpler words, they were snobs, but not even in the way I would have expected. They didn't lord their extensive knowledge of music or movies over me, but they did gawk whenever I revealed I hadn't read whichever essay they were talking about that day. Their version of one-upping seemed to consist entirely of name-dropping and gaining Twitter followers. There was a lot of whining. Still, I developed valuable skills. I got comfortable sending professional emails. I learned how to convert news items into flashy and succinct articles people would actually read. I was introduced to the wonders of Gchat. But the most meaningful aspect of my time at The Dish was my access to the occasional interview whenever actors or singers were brought into the office. One interview in particular—with a singer named Michaela Jones—changed everything.

Michaela had fronted a pop-punk band in the early 2000s, disappeared for some time, and recently returned, newly reborn as a folksy solo artist. I was obsessed with her. I knew Anthony, the guy who was spearheading the interview; he wrote pithy album reviews that ran down a sidebar on the music page, and we'd bonded over our shared tastes. He was my closest thing to a work friend, and I was nearing the end of my time there anyway, so I figured, *Well, why not?* I sidled over to his desk while he was eating lunch (this would be another lasting lesson—no one who wants to get anywhere in New York takes lunch breaks) and asked if he was looking for any assistance regarding the interview—maybe some brainstorming or research, or even, if it would be helpful, someone else in the room?

Anthony obliged, and two days later I was standing at the door of our photo studio, eyeing the office entrance. Michaela arrived with a small entourage in tow, but one woman in particular piqued my interest. I guessed she was the publicist, mainly because of the way she walked across the office—confident gait, eyes never leaving her phone. She was tall and lean, in a sheer white button-up with sleeves rolled to the elbow and flowing high-waisted pants that made her legs look about a mile long. She wore her hair natural, cropped close to her head, and her face was bare save for bright-red lips. Michaela introduced herself to Anthony, our photographer, and me, and gazed around the room while the publicist's thumbs danced wildly over her phone. It was clear she was running the show. She finally dropped the phone in her purse and offered her hand. She introduced herself as Joanna Girard, thanked us all for inviting Michaela, and then ran through a short list of topics her client wouldn't be discussing.

"No being cute," she said. "When I say she won't discuss it, I mean she will not discuss it." She flashed a shining smile and retreated to the back wall, where she stayed, eyes glued again to her phone, for most of the interview.

Anthony led the conversation, focusing often on Michaela's love and social life, frequently flirting with the verboten topics. I got some questions in about her plans to do more songwriting, and what it was like to tour without a band. When Anthony decided to push his luck and bring up Michaela's rumored affair with another (married) singer, it was as if he'd pulled the fire alarm. Within seconds Joanna had gathered up her and Michaela's bags, and then ushered her out the door, ignoring Anthony's trailing apologies and pleas for their return. Joanna didn't even look back. It was incredible. The room felt electric, and I knew: *That* was the kind of impact I wanted to have.

Now, seven years later, I channeled that energy as I walked toward the conference room where I knew the Three-Headed Dog (which was what Harper and I sometimes called Ryan Weaver, Sam Daniels, and Keiran Fitz—because they were always together, and equally slimy) was waiting for me. I'd expected to get there comfortably before Archie Fox & Team, because Archie Fox was a rock star, and rock stars get places late. I'd counted on greeting the guys, settling into my chair, and then having a few moments for additional, covert research on my phone. But when I opened the door, the first person I saw wasn't Ryan, Sam, or Keiran.

It was Archie Fox.

At the sound of my entrance, the room fell silent, and everyone, including Archie, who was seated at the far corner opposite me, and a woman in her forties, whom I presumed to be Archie's manager, looked up. I allowed myself to hold Archie's eye but only for a second for fear I might seem like a wannabe fangirl instead of a professional. It was enough time to confirm three things: One, that he looked extremely tired; two, that he was significantly broader, and slightly older-looking, than I'd imagined him to be; and three, that he was really very cute. This last part made me particularly annoyed—at him, for having the nerve, and at myself, for being just as susceptible to his face as everyone else.

"Are you planning to sit?" asked Ryan. Sam and Keiran exchanged looks, and I felt my face flush as I scrambled to pull a chair out from the table.

"As I was saying," said Ryan, "we're grateful to you both for making the time to meet with us. Archie, I know you're mid-tour, so—"

"Sorry, what's your name?" asked Archie.

I was busy setting up my laptop to take notes, so it took me a moment of collective silence to realize that Archie had been talking to me. I looked up.

"Oh," said Ryan, "that's—she's just—she's just here on Joanna's behalf. Joanna sends her apologies, of course, we—"

"Rose," I said. I was blushing again, but Archie was still looking at me, and even though I had been told not to speak I figured I was allowed to answer direct questions. This one, at least.

"Rose," Archie repeated. "I'm Archie."

"I know," I said, sounding a bit more irritated than I had intended. I was surprised to see a slight twitch around his mouth. He leaned back into his chair, folding his arms across his chest, so that the thin arrow that stretched across his tattoo-covered right forearm formed a perfect parallel with the conference table.

"Right," interjected Ryan. "So, as I was saying, thrilled to have you here. We've got a few excellent outreach ideas that will really get the momentum going ahead of the album release. I think you're really going to love them. Keiran, you want to start?"

"Absolutely," said Keiran, directing that shit-eating grin of his toward Archie before taking a folder from a small stack that sat on the table next to him. Because he worked primarily under Ryan, Keiran usually worked with actors, but I'd always had the feeling he wanted to switch to music, and now I was sure of it. "Mission 5 has shown *serious* interest in having you as a spokesmodel, which we think is a great fit." Like a slow-motion car wreck, I watched Keiran open the folder to reveal a series of mock-up print ads featuring Archie Fox's face Photoshopped onto the bodies of models wearing Mission 5's trademark bro-tastic beachwear.

"I don't know..." Archie began, pausing for what felt like a full minute before closing his mouth again.

"I don't think we're interested in the spokesmodel approach," said his manager, smiling tightly. Under the table, I did a quick Google search for *Archie Fox manager.* Maria Bird. *Right,* I thought, remembering hearing Joanna speak in half-frustrated, half-admiring tones about the blunt, no-nonsense Maria.

"It's great visibility," said Keiran, grinning again as the vein in his forehead that showed up when he was challenged by anyone appeared. "Mission 5 has great recognition for the thirteen-to-seventeen demo."

Thirteen-to-seventeen-year-old *boys,* I thought. And no one, of any gender, over the age of sixteen thought Mission 5 was cool. I didn't care what Keiran's market research said. He was wrong, and I knew it, but I bit my tongue. Joanna had told me to be silent.

"Let's hear the next one," said Archie, with a curt nod.

"Of course," said Keiran. "Modeling's not your thing. Got it."

"You sure have the hair for it, though!" said Sam. At that, I probably winced visibly.

"Ah, well, thanks, mate," said Archie. Then, before I had time to look away, he looked right at me—just for a second, without moving his head, and so fast I could have convinced myself I was crazy. I looked back at my notepad.

"All right," said Keiran, shuffling through the folders. "Sam? Do you . . . ?"

"Have you considered vlogging?" asked Sam.

Much to my horror, I snorted. I immediately tried to play it off as a cough, but one glance in Archie's direction confirmed that he, at least, did not buy it.

"Vlogging?" he asked with, to his credit, an almost-believable look of consideration. This apparently was invitation enough for Sam to dive right in.

"Video blogging. It's the most direct and efficient route to your audience," he said, passing a one-sheet around the table. "Mikey Trick, for example, started a weekly video-diary-style show three months ago—single camera, low production cost—and since then, his subscribers have nearly tripled."

"His YouTube subscribers, you mean," said Archie with one eyebrow raised. Keiran and Sam exchanged nervous glances, but Ryan apparently got the point.

"Which, of course, isn't exactly where you need more of a following."

"Right," Sam said. "Your YouTubers *love* you. I've seen the videos of the, like, ten-year-old girls going fucking *nuts* screaming and crying. Insane!" He laughed, a series of truncated honks, and leaned in toward Archie clearly hoping to bond. But Archie only replied with a close-lipped smile. "Ah, but, um—" Sam cleared his throat. "—that doesn't mean there aren't more kids out there who could fall in love with you, too!" *Kids?* I couldn't believe the tone Sam was taking. If Archie's fans had been teenage boys rather than girls, he (and Keiran, for that matter) would have taken this assignment more seriously. I was sure of it.

"You could also go multiplatform," Keiran said, jumping in. "Bring in some guests—maybe those Vine guys who are always doing those hilarious animal impressions? Then they show clips on their Vines, they get more views, more Vine traction for you."

"Okay, okay, everyone hold on," said Archie, hands raised and laughing. "Please, just—no one say 'Vine' again."

I'd never seen Sam and Keiran look so nervous. I didn't hate it.

"It's just that audience expansion on . . . a new platform like that . . . it could be good, don't you think?" Ryan said. He glanced at Maria, who did not look up from her phone.

"And I appreciate that, but unfortunately I'm not a talk-show host, nor do I care to share with the world my 'video diaries.' " On this, Archie made mocking air quotes, and I had to swallow hard to keep from snickering. He turned his glance toward me. "Rose, right? Tell me—do you have your phone with you?"

I felt blood rush to my ears. "Well, yes, um. We all do . . ." If I was going down for that, I was taking Ryan, Sam, and Keiran with me.

"Don't worry, I'm not some monster who requires his team leave their electronic devices at the door."

His team. I got goose bumps, even if it was just a figure of speech, I felt like I was finally getting a seat at the big kids' table. I would've savored the moment if his questioning expression hadn't immediately pulled me out of my reverie.

"Well? Can you pull it up for me? Your most recently played tracks."

"She's really not—" Ryan stammered.

"Archie..." Maria said, with an air of quieting condescension, a tone I guessed she'd spent years perfecting.

"No, no, I'm just curious," said Archie. "Rose...?"

"Reed," I supplied. What the hell was going on? And was there any god I could pray to who would magically place Archie Fox in my recently played tracks?

"Rose Reed hasn't said a word, and, no offense, mates, she's kind of more my demographic. So, Rose. No wrong answers here. I just want to know. Who do you listen to, and, of those artists, which of them are also spokespeople or animal impressionists or vloggers?"

I avoided the stares of the Three-Headed Dog. "None of them."

Archie turned to the room in victory. "I rest my case." He turned back to me. "You didn't answer the first part of the question, though."

"That wasn't the important part," I said. I hadn't expected him to be quite so cocky.

"We'll come back to it. So, boys, I'm sorry to be so direct, but any other ideas?" I couldn't be sure, but I hoped that Archie's use of the term "boys" there was intentional.

Keiran looked to Ryan, who wordlessly gave him permission to continue.

"Well, we think it'd be good for you to be seen with someone else who's trending right now," he said, adding, almost frantically, "Another musician, of course."

Archie leaned back in his chair and ran his hand through his hair. He looked at Maria and shrugged. She looked from him to the three men. "Who did you have in mind?" she asked.

"Madison Keener," said Keiran, his palms pressed flat against the table as if even he could not believe the genius behind the name he'd just spoken.

I risked another quick glance toward Archie and noticed, again, that same little twitch of the lips.

"What do you think?" asked Ryan, sounding palpably nervous.

"She seems like a very nice young lady," said Archie, slowly.

"And hot," said Sam. I rolled my hand into a fist and pressed it into my mouth to keep myself from saying *ew*.

"I think she's a bit... wholesome? For my client?" said Maria. She was trying as hard as Archie was to be polite, but the message was loud and clear—not to mention something anyone who'd picked up a tabloid in the last year should have already known: Madison Keener was boring as hell, a one-trick pony who'd stretched that one trick over three bubbly and impossibly grating singles.

"Understood," said Ryan. "Another direction, got it. What about..." Here he paused to read off a sheet of paper in front of him. "... Dame Wallis?"

*Oh God*, I thought. *No.*

"Ah," said Archie. "Well."

"Not into her?" asked Sam. "Not really my type, either, have to say."

"It's not that," said Archie. "It's just, I'm rather inclined to think it's her who wouldn't be into me."

"No," Keiran practically purred. "Come on, dude, don't be modest." (*Did Keiran Fitz just call Archie Fox "dude"?* I thought. I wished that I would evaporate into the air.) "What woman wouldn't be into *you*?"

"She's gay," I said. I figured I'd already broken Joanna's command once. It was too late for me, and I couldn't bear to let Keiran, Sam, and Ryan embarrass themselves—and, by proxy, Joanna—any further.

The men looked at me, and then at Archie, as if for confirmation. He simply smiled.

"Apparently she's dating that French tennis player, something Marchand?" said Maria. "There was an item in the *Star* last week."

"Ah," said Ryan. "My apologies. British gossip doesn't always make it across the pond."

It was mortifying, really. Joanna didn't work with actors, but she at least kept up to date with celebrity gossip at large. But if a celebrity existed outside Ryan's sphere, he couldn't be bothered.

"What about Raya?" I asked.

I'd heard the phrase "You could cut the tension with a knife" plenty of times in my life, but had never truly understood it until this very moment. Ryan, Sam, and Keiran looked at me with as much disgust as if I had leapt across the table and asked for an autograph. Maria and Archie wore expressions of more decided amusement. Regardless, every eye in the room was on me.

"She's up-and-coming," I said, shrugging. "She's young. She's cool." All of which was true. Raya, the otherworldly-looking singer/songwriter/animal rights activist/style icon, was infuriatingly cool.

The kind of cool that, somehow, seemed intrinsic to her personality. Like she slid out of the birth canal with pale-blue hair and a coy smile, and her mom was like, *Huh, that's it? What a breeze.* She was only twenty (I was still coming to terms with the fact that I'd reached the point in life after which every new pop star would be younger than me), but she had this air about her that suggested she was wise beyond her years. Her Instagram was filled with gray-tinted photos of mugs of loose-leaf tea and tarot cards and, like, the scarf she was knitting. I was obsessed with her.

Archie's eyebrows rose. "I didn't know Raya had reached corporate-level recognition." She hadn't; he was right. The only reason I knew anything about her was that I'd heard her song straining over the crowd at a warehouse dance party in Bushwick, one of the places I went to hear new music, and had researched her thoroughly as soon as I got home. As of now, though, Raya was still only releasing tracks here and there on SoundCloud. *Complex* had given her a little blurb as a person to watch, but it was a Web-only list. The chances of her being on Ryan's radar were slim to none.

"Oh, of course," said Sam, eyeing his phone under the table. "We're *huge* fans of... Head Bush. Rush. Head Rush."

"I think we can probably make that work. Archie?"

He was rubbing his face with the butts of his palms, his cheeks and temples flushed red. He looked exhausted by the meeting—which had been going on for roughly fifteen minutes, but felt like hours—and I didn't blame him.

"I like Raya," he finally said. "I'm a fan of her music. We've crossed paths once or twice, and I've found her to be good company." He chuckled. "But what are we going to do, have my people hand a note to her people: *Does Raya like Archie? Check the box, yes or no*? Couldn't I just give her a quick ring?" *There* was that charm he was famous for, I thought. It had been a while since anyone had seen it.

"In a simpler world, yes." Ryan rose from his chair and patted Archie on the shoulder with an almost-wistful look—like he was a father giving his son dating advice, unaware that his son had been messing around with girls in the backs of cars for years. I caught a glance from Archie and tried to stifle a laugh when his eyes widened slightly in bewilderment. "But that's what *we're* all here for," Ryan continued, gesturing to the room. "Besides, it'll make much more of an impression on her if she's contacted by your team. She'll know she's playing in the big leagues. Really wow her."

I doubted any woman with even an ounce of heterosexual interest in her body needed much wow-ing to be convinced to have dinner with Archie, but I held my tongue.

"Are we sure this is the *best* choice, though?" Keiran piped up. "I mean, personally, I'm a huge fan, but it's no secret that she isn't exactly topping the charts, right? And the whole point is to increase visibility, is it not?"

I rolled my eyes without thinking, and hoped no one had noticed. That bubble burst in a microsecond when I heard Archie snicker and saw Ryan shooting daggers in my direction. "Is there something you wanted to say, Rose?" he asked, turning the room's attention to me. I'd never heard my name said with such precise derision.

"Enlighten us," said Sam. He and Keiran—both just a few years older than me and forever resentful of the fact that I seemed to be moving up the ranks faster than they ever did—shared a look of anticipation, sure I was about to dig myself into a deeper hole. Unfortunately for them, I was promoted for a reason: I'm *really* good at my job. Even though I wasn't typically one to veer from my own strict, ordered, deliberate vision of my professional path, and even though I feared a swift retribution from Joanna, something deep inside me told me I needed to speak up, to trust that I had something worthwhile to say.

"Actually, yes, since you asked," I said, rising out of my own chair and walking across the room to stand directly behind Sam and Keiran.

My heart and mind were racing; my adrenaline was pumping. Since being hired at Weaver-Girard, the only other time I'd spoken out of turn so publicly—at an all-hands staff meeting, when I'd delivered an impromptu and impassioned tirade about the legitimacy of teen bloggers as tastemakers in fashion and music—the outburst was followed shortly thereafter by my promotion. I had never spoken so freely in front of a client, though, and there was a chance the consequences could be a little less positive. But at this point, I was all in.

"We're worried Archie isn't going to sell enough copies of his next record, right?" I saw varying levels of shock on the faces around me. "I'm sorry to be blunt, but we all know that's why we're here."

Archie shrugged but made no move to interrupt me.

"That's not, on its own, a bad thing. Fear is good! Better to have this discussion now than after the fact, when we're figuring out how to come back from an album that's already tanked. Like your last one." Archie's eyes widened ever so slightly.

"Yes, that is our job," said Ryan. I'd struck a nerve. It was always the male higher-ups who so easily turned defensive; honestly, I was never sure how they'd made it up so high with egos so fragile. "Thank you for explaining how PR works, but unless you have any thoughts on this specific idea..."

"You're right, I'm sorry, I do." I wasn't about to stop now. There was a decent chance I was speaking in my very last meeting as an employee at Weaver-Girard, so I figured I'd make the most of it. Besides, what I was about to say was right. It was my job to make them realize that. "We know better than anyone else: If someone is famous, it means their peak is behind them. Archie's held international attention for a few years now—which is admirable—but the audience who loved him from the beginning are aging out of the music-buying, concert-attending demographic."

I looked at Archie, who seemed more skeptical than he'd been just a moment ago.

"I know, this is more calculated than you want to believe the life of the artist is, but you started in this business when you were, what, nineteen? You know it's the truth. And contrary to what I *think* you're thinking, fame doesn't have to mean sacrificing substance. Which is why Raya is perfect. She's going to be huge. She's been seen at every big summer festival. Last year because of what she was wearing, but this year because she's popping up on stages. There isn't one big-name DJ who doesn't have her in his set list. But she also writes her own music—which you've already said you like—and her songs are also selling this idea of...self-sufficiency, self-respect. Smart rebellion. Young girls are obsessed with her. They feel like they know her because she's constantly engaging with them on Tumblr and Instagram. And so if this girl, this fantasy stand-in for themselves, is suddenly seen all over the place with that British singer their older sister used to love? Well, maybe that guy's worth checking out, too."

If my life were a movie, this would have been the point at which someone (Ryan, probably? Or Archie—more handsome) led a gradual standing ovation with nothing but a slow clap. The reality—"Sounds good to me," from Maria, and a shrug from Archie—was exponentially less exciting, but satisfying nonetheless, if only for the fact that I could tell it really got under Sam and Keiran's skin. Ryan wasn't happy to be upstaged, but still, a win for me was a win for the firm, which, most important, was a win for him. It didn't matter who presented the idea, necessarily, as long as it was well received as our collective genius.

"Well!" Ryan lifted his arms in pride, as if everything that had happened in the last six minutes were exactly what he had planned. "It sounds like we have a winning idea."

Archie shifted his weight in his seat. "If the idea is that I hang out with an artist I've met before, whose company I would've likely sought out regardless, then I suppose so." He tossed his head back and muttered to the ceiling, "But I still think we could have executed this on our own."

*Aww*, I thought. *It's like a little sex-idol temper tantrum.*

Maria's already-dwindling well of patience had apparently run dry. "But you didn't, kid," she said, simultaneously typing on her phone and flipping through the pages of the old-fashioned analog day planner in front of her. "So Archie's got five days here in New York, then it's pretty much a show a night up and down the eastern seaboard."

"He's got that seventy-two-hour window between Montreal and Boston?" Ryan's eyes were glued to his phone; Sam and Keiran were scrolling wildly just trying to keep up.

"Not the most exciting spot," said Maria.

"Or romantic." Ryan and Maria shared a laugh without even looking at each other. It was almost mesmerizing.

"What about pushing to August?" Maria suggested.

"That's too late," said Ryan. "We want him still on tour. We want the rumors already confirmed by then." It was the least romantic way I could possibly imagine discussing a new, young relationship, but these celebrity couplings were never much more than business dealings anyway. The thing was, Raya was actually doing a show in New York in a week, opening for Brigantine, the latest chart-topping four-piece of white dudes with asymmetrical haircuts and neckbeards. I knew this because I'd been desperately Googling her under the table. I'd sort of hoped I wouldn't have to be the one to announce it—certain, or at least hopeful, that someone on either team would figure it out—but at this point I couldn't just sit with it any longer.

"So, Raya's actually doing a show at SummerStage in a week?" I offered, wincing at my nervous upspeak. "Well, opening a show."

"Oh, duh!" Maria shut her planner.

"Great," said Ryan, with a too-wide smile and slightly flared nostrils. I knew then that it would be in my best interest to get out of that room as quickly as possible. "We'll reach out to Pilar, Raya's manager—old friends from my time in the LA office. And Keiran will be your point person, so let me make sure you have his direct line."

"Oh no, we want the girl," said Maria. My heart stopped. She couldn't mean me, right? Surely she was referring to Joanna... but with an incredible lack of professionalism?

"Unfortunately, Joanna simply has too much on her plate

with Trevor." It appeared Ryan was hoping for a rude client rather than an insubordinate one.

"You know I don't mean Joanna, Ryan," Maria shot back.

Okay. Archie Fox's manager was requesting me as his point person. Sure! I tried to remain calm. I could do this. It was my idea that had won her over to begin with. I mean, that *was* it, right? *Of course that was it,* I told myself. *This will be a* good *thing.* Still, I couldn't ignore the nagging hope that Ryan would shut it down. I looked from Maria to Ryan—both looking at each other—to Archie, who was looking squarely at me. I swallowed hard.

"Maria, you know I have the utmost respect for you," said Ryan, "but Rose really doesn't handle these sorts of projects. She works more in an assistance capacity for Joanna. Keiran has much more experience in this arena. Rose understands—right, Rose?" He winked at me.

*Fuck this, and fuck Ryan, and fuck Keiran,* I thought, beginning to grin like a crazy person. Now I actually wanted it.

"To be quite honest, it seems like Rose is more experienced in this 'arena' than any of you," said Archie. Again with the air quotes. "I don't mean any disrespect. And I'm not saying the idea's a terrible one, but if I'm going to do it, I want to work with her."

I was simultaneously vindicated, terrified, proud, and slightly nauseated. It was, needless to say, a new sensation.

"Archie," began Keiran, quickly seeing his misstep in Ryan's eyes. "I'm sorry, Mr. Fox. I know we don't know each other well—"

"Quite an understatement, mate, we've met just once before."

Keiran laughed nervously, and Sam squirmed in his chair. "Right, yes, well. What I mean to say is, you can still trust me."

"I'm sure," said Archie. He swiveled to face me and shot me that deadly smile. "But I don't know, I just get the feeling I'd get on better with Rose. What do you say, Ms. Reed?"

"Um, sure," I said. "I mean, yes. Agreed." I wished for swift death. It didn't come.

"Great," said Maria, standing up and signaling the end of the meeting. The rest of us followed suit. "Ryan, always a pleasure."

She walked over to shake my hand. "Rose, we'll be in touch."

She ushered Archie toward me, and it was only then that I realized just how tall he was. He loomed close enough—maybe a little too close? Was this a British thing?—that I could see he had faint freckles across his cheek; his long hair was, I'll admit, kind of greasy; and Jesus Christ, someone needed to give his childhood dentist a medal because his teeth were a true feat. He held his hand out to mine, which I hoped wasn't trembling.

"And you, Archie," said Maria. "Be nice."

# 3.

After we'd walked Team Archie to the doors, and I'd watched him get on the elevator and seen the doors close, I resumed breathing. I hesitated in the entryway, mentally steeling myself against the verbal spanking I was sure was headed my way. I glanced nervously at Ryan, Sam, and Keiran, who stood in a tight cluster closer to the doors, but they seemed to have forgotten I was there. I was dying to get back to my desk and recuperate, so I took a step back, and then another, waiting for them to notice and stop me. Ryan was the only one facing me, and when he looked up, I froze. But he only gave me a short nod with a tight, unhappy smile—the Ryan special—so I turned around, taking his gesture as a sign that I was free. For now.

Before I could get to my desk, Harper met me outside our cubicle, her arms folded across her chest and her dark, perfect eyebrows raised almost clear off the top of her head. A head that at present was adorned by a meticulously wrapped topknot, her hair, this month, dyed a deep forest green.

"I can't believe you didn't text me *once* while you were in there," she said.

"I couldn't," I said, "I was talking practically the whole time."

"What?" she yelled, so loudly that several heads popped like prairie dogs above their cubicle walls to assess the situation. I grabbed Harper by the elbows and steered us both into our cube.

"You weren't supposed to talk!" hissed Harper. "Joanna is going to murder you, and then who will I have to share my cube with?"

"*Our* cube," I said. "I'm sorry. It'll probably be Ethan."

Harper held a finger over her top lip, mimicking Ethan's creepy, tiny little hipster mustache. "Hey, Harper, have you been to Niku Hus yet? It's Japanese-Danish fusion. Supposed to have great, like, Zen-but-modernist design. It's, like, impossible to get in, but I know a guy." Ethan was desperately in love with Harper but too afraid to ask her out directly, and somehow completely oblivious to the fact that she was gay. She said she'd told him once and he hadn't "gotten" it, which I didn't understand. It seemed he either hadn't heard her, or had refused to believe her gayness was permanent. He'd talk about restaurants (or shows, or museum exhibits) like he was an event listing, hoping, apparently, that she'd fill in the rest for him. Instead, she'd become a true master of elaborate, irreversible excuses—she'd once told him she had misophonia after he kept bringing up some summer concert series he'd totally go to if he knew anyone going. Now, whenever he was around, she had to wince at the slightest noise.

"He's always gonna be able to find a restaurant whose cuisine you haven't claimed an allergy to yet," I said.

"I know," she said. "Stupid New York. Wait—don't distract me! Go back to the part about you talking to Archie Fox for an *entire meeting*? God, what did he look like? I tried to get a glimpse when he was leaving but his manager was in the way. I hate her. All I could see was his beautiful hair." Though Harper had no interest in actually dating men, she wasn't completely impervious to the effects of Archie Fox. He was just one of those people who can be incorporated into *anyone's* sexuality.

I laughed. "He looked...great." For a second earlier I'd thought I might downplay the entire exchange, knowing how many people Harper probably would have killed to get a chance to sit across the table from Archie Fox—let alone be his personal public relations representative—but now that I was in front of her, I couldn't have minimized my excitement if I'd tried. My whole face was red, and I couldn't seem to get myself to stop smiling.

"Oh my God," she gawked. "You love him now."

"No," I said. "It's not even that. He was actually kind of petulant."

"No way. You're just trying to keep your cool because you don't want to be as into Archie Fox as every other person on the planet."

"No, seriously," I said. "He's hot and charming when he wants to be, but he's got a pretty sizable chip on his shoulder. There's a reason he was here for an image redux."

"Okay. Fine. You still haven't told me what you said to him."

"Well," I said, scooting my chair closer to hers and lowering my voice, "let me first just say that I was *planning* on following Joanna's orders." I paused for Harper to nod, and therefore grant me imaginary immunity. "It's just that everything Keiran and Sam were saying was extremely idiotic. Even for them."

"Like what?"

"Like that Archie should model for *Mission 5*."

Harper's eyes widened, her mouth dropping open into a

round O. As someone with roughly one million times the fashion sense I had, she would be gravely wounded by this part, I knew.

"Shut up," she finally said.

"It's true."

"My God, can you imagine? Archie Fox in camo-tropical board shorts?" Harper looked like she wanted to cry.

"Truly I do not want to," I replied solemnly. "And *then* Ryan suggested Archie consider *vlogging*."

"Oh my God," she said. "Tell me he didn't say that word."

"He did. And they couldn't stop. They were all, 'Make Vines! Do more on YouTube, even though that's literally where you started and where you have more fans than anyone in history!' Harper, it was a shitshow."

"How did Archie respond to all this?" she asked.

"Well..." I pictured our few moments of shared eye contact, his subtly disdainful expression. "He was relatively polite about it, but it was clear he thought they were out of their minds. But then they started suggesting girlfriends."

"Whoa," said Harper. "I didn't know they were going that route."

"Me neither," I said. "I'd assumed they had a more comprehensive package planned out, but everything they had was completely slapdash and awful. And their romance candidates weren't any better."

"Who?" breathed Harper.

I grinned. "Madison Keener—" I paused for Harper to stick out her tongue in disgust. "—and Dame Wallis."

"Obvious lesbian Dame Wallis?"

"That's the one."

"I want to be shocked," said Harper, "but I'm not. What did Archie say to that?"

"He was like, 'I'm not sure I'm her type,'" I said, smiling again. For God's sake.

Harper sighed. "So witty."

"So then, I *had* to say something."

"No kidding."

"Soooo, I suggested Raya," I said.

Harper nodded slowly. I'd sent her a link to Raya's tracks a few weeks earlier, so I knew she knew who I was talking about.

"Say something!" I shrieked.

"Sorry," she said. "I was just picturing the tabloid shots. They'd look *good*."

"Right?"

"Yeah, I'm impressed. She's *so* cool."

"I *know*," I said, sounding just *slightly* jealous.

"What did Archie think?" Harper asked.

"I'm not sure," I said. "He likes her music and thinks she's 'good company,' I think was the phrase. But he was also running out of options by that point, and his agent sort of agreed on his behalf."

"Wait," gasped Harper, reaching out to grab my arm with her hands. "*Wait.* Are you telling me that Archie Fox is going to publicity-date Raya on *your* suggestion?"

"It's looking that way, yes." I grinned.

"Oh my God. This is too much," she said. "I can't process this and it's not even me."

"Well, hold that thought, because there's more."

Harper covered her eyes like an audience member at a horror movie, peering out at me between her fingers.

"Are you holding your breath?" I asked.

"Yes, it's fine, just tell me."

"I'm going to be his point person."

"*What?*" she yelled.

Ethan popped his head over the wall between his cubicle and ours. "Are you okay?" he asked Harper. Reflexively, she slapped her hands over her ears.

"Yes, she is, thanks, Ethan. She's just having a, uh. A bad sound day," I said.

He pulled a sympathetic face and mimicked closing his lips with a zipper. Harper removed her hands from her ears and gave him grateful prayer hands. He nodded, and his head disappeared below the wall.

"*Let's go get lunch*," I whispered to avoid further probing by Ethan, and we tiptoed out of the cube until we reached the front doors.

---

At lunch, over hastily and therefore badly assembled cafeteria salads and Diet Cokes, I explained everything to Harper as best I could, given that I hardly understood what had happened myself. I was supposed to be at least a year or two off from working directly with clients and Ryan knew it, but it was hard to argue with Archie Fox's agent. I'd been nervous to tell Harper that I'd be working with him, worried that she'd be jealous—she was, after all, a much bigger fan of Archie's—but she wasn't. At least, not too jealous to be thrilled for me. She was a rung lower than me at Weaver-Girard, not because she wasn't more than capable and totally savvy, but because she didn't care. PR was a holdover for her; she wanted to work in fashion. So for her, this wasn't a lost job opportunity. She just wanted to know every last thing that Archie did, so I promised her I'd forward her every last curt and boring text and email that he would inevitably send me. After we finished our salads, at Harper's suggestion, we shared one of the caf's human-head-size brownies in celebration of what was inarguably a huge boost to my career.

On the walk back to the office, my joy started to curdle into terror. Just because Maria had said she wanted me to be their point person and Archie had agreed didn't mean that Ryan was going to actually let it happen. What if he took advantage of Joanna's being gone and fired me? He could simply tell Maria that I wasn't available to be their contact because I'd recently been let go. My heart pounded in my chest, and I barely heard a word of what Harper was saying. (I gathered at least that it was a story about some cutesy cake pop recipe she'd found on Pinterest and tried to replicate to disastrous results.) Part of me thought the worst thing that could happen would be for me to get in trouble, or fired, but the other part of me was even more afraid that they'd let me do it. I'd never even assisted Joanna on a celebrity as A-list as Archie Fox before. How would I be able to manage it myself? Then I remembered what Archie said—"To be quite honest, it seems like Rose is more experienced in this 'arena' than any of you"—and I knew this opportunity was mine to lose, even as my entire body blushed. The Archie-effect was ridiculous.

"Are you okay?" Harper asked, pulling me to a stop just outside the office doors. "You've gone silent and you're sweating."

"I'm fine," I said. "I'm sorry. I'm just nervous."

"It's going to be fine. From everything I've read, Maria Bird is like Archie's ultra-fierce pseudo-mama-bear."

"How is that supposed to make me calm down?" I asked. I thought I might be sick.

"Because she wouldn't have asked for you if she thought you couldn't take good care of her cub," said Harper.

I nodded. I knew Harper was right. I'd done well enough in that meeting for Maria to *think* I could do a good job. It was just that there was still plenty of time for her to be proven very wrong.

Harper pushed open the door and I followed close behind, ready to get back to my desk and begin a several-hour period of panic-induced research. But I'd only taken about ten steps in that direction before I heard a door open behind me, and someone call my name.

"Rose?"

I turned to see Ryan, leaning partway out of his office. He did his annoying little thumb-and-two-fingers come-here wave. I turned to look at Harper, who'd stopped to wait. "I'll see you later," I said, trying to communicate *Please save me* by telekinesis. But there was nothing she could do. She mouthed *It's okay!*, gave me a thumbs-up, and, turning around, left me there to face Ryan.

As I followed Ryan toward his large, comically swanky-looking office—the rumor was that he'd had his French Heritage furniture custom-made and flown in from Provence—I ran the events of the past two hours through my head. I'd set my first PR relationship into motion, and it involved Archie Fox. The whole situation was surreal—the fact that I'd suggested it, the fact that it was actually going to happen—but it also, honestly, felt inevitable. Part of me believed Joanna must have known I wouldn't be able to keep my mouth shut; after all, my lack of restraint was basically what got me hired.

I'd ended up in an internship at Weaver-Girard the summer after junior year (I'd never forgotten that first encounter with Joanna and stalked her after a disappointing second internship at The Dish) and only lasted a week before blurting out the fact that Joanna and I had already met. She'd wandered into the copy room while I was stapling packets for an upcoming presentation, her eyes glued to whatever figures were on the papers in her hands, and she probably wouldn't have even noticed I was standing next to her if I hadn't addressed her.

"We've met before," I said, immediately regretting it. She raised an eyebrow, and I registered some distant recognition.

"Was I in the room for your interview?" she asked. "I usually don't sit in for interns."

"Oh no, it was at a different internship, at The Dish—you were there with Michaela Jones?"

"Oh, that shitshow," she said. "How'd you like it over there?"

"It was, uh..." I considered my response, torn between not wanting to talk badly about my previous employers and not wanting to be associated with their poor judgment. "It wasn't for me."

Joanna nodded, and then turned her attention to whatever was on the papers in her hand. I hovered for another moment.

"It worked out pretty well, though," I said. She looked back up at me. "For Michaela." Another unreadable pause. "I just mean, that was why she went on that whole Twitter rant, right?" I pressed on. "About interviewers disrespecting women in the music industry? Which obviously got everyone talking about her as this, like, feminist icon and not someone who was maybe sleeping with someone else's husband. But of course you know that. Um."

I bit my lip to stop my rambling, but her perfectly stained lips loosened into a (small) smile.

"You're right," she said. "It did work out. What did you say your name was?"

After that, I got curt nods from Joanna whenever I saw her around the office. This was her version of a wave, and a gesture no other interns seemed to receive. During my last month, I was invited to sit in on client meetings, and was even allowed to throw out some ideas in brainstorms. All but one of those early ideas went nowhere (the one success: teasing an album release on Instagram with nothing but a screenshot of the words IT'S COMING), but I was addicted to the energy. On my last day, Joanna congratulated me on a job well done and told me to stay in touch. I applied for and was offered an assistant position before I even graduated, and in the four years (and one promotion) since, I'd shadowed Joanna studiously and tried my best to trust my gut when decisions started falling on my shoulders. I'd assisted Joanna on steadily more and more important clients, but none as big as Archie, and certainly none for which I'd had this much control. I had to believe that Joanna was grooming me for this very moment; I only hoped her approval would be enough.

Ryan held the door open for me, his face stretched into a smarmy smile, and I walked in only to see Sam and Keiran sitting on the gray-and-beige Auteuil sofa. At our entrance they rose, closing around Ryan in V-formation as he stood behind his nine-foot-long, three-foot-deep desk. Ryan gestured for me to sit down, and once I had, he followed suit. Keiran leaned against the back window, and Sam went to sit on the edge of Ryan's desk.

"Don't," said Ryan. Sam jumped up and, looking a little lost, finally crossed around the desk and sat in the empty chair next to me.

"What's up?" I said, trying to sound casual. I knew now that I'd been right to feel uneasy. There was no way I could be appointed Archie Fox's official point person, especially when Ryan had wanted Keiran to do it, without retribution.

"That was some meeting, huh?" said Ryan. He forced a chuckle, plainly attempting to appear relaxed himself.

"Yes," I answered. "It was certainly not what I expected to happen."

"I would think not. But the talent can be so finicky, you know. That's something you learn when you've been around as long as I have." *Yes*, I thought. *Definitely only fifty-something PR executives know that professional entertainers can be temperamental.*

"Mmm," I said.

"I imagine you're feeling overwhelmed," said Ryan. "This job is obviously outside the typical range of duty for someone in your position. That's why I wanted to call you in, to see if there's something I—we—can do."

*Ah*, I realized. So that's why he wanted to talk. Ryan wanted me to tell him I wasn't up to the task, to say that I was underprepared and unready and unwilling. If I refused to be Archie's point person, Ryan could tell Maria that he *had* to appoint someone else. I looked from Ryan to Keiran to Sam—all of them wore the same expression: barely concealed anger at my insubordination, and half-faux sympathy for my predicament.

"I understand that this is a bit of a leap for someone at my level," I said, figuring what I was about to say would go over better if I reiterated my inferior position at the company. "But I'm not overwhelmed. I've learned a lot from Joanna, and I am on the music side. I'm confident I can do this well."

Ryan nodded slowly. "I know this is an exciting, fun-sounding project for you, but I'm afraid it might involve a lot more work than you realize. Joanna tells me you're bright and hardworking, and I don't doubt it. I just think that someone with more experience would be better suited to working with Fox at this time."

I felt my heart rate pick up speed. "With all due respect, I think the person best suited to working with Fox is the person he and his management asked for."

Ryan stared at me for a moment before giving me a tight smile. "I know that Archie Fox is a charmer," he said, and I felt my neck flush red with anger. "But—"

"But *what*?" I interrupted.

Ryan paused. He cleared his throat. "But he's a musician, not a public relations professional," he finished.

"Well, then it's lucky he's just hired one."

Again, Ryan nodded slowly. He looked down at his desk and began tracing a finger over the dark mahogany in a figure-eight, the office so quiet I could hear it slipping and squeaking over the wood.

"In that case," he said, "I think we ought to get Joanna on the phone."

I paused. "Right now?" It was after 10:00 p.m. in Dubai. Even Sam and Keiran shifted nervously from their relaxed positions.

"I think that would be best," said Ryan. He picked up his desk phone and dialed, pressed the machine's SPEAKERPHONE button, and placed it back in the receiver. While the four of us waited for Joanna to pick up, I held my breath.

Finally, there was a click, and then her voice.

"What is it?" she said.

"Joanna," said Ryan, "you're on speaker."

"With whom?" she asked, politely cautious, I knew, in case one of the people on the line was a client.

"Me, Sam, Keiran," he said, "and Rose."

"Oh, for fuck's sake," she said. "I'm in the Middle East. Group huddle can wait."

"I know, I'm sorry," said Ryan. It was thrilling to watch him apologize. "It's about Archie."

There was a pause, and a small, barely audible sigh. "Go on."

"His team was in earlier—"

"I'm aware."

"They've gone the mutual association route," he said. "With Raya."

"Ah. My daughter likes her," said Joanna. I tried not to openly beam.

"Yes, she's fantastic," said Ryan, glancing at me and then quickly away. "That's all well and good. It's just that they've... well, everything was squared away for Keiran to handle, but Maria sort of requested that their point person be... Rose."

Another pause.

"Rose?" said Joanna. "You there?"

"Yes," I said. "Hello."

"You spoke?"

I felt like I was going to pass out.

"Yes," I replied. "I did."

"Was Raya your idea?" she asked.

I looked across the desk at Ryan, knowing full well he expected me to demur.

"Yes," I said. "It was."

"Mmm," said Joanna. "That was rather bold, don't you think?" My heart sank; I could practically *feel* Sam and Keiran brimming with schadenfreude.

"Of course, we *so* appreciate Rose's suggestion," said Ryan. "I just feel Keiran is more equipped to carry it through."

"Ryan," said Joanna. "Take me off speakerphone."

Ryan paused, glancing around at the three of us before clearing his throat. "Sure thing," he said. He pressed the SPEAKERPHONE button again and picked up the receiver. My stomach dropped as I imagined the various things Joanna could be saying to Ryan. *Fire her* was the main one that came to mind. I watched Ryan's face, hoping for any clue, but he remained impassive and completely silent. After what felt like twenty full minutes had passed, he finally spoke.

"Yes," he said softly. And then, a bit louder, as if asked to repeat himself, "*Yes.*" He nodded to himself, looked up at me then quickly away. "Right," he continued. "I will... Right... Safe travels."

Ryan gently placed the phone back in its cradle.

"Well!" he said. "Let's get back to work, shall we?"

*Wait, what?*

"So..." I ventured. "Is everything... fine?"

"Mm," said Ryan. He rubbed his forehead and gave a single short nod.

"I'm sorry, I'm a little confused as to what's just been decided," I said. Truthfully, from the look on his face, I had an idea as to what was happening—though I had no idea why—but I wanted to hear him say it.

"You were at the meeting, weren't you?" snapped Ryan.

"You'll run point. Get in touch with Maria to set something up, and soon. She should have all your information—email, work phone, cell phone, everything. She's probably wondering why she hasn't already heard from us."

My outrage at Ryan's truly extraordinary ability to delude himself was tempered by the realization that I had *won*. One of the firm's top two executives had wanted me off a project, and I was going to do it anyway. I desperately wanted to know what Joanna had said to him, and why she had spared me after I'd willfully disregarded her orders. But I knew, of course, that Ryan was much too proud to tell me. It was better to get out of his office before he changed his mind.

"Will do," I said cheerily. I got up from my seat—neither Keiran nor Sam would look at me, but I didn't care. I turned on my heels and walked out of Ryan's office feeling more determined than ever. Archie Fox and Raya were going to be *the* It Couple of the year if it was the last thing I ever did.

# 4.

WHEN I GOT HOME THAT evening, I was more tired than I could remember being in years. I walked in the door of my two-bedroom Brooklyn apartment, dropped my bag, and listened for any sign that my nearly permanently absent roommate Chelsey was home. Mercifully, I heard nothing—Chelsey was three years younger than I was, a pothead who'd just graduated from NYU and slept over at least five times a week at her skateboard-shop-owning boyfriend's place on the Lower East Side. And because her parents mailed in her rent each month and had furnished our place with premium cable, she was pretty much the perfect roommate. I reached up under the back of my blouse, unhooked my bra, and threw myself onto the couch to wait for the Thai delivery I'd ordered off Seamless the second I stepped off the subway. I was actually a pretty good cook—having decided two weeks into an idle high school summer that I had no relaxation left in me, I'd checked out cookbook after cookbook from my local library and started taking over my family's kitchen while my parents were at work, preparing elaborate three-course dinners until they'd finally asked me to chill out—but my tiny apartment hardly allowed room for a single saucepan, and so, most often, I ordered in.

After I'd left Ryan's office I'd practically run to my desk to update Harper, who'd been so thrilled by Joanna's intervention and Ryan's being put in his place that she'd clapped. After turning to my computer and giving myself a silent, five-minute-long pep talk, I'd emailed Maria Bird. Her response had been brief and borderline curt—she'd cc'ed Archie so he had all my contact information—and she'd misspelled my name as "Rosa," even though it appeared correctly in the address field and my original message. Still, it didn't matter. I was over the moon. She'd given me the details for Archie's whereabouts and scheduling over the next five days, suggesting a couple of places that might work for a public rendezvous. I'd then called Raya's manager to follow up. Naturally, she was *extremely* eager to find time for her client to meet mine.

---

It turned out my client had gotten around.

That was the main takeaway from roughly four hours spent researching Archie that night in my favorite working-from-home position: laptop on lap, phone resting on laptop, and TV running through episodes of the second season of *The X-Files* on the wall in front of me. According to the Internet's most reliable tabloids, he'd had three rumored relationships (and six or seven "flings") since anyone started caring who he was, and I had separate windows on my laptop open for each of them, and an Excel spreadsheet to which I added copious notes and a color-coding system. His first "girlfriend" as a famous person was Lila Holmes, an entertainment news anchor not quite old enough to be his mom, but certainly old enough to be a cool aunt. This liaison had lasted about four months. Every single headline attached to their photos—Archie at nineteen years old, all awkward smiles and half-raised waves, stuck somewhere between posing for the paparazzi and ignoring them; Lila, always beaming and walking tall—included some cheeky reference to their age gap, and every interview of him from that period included an awkward question about his apparent penchant for older women. It wasn't *not* creepy, but he was legally an adult and, to be fair, didn't look like any nineteen-year-old I'd ever seen. Who could really blame her?

Archie's second famed fling was believed to be with Amanda Jackson, Victoria's Secret Angel extraordinaire, but their relationship was never confirmed. It rested solely on some photographic evidence that was, quite frankly, unconvincing: a handful of blurry views of them through ritzy restaurant windows, seated in positions that suggested that vague catchall activity, "canoodling," and another few washed-out shots of them emerging, hunched, from exclusive bars. The Internet cared about them for a month, tops. They parted ways with little ceremony. After Amanda there was a string of vaguely related-looking rebound models, a Swedish DJ, and another few models.

And then there was the most recent (and by far, most famous) relationship: Chloe Tan. And *man*, did that relationship look good. Archie and Chloe were an item for an estimated eighteen months, and during that time they were the darlings of the gossip industry. As a then-twenty-two-year-old, Archie had met Chloe (then twenty-six, the rags were delighted to report) on the set of the paranormal drama on which she played a high school junior. Archie was doing a cameo as a charming singer-songwriter who offers Chloe's character unexpected but sage romantic advice when they miraculously end up at the same café after his show. It was that whole what-are-the-chances shtick, the joke being the fact that the non-famous character ends up making the miraculous exchange all about her mundane life. The spot was a terrible call for him, I thought, and never would've been made had he been my client (already I was getting used to the phrase) at the time. Cameos like that never seemed anything but desperate.

I remembered the episode; he'd done a lot with what little they'd given him, but it was still fairly silly. But his performance must have worked some kind of magic, because they were inseparable from that point forward. I opened tab after tab of news items and blurbs: Chloe and Archie caught at brunch in Los Feliz; Chloe and Archie laughing in the waves on their Hawaiian vacation; Chloe and Archie walking the cutest goddamn puppy I'd ever seen like some picture-perfect nuclear family designed by the government to distract the masses.

I was lost in a profile of Chloe from three months before their breakup, which was now a bit over a year behind us, when Harper's face popped up on my screen. I answered the Skype call but didn't even let her say a word.

"'Archie came into my life when I'd just about given up on love,' Chloe says, stirring her tea but looking straight at me with tear-glistened eyes,'" I read. "'He saved me.' Come. On."

"Oh God, shut up. Was that the *Cosmo* profile?"

"*Vanity Fair.* There's no way she believed that. She was *twenty-six years old* when they met. My age."

"Maybe people mature more quickly in Hollywood. Maybe

full disillusionment comes way before middle age, because their middle age is actually, like, thirty."

My lips pursed. "Maybe. What are you up to?"

"Working on some sketches. You didn't answer my texts—would you say you look back fondly on flare-legged jeans?"

"Gross, no," I said, too quickly. "I mean, unless you like them. I don't know. Don't ask me." I panned the camera across my after-work leisure outfit: black T-shirt, worn black leggings, an opened bag of Goldfish resting on my chest.

Harper laughed. "So Chelsey's out, then?"

"I haven't seen her in days. The only reason I know she's alive is because of her Snapchat. She had dinner at Buffalo Wild Wings, if you're wondering."

"Great, yeah, I definitely was." She paused, reached out of the frame, and pulled back a mug full of colored pencils. "So, where are you on the freaking-out scale?"

I minimized the chat and clicked back to my Chloe window. "Coming down. Maybe I'm just getting tired, though. Do you think if I looked like Chloe Tan, I, too, would have so much romantic activity in my life that I'd have already reached a point of utter *exhaustion*?"

"No."

"Cool, thanks. Good conversation, bye!"

She rolled her eyes. "That's not what I mean, and you know it. You're a vision, Goldfish crumbs and all. I just think maybe Chloe Tan is more open to the *idea* of romance. Or at least, her people want us to think so."

I grimaced and continued scrolling through shots of Chloe walking through sunny LA—her long, pin-straight black hair flowing behind her, her tan legs popping out of a beige, airy dress that I knew, on me, would look like a potato sack. She was rarely caught without some impossibly bright red lipstick swiped perfectly across her mouth. I funneled some more crackers through my fist into my face.

"It might be tougher than I thought to get the world to care about Archie and Raya after Chloe," I said. I thought back to all of the melodramatic tweets following the announcement of their split, all of the people who'd come to view their relationship as evidence of true love and experienced true grief over its end despite knowing next to nothing about either of them.

"Nah," Harper said with a shrug. "She cheated on him. The world will sigh in collective relief if they can believe their sweet golden boy has found love again."

"Yeah, you're probably right," I conceded, but my mind had already started drifting away from the conversation. Archie had dated Chloe before he'd moved to Weaver-Girard, so it was unclear whether or not theirs was a manufactured relationship. Regardless, its very existence convinced an international audience that fairy-tale romance does exist, and it would be difficult for me to pull it off a second time. Archie's relationship with Raya couldn't represent romance alone; it would have to project something else. Creative inspiration, maybe. Reinvention. Even lust. But another happily-ever-after? Archie fans had already been burned. I knew they'd need some warming up to the idea.

"All right, I'm gonna get back to it," said Harper.

"Show me?" I asked. She grinned and held her sketch up to the camera. The page was covered with three different perspectives of the same outfit—a floral, cropped corset and flowing, high-waisted pants. Two of the three were finished with a long pink blazer.

"Damn, Harp," I said. "I'd buy it."

"Eh, we'll see. Get some sleep."

I said good night, shut my laptop, grabbed my phone, and opened up Tinder. I'd begrudgingly downloaded the dating app at Harper's behest, but had yet to find even a fraction of the success she'd had on it. These days, I logged in mostly out of a sense of obligation. Perhaps some boredom. Certainly not any hope.

It had been five years since my only significant relationship ended, and I'd been unimpressed by post-breakup dating to say the least. Dave and I split up in the middle of junior year, technically because he cheated on me. Which, to his credit, I suppose, he'd confessed to me willingly and unprompted—though after years of distance, I was able to recognize that by then the magic had been missing for a long time. Our plan had gone off track, as plans—especially teenage ones—tend to do. We weren't living in some high-ceilinged fantasy studio. Dave had gotten swept up in the capital-c College experience in a way that evaded me, and when he moved into a suite with friends who needed a sixth roommate we became less of a dynamic duo and more of an ensemble cast. This had made the breakup doubly devastating—not only was I losing the partner with whom I'd spent nearly a third of my life, but my group of friends had gone with him, too. It was hard not to be guarded after such an upheaval, and besides, getting to that level of comfort with someone new just seemed like so much *work*.

If I was ever going to let another guy get so fully enmeshed in my life, I'd decided, he'd sure as hell have to be worth it. The most promising thus far had been a graphic designer I matched with on Tinder, who also loved Otis Redding and *The X-Files*, with whom I'd had engaging conversations across two seemingly great dates, and who knew the exact right amount of tongue to use in a second kiss. Then he sent me an unsolicited dick pic at 3:00 a.m. in the middle of the week, and followed it up with a drunken phone call asking me what I "wanted to do with it." When I'd snapped at him about how inconsiderate and inappropriate it was to wake me four hours before I had to be up for work, he'd laughed and told me to lighten up. Suddenly I was twenty-one again, and it was Dave telling me he knew he'd done something wrong in cheating on me, but wasn't it partly my fault, too? That I'd thrown myself into school and work, that I'd stopped going out as much, that I wasn't as *available*, if I knew what he meant, and what else was he supposed to do? I deleted the app immediately after ending the call.

I'd spent years since in a cycle of signing on, hating everyone, deleting the app, getting lonely, forgetting I hated everyone, redownloading the app, and starting the whole cycle again. Tonight a bright-red envelope shone in the bottom right corner of the Tinder app, indicating new messages waiting for me. I steeled myself and clicked.

`let me get lost in those deep blue eyes`

Maybe four months ago, dude, but now I know better. Delete.

`420 friendly?`

Thank you, but no thank you. Delete.

`u look like u work hard why not take a break`
`i got a seat for you :)`

Jesus. Delete. I closed the app.

My suspicion was that Harper's continued optimism for Tinder was made possible by the fact that she was only talking to and dating women. She had her own romantic woes, of course, but I couldn't imagine a woman opening up a dialogue with a smiley-faced offer for a trip to third base. But maybe I was wrong! And maybe that kind of thing was exactly what this app was meant for; what dating in one's twenties was destined to be. Maybe I was the one doing it wrong, and Harper was right, maybe Mr. Smiley was genuinely concerned about my stress level. But would he be worth the risk and hassle of finding out? I doubted it.

I settled into the couch and pulled my computer back onto my lap, reopening the Chloe-Archie window. They looked happy. The evidence was there: the way they gazed into each other's eyes on red carpets, the way he held her bag while they walked down the Venice boardwalk. I, more than most people, knew that the majority of celebrity relationships could be manufactured to look real, but this one looked *really* real. Except, of course, for the little fact that Chloe ended up leaving Archie for a different co-star, whose baby she was pregnant with now. It didn't matter so much if it was real or fake; it was over. All the available evidence suggested that love—natural or staged—was simply too fragile to last.

I was opening up a new window when my phone vibrated right off my laptop. I caught it before it fell—unknown number. I stared at the screen. As a rule, I let unknown numbers go to voicemail, and then let those voicemails pile up until, months later, I deleted them all in one fell swoop. But it was well past midnight—what if something was wrong? Wasn't this exactly the time people called with emergencies?

"... Hello?" I stuttered.

"Hi, is this Rose?"

That unmistakable British purr. *Dammit*, I thought. *This is why you answer the phone with your name and some confidence, like a special agent.*

"This is she," I said, trying to recover.

"Right, this is Archie Fox."

My heart raced; the phone felt slippery in my hand. I couldn't believe he'd actually taken my number from that email exchange with Maria. I couldn't believe he'd even *looked* at the emails. "Yeah, I know," I said. "Do you always make professional calls at one in the morning?"

"I don't know—do you always answer?"

I chewed on my lip and smiled, proud of, albeit surprised by, my own brass. Turns out it was much easier to talk to Archie Fox when I wasn't looking him in the face.

"What can I do for you, Mr. Fox?"

"I'm just awake thinking that if this is going to happen, we're going to need to make some ground rules, yeah?"

My mind wandered. Where was he calling from? A balcony off his Manhattan penthouse? His kitchen table, holding a steaming mug of tea?

"Uh-huh," I replied. It was late—maybe he was calling from his bed? What kind of sheets would Archie Fox sleep in?

"This will be purely business. Raya's a nice girl, and, as I said, I will be happy to spend time with her. But it won't go beyond that," he said, with a sudden sternness.

The moment felt delicate. I waited to see if he would continue the thought, but it was apparently all that he was willing to give.

"So anyway," he said, clearing his throat and resuming his

typically deep tone. "I just say this so that you can make it very clear to Raya. Or her people, whichever. She's young, you know? She might not know how this goes."

"You say this like you're a wizened old man," I said. "I know you're famous and everything, but you're, what, twenty-four?"

"Well..." he said with a lilt.

"Wait—are you not?" *Of course*, I thought, annoyed I hadn't already guessed.

"You seriously don't know? Listen, it's not as if I'm in middle age."

We both waited.

"I'm actually twenty-seven," he finally said. I could hear him smiling.

A sharp laugh escaped from my throat. "So wait, Lila..."

"Not *quite* as odd as everyone thought," said Archie. "There was still a bit of a gap, but it wasn't so, you know... robbing-the-cradle-esque."

"Well, I'll be sure to add this information to my file," I said. "Any other secrets I should know?"

He hummed, meditating on the question. "I'm not actually British."

My heart fell.

"Christ, I'm kidding," he said through laughter. "Are you really that gullible?"

"No!" I squeaked, immediately defensive.

"Right, this will be fun."

*So Archie has a sense of humor*, I thought. Good to know.

"Stop it. I definitely knew," I said. "I was just distracted. You know, I was doing other things before you called."

He sighed, as if settling into a seat. "And what was Rose Reed doing on a Thursday night at one in the morning just before her pesky client interrupted?"

*Be professional*, I reminded myself.

"What does anyone do at one in the morning?" I said. "Bullshitting on various social networks."

"Ah, see, no one lets me do that. I've got to delegate my bullshitting," he said. "Listen, love, I'm going to put you on speaker for a second."

I was thrown off by the use of "love," but then, I supposed, British people call everyone "love." I was pretty sure he'd called Ryan "love" in our meeting.

"Right, I'm back." His voice was suddenly so close I could almost feel his breath on my ear.

"Hello again," I said. What was even happening? What was he doing now?

"So tell me what your preferred networks are," he continued. "Are you a Twitter gal? You seem like a Twitter gal."

"What does *that* mean?" I asked, vaguely offended but disarmed by his extremely effective use of the word "gal."

"I don't know, all you New York media industry types are always tweeting."

He was right—Twitter was, as always, waiting in its own tab for my frequent return. But something in me wanted to test the boundaries of the conversation. "Well, I hate to disappoint you, but no, I wasn't on Twitter."

"Tumblr, then. Exploring your emotions."

I laughed. "Sometimes, but not tonight."

"Where then?" he asked.

I hesitated, but something about talking to Archie made me

want to be as forthright as possible. "Tinder? You probably don't know it." I could hear my pulse in my ears.

"Rose Reed!" His tone was indecipherable, but there was something about the way he said my name. It was almost, maybe, a hint of fondness. A business-like one, surely, but still.

"What?" I asked.

"What are you doing on *Tinder*?"

I could feel defensiveness rising up my chest. "Don't tell me you're some love expert just because you sing about it. It's not like *I've* got a team whose job it is to find me people who are beautiful and brilliant enough to be my potential mate."

He paused, and I worried I'd gone out of bounds.

"Well, I'd say your first problem might be the term 'potential mate,'" he said, and my face relaxed into a smile. Was this really what working with Archie would be like? It could not possibly be this easy. *You haven't* done *anything yet*, I reminded myself.

"Well, anyway..." I said, trying to signal the end of a conversation I was too anxious to continue. Something could go wrong; I could say something embarrassing, or, more likely, I'd stay on the line long enough to convince myself that some random thing I'd *already said* had been too weird. My nerves couldn't take it.

"Oh, are you leaving me?" he asked.

"Well, I—you know, it's late, and I do have to work tomorrow." I pulled myself together, grabbed the remote, and switched off the long-muted TV. "On your account, let's not forget."

"That's fair," he said. "I don't suppose you could give me any hints as to what's to come?"

"I've got some ideas." This wasn't a *complete* lie; more like an exaggeration. I did have some vague notions, which would surely form into bona fide ideas by morning. I just needed to get him off the phone so I could think and breathe like a normal person again. I snatched my favorite throw blanket and balanced my laptop on my open palm as I carried both from the couch to the bedroom.

"Just know that I don't do discotheques," he said.

"*Discotheques*?" I said, mimicking his accent.

"Clubs, fine. Whatever you want to call them. You know, grinding and all that."

I attempted pulling off my shirt without dropping the phone, my laughter muffled. "You know, I take it back. Maybe you really are an old man."

Archie scoffed in what I hoped was mock annoyance. "Well, if that's all, we'll talk later."

"Sounds great, Mr. Fox."

"You can call me Archie."

"Sounds great, Archie." My cheeks were beginning to ache from smiling.

"Good night, Rose Reed," said Archie.

"Good night," I replied.

I hung up, took a deep breath, and stared blankly at my phone for a full thirty seconds before dropping it to dig my favorite holey sweatshirt out of my hamper and, deciding it didn't smell bad *yet*, settle into bed.

# 5.

I WOKE THE NEXT MORNING with a start. Heart racing, I leaned over the edge of the bed and picked up my phone from the nightstand. When I saw that it was only 6:47, thirteen minutes before my alarm would go off, I groaned and rolled back into bed with my phone in hand. Under the covers, I scrolled through the emails that had built up in my inbox overnight: Half a dozen of them were from clothing companies I'd bought something from once, and another handful were the result of Google alerts I'd set up to automatically email me each time one of Weaver-Girard's clients made headlines. Most were irrelevant, trivial items—Mackenzie Bayer said to be shopping for an apartment in Tribeca—but I noticed there was one from *People* on Trevor James. Apparently, he'd just been named a youth ambassador for a lesser-known international human rights organization. I grinned. Nobody but Joanna could make something like that happen for someone like Trevor James in the span of twenty-four hours, much less from his secret rehab stint in Dubai.

I scrolled through all the way to the earliest new email in my inbox, which had come in just after 1:00 a.m. It was a calendar invite from Alexis, one of Ryan's assistants, for 9:00 this morning, for breakfast with Raya and Raya's manager. I sat up straight in my bed in panic. When I'd talked to Alexis the evening before, I'd told her to shoot for 10:30, but apparently that hadn't worked for Raya. I'd thought, if anything, that it'd end up being later—musicians, as a rule, did not meet anyone for anything before 10:00 a.m. What was I doing late last night that I didn't remember to double-check the schedule with Alexis?

Oh, right. Just chatting on the phone with Archie Fox.

I threw my face into the pillow and let out a muffled scream. How was any of this real? I tried to remember every last thing I'd said, wondering how much of it (if any) was unprofessional and/or embarrassing. *How* had he gotten me to talk about my dating life? Thinking about it more, I wondered, did he even really "get" me to? Or had I volunteered it freely, for no reason other than my apparent desire to humiliate myself in front of one of the hottest, most famous rock stars on the planet? Why had I felt so compelled to make sure he knew I was single?

(I knew "why," but still, *whyyyyyyyyyy?*)

I lay there in a motionless heap until the soft harp of my alarm sounded, and then I threw off my comforter and sat up, sliding to the edge of my bed. I had a little over an hour to get myself together before breakfast with Team Raya on the Lower East Side. More specifically, at Basile, an extremely expensive, extremely new French restaurant that had just opened last week, and was therefore not trendy, but pre-trendy. At least, I hoped it was. I was using my breakfast meeting there as a way to scope it out and see if it might eventually make for a cool spot in which Archie and Raya could be seen together. By introducing Raya to the chef now, in its soft opening, I'd make sure she was all the better positioned for VIP service in the weeks ahead. Any table she wanted was hers—as long as it was near a window.

By 8:47 I was settled into a chic, grayish-white picnic-style table in Basile's airy, enclosed courtyard. I surveyed the scene: indoor dining on opposite sides, kitchen behind me, entryway and bar ahead. The windows were dark and burnished with a kind of brassy finish, making it much easier to see the courtyard from within than to see inside from where I sat now. It was perfect: Celebrities who not-so-secretly wanted to be gawked at could sit outside—which was, after all, being marked as VIP seating—and celebrities who just wanted to eat in peace could sit in one of the booths inside, allowing the people who saw them anyway, while walking through the restaurant, to think of them as private and humble. If and when I sent Archie and Raya here, I would have them seated cozily inside.

The server was refilling my water glass for a second time when Raya and her manager showed up. I quickly slid my phone into my pocket, checking the time as I did—9:03. I was almost surprised by how punctual she was, but then, I supposed, she was still working her way up. A few hit singles, and a few months with Archie, and she wouldn't have to be on time for anyone or anything.

I stood up from my seat and extended my hand toward Raya. She took it and shook—delicate, but not limp.

"Raya," I said. "Such a pleasure to meet you. I'm Rose."

"Likewise," she said. "This is Pilar." She gestured to her manager, who ignored my outstretched hand and went in for a hug.

"*So* nice to meet you," she gushed. "We're so excited about all this."

I took a quick glance at Raya's face, gathering from her

expression that Pilar's "we" was something of an exaggeration. *Wonderful*, I thought. *Two* ambivalent clients.

We took our seats, our butts hardly grazing the wood before our server was back, pouring Pellegrino and welcoming us all to Basile. She asked what else we'd like to drink, and while Raya and Pilar made their orders—tea and honey for Raya, a mimosa for Pilar—I surreptitiously (I hoped) stared at Raya's outfit: a 1990s-era spaghetti-strap floral dress under a sheer, lacy, long-sleeved black top. Her face was only minimally made up—with eyebrows, eyelashes, and cheekbones like that, who needed makeup?—and she wore almost no jewelry, apart from a tiny silver septum ring and a thin silver band she wore as a choker. Her hair was a cascading curly mane, now dyed a Little Mermaid–esque bright red. She wrapped long fingers around her tea mug, and I could see that her nails were bitten down and bare of polish. Despite being six years younger than me, she could have passed for thirty—and not in a way that would bite her in the ass when she actually neared thirty, but in a way that made her seem ethereal, wise, and already over the various trappings of youth.

I realized I was on the verge of gawking, took another sip of my water, and cleared my throat.

"Before we get started, do you have any questions or concerns you want to go over?" I asked. Joanna had always said it was important to give celebrity clients the opportunity to complain about what you're doing before you even do anything. It makes them feel heard. But Raya just tilted her head back and shook it, her red curls swiping across her back. She closed her eyes, and for a moment I wondered if she was going to be one of those clients who doesn't say anything out loud, instead whispering each thought to a manager or assistant, who must then pass it along like a grown-up version of the game Telephone. But then she sat up and opened her eyes, which were a striking shade of golden hazel. *She's going to be such a star*, I thought. Nobody out there looked like she did.

"I just want to be clear about one matter in particular," she said, and I gave my practiced sympathetic nod. "This is, for me, entirely and exclusively an undertaking meant to disseminate my music. I'm willing to entertain this because I understand the difference it can make. However, if it becomes clear that it's not having the effect I desire—regardless of how it's affecting Archie's career—I'm ending it."

In spite of myself, and every piece of feminist thinking I'd consumed in my time thus far on Earth, I was impressed and surprised by how smart Raya seemed. Partly because she was stunning and a phenomenally talented musician, and it struck me as mildly unfair anytime someone had literally everything going for them, but also because she was so young. She had to have been the type of kid teachers lovingly call "precocious." Or she would have had she not been homeschooled by her Quaker parents.

"I totally understand," I said. "Obviously I haven't been part of one of these contracts myself—" Here I paused for a *Lol, we both know you're merely a serf* laugh from Raya, but got nothing. "—but I've worked on enough of them to have a sense of how strange and clinical it can feel for the people involved. It's my job to make this as easy and rewarding for you as I possibly can." I was careful to sidestep any mention of tangible results; there were celebrities who entered contracts with Weaver-Girard expecting certain outcomes, like an Academy Award or a platinum record or even bona fide true love with an equally successful, equally beautiful movie star. Some of them seemed to forget that, even though we were experts and could certainly help, there was only so much we could do. If your movie sucked or your music sucked or your sitcom-star boyfriend got a Marvel role and decided he was too A-list for you, you were still, no matter what, going to suffer.

"Absolutely," said Pilar, beaming from ear to ear. Her client might not be shrewd (or cynical) enough to fully comprehend the opportunity she was being presented, but it was clear from that manic smile that Pilar did. "As an in-demand new artist, you'll understand, Raya has a very busy schedule." (I nodded sympathetically.) "But we want to make this work, so, we're totally willing to be flexible whenever possible. Right, Ray?" Raya gave Pilar a close-lipped smile and looked back at me.

"So how many days have you been on the job?" she asked.

I smiled, hoping the flames in my eyes weren't showing. "I've been with Weaver-Girard for just about four years," I said. "I graduated a little early and started right away." Raya said nothing, so I continued. "I promise you, I'm the right person to work with you both. It's to your advantage that I'm young. I understand the media landscape and the Internet at large. I'm a public relations consultant, but I'm also a fan who spends pretty much all her free time reading what other fans—of yours, of Archie's, of pop music more broadly—are saying online. I know these people, and I know the kinds of things they love to see from their idols. And I can tell you right now that they're going to lose their *minds* when the first photos surface."

I paused, wondering if I'd said too much. I'd used the term "media landscape" for possibly the first time ever, for one thing.

I'd also maybe insinuated that my youth and savvy set me apart from the rest of Weaver-Girard. Privately, of course, I thought this was kind of true, but I didn't want a client losing faith in the company I worked for.

"What's your Tumblr?" asked Raya. I was so stunned that it took me a moment to speak.

"Oh, um," I said. "It's 'GeorgiaRose.' "

"Ah," said Raya. " 'Best Song Ever.' " She typed it into her phone with a little smirk. I laughed and tried to control the pink spreading across my face. I'd made the account when I was about her age.

"It's mostly reblogs," I said, wanting to fill the awkward silence while Raya paged through my Tumblr and Pilar leaned over her, trying to get a glimpse at the screen. I racked my brain trying to remember my most recent activity—puppy videos, alien gifs, and Harper's sketches—and was grateful for the fact it was mostly inoffensive.

"Reblogs are an incredibly meaningful window into a person's true nature," Raya intoned, still staring at her phone. I wasn't sure how to respond; it was impossible to gauge her seriousness. But then she peered up at me, and smiled, and I felt free to laugh. "I'm joking," she said. "I'm earnest, but not *that* earnest." She set her phone down on the table and rested her elbows on the table. "But you do have good taste," she added. Pilar nodded and beamed in agreement.

Someone with a septum ring thought I had good taste. I felt so honored I thought I might pass out. I took another sip of sparkling water. *Keep it together, Rose.*

"Thank you," I said. "So, let's talk logistics, if that's all right with you both?"

Pilar nodded and Raya shrugged, which I decided to take as tacit acceptance.

The plan was this: The following Tuesday night, after Raya's show at Central Park's SummerStage, a driver would bring her here, to Basile, to meet Archie for dinner and a drink. We'd have to time their arrivals meticulously because their walking in together was one of the two short periods in which it was most likely they'd be photographed—the other, of course, being their exit. Luckily for me, whoever got there first could camp out in his or her car to wait, and it would look like they were psyching themselves up to deal with the paparazzi. I knew there would be paparazzi standing by because I would call them myself. Or, more specifically, I'd call one: Lucas, a paparazzo with whom Joanna had something of an arrangement. He was kind of an overconfident ass, but he was (relatively speaking) tame and polite in his celebrity pursuits, and if I gave him the exclusive tip-off I knew I could count on him to send high-quality images to the firm in record time. (For an absolutely insane fee, of course.) Later, when news spread, it would get harder to obtain clear, close-up shots of Archie and Raya together, but later it wouldn't matter. All we needed to get the ball rolling was the classic three-photo new-romance spread, tailor-made for the middle section of *Us Weekly* and *In Touch*: one shot of them walking in together, one shot of them sitting together—bonus points if at least one of them is lifting a forkful of food to his or her mouth—and a third of them leaving, together, to an implied mystery second location. Though my politics pained me to say it, I told Raya she should walk behind Archie with her eyes on the ground and never directed at the cameras. Archie could look up if he wanted, because he'd been around for longer, and it would make him look defiant rather than startled, or hyper-aware. If Raya looked at the cameras, I knew, it could quite easily end up looking like she knew what she was doing by being seen with Archie Fox, and there was nothing more likely to kill the public's thirst for a celebrity item than visible calculation.

At this, Raya rolled her eyes and smiled, which was probably the best I could hope for. When they'd left—heading off, Raya said, to see her vocal coach and "a guy about these totally sick pedals"—and I'd handed the server my card, I attempted to calm my nerves by reminding myself it was in Raya's best interest to do what I'd said. Plus, I knew I had Pilar firmly on my side, and Raya seemed to trust her implicitly.

The server returned to my table and hovered for a moment with her hands behind her back, waiting for me to hand her the check but trying not to look like she was asking for it.

"Actually," I said. "Can I get a mimosa? I'll pay cash."

It was after 10:00, I reasoned. And mimosas were a breakfast drink.

The server nodded and took my card. When she returned with my drink I swallowed a third of it in one gulp, and then sent a quick email to Joanna and Ryan, letting them know that I'd met with Raya and Pilar and that everything was ready to go for Tuesday. `We're all set!!` I wrote, first with four exclamation points and then, because it looked insane, scaling it back to a modest two.

I just hoped I was right.

# 6.

THAT NIGHT WHEN I GOT off the subway it was almost 9:00, and the sun was setting in a brilliant pink-orange sky over the rooftops along my block, where it seemed like everyone but me was settling into a night of summery barbecuing and beer drinking. I snarled at them as I pushed through the PVC strips that hung in the doorway of my corner bodega. I took a Diet Coke from the refrigerator in the back, and then, thinking better of it, put it back, grabbing a Diet Red Bull instead—even though it was a Friday night, and I knew there was only so much I could reasonably accomplish on Project Platinum. This was my new nickname for the Archie Fox contract, which had seemed much cleverer at 8:00 in my why-am-I-still-in-the-office hysteria—Harper had suggested I call it Project Pailey 2.0, after another, super-successful PR relationship Girard-Weaver had manufactured years earlier between then-blossoming movie stars Hailey Riker and Patrick O'Rourke. It was weird to think about "Pailey" (as the tabloids had called them) now as having once been *the* aspirational It Couple. They'd divorced three years ago after Patrick fell in love with Olivia Deniaud on the set of an Elizabethan period drama I couldn't even remember the name of. In a *GQ* profile just months after the divorce, he'd had the nerve to say he'd fallen in love with Olivia the first time he saw her in a corset. That they were both reasonably well liked among the public and in the press—though, of course, Hailey's coverage always came tinged with a heavy dose of paternalistic sympathy—was entirely owed to Ryan's handling of their PR in the year after the divorce. For that, I had to give him credit.

After a solid thirty seconds' worth of struggle to unlock my temperamental front door, I walked into the apartment, screamed, and immediately walked back out, backward, letting the door slam closed in my face.

It had only been a second, but it was somehow enough time (more than enough time, really) to take in the sight of Chelsey and her boyfriend having sex on the couch (*our* couch) in a position I felt safe saying would fall under "Advanced to Expert" in a hypothetical compendium of sex positions a pair of humans could accomplish on a crappy IKEA couch.

"Um," I said aloud, to myself. "Okay. Well."

Inside I could hear scrambling, and then giggling. I wondered for a moment if I could just walk away, maybe find an apartment in Bushwick or Queens or the Upper West Side, and live there instead. But no. I could buy new clothes, but I could not and would not abandon our cable package like that. I waited for another moment, took a deep breath, and knocked on the door.

"Yeah!" said Chelsey. I held my hand on the knob for another twenty seconds just to be safe, and then, slowly, I turned it.

"You're safe," she said as I—gradually—pushed the door open.

Chelsey stood in front of the couch wearing an oversize T-shirt and basketball shorts, her arms crossed in front of her.

Behind her, her boyfriend, Jay, sat on the couch, shirtless. My eyes fell to his lap, which was covered with one of the beautiful gray throw pillows I'd found on sale at West Elm.

"Are you naked under there?" I asked. I couldn't help it; it just came out.

"He has boxers on," said Chelsey. Around me, at least, Jay was functionally mute. I assumed he spoke at least a few words to Chelsey each day, but I couldn't be certain. Chelsey rotated around to look at him, and they started giggling. After it had been nearly a minute, I became worried they had forgotten I was just standing there, and I let my oversize leather bag fall from my hand to the floor.

"Sorry," Chelsey said, "sorry." She spun around, wiping tears from her red-rimmed eyes.

"It's fine," I said, probably too brusquely to be believable. "I mean, I don't need a repeat viewing or anything, but. Um."

"No, *totally*, won't happen again. I'm really sorry." Chelsey's face flushed, and I saw that she meant it. She turned to shoo Jay, still laughing, into her bedroom, and I took the opportunity to pick up my bag and sidle past them to my bedroom on the other side. Holding back the lecture I wanted to deliver about personal boundaries and impropriety was physically painful, but I also knew they weren't exactly in a position to absorb whatever I told them. Instead, I added "strip and dry-clean sofa" to my mental to-do list.

Once inside my room I closed the door and collapsed onto my bed, wincing as the cheap slatted boards underneath the mattress squeaked and shifted. Someday I would buy a queen-size bed instead of a double, and someday I would live in a place that could accommodate it with room to spare (and without a roommate whose vibrant sex life would be on display). But for now, even though it was loud and a little too firm, I was happy to be in my bed and off my feet. I used the toes of each foot to push off my stacked-heel sandals, wincing as they slid off and clattered against the floor. Not that *I* should be worried about making noise.

After fifteen or twenty minutes of aimless scrolling through various social networks on my phone, I pulled my laptop out of my bag and opened my Excel spreadsheet and PowerPoint-in-progress, empty so far save for a title (PROJECT PLATINUM, though I'd probably end up changing that) and a slide filled with a few blurry, grainy pictures of Raya I'd found online. Rumor had it that she didn't like being photographed. *Good luck with that now*, I thought. I dug back into my bag and produced a small stack of tabloid magazines I'd collected over the past few months. The office received about twenty copies of each of the major rags each week (or month, as the case may be), and I'd grabbed as many as I could find from the stack that accumulated in the bin next to the refrigerator in the break room. For the next hour I slowly paged through each of them, earmarking every reference to and picture of Archie I could find, entering the language used to describe him in the spreadsheet in POSITIVE and NEGATIVE columns, respectively. Raya, of course, could not yet be found in the magazines' pages—but it wouldn't be long now.

Halfway through the stack I started taking more notice of Archie's outfits. Of late, they were tending toward the sloppier side of the celebrity-seen-about-town spectrum. Strictly speaking, Archie's sartorial choices were not within the purview of this contract, but I was of the opinion that the best image overhauls were ones that signaled visually. It gave the public a clear demarcation line: There is, for instance, Hannah Montana brunette Miley, and then there is Pansexual Nudist and Weed Enthusiast blond crop Miley. And while Archie Fox had been known, especially early on, for his style, he had lately been seen wearing too many stretched-out T-shirts and insufficiently tight jeans.

Together Archie and Raya would look undeniably beautiful, but I knew there was some unifying element that could elevate them, that could make people's jaws drop when they flipped the pages of their *Us Weekly* magazines and landed on a picture of them together. I might not be stylish enough to know exactly what that was, but Harper would. I leaned across my bed and picked up my phone to call her. She answered after a single ring.

"Can't get enough of me?" she asked.

"Never," I said. "Oh, wait—aren't you supposed to be on a date right now?" Harper had left work a few minutes before I did, telling me as she packed up her things that she was meeting a girl from Tinder at a dive bar on the Lower East Side.

"I texted her to cancel, like, the moment I stepped outside."

"Harper!"

"I knowwww," she whined. Harper was something of an inadvertent heartbreaker, with a constantly full inbox and a seemingly never-ending string of late-night texts from girls she'd gone out with once or twice and then called it off with. But because she never just disappeared on anyone, and because she always gave at least an hour's notice when canceling on a date, it was hard to fault her. "I just really wanted to go home," she added. "I should stop scheduling dates on Friday nights. All I ever want to do is go home and/or die."

"I don't relate to this crisis," I said, "but I sympathize."

"Any word from Hot Doctor yet?" Hot Doctor was Neil, a surprisingly cute and relatively normal-seeming guy Harper and I had come across in our obligatory trip through my Tinder, at Harper's insistence, each day at lunch. I would halfheartedly protest as she commandeered my phone, swiping right on all kinds of guys I would have rejected if left to do so myself. Earlier, though, when she'd come upon Neil—tall, tan, dark-brown hair, with five pictures that managed not to feature ex-girlfriends, dead animals, or partial nudes—she'd paused and showed me the phone. "Oh," I said, which was the most enthusiasm I could muster for Tinder. "Yeah, he's cute." A few hours later, when my phone buzzed to alert me to the fact that I had a new Tinder match, I'd been surprised to find myself hoping it was Neil. When it was, I'd even squealed a little. I'd showed Harper, who'd launched into strategy mode, and told me that I had to give him twenty-four hours to message me before resorting to messaging him myself. So far, nothing. I knew—or, at least, I'd heard—that tons of guys on Tinder swiped right on *everyone*, just to find who'd matched with them. Nothing really counted until a message. I found myself getting vaguely angry with Neil. *Typical Neil,* I thought. *Thinks he's sooooooo hot just because he's a brain surgeon.*

(I did not know if he was a brain surgeon, but in my mind, he'd become one.)

"Not yet," I said, sighing.

"Okay, calm down," said Harper. "It's been four hours."

"You're riiiiight," I whined. "See? This is why I hate this stupid app. It makes me stressed out about people I haven't even met yet!"

"Don't be stressed," said Harper. "He's just some dude named Neil."

"It's not the *sexiest* name in the world," I agreed.

"If he were named Graham or Xavier or something, it'd be way better."

"Or Eddie," I said. Eddie had been the name of the fake Canadian boyfriend I'd told my friends I had in elementary school. We'd allegedly met at summer camp, where he was best known for winning the talent contest by playing guitar in a band. I never came up with a very good backstory for why a visiting Canadian was attending a Bay Area summer camp, so the romance fizzled. Still, I thought, he might be out there somewhere.

"I feel like innovation in male names is so far behind female ones," said Harper. "I saw a Chrysanthine on Tinder the other day."

"Oh wow, that's really something."

"I could call her Chrys," said Harper. "It'd be adorable." I laughed—Harper, without fail, went for girls who looked and acted like they'd just gotten off the bus from Burning Man: shredded clothing, dirty hair, tattoos, and, usually, an extremely flaky disposition. My not-so-secret hope for her was that she'd one day fall in love with, like, a librarian. Or an accountant. Or really anyone whose living did not in any way rely on selling handmade crafts or her ADD prescription pills.

"Did you match with her?" I asked.

"Not yet," she said. "Her profile said she hadn't been on in two months. I've decided she's on a spiritual retreat in the Himalayas."

I laughed. "Wait, I called you for a reason."

"What?"

"I want you to help me style Archie Fox." I grinned, knowing as I said the words how excited she was going to be to hear them. Sure enough, she screamed, so loud I had to hold the phone away from my face.

"Are you serious?" she said. "Like, for real?"

"Yes," I said. "I need you. He needs you."

"Okay, but, don't you think his manager would have to approve it? Doesn't he already have a stylist?"

"I was sort of thinking I'd just…sidestep Maria on this," I said as lightly as possible. "And no, he fired his stylist last year. I saw her Instagram post about it." In truth I hadn't thought of the manager question until Harper had brought it up, but I was sure (or pretty sure) that it would be fine. Why wouldn't Maria want Archie to look better than he did now? What reasons could she (or my own bosses) have to object? I felt suddenly nervous, wondering if I was stepping out of bounds. Maybe I *should* email Joanna, I thought. But then I remembered all the times I'd annoyed her by asking for her input on things that didn't concern her. She *wanted* me to take initiative, to follow my instincts. As long as they were good ones. And I was pretty sure this one was. I took a breath, reminding myself that it wasn't like I was going to charge a brand-new wardrobe to Weaver-Girard, or make him shave his head (I shuddered to even think of it)—I was simply going to take him shopping, along with Harper, and then we would just gently suggest he try on a small number of items. A moderately small number of items. Besides, he was going to be doing more appearances soon, and touring, and he would need new stuff for that anyway. I was merely being thorough.

"What's his budget like?" Harper asked, bursting into laughter before she could even finish the question. "God, I'm funny."

"Any thoughts as to where we should take him?" I asked. "This is all assuming he agrees, of course. I plan to be very convincing."

"How?"

"I don't know yet," I said.

"Well, give me the night to think about it," said Harper. "We'll want a flagship store, obviously. If he's free, Sunday night after close or Monday morning before opening would be ideal. Luckily for us, I don't think there's any store in New York that would require more than five minutes' advance notice that Archie Fox wants to make a private visit."

"I should hope not," I said. "I'll talk to him and find out when he's free. I'll just be vague as to where we'll be going. And what we'll be doing."

"Cool, that won't make him suspicious," said Harper.

"It'll be fine," I said. "Right? It'll be fine." I closed my eyes and pressed my fingers to my left temple, which had started to pulse. I'd been reassuring myself an awful lot lately.

"Yes. Everything will be fine," soothed Harper. "We're gonna take Archie Fox shopping. Everything will be fucking *fantastic*."

"Okay." I took a deep breath. "I should go. Think about stores. And text me when you know."

"You got it. And good luck."

I flopped backward onto my bed. Outside my room I heard the front door slam closed—Chelsey and Jay heading out for the night. I waited for a minute, until I felt sure that she hadn't forgotten anything and wasn't about to walk back in, and I let out a long, low-pitched groan. The image of them on the couch floated back into my mind and I grabbed my phone, desperate to erase it. I tapped on the Gmail icon, sat up, and opened a new email.

`Dear Archie`, I typed, and immediately erased.

`A`–I typed. But no. Maybe he could get away with addressing *me* as "R"—not that he had, or ever would—but I couldn't pull it off.

`Hi there.` (*Ew*, I thought. Too weirdly flirty.)

`Archie`, I typed. *Whatever*, it'll do. I went on.

`What's your Sunday evening like? Alternatively, your early Monday morning? I know this is a bit last-minute, so I'll understand if you're not free, but if you can find some time to meet with me, that would be awesome.`

I deleted "awesome" and wrote "great."

I hesitated, and then I sent it. The message was willfully vague, but at least none of it was *false*. I just hadn't mentioned where I wanted to meet, or why. He might not even be free anyway.

But a moment later, my eyes were drawn back to my phone screen by the appearance of a new email. From Archie Fox. Late on a Friday night, when he should (or at least, I thought, would) be out partying with various supermodels, on a rooftop bar normal people weren't allowed into.

`Sunday evening works. I'm not much of a morning person. When and where?`

I paused. I knew most high-end stores closed at 6:00 on Sundays, so I decided to make an educated guess. They'd want at least an hour to get the store in shape, I figured, and the closer we got to sunset, the easier it'd be to make Archie's arrival a private one.

`How's 8:00? Exact location TBD, but I'll email you soon.`

I pressed SEND, and when his reply arrived, again just moments later, I laughed. I couldn't believe he wasn't doing something cooler.

His message read: `Mysterious! TTFN.`

I laughed again. My thumbs hovered over the phone keyboard. I wanted to write *HAGS* or *CUL8R* or, illogically, *LYLAS*, but I couldn't bring myself to type them out. Instead, I typed `Talk soon!` and pressed SEND. At the sound of the little *whoosh* I felt a tiny wave of guilty panic for having been somewhat misleading. I didn't want Archie to be annoyed—or offended, or mad—when we got to whatever store Harper picked out, and he realized what I'd had in mind. But then, I thought, my job was not necessarily to make Archie *happy*. It was to make him beloved.

# 7.

"Are you sure this is right?"

I peered through the door for the third time in the five minutes since we'd arrived, but the view hadn't changed. All I could see of the store was a blank white wall, at the end of a dark, somewhat ominous, tunnel. It was the same tunnel I was currently standing in, encircled by narrowing metallic walls that led from the sidewalk, to the front door, and then seemingly beyond. "The whole thing kind of has a Hobbit hole vibe."

When I'd first imagined an exclusive shopping spree, this wasn't exactly what I'd had in mind. I was thinking glitz, luxury—a sprawling Fifth Avenue megastore open to us like an after-hours amusement park. What I got was a graffiti- and flyer-laden brick building, on a quiet Chelsea street mostly inhabited by art galleries, with no evidence of any store's existence other than the small block letters written across the circular glass door: DU ROI.

Harper had called me early Saturday morning, uttering only those two words in lieu of a hello, as if the name itself were all the explanation I'd need. When I met them with silence, she launched into her vision—which had apparently kept her up late into the night—while I did my own investigating online, scrolling through images of silky shirts, tight, beaten-up-looking jeans, and elaborate boots. Harper assured me the edgy French brand would lend Archie a "cool factor" that was "utterly necessary" for legitimizing his pairing with Raya; that the line's brazenness would return him to a time when he "actually seemed fun"; that its trademark androgyny was "*perfectly* in line" with his early experimentation in girls' jeans and felt hats; and that, frankly, he'd just look super-hot in it. Of course I went along with it. Harper's reasoning made sense, and if her plan involved getting Archie back into painted-on pants, well, the rest of the world could thank me later. But now, looking at this brick-and-mortar manifestation of hipster, I was having second thoughts.

"Listen." Harper pulled me away from the front door to join her at the sidewalk's edge. "It's supposed to be weird! It's part of its whole"—she waved her hands impatiently—"thing. Samantha's right in there. She's waiting on a text from us. Just trust me."

I took in a slow, deep breath and then let it go. Samantha, a college sort-of-friend of Harper's whom I'd never met, was one of the managers of the shop, and would be our dedicated sales associate for the evening. We were to let her know when Archie arrived—because, unsurprisingly, his presence was the only one that warranted after-hours access—and then we would run through our very own shopping-slash-fashion-show montage. At least, that's how I pictured it. Harper assured me we were in great hands, and I trusted Harper. Everything was fine. This was just the first big, experimental decision I'd made without consult, on the first real project I'd ever run on my own, and the success of this decision *could* dictate the tone of my working relationship with my first real client, and perhaps the success of the rest of my career, but, yeah, it was fine. It was going to be fine. Probably.

I checked my phone: 7:48. Still early, but we'd arrived earlier than early, having counted on Archie—surprisingly punctual—to do the same. And we were right. Before I could even take my eyes from my phone, Harper was jabbing me in the ribs.

"Is that him? Oh my God, it is. Is it?" she whispered in a tone about a full octave higher than her normal voice.

"Harp!" I laughed and shoved her slightly. "That hurts!"

Her jabs relented, and her nervous energy channeled into what could only be described as a quiet, drawn-out squeak. My best friend had been replaced, instantaneously, with a prepubescent fangirl, and the source of all this excitement was just a few paces away. I was surprised by my relief when I realized he was alone, but decided not to question it.

"No car?" I asked. "I didn't think you were allowed to roam freely in this city."

Archie shrugged. "My driver has the night off for his twins' birthday."

Likely as a result, he was dressed to blend in: the hood of his too-baggy sweatshirt (reading, ironically, TALL PINES SUMMER CAMP) was pulled over his head; his hair was hidden under a Yankees baseball cap. His jeans were torn and just a tad too loose, and he'd topped it off with a pair of nondescript sneakers. If I hadn't been expecting him, I wouldn't have given him a second look. The only suggestion of celebrity came from his sunglasses, unnecessary in the dimming light.

Harper sidled up next to me and thrust out her hand.

"I'm Harper. Colleague of Rose's. Big fan of yours. Super

fashion nerd. This was my idea. I mean, the venue was my idea. The activity was Rose's."

"And what is that activity, exactly?" he asked. When I'd emailed him after speaking with Harper, I'd offered as little information as possible: namely, the cross-streets, and a reiteration of the meeting time.

"You didn't tell him?" Harper spun around to face me.

"I didn't specify the *exact* nature..." I trailed off as Archie looked past me, sizing up the building.

"Now I'm *very* curious," he said.

"Okay, well, it's not incredibly exciting, so don't get your hopes up," I said. "I just thought we might do some... shopping."

Archie's eyebrows rose.

"She's underselling," gushed Harper. "It's gonna be amazing. I'm not sure if you're familiar with Du Roi, but it's super cool. Like, definitely Raya-cool. Not that you aren't already cool! But, you know. Ah!" She blew out a deep sigh, turned to me and then back to Archie. "Am I talking too much? I feel like I'm talking too much. It's just. You're Archie Fox, for fuck's sake!"

I felt my eyes go wide, and my jaw tightened. Harper was definitely more celeb-crazed than I was—"This is why they don't let me work with the talent," she'd joke whenever an especially famous and/or attractive star walked past our desks, causing her to briefly lose all focus—but she was in rare form tonight. Archie's inscrutable expression made it difficult to tell whether he was charmed or horrified.

"Forgive Harper's... salty language," I said. Harper nodded wildly, expectant. "She's, um. She's enthusiastic."

Archie smiled, and I felt all the muscles I didn't know were tensed relax. "She's great."

Harper beamed and texted Samantha to tell her our full party had arrived. Moments later, the big glass door slid open. Our host was tall and lean, all hard angles draped in sheer linen, with a platinum-white bob and jet-black lips. She greeted each of us with a curt nod, ushered us in wordlessly, and then followed as we made our way slowly through the tunnel, which extended about ten feet past the door. I looked back to gauge Archie's immediate reaction, but his head was tilted up toward the ceiling, his fingertips grazing the metallic veneer.

"You know, it's so odd," he said. "This reminds me of this place I loved as a kid. It was like an arcade, but with rides—bumper cars, ball pits, that sort of thing. Horribly dirty if I think about it now, but rather fun then. Anyway, it was space-themed. There was a tunnel at the entrance, with flashing lights. I always used to pretend I was entering a black hole."

Harper and I exchanged a quick, blank look. It was the most I'd heard Archie speak without prompt, and I didn't want to risk ruining it by cutting him off. It was like he was sleepwalking, and we just needed to let whatever he was dreaming play out. I tried to transmit this message telepathically to Harper.

"Dude, are you a closet sci-fi nerd?" she asked over her shoulder. Evidently, our best-friend mind reading still needed some work. "You and Rose will get along *very* well."

"Is that right?" he asked. "Trekkie?"

"Too highbrow. Rose likes the cheesy stuff."

"I'm sure Samantha—who very graciously has taken time out of her day to let us shop—would love for us to get right to business." I smiled at Samantha, hoping for an ally, but her expression remained stony. Probably she didn't give a shit what we were talking about, or how long it took us, as long as we left with money spent.

"We've made her mad, haven't we?" Archie stage-whispered to Harper, who actually *giggled*. In our three years of friendship, I'd never seen her laugh in a way that even remotely resembled a giggle. I'd envisioned many varied scenarios that might come of this shopping trip, but the teaming-up of Harper and Archie against me was not among them.

Harper made a show of composing herself, straightening her smile. "You got it," she said to me. "Serious. Shopping."

I looked around us. The interior was exactly as strange as one would expect of a store whose entrance suggested a portal to another dimension. Said portal dropped us in the center of a cavernous space, where we were surrounded by freestanding gold-painted walls. Some angled toward the outer walls, some expanded toward the ceiling, some curved in a semicircle. As for the merchandise, it was elegantly sparse—three racks, maybe four, of brightly patterned shirts and gigantic frocks. A rack of mannequins wore dresses that looked like they were either unfinished or falling apart. A low, long shelf presented a single pair of shoes, one bag, and three fuzzy spheres lined up in increasing size. A statue of what appeared to be a dystopian Mickey Mouse stood in the far corner. It was unclear if the spheres or the statue were for sale.

*Welp, this is it,* I thought. *I had a shot to style Archie Fox, and I took him to a carnival fun house. Cool. It's cool.*

I turned on my heel to offer up an alternative suggestion (though I hadn't gone so far as picking one—Gucci was a thing celebrities wore, right?), but Archie clapped his hands together before I got the first word out.

"Well! Where should we begin?"

*Never mind*, I thought. *I guess this looks normal to him?*

I lifted my hands in surrender. "Go for it, Harp—you're running this show."

She gave Archie the Cliffs Notes version of the speech she'd given me, softening the parts about how people would need to be nudged in order to believe he was cool enough to get Raya, and instead emphasizing how, when deployed effectively and strategically, a person's wardrobe could highlight or suggest certain aspects of his personality. It could guide people into seeing him the way he *wanted* to be seen. He could literally fashion himself into an image of his making. It was all very rousing.

"So, I think there should be a unifying element of your style," she said. "Something with intention. Whether or not your fans pick up on it. Like, *the* shirt or hat or jacket or jewelry—but honestly, like, be careful with jewelry, because you wear a bunch of the wrong necklaces and suddenly the message you're sending is *I'm secretly a contributor on a bunch of pickup artist message boards*. But anyway, it should be something people see you in, over and over again, enough that even those people who don't give two shits about you can summon a clear image of you in their heads. You get it?"

"I get it."

"So let's see first what you're drawn to," said Harper. "Walk around, pick things up, see how it feels." I remained silent, surprised and impressed by the way talking about clothing had brought Harper to life. At work, she was smart, and quick, but here she was a genius.

I watched as Archie paused in front of a pair of black loafers, but then he quickly gravitated toward a rack of men's shirts. He pulled out a button-up with a white torso and pink sleeves, held it up to his chest, and then returned it. Same fate for a patchwork denim pullover. He grabbed a black-and-white polka-dot button-down and twirled it around for our opinions.

"I like it!" said Harper. I offered an enthusiastic thumbs-up.

He made the rounds, adding a floral button-up, black jeans, and navy velour blazer to the pile. Finally, he returned to the original rack and pulled out a previously dismissed black silk shirt covered in flamingos.

"Too much?" he asked, his face scrunched in indecisiveness. It was annoyingly cute.

"No, oh my God, I love it!" Harper's hand flew to her chest, as if unable to contain her joy.

"Really?" I grimaced. I was less of a fan, to say the least. "You don't think it's a little, like… resort-wear-y? Like Tommy Bahama or something?"

Harper rested her hands on my shoulders and locked her eyes on mine. "Rose? You are not allowed to compare Du Roi to Tommy Bahama. Okay? I will revoke your opinion rights."

"But, like, what is he, the new guitarist for the Beach Boys?" I asked. "I'm sorry, I just think it's kinda… loud." I stopped, turning around. "No offense, Samantha."

Samantha, preoccupying herself with folding one of three sweaters on a small table, sighed. I was beginning to suspect she was mute.

Harper groaned. "You're killing me." She pointed to Archie. "You—try it all on. Don't listen to a person who hasn't worn color since 2005." He disappeared into a room and pulled the curtain closed behind him.

"Black is classic!" I said, sounding slightly shrill.

"It's also for mourning."

I was about to shoot back when Archie stepped out in the first shirt—polka dots. Simple, good. Harper squealed and walked over to cuff his sleeves.

"This is good. Like, so good. Do you like it?"

"Well, it feels all right, but there wasn't a mirror in the stall. Do you . . . ?"

"Samantha, is there a mirror we can pull out?" Harper called without leaving Archie's side. "They don't really do mirrors here. Lorin Pouliot says it's about how clothes make you *feel*. But they probably have something in the back."

"Harper," I said. "They don't 'do' mirrors? Come on."

"What!"

"You know, Rose, you're doing an awful lot of raining on our parade for a person whose idea this whole thing was," Archie chimed in, adjusting his collar.

"*Thank you*," said Harper. She turned back to me and winked. "An *awful* lot of raining."

I rolled my eyes as Samantha arrived at Archie's side with a vanity mirror no bigger than a piece of paper. "It's all we have," she said, confirming she could, in fact, speak, and in a voice much deeper than I'd imagined.

"Well, you and Rose will just have to be my eyes," said Archie. He turned to me.

"Okay, yeah, I like this one," I said.

"Great, there's one done."

I felt my phone vibrate in my pocket and stole a quick glance as he returned to the changing stall. A Tinder update: a message from Neil. I returned my phone to my pocket, and then pulled it out again. I tried, very quickly, to gauge the level of unprofessionalism in using my phone for personal business while with a client. If I'd learned anything from Joanna, it was that celebrities are a bunch of babies who need to feel like they're the most important—ideally, only—thing in your life. But Archie seemed different. And he needed Harper's opinion more than mine anyway. And besides, how often did I encounter someone on Tinder who didn't seem absolutely terrible? I needed to know if his message would change that. I clicked on the envelope icon.

> Hi there! I'm not totally sure the best way to start these things (I know everyone says this, but I don't really use this thing a lot...) but I saw that we matched, and you seem really interesting! Could I buy you a drink sometime?
>
> xx
>
> Neil

I read it again, and then a third time for good measure. It wasn't the flashiest message I'd ever received, but it was the first in a very long time that didn't immediately make clear the sender was either an idiot or an asshole, or both. I'd gotten so used to dismissing matches out of hand that I'd apparently forgotten how nerve racking potential interest on my part could be.

"Rose? Where'd you go?" Archie was standing in front of me, arms spread wide, wearing the flamingo shirt. Harper was behind him, wrapping a thin, black silk scarf loosely around his neck. I shoved my phone back in my pocket.

"Oh, ah, I'm sorry." I took a moment to study his appearance:

less Dad-after-shopping-the-beachwear-sale, more gender-bending glamazon. "I like it!"

"You like it?" Harper asked. "Cool, right?"

"I mean, I don't know. Sure. It's not as bad as I thought." In truth, while I did like the look, my mind was still mulling over that message from Neil. "I'm sorry, yes. It looks good!"

Archie and Harper caught each other's eyes. They'd literally met two hours ago, and they were already sharing meaningful glances.

"What's going on?" Harper asked. I raised my eyebrows and glared at her as hard as I could, but instead of taking my meaning—*Shut up, move on*—her eyes went wide. "Is it Hot Doctor?"

I felt my cheeks flush. "Harper!"

"Wait, who's the hot doctor?" Archie asked.

"Just, like, a brilliant brain surgeon who's also super-hot and basically in love with Rose." She unraveled the scarf and swapped it with a hot-pink handkerchief that she tucked into Archie's shirt pocket.

"That's not true," I said.

"Ooooh," Archie cooed, I thought, somewhat derisively. "Tinder?"

"Jesus Christ," I said. "Can you try on your next outfit, please?" I glanced quickly at Archie, too embarrassed to meet him in the eye but too panicky not to try and change the topic. He chuckled and turned, returning to the stall.

"Tell me what it said," said Harper.

"I don't know. It's stupid. He's probably stupid." Harper glared until I pulled out my phone. "Okay, so first of all, he used *ellipses*."

"Uh-oh," said Harper. She knew how seriously I took text and email grammar, and how angry the misuse of ellipses made me. She didn't agree, but she at least understood.

"What's wrong with ellipses?" Archie asked from behind the stall door.

"I'm not getting into this," I said. But I couldn't resist. "They just make everything so ominous! And this next part, like, okay, acknowledging that 'everyone' says the thing you're about to say doesn't make it any less cliché when you say it."

"Just let me see," Harper said, and grabbed my phone.

"Share with the class," said Archie, who'd emerged in a black tee, plain save for a small crown logo on the bottom right hem, and distressed black jeans. He looked great; even Harper was momentarily distracted from her single-minded pursuit of ruining my life. We both watched Archie take a seat on one of the gold tables, and Samantha approach as if to ask him to move, but then she thought better of it and retreated.

"Okay," said Harper, and I covered my face as she began to read through the message in her all-purpose male-impersonation voice.

"This honestly seems fine," she said at the end. I reached for my phone but was intercepted by Archie.

"She's right," he said.

"But the ellipses!" I protested.

"You've gotta let that one go, Rose," she said.

"He said I seemed 'interesting.' Interesting doesn't mean anything. It's like the least valuable qualifier."

"How do I get to his photos?" asked Archie. *Celebrities,* I thought. My mouth dropped open in horror as Harper leaned over to help him, but I was powerless to stop her. The day had already gotten so far away from me. Archie studied the photos for a moment, and in my head I visualized what he saw—the best man at a wedding candid, the med school graduation, the soccer team action shot, the obvious woman bait (him with a puppy, him making a snow angel with a niece). "Seems like a... nice young man," he said, the pause between "a" and "nice" held for so long that it had to be at least partly pointed.

"He's a *doctor*," said Harper.

"Yeah," I said. "Not everyone can be a multimillionaire rock star with their own private jet." It was fine if *I* said Neil seemed stupid, or kind of boring, but Archie was not allowed.

"Those *are* my best qualities." Archie was grinning, but his eyes looked steely, almost cold. He stood up from the table, fidgeting in his jeans. "I know we're going for tight but if I wear these any longer I'll faint, and that would not be very trendy of me." With that he turned into his stall and pulled the curtain closed behind him.

I looked at Harper, who was very evidently trying her hardest not to press the matter further but who, also very evidently, could not stop herself.

*It's just a drink*, she mouthed, silent. We'd gotten pretty good at lipreading from carrying on silent conversations in our cubicle in order to avoid being noticed by Ethan.

I rolled my eyes, mouthing back, *I don't have time.*

"Netflix suggests otherwise."

In that moment I deeply and sincerely rued the day I gave Harper my Netflix password.

"I don't have anything to wear," I said. This was not *strictly* true, of course; I had a closet that was moderately full of clothing items, many of which even went together by virtue of being almost exclusively black. But it was *figuratively* true, in a way even Harper could not argue with. My wardrobe consisted almost entirely of structured business separates and slightly more casual, also-black weekend wear. With the arrival of each new season I bought a few new blouses and sweaters and skirts from Ann Taylor Loft or J.Crew, and after that I more or less called it a day. I knew how to look put-together and professional, but I did not know how to go, as the magazines would say, *from day to night*. I knew this because every time I texted Harper a date outfit for her approval, she texted back something like, "Isn't that what you wore to work today?"

Harper stared at me in response, thinking it over. I knew she'd have offered to lend me anything, including the clothes off her back, if we were at all comparable in clothing size, but we weren't. She was a hair over six feet tall and fit, a volleyball player's body. I was six inches shorter and, um, slightly less fit.

"Samantha," said Harper. "Can we get one each of your ready-to-wear dresses in an... eight?" She looked at me, waiting for my confirmation, and it took every ounce of personal strength I had to keep myself from both looking at Archie to see if he was listening, and striding across the floor to punch Harper in the face. I jerked my head up in a tiny nod, then looked at Samantha, who looked back and forth between Harper and me.

"Of course..." she said. It was obvious she wanted to say more—like, *For you?* or *Does someone in Steve Madden boots really have the budget?*—but she sucked them in along with her cheeks, creating cheekbones even more prominent than before. Once she'd disappeared into the back room, I crossed over to Harper and grabbed her by the arm, hard.

"Ow!" she yelped.

Archie, previously immersed in his phone, looked up at us both. I forced a smile. "Do you maybe want to go browse the shoe collection?" I asked, pointing behind him to the little shoe room off the back of the store. He looked behind him, gave a slight nod, and got up without a word. Once there were twenty feet between us, I whirled around to face Harper again.

"Harper," I said. "I do *not* have the money for a Du Roi dress. I don't have enough money for a Du Roi button."

"Relax," she said. "You're just trying them on."

"What's the point of that?" I said. "If I love it I'll just be mad I can't buy it. And if I hate it, then I'll just feel sad that rich-people clothing doesn't look good on me."

"The point is that it's fun!" said Harper. "And if you find something you like, I will find you a cheap version. Just like in the magazines. This is the splurge, and I'll find you the steal."

I sighed.

"Come on," she continued. "Besides, I can help Archie with shoes while you're trying them on. I think he'll feel less overwhelmed if he only has to deal with one of us at a time and I can just tell him what to do."

I turned to look at him across the store, where he was once again immersed in his phone screen, surrounded by shoes he wasn't looking at, leaning against the store window.

"That's probably true," I said. Just then Samantha emerged from the back with an armful of dresses, which she hung from a row of hooks in the changing stall next to Archie's.

"Holler if there's anything you want me to see," said Harper. She turned to face Archie. "What are you doing?" she yelled across the store. "Stop texting and pick up a shoe!" Before I could see how he responded to her I closed myself into my little room, sat on the tiny bench inside it, and cupped my face in my hands. I took a few deep breaths, trying to remind myself of where I was and why I was there. Part of me worried that it was unprofessional or unsavvy for Harper (or me) to boss him around like this—as if telling him what to wear was somehow different from telling him who to go out with. But as I breathed in and out, I reminded myself what I'd been taught: Sometimes celebrities needed to be corralled. Still, when I stopped to think about the situation at hand, it was pretty weird. How was it possible that Archie Fox was now, in addition to being an international pop phenomenon, a guy my best friend casually scolded in a clothing store? I thought of something Joanna said to me a few times, half-jokingly, when I first started. "Remember, they're just people." A beat, and then: "Sort of."

I stood up to face the stack of dresses hanging from the metal bar that lined the wall separating my stall from Archie's. I checked the curtain once more, tugging at one end to cover the inch-wide sliver of light shining in from the store outside, and then doing the same to close the now-*two*-inch-wide opening on the other side until I realized there was no way to cover it completely, and maybe that was also part of this stupid store's philosophy.

I turned back to the dresses; I was slightly afraid I would touch one and somehow accidentally pull on a loose thread and the whole thing would unravel, and Samantha would tell me I had to pay for it, and I wouldn't have enough money on my credit card to cover it, and Archie would overhear us and end up paying for it out of pity, and then the tone of our entire working relationship would be thrown off because I would feel like I owed him something, and he'd back out of his contract with the company, and I would get fired, and I would have to move back to California and into my parents' basement and get a job at the Olive Garden where I worked in high school because it would be the only place that would take me.

Feeling warm, I closed my eyes and reached out a hand toward the wall to steady myself, but as my fingers made contact with one of the dresses—a fabric so crisp, so thick, it was like touching an actual stack of hundred-dollar bills—I opened them again. The dress was still intact, and it was incredible-looking. I slid the hanger down the rod and looked at the next one, which was also incredible, as was the one after it. I stepped out of my boots and pulled off my dress. I carefully pulled the hanger out of the first dress—a short skirt with a wide neck and long sleeves, all made of a bright-yellow fabric, geometric black stripes sewn across the shoulders and waist—and tugged it down over my body. From what I could tell by looking down at myself, the dress actually sort of fit. But I knew that didn't count for much without a mirror, and again I cursed this store (beautiful dresses and all) for being so willfully difficult.

I reached a hand around the curtain and pulled it back to see Harper and Archie still standing on the far end of the store. Harper's back was to me, and she held up a different boot in each hand, lifting one and then the other, while Archie listened with his arms crossed in front of him, occasionally nodding or furrowing his brow.

"Harper?" I hissed. She didn't hear me, but I refused to step all the way out of the stall. "*Harper.*"

She turned to face me, and Archie looked over, too.

"Can you...?" I said, willing my face to transmit the rest of my plea for me. *Please don't make me clarify that I want* only *you to come over here.*

Much to my relief, she plunked the shoes in Archie's hands and walked over. When she was within arm's reach I grabbed her and pulled her into the tiny stall with me.

"Oooooh!"

"Yeah?" I said. "I can't see it, so."

"Yeah! Well. I like it, but. It's not super *you*."

"Well no shit," I said. "I thought that was the point."

"It is," she replied. I rolled my eyes. "But the right dress should just make you look like some version of you, even if it's a version you haven't seen before."

"Um," I said. "Sure. I don't have a mirror so I'm just going to trust you on that."

"Good." She glanced over the rack, picked one out from the middle, and handed it to me before slipping through the curtain.

I examined the dress she'd handed me—solid, velvety black, and short, with a row of bright-silver buttons running down the middle of the front and rows of four each at each wrist, and a high crew neck with squared, lightly padded shoulders. It was gorgeous, and—if I were the type of person who spent two thousand dollars on dresses—very me. I yanked off the yellow dress as gently as I possibly could, and pulled the black one on in its place. I ran my hand over the buttons and the high neck and thought that if for some reason I were forced to wear one tight, black dress for the rest of my life, I would want it to be this one.

I pulled back the curtain and Harper, waiting dutifully just outside, squeezed back into the stall. For what felt like a full minute, she examined me in silence.

"Well?" I said finally.

"Jeez, Rose," she said.

"Good?" I said. "Or bad?"

"Um, good, obviously. I am literally speechless."

"Well."

"I mean, almost," she said. "You look magnificent."

"Really?" I gushed. "I *feel* magnificent. I feel like I could be in a music video. Like in the background or something."

"Definitely at least in the background," she said.

"I want a fucking *mirror*!"

"I know," she said. "Oh! I'll take a picture of you." She pulled her phone out of her purse and backed up, the entire four inches left in the stall. She held up her phone and frowned. "Okay, no. Let's go out there."

"Um," I said. And then, quietly: "I don't want to."

*Because of him?* she mouthed.

I shrugged. *Yes.*

"He doesn't care," she said. "He's shoe shopping. Turns out he loves shoes."

"Oh," I said. "Okay. Ugh. Fine."

She pushed the curtain aside for me and I walked out first, making instant eye contact with Archie. It was only a second and a half before he turned, and I looked away, but that last half felt long. Then Harper pushed past me, and began arranging me into place for a photo, and I focused instead on her. She stepped back from me and I stared, unblinking, wanting badly to see if Archie was looking at me again, the way it felt he was, or if I was imagining it.

"Try not to look so manic," said Harper. I felt my neck flush pink, but I forced my eyes to relax, and my mouth into my best closed-mouth model smile.

"Perfect," she said. She walked back, holding up her phone for me to see. I'd sort of hoped that my initial impression was wrong, and that the dress fit me horribly, and looked all wrong, so that it wouldn't be tragic when I had to take it off and walk out of the store without it. But as pretty much always happens when one is trying on items one cannot in any way afford, it looked amazing, like it was meant for my body, like I had been an idiot for ever wearing anything else.

"Dammit," I muttered.

"I know," said Harper. Then, before I could stop her or, better yet, kill her, she called out, "Archie! Doesn't Rose look amazing in this dress?"

Very reluctantly, I followed Harper's lead and turned to look at him. His eyes flitted from my face to the hem of the dress and back up, his expression unreadable.

"Bit posh for a first date, isn't it?"

"Great," I said. "Thank you *so* much."

Harper scoffed. "First of all, no, it's not. And second of all, that's not what I asked."

"Right," he said, looking from Harper back to me. "Then yes, she looks quite all right."

"Okay!" I said. My head felt hot with a mixture of embarrassment and anger. "All right"? I looked fucking amazing. Maybe I did not look like *Raya*, but for me at least, I looked amazing. "Cool. I'm just going to—" I trailed off, gesturing toward the stall with my thumb and walking backward toward it at the same time.

Inside the stall I took off the dress and hung it carefully back on its hanger. I stood there for a few minutes in my bra and underwear, my arms crossed in front of my chest. I could hear Archie and Harper talking about shoes again, but I tuned them out, trying to push the mortification deep down in my body. When I emerged from the fitting room I would make myself be cool and composed, bright-eyed and professionally friendly. I would no longer allow for group discussion of my personal life, or lack thereof.

I exited the stall with the stack of dresses piled high over one arm. As I handed them to a grimacing Samantha with my best thank-you-but-no-thank-you smile, Harper looked over and asked, "Hey, why didn't you show me any of the others?"

"Didn't fit," I said with a shrug. She frowned and furrowed her brow. If she knew I was lying she decided against saying as much, and instead she just nodded.

"So what've we decided on?" I asked.

"The polka dots in both colors, the black tee, the jeans, the flamingos, and the boots," said Harper, sweeping her arm across the shelf behind her like Vanna White. Three pairs of ankle boots, all with stacked two- or three-inch heels, sat in a row atop it—one, a simple camel-colored suede; another in black leather with biker-style buckles; and finally, the showstoppers: a cowboy-style pair in bright silver with a metallic turquoise color-block near the ankles. All three pairs were cool, fashion-forward, and androgynous. On some (maybe most) men they would have looked silly, or calculated, but I knew that on Archie they'd look natural yet edgy.

"Those are great, Harper," I said. "Especially the silver."

"Those are all Archie," she said.

I looked up at him and he shrugged. "Well, great," I chirped. "We ready?"

"Yes!" replied Harper. "Samantha, I think we're ready!"

We gathered at the cash register with a visibly relieved Samantha, who folded Archie's shirts into tissue paper, slid everything into a large paper bag, and accepted his credit card with a pinched smile—the happiest she'd looked all day. When we walked outside a black Escalade was parked just in front.

"Pete put his twins to bed," explained Archie.

"Ah," I said. "Well, thanks so much for making time for this."

"My pleasure," he replied, tipping the brim of his baseball cap. "Thank you both for your invaluable fashion guidance." He grinned widely, a dimple appearing in each cheek. I couldn't help but smile back. He climbed into the backseat of the car, carelessly tossing the bag—with its four thousand dollars' worth of contents—into the seat next to him, and waved.

# 8.

ROSE! PLEASE!"

I didn't realize I'd started doing it again until Harper hissed my name.

"I'm sorry, I'm sorry!" I said, shoving aside the pen I'd been tapping rapidly against my desk. I turned my attention back to the screen in front of me. It was well past lunch and Joanna hadn't left her office once all day. I knew because I'd barely taken my eyes off the door. It was rare that I arrived before her, and when I'd realized that was the case this morning—8:55 a.m. as always—I'd hovered in front of her door like a lost child, coffee in hand, until Harper pulled me away.

"Why are you being such a creep?" She'd taken the coffee from my hand and brought it to her mouth, dropping down in her seat.

"That's Joanna's!" I shrieked. Harper brushed my concern away with a wave of her hand.

"It's already room temp. I'm doing her a favor. Anyway, she's late. It's her own fault."

I groaned and sank my head into my hands. "When you own the company you're never late. Everyone else is just early."

Harper shrugged. "Then you can also get someone to bring you a fresh cup of coffee."

When Joanna did breeze in at 9:30, I jumped from my chair to meet her at her door, fumbling over an explanation while she plopped her bag down and settled into her desk—I'd had her coffee, but tossed it because it had gotten so cold, not that I was blaming her for being late, not that she even *was* late, really, but anyway, did she want me to run out and get her another?

She looked up at me as if she was just realizing I was in the room, pointed to the earbuds in her ear with her free hand, and then raised the other—which was holding a steaming travel mug. I laughed and apologized and slinked out, while Joanna told someone named Rob she didn't give a shit what *Us Weekly* was offering, they "weren't running the pictures." It was her first day back from Dubai, clearly still embroiled in Trevor drama. I knew, realistically, that she was just distracted—and now, four hours later, I understood it was a good sign that she hadn't yet called me into her office to talk about Archie. Positive reinforcement wasn't really Joanna's thing; she was more of the mind that you'd know you were doing a good job as long as she wasn't yelling at you for doing a bad one.

Sometimes I forgot this. Not always, but sometimes—like, for instance, when I'd talked myself into a position I maybe wasn't *totally* qualified for, and then decided to go rogue with the decision making anyway. So here I was, with the morning gone and nothing but intense staring and pen tapping and cubicle-mate-irritating to show for it.

"You need to chill," Harper said. "Have you heard from Maria?"

"Yes." She'd emailed before I'd even woken up to tell me what a wonderful time Archie had on our shopping trip (a sentiment that no doubt came from Maria and not Archie himself), and how excited he was for tomorrow night's date (same), and that she'd love to get on the phone sometime today to nail down "the particulars."

"And?"

"We're talking later today. Apparently Du Roi was a hit."

"Cool, I'm glad." She was trying to play reserved—a tactic of Harper's that was always strongest on Mondays and weakened as the week progressed—but I could see her whole face beaming behind her computer.

I clicked over to my Gmail tab and opened a new message to Archie. I was accustomed to messengering thank-you notes and the occasional gift to clients who'd taken the time to meet, but I wasn't exactly sure what the rules were around an unofficial, off-the-books styling session—one that I'd coordinated, he'd bankrolled, and ultimately felt like a shopping trip among kind of awkward friends. A quick email? A phone call? Was there an e-card for that?

I decided on an email and was in the middle of drafting a message that was both breezy and emphatically self-assured when a little Gchat window popped up from Joanna.

`Hi, you there?`

The scariest three words.

`Yup! What's up?`
`Could you step in for a min?`
`Sure! Be right there!`

My heart was racing. I wanted to go back in time to the hours in which Joanna had seemingly forgotten all about me. I wanted to yell at the version of me who had wished this very message into existence. I desperately hoped my exclamation points had masked my fear.

"Shit, shit," I muttered, gathering up papers for no real reason, opening and closing drawers of my desk.

"Uhh, what's the deal?" Harper asked.

"Joanna wants to see me." I stood up and smoothed the front of my silk blouse.

"That's good! Right? You have good things to tell her."

I knew Harper was right, but Joanna had a way of disappearing my confidence without really doing anything. It was something I'd been trying to figure out since I'd started working closely with her. Joanna respected me, and I understood that. I appreciated that she'd promoted me fairly quickly, and I reminded myself often of the unlikelihood that my promotion was part of some very long-running and elaborate prank. When my trust in this faltered, I went to Harper for reassurance. But I'd also never before embarked on a project that could be seen as risky, or one in which I had so much independence.

Harper flashed me a thumbs-up, and I grabbed a notebook, stuck a pen behind my ear, and walked across the hall.

Maybe I was biased, but Joanna's office was my favorite of all the partners'. It wasn't huge, but its rear wall of windows offered a view of Madison Square Park that was basically a work of art, complete with the Empire State Building peeking out in the distance. It always seemed incredibly clean, but never intimidatingly so. Natural light flooded the space—which, luckily for the rest of us, also filtered past the striated glass doors that faced the rest of the office—and it was almost completely white, save for the burgundy wall on the left, in front of which was Joanna's desk, and the few matching pillows scattered on the white couch right smack in the center of the room.

My favorite part, though, was the wall opposite Joanna's desk: that one, with its built-in floor-to-ceiling shelves, presented both Joanna's massive record collection *and* her truly covet-worthy Pioneer turntable, a circa-late-1970s PL-610. It brought me physical pain that increased in direct relation to my proximity to it. In my wildest dreams, Joanna and I would find ourselves the only people left at the office late one night, and she'd shout an invitation across the hall for me to join her for a beer, and I'd casually stroll over to the wall and make some knowing comment about Pioneers, and she'd say, "Oh, you know it? Play something!" and I'd impress her by choosing *Rumours* by Fleetwood Mac.

Of course, I'd never seen Joanna drink a beer, and I'd never gotten close enough to her collection to rifle through it. Maybe she didn't even like Fleetwood Mac. For all of my time working closely as her assistant, I'd never had a glimpse of what a friendly relationship with her might look like. I knew her client list, but not much about her personal preferences. I knew the names attached to her lunch dates, but had no idea if they were *date* dates. I wasn't generally, or at least immediately, worried about my career, but what I hated to admit was that beyond doing well here, I also just wanted Joanna to *like* me. Whether or not she did was the most inscrutable aspect of our working relationship. I knew I was lucky to be at all part of her inner work circle, but to be honest, I was greedy. I wanted a little bit more.

So my heart fell when, without raising her eyes, she welcomed me with, "Du Roi was a risky move, no?"

I smiled, trying not to let on to the fact that my inner monologue was, for the moment, just a high-pitched, never-ending shriek.

"Was it? Honestly, I was inspired by you and Salome Diaz." In truth, I hadn't thought of that bit of Joanna's history until just this second, but the defense held water. Two years back Joanna had strongly suggested that Salome Diaz, then only recently of "former Disney" fame, chop her famous wavy locks into a close-cropped pixie cut without checking in with her stylist or manager first. She knew it made sense to match her physical appearance with musical reinvention, but also knew Diaz's team would fight for a tamer, more easily reversed change.

Joanna settled back into her chair and folded her arms across her chest. "I was in a much more senior position then than you're in now."

I sat in one of the two hard plastic chairs facing her desk. It was unclear yet whether she was mad or impressed. Possibly, it was both.

"True, but I'd argue this was less of a risk—Salome had a stylist. Archie's a free agent."

Joanna smiled. "I don't think that's what that means, but okay."

She paused.

"He spent his own money?"

"He did. I presented it as a casual shopping trip," I said. "Harper gave him some advice but didn't tell him what to buy."

"Oh, you brought Harper." Joanna's face relaxed, and I would've been offended if I weren't so relieved things were apparently turning in my favor. Joanna and Harper didn't work closely, but there wasn't anybody in the office who didn't see how well Harper dressed herself.

"So it's going well so far, then?" she asked.

"*Really* well," I said, opening my notebook on my lap. I gave her a quick rundown of the progress so far. She was happy about the venue for the date, less enthused over the actual day. (She grimaced: "Tuesday? For what's supposed to be their first big date?" I explained that it was the only day that worked with both their schedules—a justification she found only partly satisfying.) She seemed cautious but happy about the decisions I'd made on my own, and seemed quietly pleased when I mentioned Maria's shared enthusiasm. Without saying as much, it seemed we both knew any success I had was also a small *I told you so* to Ryan and Co. Finally, her voice softened.

"And you're doing okay?"

"Oh yeah! Really excited, so grateful for the opportunity." I knew I was gushing.

"You don't have to do that."

I was taken aback. "Oh, no, I mean—I am, though. It's exciting to take the reins."

She held my eye contact for a beat and then swiveled back to face her screen. I couldn't help but feel like I'd done something wrong. "Get something in the calendar for after the date, so we can discuss next steps," she said.

She paged her assistant to get Trevor's manager on the line, which was my cue to leave. I shut the notebook in my lap, nothing new on its pages, and headed back out the door.

Back at our desks Harper wasn't even pretending to be

working, her chair turned to face the opening of the cubicle walls and her hands clasped tightly together in her lap. She raised her eyebrows by way of greeting, and I responded with a somewhat dejected shrug. I slid my notebook onto my desk and slumped into my chair, covering my face with my hands.

"That bad?" Harper whispered.

"I don't even know," I said. "I think I already forgot everything either of us said. But it didn't *feel* great."

"You have to remember so you can tell me, though."

"I know," I said, rubbing the skin along my hairline where I now felt that I'd broken out in a fine line of stress acne. *Wonderful.* "I'm trying."

I took my hands away from my face and saw Harper staring at me expectantly. Just as I was about to attempt a retelling, though, I heard my phone buzz loudly against the desk. I reached over my shoulder to grab it, hoping (perhaps ridiculously) that it was Archie, or even Maria—someone who'd confirm for me that I still had my job and that I wasn't terrible at it.

Instead, I saw a notification from Tinder. Neil had sent me another message. I definitely didn't want to deal with that now, but before I could return my phone to its spot, Harper snatched it out of my hands. How she was always able to know the type of message I'd received from the way I looked at my phone I wasn't sure, but then, I supposed, I could do the same thing for her, and I couldn't explain that, either. She stopped just shy of reading the message, looking at me for approval first and proceeding only when I gave a defeated nod.

"Oh my God," she said. "You guys have been *chatty*!"

It was true, sort of—since I'd replied to his first message

the night before, after getting home from the shopping expedition, Neil and I had exchanged a dozen or so messages. Most of them were short, no more than three or four little lines, and most were sent with an hour or more between them. But still, for me at least, it was a lot. To even be in the "talking" stage—as in, "Yeah, I've been talking to this guy..."—felt significant, at least now that Harper was pointing it out. I'd responded to most of the messages while doing something else: ordering Seamless, eating Seamless, between washing my face and brushing my teeth before bed. It was weird, the way online dating worked; how you could be going about your own boring daily routine alone and at the same time meeting someone you might one day love. Not that I thought, at this point, that I could love Neil. I wished, for one, that his name was something other than Neil.

Still, his messages were nice. A little charming, even. I watched Harper's face as she read them over and smiled when I saw that she was smiling, too.

"See, you always say you don't know how to flirt," she said. "But you totally do."

"I wasn't flirting! I was just talking."

"First of all, same thing, basically. And second of all, yes you were." She held out the phone with one hand, using the other to point at one of my messages. "You mentioned his body."

"Yeah, but like, in the context of what clothes to wear when it's so hot out."

"Doesn't matter," she said. "You wrote the words 'your arms.' That makes them think you're thinking of their arms."

"I don't know..."

"It does," she said. "I know you don't think I get it because I'm gay, but there is not really that much to get."

"Okay, well, what does the new one say?"

"Read it," she said, and finally let me take the phone from her hands.

The message read:

Hey—so this is kinda last minute, and maybe kinda sudden seeing as we've been talking for, oh, about 24 hours now, but I'm wondering if you'd be up for getting dinner with me tomorrow night. The short version of the medium-size story is that a friend who knows a chef got us a 7:30 pm table for two at this new place on the LES called Basile, but today tells me he's got to take a business trip to Philly on short notice. The restaurant sounds great, and you seem great, so I figured, why not ask? No pressure.

—Neil

I looked up at Harper, realizing only then that my mouth was hanging open.

"I know," she said. "I know."

"How—"

"I know."

"This has to be, like, some kind of cosmic prank or something," I said.

"By whom?" asked Harper. "God?"

"Yes, or Satan."

"It is definitely strange," said Harper. "I mean, Archie and Raya's rez is at eight, right? There's no way you won't see them."

"There's no way I'm *going*. Are you kidding?"

"Are *you* kidding?" said Harper, her voice rising dangerously close to an audible volume. She paused to peer at the top of the cubicle wall, but when Ethan didn't appear over it, she continued. "This is the first guy you've been even remotely interested in talking to in approximately centuries, and he's just asked you out to dinner at the coolest new restaurant in the city. You're an idiot. You're going."

I sat there silently for a moment, smoldering and trying to think of excuses.

"This is their first date. I need to be available, make sure it goes off without a hitch."

Harper rolled her eyes. "Okay, you know that's not true. What are you going to do beyond making sure they arrive? Trail the waiter? Send over a tableside violinist?"

I couldn't help smiling. She was right. I hated to admit it, but there was only so much I could control about the night.

"I don't have anything to wear. I know I said that before, but truly, I do *not* have anything I can wear to *Basile*." I dragged the name out in an exaggerated fake French accent: bahhw-*zeeeeel*.

Harper didn't say anything. Instead she wheeled her chair around, hunched underneath her desk, and began rooting around in the pile of plastic and paper shopping bags that formed the natural landscape of her work space.

"Harper," I started, but she hissed, shushing me.

Seconds later, she emerged from her hovel holding a bag, which I quickly realized was the trademark dark purple of Du Roi.

"What... is that?"

"Open it," she said, holding it out. I took it carefully and peered inside, like someone expecting to find a snake. But it was almost worse: At the bottom of the bag was the black military dress I'd tried on a day earlier.

"Harper," I said. "How—"

She held up a hand to stop me. "Samantha owed me one."

"She owed you two thousand dollars? Why?"

"It didn't cost her two thousand dollars," she said. "She lent it to me."

"Just like that?" I said. "But you're just... you. No offense."

"None taken," replied Harper. "I'm cool. But no, she lent it to me... for Raya." At this last bit Harper paused, looking sheepish.

"*What?*" I yelled, forgetting where I was. Before Ethan could pop over the cubicle wall Harper grabbed my arm, yanked me out of my chair, and pulled me down the hallway to a tiny, empty conference room.

"Harper," I said, once she'd closed the door. "You said this was for Raya? Are you trying to get me fired?"

"Obviously not," said Harper. "And I really thought it maybe *could* be for Raya, you know? Like maybe you wear it tomorrow, and then she can wear it out after her next show or something. It's not like anyone's going to take your picture in it. *No offense.*"

"There are so many problems with this plan that I don't even know where to begin," I said.

"Come on. It's flawless."

"It's the opposite of flawless. It's flaw-full."

"Falafel?"

*"Harper."*

"Sorry."

"This is probably the least of the problems, but there is *no way* that Raya and I are the same size," I said.

"I kinda think you are," Harper said with a shrug. "She's pretty tall, and tall people always wear a size or two bigger than you'd think."

I paused to consider this, and ran my fingers along my hairline.

"Rose," she said. "I know it's maybe a little…borderline. But you have nothing to worry about. Samantha owed me. You'll have an awesome date outfit, we'll have it dry-cleaned, she'll get her pictures of Raya in it, and it'll go back before the week is out."

I looked at her pleading face, and at the same time remembered how I'd looked (and felt) in the dress. Maybe it would be okay, I thought. She had a point about pictures. But then I thought of another problem.

"What if I run *into* them?" I said. "And Raya sees me in it?"

Harper's face fell. "…Huh."

"It's not that big a restaurant," I said.

"Okay, look," she offered. "I don't know. Either she sees you and notices your dress and likes it, and then we say we'll get one for her, too, or she sees you and notices your dress and doesn't say anything about it, and then we tell Samantha that Raya appreciated the loan but didn't think it was her style. Or you don't see her and we send it to her and see what happens. I don't know. Samantha can deal with it. I got this dress for *you*."

I rolled my eyes. It was typical Harper—I couldn't stop loving her even when she was driving me up the wall. She clasped her hands in front of her face, mock-begging me. "Fine," I said. "Thank you."

"*Yes*," she screamed, clapping her hands together.

"But if this doesn't go well, you don't get to pressure me into a date for at least *six months*, got it?"

"Deal," she said, and together we walked quietly back to our desks.

# 9.

I COULDN'T DENY THAT I looked good. At least, my bottom half looked good. My full-length mirror had fallen off the wall a few months back (crashing down in the middle of the night, proving that if I was ever woken by some real disaster, my reaction would be to throw a pillow at it) and I kept forgetting to replace it. I'd gotten into the habit of stealing into Chelsey's often-vacant room and using hers, but tonight—the night I actually really *cared* what I looked like—she was holed up with Jay. I didn't want a second viewing of the little performance I'd caught last week, so I did what any rational adult would do: I pulled the portrait-size mirror off the wall near our front door, leaned it gingerly on my dresser against the wall opposite my bed, and then hopped on my bed and tried to contort my body so that I could get a decent look at the outfit as a whole in that little rectangle. It was working. Kind of.

I heard my phone buzz from across the room, and hopped off the bed—a feat that, in a skintight dress, was much more difficult than I'd anticipated. It was a text from Harper.

`Are you excited??`

I was excited, against my better judgment, but I was also anxious, and it was hard to figure where one nervous energy ended and the other began.

`Yes!`

I decided to go the simple route.

She requested a selfie; I obliged and then told her to get off her phone. Harper had planned to be with me for date prep but had to cancel, begrudgingly, to go on a date of her own—one I'd made her pinkie-swear not to wuss out on. Hers was a more low-key affair (a reading at the Strand, followed by some coffee and sweets at The Cocoa Club) but also one I found vastly more appealing. A first date at Basile would've been a lot for me under any circumstances, but my hands started sweating whenever I let myself realize I'd orchestrated the night to be a veritable celebrity gossip Event.

Of course, not everyone knew about this (perhaps ill-advised) overlap of my personal and professional lives. I'd told only the people who absolutely had to know (Archie, Harper: yes; Joanna, Raya, Maria: no) and had made sure, beyond a doubt, that Archie was comfortable with it. I'd left him a voicemail that was probably more ominous than it needed to be, because when he called me back just ten minutes later, his reaction to the news that we'd be on a quasi-double-date was almost annoyingly chill.

"Oh, you made it seem like this was a big deal," he said with a sigh.

I felt myself get defensive. "Well, I'm just keeping the client in the loop. Generally good practice to avoid surprises." I paused. "Plus, you know, it would've been weird if you'd shown up and I was just there. Like I was stalking you."

"Mmm, but I'm not quite sure that you aren't. I mean, it's still weird, isn't it?"

"I can cancel—that's why I called you to begin with! Listen, I'm messaging Neil right now."

He laughed. "Rose. I'm messing with you." He paused. "So it's the surgeon, then?"

"Yes, the surgeon."

"Huh."

"What?"

"I'm just impressed. *Basile.*"

"Believe it or not, we plebeians also enjoy good food." He didn't have to know it was actually Neil's friend he should be impressed with.

I pulled up the minute-by-minute time line I'd put together, and we did a final run-through of the night's details—his car would pick Raya up between 7:30 and 7:32 and take them to the restaurant, where they should arrive no later than 8:09; Lucas, at the very least, would be ready for photos around the entrance by 7:45. I reminded Archie that he should try to make it seem like he and Raya were at least comfortable with each other (his arm around her shoulder wouldn't hurt); oh, and he should strongly consider wearing those new boots; and then I offered to cancel my own date one last time. Part of me hoped he would take me up on it. There was something so comforting about being able to get out of a social engagement without taking any of the blame.

He didn't. So I ran through the schedule with him one more time (ignoring his theatrically exasperated sighs), and when he promised me (twice) he understood, we said good-bye and hung up.

So, here I was. I returned the mirror to its rightful place on the wall and leaned in to examine my face. The curls I'd attempted had flattened, leaving me with sort-of-wavy, sort-of-messy hair that was stiff with hair spray. It was too late to do anything about it, and besides, if Neil decided to lean over and run his hands through my hair, I'd be out of there faster than you could say "personal space" anyway. I swiped some berry stain on my lips, brushed on some mascara, and tamed my brows. Harper had told me to keep the makeup simple and let the dress make the statement; it was an easy directive to follow. I checked my phone. If I wanted to be on time, I'd have to have left at least five minutes earlier, so I texted a slight fib to Neil (`Running a bit late, on the train now!`) and *almost* left. I just needed to double-check details with my paparazzo first. Again.

---

I wasn't sure how it was possible, but Neil was better-looking in person than online, and looked younger than his thirty-six years. The outfit didn't hurt: skinny black jeans, skinny black tie, white button-up with the sleeves rolled to the elbow in that nonchalant, *Oh, do my forearms look good like this? I hadn't noticed* way. He had the beginnings of a beard, or just a well-maintained permanent stubble, and his hair was almost jet black, curled in the front like an old-fashioned movie star.

I needed to know what was wrong with him.

He was waiting at the bar when I arrived—to my credit, only

three minutes late, which is barely late at all—and jumped from his stool when he saw me.

"Hi! You look—wow. It's, um, it's nice to meet you."

He turned back to the bar to grab something, and then thrust a modest bouquet of red roses toward me. "I'm Neil."

*Don't be a jerk,* I thought to myself, hoping my face was more smile than grimace. *This is a nice gesture. Who cares if you're at an overpacked restaurant without a vase and nowhere to put these already-dying flowers.*

"Thanks so much, Neil! It's great to meet you, too. This is... super nice of you."

*Super nice?*

"Oh, it's nothing," he said, smiling somewhat bashfully. "So, be cool, but I'm pretty sure that guy who played that detective in *Law and Order* is sitting a few stalls back."

"Oh, no way!" I snuck a look; he was right. "So cool." I tried not to dock him points for knowing neither the name of the character (Munch) nor the branch of *Law & Order* he was in (SVU, of course). We nodded, smiling meekly at each other long enough for me to consider dropping the flowers and running, until he leaned in closer and I realized just how good he smelled. Like the woods. But with a hint of vanilla? He held his arm out in front of him as if to clear my route, and directed me toward the host.

"They wouldn't seat me without the full party, even though the full party is two people. You know how it goes," he said.

When we got to the host's stand, though, the host—who didn't look a day over sixteen—was in the middle of a conversation with Greta, the manager who'd helped me coordinate Archie and Raya's night out.

"Rose!" She grabbed my shoulders and planted a kiss on my cheek, suggesting a friendship going way beyond our three interactions, two of which were on the phone. "I wasn't expecting you tonight! Spying on your man? Holy shit, you look amazing."

"Oh, um, I—"

"We're actually here for a seven-thirty reservation," said Neil, his brows furrowed in confusion. "But now I'm wondering if we really needed one?"

"Ah, shit, I'm sorry," Greta said, looking from me to Neil and rolling her eyes. "Big mouth. Let me get you to your table, and Matt"—she nudged the nervous-looking host—"tell Sandy to send these two over a couple glasses of champagne, on the house."

"Oh, you don't have to—" I said.

Greta raised her arms in front of her face. "Nope, don't even think about it. I can't tell you how psyched my boss is for tonight."

She directed us to our table—a tiny square in a dimly lit corner, the kind of table whose size requires a constant rotation of dishes and drinks since it was incapable of fitting them all at once—threw me a wink, and told us to please let her know if there was *anything* we needed, before disappearing into the courtyard.

I stared down at the single-sheet menu, a sheet so long it was overflowing into my lap.

"So do you have a secret identity, or something?" Neil asked. I looked up to find him smiling.

"Ah, I'm sorry," I started. "I should've mentioned this to you, but I didn't want to seem, like, braggy, and now even *that* sounds braggy...but, um, you know how I work in PR?"

He nodded.

"Well, so, I'm kind of in the middle of this big project involving Archie Fox—"

"The YouTube guy?"

"Yeah—well, he's done a lot since then, but, not important. Yes. Basically I coordinated a date between him and another singer. Here. Tonight."

Neil frowned, nodding slowly. It was like I could see his brain putting the pieces together in real time.

"So you're, like... Cupid."

I laughed. "I mean that's like... an endearingly sentimental way of putting it, but sure. In a very small way. Honestly, if you knew all the machinations behind it, you'd probably find the whole thing a lot less romantic."

He nodded, then poured a little pond of olive oil on a plate and dragged a piece of bread through it.

"So is this for the restaurant?" he asked, his mouth full of bread, but not, somehow, in an altogether unpleasant way. "What does Archie get out of it?"

"No, I mean, it's good for them for sure, but yeah, it's more an image thing for him. And for Raya."

"Ooh, Raya. Sounds very hip," he said. He paused. "Did that just make me sound a million years old?"

"Yes," I said, taking my own bite of bread. "But at least you recognize it. Sorry, we definitely don't have to talk about my work right now." I had gotten used to friends and acquaintances showing interest once they heard I worked with celebrities, but quickly losing it once they realized that didn't translate into either partying or hooking up with said celebrities. When it came to romantic interests, I'd found men to be less than thrilled about my professional life—from Dave, who was forever complaining that I made him feel like he was less important than my internships, to all of the many dudes who felt it necessary to balance my success with negs about that success being in such a "frivolous" and "fun" field. I'd grown accustomed to avoiding the topic altogether.

"No, I'm curious!"

I narrowed my eyes at him, trying to gauge his sincerity. *Well, he asked for it.*

I gave him the short-ish version of the story: how we all know public image is manufactured but we often don't realize to what extent; how Archie had been disrupting his previously immaculate image by shrugging off the media; how with this new setup Raya's career would get a boost, Archie would earn some new cool points, and, incidentally, we'd put Basile on the map. "It's a win-win-win."

Our champagne arrived and we clinked our glasses; he mulled everything over while taking a sip.

"So what you're telling me is you can maybe get me into a Leonardo DiCaprio party."

*Ah*, I thought. *There it is.*

"Ha," I half laughed. "Well, we don't represent him..."

"I'm kidding," he said. "But that would rock."

"He strikes me as something of a, uh..." I paused, debating just how diplomatic I cared to be. "...dick," I finished. So, not very diplomatic.

To my relief, Neil laughed. "Fair enough," he said. "I just bet the dude throws a good party."

"I'm sure you're right," I said.

Soon the server (another very-young-looking guy, this one

sporting a sleek undercut) was at our table to take our drink orders. Neil selected a mid-range bottle of red wine ("When in Rome," he said, and I half smiled, half winced) and, when it was brought to the table, sniffed and swirled it with convincing expertise. As soon as it had been poured, I picked up the glass and drained about a quarter of its contents. Neil raised his eyebrows.

"Nerves," I said, trying to look coquettish rather than insane. He smiled down at his lap and I thought, *Good*—he thought I meant for our date, and not Archie and Raya's.

Knowing it was nearing 8:00, I could barely focus my eyes on the menu, and was therefore atypically grateful when Neil offered to order for me.

"Any dietary restrictions I need to know about first?" he asked.

"Not one," I said. "I'll eat anything." The truth was I didn't know if I could eat *anything*, but it would come off better to pick at something he'd chosen than for me to say something dainty and girlish, like that I just wanted the Niçoise salad. The standard Basile meal was four courses, and it seemed to take Neil nearly an hour to order for us both. I thought I heard something about yellowfin and something about tagliatelle, but other than that it was a blur. My ears were trained on the front door behind me, and whenever I thought I could risk it, I turned to look over my shoulders, too.

"Gettin' antsy, huh?" he said.

*Dammit.* Caught red-handed.

"I'm sorry," I said. "I'm being so rude. Maybe I should have canceled."

As soon as I'd said it, I knew it was the wrong thing to say.

"I just mean that I have this crazy annoying work thing," I backtracked, "but I really didn't want to turn you down for tonight. I wanted to come." I was surprised by how much I meant it. Neil was kind of a doofus, at least so far, but he was handsome, and sweet, and the flowers—now sitting sadly on the floor by my feet—really were a nice thought.

"Well, I'm glad you did," said Neil. Just then the server returned with our appetizer—the yellowfin—and, pretending to drop my napkin from my lap to the floor, I reached into my bag and touched my phone so the screen lit up. I was startled to see that it was actually 8:06, and Archie and Raya had yet to arrive. Nor had I apparently received any word from either of them: My home screen was completely, unnervingly empty of notifications. They had three minutes.

"May I?" Neil asked, and I surfaced to find him holding out a small serving of yellowfin on a piece of toasted bread. For a moment I panicked, thinking he was trying to feed me like a baby, but then I realized he only meant to put it on my plate.

"Yes, thank you," I said. Though my limbs felt gummy and my stomach roiled, I lifted the toast and took a tiny bite. Even in my heightened state of fear that my entire career was on the brink of destruction, I recognized that it was perhaps the most delicious bite of food I'd ever eaten.

It was then that I heard a commotion behind me—the brisk entry, the clicking of a camera, Greta's overly enthusiastic greeting—and I knew, without turning around, that Archie and Raya had arrived. This was made all the more obvious when I saw Neil look up and over my shoulder, craning his neck to get a better look.

"Oh wow," he said. "I think your dude is here."

*My dude*—as if. I still didn't turn around, and only smiled and nodded in reply.

"Aren't you going to go say hi?" asked Neil.

"Absolutely not," I said, so severely that Neil looked a bit chastened. "I just mean, it might ruin the facade, you know? I have to be careful in case anyone's snapping photos on their phones. If I go up to them it's like, who's the random talking to Archie Fox and that singer my teenage sister loves like she knows them? Is she a publicist? Something fishy is happening. You know?" I cringed a little, knowing I was rambling.

"I hope this doesn't seem too forward," said Neil, "but I don't think anyone who sees you in that dress would think you're a random."

In spite of myself, I blushed. "Thank you," I said. *It's not mine*, I almost added, but managed to keep it in. The server came by and cleared our plates (his empty, mine with only that small bite removed) without asking if I was done with mine; presumably, he was trained to get used to female diners not finishing their food. I took the opportunity to lean over for my phone once more. This time, Neil noticed. "Sorry," I said, "I just gotta make sure the arrival went off without a hitch."

"Of course," he said. "Believe me, I understand what it's like to be tied to your work phone." It was obvious he meant the comparison sincerely, but I couldn't help but think, *But your work is literally saving people's lives.*

I sent a quick text to Lucas, who was probably still lurking outside and would be for upward of two hours, waiting for Archie and Raya to emerge: `Get the shot??`

"It's not usually this crazy," I said. "But this project is sort of the first one I've ever led." I felt my phone buzz in my lap and looked down. Lucas had replied. `You know it. More like 20 of them.` For the first time all day, I breathed a sigh of relief.

"All right?" asked Neil.

"Yes," I said. "Thank you so much for being so patient with me." Also for the first (real) time all evening, I actually looked at Neil sitting across the table from me, and reminded myself of where I was: on a very nice date, with a very nice man—a rarity, if recent years' experience taught me anything. I dropped my phone back into my purse, vowing not to look at it again. At least until after dessert.

Over the next two courses—each plate more delicious and beautifully arranged than the last—we talked: about his work (he was a vascular surgeon and not a brain surgeon as I had, for who-knows-what reason, automatically assumed), about the upstate farmhouse he wanted to buy and renovate and rent out, about our respective high school personae (he was a bit of a Casanova jock, he told me apologetically; I took this to mean he dated two girls from the cheerleading squad), about diet pseudoscience and whether coffee was actually very good for us, or very bad. He was easy to talk to, and smiley; I made him laugh easily, which made me laugh, too. He had a nervous habit of running his palms down his thighs as if to smooth out his pants, which I could tell he was doing even though his hands were below the table. For nearly an hour I forgot (well, almost forgot) about Archie and Raya, seated some twenty or thirty feet away in the twinkle-light-lit courtyard.

Then, when our entrée plates were cleared, and before dessert arrived, I excused myself to powder my nose. That's what I said, out loud: "Will you excuse me? I need to powder my nose." He nodded, and once I'd walked out of sight I clapped my hand to my forehead.

I found a small line outside the bathroom door and was mid-internal-chastising (*why* were women incapable of peeing quickly?) when I noticed the queue was led by a guy (served *me* right for stereotyping). Single unisex bathroom, and, from what I could tell, only one for the whole restaurant. I was clearly going to be here for a while, but at least I had my phone.

I typed out a quick text to Harper (my version of gushing: `Hot doctor seems kind of OK???`) and then switched over to Twitter. The only reason I looked up was the sharp gasp I heard from the young brunette in line ahead of me.

"Well that dress looks familiar."

I whirled around to face Archie, whose cheeks were redder than usual—either nerves or a wine blush. I guessed the latter.

"Hello, Archie."

More excited whispers fluttered ahead of me, this time from the blond woman standing in front of the brunette. Both were holding up their phones as if looking for a signal, trying desperately to frame Archie in a creepshot without revealing that's what they were doing. I shot them a glare and their hands rocketed to their sides.

"How's it going?" I asked.

"Oh, you know..." said Archie, waving his hand dismissively. His mouth was smiling, but his eyes gave away a definite frustration.

"Well, no, I don't, that's why I asked."

"Your date is *quite* handsooome," he said, dragging the last syllable in a nasally drawl. *Definitely drunk.* I ignored the comment and lowered my voice.

"Are you guys hitting it off?"

"Yes, Rose. She's immensely charming, and smart, and beautiful, just like you said she would be; and I'm being charming, and funny, and handsome, just like you wanted me to be."

The words dug into my skin. "Well, good."

I heard a flush, and then the faucet, and then the bathroom door open, but the line didn't move. I turned around to face the women, who quickly averted their eyes.

"I think the bathroom's available," I said. Archie moved in closer and shone a gleaming smile at the women.

"I've got this—pardon me, how's your evening, ladies?"

The brunette giggled; the blonde whispered, "Fine."

"Forgive me if I'm being presumptuous, but would you like a picture?"

This was followed by a chorus of oh-my-Gods and are-you-sures and thank-you-so-so-muches. The three huddled together for a selfie—Archie reaching one arm around them, the other stretched with phone in hand—and I shimmied past to the bathroom as they were deciding whether the shot was good enough or if they should get another. "My pleasure," said Archie, his eyes on me.

I shut the door behind me and stared into the mirror. *What is his deal?* I thought. Didn't he know I was trying to save his career? I sighed at my reflection. At least he was on the date. He was engaging with fans. He didn't *have* to like me while doing it. I brushed some powder on my forehead and stepped out. The two women were waiting, gushing over their phones, but Archie was gone.

"Sorry that took so long," I said when I got back to the table, settling back into my seat. "I wasn't in the bathroom the whole time—there was a line." *Stop talking, stop talking.*

"No worries," said Neil. "I tried waiting, but..."

I looked down and saw a plate of mostly eaten chocolate mousse, sitting in a sad pool of melted whipped cream.

"Oh, it's okay! I don't even really like chocolate that much." This was a lie.

Our server brought over a credit card receipt, and removed the plate before I could even get a bite. Panic bubbled up in my chest. He'd asked for the check while I was gone. Did he see me talking with Archie? Did he read into it? He obviously wanted out, ASAP. He signed the slip, dismissing my offer to give him some cash, or at least leave the tip, and stood.

"Well!" he said.

"Well." I was horrified to feel the sting of tears welling in my eyes. I wished I hadn't texted Harper that it was going well because now I'd have to explain that I was wrong, as always. "It was, uh, really nice to meet you."

I extended my hand to shake his, and to my surprise he smiled.

"Oh, is this good-bye? I was kind of hoping we could go find you a better, not lukewarm and half-eaten dessert? I know it's a weeknight, but it's only just after nine thirty, and I'm feeling a little crazy..."

I laughed. "No, that would be great!"

I reached down to grab my roses, and Neil guided me toward the door. We passed Archie's table on the way out, and I could feel his eyes on us without looking down. A tiny, quiet part of me hoped he noticed Neil's hand on my back.

# 10.

"So?"

I'd been in the office for at least five minutes and hadn't yet given Harper an inkling of how the previous night had gone. This was partly because I was settling in, but also because I so rarely had developments in the romantic department, and it was fun to really milk it. And it was working.

"One sec!" I said.

"You are *killing* me."

I opened all of my necessary tabs—Gmail, Gcal, TweetDeck, my four favorite celebrity gossip sites—and then settled back into my chair.

"Okay. It was . . . pretty good."

Harper squealed.

I told her about Basile, leaving out (for the moment) the awkward Archie exchange. I told her that Neil had asked me what my favorite dessert was, and when I told him rice pudding, not only did he not judge ("Rice pudding is still disgusting, but, okay, fine," from Harper), he actually hailed a cab and directed it to Rice to Riches (the best, if only, rice pudding spot in the city) even though we had to walk more than a mile to get there. I told her that he actually made me laugh a few times, if in a dorky, he-doesn't-know-he's-being-funny kind of way, and that when we said good-bye, after he walked me to the Q stop at Canal, he went only for a kiss on the cheek.

"You like him." Harper smiled slyly.

I blushed. "He's fine!"

"If I told you about some other random guy ending a date with roses and a kiss on the cheek, you'd strain yourself from rolling your eyes. So you must like him."

"Technically, he started the date with roses."

"Whatever. How did the other date go?"

I groaned. "Good, apparently, though I wouldn't have known based on Archie's behavior."

"What does *that* mean?"

"Nothing. It's fine." I shrugged it off. It wasn't like people never voiced their frustrations with clients in the office—in fact, sometimes, it was an effective way to emphasize your success, prove that you were part of the club—but I didn't want to risk one of Ryan's lackeys overhearing and running to tell the boss what a difficult time I was having. "I'll tell you later."

I'd checked my email (finding short but enthusiastic missives from both Maria and Pilar, assuring me their clients had both had a wonderful time) and the gossip blogs before I'd even left the bed that morning. TMZ ran first:

FOXY DATE? ARCHIE FOX AND SEXY SINGER SHARE ROMANTIC DINNER IN NYC

Looks like British babe Archie Fox is back in the dating pool, and as usual he's keeping quiet about it.

Archie and 20-year-old LA songstress Raya were spotted at Basile last night...and the two were looking *very* cozy. Sources say they were touching each other more than their plates.

Raya looked extra sexy in a skintight white dress, and we can't help but wonder if Archie ex (and new mom) Chloe is missing the days she could pull off something similar. Can't wait to see what this new fling brings...

The photos were perfect, even if Raya didn't follow my instructions to the letter—she'd walked behind him, but then entered the restaurant before him. She didn't look down, but she also didn't look directly at the camera. Instead, she was looking intently at him. Whether she was a PR mastermind on her own, or she was genuinely mesmerized by him, the end result was good. She pulled off intimacy without showiness, as if she were just gazing up at him—like hundreds of thousands of women would do in the same scenario—wondering at her luck to be so close.

And who could really blame her? Our shopping trip proved more than worthwhile. Archie looked better than he had in years: The black tee was just tight enough, rippling slightly across his chest; his jeans fit like a glove; the heeled boots looked so good I considered buying a pair for myself; and he'd topped it all off with a single silver chain dipping way down toward his stomach. I hadn't noticed in the dimly lit restaurant hallway how well the whole thing came together.

I felt a pang of something not totally unlike envy.

When I'd read through that morning, the comments were just coming in. I scrolled down to see what had developed since, bracing myself for the feedback. We could pump as many items through as many gossip editors as we wanted, but it would be these people who would decide whether any of it would stick.

"Who the fuck is Raya?"

*Oof.* I read on.

"Raya, girl, just step away from my husband and no one will get hurt."

"This is gross."

"OMG he looks so weird?????? Cut your hair Archie PLEASE!!!! 1D is over, did you miss the memo..." And, in reply, "No. JUST NO. if archie cuts his hair i might as well just die."

Not great, but not surprising, either; I'd expected some die-hard Archie fans to reject any evidence of a change, much less a new love interest.

"am I supposed to care about these people?"

"how is this news"

I bristled, but moved on.

"ok so who wants to join me in camping outside basile until he comes back lol but really"

"omg is that a bulge or something in his pockets?? someone zoom in i heard its big ;) ;)"

Ah, yes—the comments that still managed to scandalize me, after all this time. And then, there it was: exactly what I was waiting for.

"I LOVE THIS COUPLE!!!!!!!"

"omfg raya is a GODDESS and archie looks amazing"

"Toooo cuuuuuuute"

"guys but their kids can u imagine sldhlshvlasv i'mdead"

"YAAAAS RAYCHIE SLAAAAAAAY"

"Raychie" didn't exactly roll off the tongue, but it was a good sign that a fan-made couple name had already emerged. It would do. I took a screenshot, added it to my PowerPoint, and, after a moment's hesitation, Gchatted it directly to Joanna, too. Then, from the fake-fan Twitter account I'd set up just for things like this, I tweeted the pictures, plus the hashtag #raychie, at every major fan account I had bookmarked. They'd almost certainly already seen and shared the images themselves, but hopefully I could get the hashtag picked up. Bigger fan accounts than mine would see it, use it, search for other mentions of it, each action building on every other until the name started trending, and the couple name was accepted as official.

"How's the peanut gallery?"

I swung my chair around and Harper, who'd been reading over my shoulder, rushed back to her seat. Joanna stood behind me, hand resting on her slightly jutted-out hip. She tilted forward, her eyes squinting to read the small print on my screen.

"Oh, um, mixed to positive," I said, my heart racing. Surprise visits from Joanna were rare, but when they did happen they were similar to a shot of adrenaline. I scrolled through the comments, glancing at her face for any reaction, but her mouth remained pursed in a tight frown.

"They're calling them Raychie."

"So you said."

"It's better than Bennifer," Harper added, her eyes glued to her own screen. Joanna smirked and straightened up.

"Let's chat in my office," she said.

I followed a few paces behind Joanna down the hall, partially because she walked so briskly that it was hard to keep up, and partially because, at this distance, I had no obligation to force small talk (or even to feel anxious about the possibility). She held the door open for me and I sank into one of the two chairs facing her desk. Joanna circled around the desk and paused at the windowsill, examining the browning leaves of a small potted plant. She ducked under her desk to pull out a spray bottle and misted the leaves, a few falling into the dirt from the pressure. I cleared my throat. Joanna spun around and looked at me as if suddenly remembering I was in the room with her.

"I'm sorry, Rose," she said. "My daughter got me this fern at her school fair and I'll be damned if it isn't tougher to keep alive than an actual child." She shook her head, sighing, and took a seat. "I should probably just have the office plant guy take care of it, but that feels a bit crass for a Mother's Day gift, right?"

It was the closest thing to a personal anecdote Joanna had ever told me, and my mind raced for the appropriate response. Here was the opening, the baby bonding step that would take me that much closer to my beers-after-work dream! And then, just as quickly, the moment was gone. Her face hardened and I could tell her brain was back at work. She leaned back in her chair, arms crossed over her chest.

"Anyway," she said. "Tell me about the date."

I gave her a brief recap of the night, skirting around the fact that I just so happened to be at the restaurant, too. Since the date had gone off relatively without a hitch, there wasn't much to add beyond what I'd already told her when I first filled her in on the plan. She offered notes—evening photos were sexy, obviously, but sunny photos were more romantic, so let's get a brunch date on the calendar soon—and raised a few questions: Would it be too on-the-nose to have them do some kind of Make-A-Wish-esque charitable event together? Can we get him in a hat that's not a baseball cap? (Yes, I'd said, and absolutely)—before we dove into the second date.

"What are you thinking?" she asked.

I actually had an idea that I had been really confident about, at least until Joanna had emphasized the importance of the day date. The thing was, I'd been *so* confident about it, I'd already emailed my contact at the venue that morning and set it up.

"So I wanted to move quickly, take advantage of the momentum..." I started. Joanna watched me expectantly. "So I reached out to a friend at MoMA, who linked me up with their events coordinator. I'm thinking an after-hours visit on Thursday night—exclusive, private."

Joanna nodded slowly, her expression unchanging.

"It's romantic," I continued, "but mature. A departure from Archie's wilder days, and perfect for Raya's art-girl vibe."

Joanna sat forward. "I like it."

My entire body sighed in relief.

"Lucas knows?" Joanna asked, turning to her computer monitor.

"Not yet, waiting on confirmation from Maria."

Joanna waved her hand dismissively. "Don't worry about that. Better to get him now and have to cancel than wait too long and miss him."

"Okay, I'll text him right now." I pulled out my phone and rose from my seat.

"Wait, Rose, one more thing."

"Yes?"

"You know Carolyn Mullens?"

"The folksinger, right?" Carolyn was a rosy-cheeked, curly-haired, emerald-eyed seventeen-year-old folksinger from Ireland who had recently piqued US interest after being featured on a sleepy, romantic duet with Ed Sheeran. Her voice was smooth and angelic, with a slight twang, and I'd fallen slightly in love with her after exploring the lo-fi tracks on her SoundCloud. As far as I knew, we weren't working with her, but I was excited by the prospect of it. "What about her?"

"I had a call with her manager. What do you think of her for Disney?"

"You mean, like, in a show?"

Joanna shrugged. "They've expressed some interest. Like Hannah Montana, revived."

I couldn't help wincing.

"So, no then?"

I realized I was awkwardly hovering halfway between the desk and the door and wondering if it was worth backtracking. Instead, I just shifted my weight.

"No, not a definite no. I don't know. Just... a Disney show? It makes no sense. I mean, yeah, it'll make her some money, but she's not someone who's struggling to get noticed. She's been noticed! And then, what, she does it for a couple years and then has to redefine herself to separate from it?" I paused, shaking my head. "I think she's too good for it. She knows her sound. She knows her identity. She doesn't need it."

Joanna smiled. "I agree."

I paused, waiting to see if more of an explanation was coming, but Joanna went back to her monitor and a frenzy of typing filled the room. "Well, sounds like you've got everything under control, Rose," she said without shifting her gaze. "We'll regroup on Friday?"

"Sure thing," I said, and walked out the door. I headed back to Harper, still puzzling over the Carolyn Mullens question and ready to fill her in, when my phone started buzzing in my hand. I looked down and gasped. Harper jumped.

"What?"

I held the screen out to her and she rushed toward it.

"Oh my God!" she squealed.

I groaned. I was not ready for this; I'd barely had time to process my date with Neil or, now, my meeting with Joanna, let alone the mysterious attitude Archie had sent my way.

"Answer it!"

I picked up the phone.

"This is Rose."

"That's a relief," said Archie.

"Yes, well." I didn't know what else to say.

"You all right?"

"I am. And you? The press is responding very well to your date." He didn't need to hear the critiques about his hair. Besides, they were wrong.

"I'm hungover," he said, "and hungry. Considering a bit of a haircut, as well."

*Wait*, I thought. Was it possible that Archie Fox read the comments? But, no. No way. Surely it was just a coincidence.

"I like your hair where it is," I said, thrilled he couldn't see me blush.

"Good," he said. "That was a test. What have you got to do today?"

"Well, I'm at work..."

"I'm your main responsibility now, though, right?" he said. I could *hear* his dimples.

"That's one word for it," I replied.

He chuckled. "Right, well then I'm going to have to borrow you for the afternoon."

I paused. "Do I even want to know what for? Is everything okay?"

"Everything's great," he said. "I'm in the car now, I'll pick you up in twenty minutes."

"Do you remember where I work?"

"No," he said, "where do you work?"

---

Archie—or, perhaps more accurately, Archie's driver Pete, whom Archie introduced to me as "Big Pete"—picked me up twenty-three minutes later outside the office. The SUV's side door slid open automatically, and after peering in, I climbed into the backseat next to Archie. He was wearing the silver boots from the night before with another pair of jeans from Du Roi (dark gray and tight), a scrubby white T-shirt, and his hair pulled back into a messy bun. The mix-and-match, high-low effect was pleasingly and effortlessly cool. I felt proud.

After we'd said our hellos, Archie launched into what felt like a semi-rehearsed speech.

"I wanted to apologize for my rudeness last night," he said. "I got a bit drunk and I don't know what got into me. I think I was a bit nervous, to be honest."

"For the date, you mean?" I said.

"Well, yeah," he said. "I mean, Ray's great." (*Ray?*) "But more than that, I just meant, being out like that again. Returning to that kind of life for the first time in a while."

"I understand," I said. He looked at me, cocking his head.

"I mean, I really don't, but, um. It makes sense that you'd feel that way."

"Anyway," he continued, "Doesn't excuse my attitude. As Maria so often tells me"—and here he adopted, with surprising accuracy, Maria's nasally Californian accent—" 'You can't change your circumstances, but you can change your perspective.' "

"That doesn't even make sense," I said. "Of course you can change your circumstances."

"I know," he said. "But one has to pick one's battles."

We looked away from each other and squinted out our windows at the sunny streets flying by. We were headed south, away from Flatiron and toward Soho.

"Where are we going, anyway?"

"Fawn," he said.

"The baby store?" I asked. "Should I be worried?" I'd started saying it as a joke, but halfway through I actually started to get a little anxious.

Archie turned to face me, an amused smirk on his face. "The date went well, but not *that* well."

"Okay, then whose baby are we shopping for?"

"Charlotte's," he said.

I nodded, but in my head I was running through the list of every possible woman I knew to be associated with Archie Fox, and wondering which one was Charlotte.

"My drummer?"

"I know," I lied.

"Lark is about to turn a year old," said Archie. "I'm her godfather."

"That's adorable."

"I like to think so." He grinned, including dimples, and I had to turn away to look out my window.

Fifteen minutes later, we were inside Fawn, a veritable mommy wonderland: its walls painted with elaborate fairy-tale-like illustrations, and very tiny, very expensive clothing arranged in pristine stacks and racks around the perimeter. In the middle was a large play area complete with a tiny castle and a tiny fake moat, all watched over by three or four young employees functioning as babysitters for shopping parents. The store was nearly empty save for the employees and a few rich-looking moms, all of whom immediately and visibly noticed Archie's arrival in the store and then, as befitted their upper-crust etiquette standards, demurely looked away. Archie nodded and smiled at the girls standing behind the counter, and after he'd moved on to a pajama display toward the back of the store I watched them exchange alarmed glances and whip out their phones. When I felt Archie was sufficiently engrossed in his errand, I approached them.

"I'm not going to stop you from taking photos," I said. "But you will not text, tweet, or Snapchat any photos you might take until an hour after we've left this store." I knew that, among the many venues in which Archie Fox could be photographed, a baby store was probably inferior only to a children's hospital or a war memorial insofar as public perception was concerned, but still, I didn't want a swarm. "If you do, I will trace it back to you," I added. It was an empty threat, but the girls' eyes widened, and they murmured their compliance.

I felt *extremely* cool. I wondered if this was how Joanna felt all the time.

I looked back to Archie, who had migrated from the pajamas

to the fall display, its miniature scarves and orange-and-red knit caps admittedly a tad early, but too adorable to criticize. Archie held two pairs of tiny mittens in his hand, one a simple pastel yellow, the other dotted with various sizes of jack-o'-lanterns.

"So what is Lark trying to say with her style?" I said. "What's her *look*?"

I'd meant it as a joke, mimicking the tone and stance I'd seen Harper use (fingers steepled, resting against the nose) whenever she was in her shopping zone, but Archie responded without skipping a beat.

"I'm torn, because she's a bit of a free spirit—really passionate and bright—but then she has a quiet, introspective side as well. So, you know, do we go the playful route"—he lifted the jack-o'-lantern mittens—"or more subdued?" He raised the yellow mittens, looking genuinely pained at the prospect of making this decision.

I paused, squinting at him and trying to gauge his sincerity. "You're kidding, right?"

"Rose." Archie looked down at me as if he pitied such narrow-mindedness, dropping both pairs of mittens back on the display table. "Babies are people, too."

"Are they, though?"

"Of course." He picked up a fuzzy green scarf, tested its texture on his cheek, and then handed it to me. "Feel this, it's heavenly."

I nodded. "Very soft."

"See, Lark is already her own person. *So* different from Charlotte. Just the other day I was over for dinner and Charlotte was flipping through the radio, and Lark starts fussing—*until* Charlotte lands on a Drake song. Lark loves it. Charlotte scrolls past it—she's not a huge Drake fan—and Lark cries again. So she goes back to Drake, and Lark's happy as a clam."

"So you're saying…"

Archie shrugged. "Lark has her own taste in music."

"Sure." My mind raced, already wondering how I would capture the supreme strangeness of this whole experience in a text to Harper. "But, like…she still can't talk, right?"

"Right." He held up a white sweater emblazoned with a fox's head. "What do you think of this?"

"It's cute! I'd buy it for myself if they carried my size."

I felt my phone vibrate in my purse. I planned to ignore it, but then it happened again, and I experienced a surge of panic that someone at Weaver-Girard had noticed my absence and had a major problem with it. When I pulled my phone out and saw the name that was actually on the screen, I said aloud, accidentally, "Oh, for *fuck's* sake."

"Beg your pardon?" said Archie.

"I'm sorry." I looked over both shoulders and mouthing an additional *I'm so sorry* to each shopping mother who was looking over at us. I realized, though, that they were looking at Archie, not me. They hadn't noticed that I'd sworn, or even that I existed at all. I looked back at Archie, who was still waiting for an explanation.

"Just work texts," I said.

"Liar," he said. "It's him, isn't it?"

If I hadn't given it away before, the scarlet-red flush that flew from my neck to my cheeks sure did. He was right. Neil had texted me—twice.

"Ahhh," said Archie. "The casual, afternoon-of-the-day-after temperature gauge text. I know it well."

I frowned. I found the idea that Archie had to gauge *anyone's* temperature incomprehensible.

"There there," he said. "Only teasing. What's it say?"

I sighed. There was no use refusing to read it now; the jig was up, and I was trapped here in this baby store until I gave him what he wanted. Plus, he was my ride. In a reluctant half whisper, I read, " 'Rose! So nice to meet you last night. I'd love to take you out again if you're up for it.' " Here I stopped, pretending I'd gotten just the one because I could not read the following aloud: `As much as I love being seen with you, maybe next time we can go somewhere without paparazzi outside. ;)`

"Well?" said Archie.

"Well what?"

"Well, are you up for it?" he asked. "Round two with..."

"Neil," I reminded him, defensively.

"*Neil*," said Archie. "Rose and Neil. Sounds lovely."

"Thank you so much," I said. "I know it's no *Raychie*."

"Ah," replied Archie. He shook a finger at me and rolled his eyes, but I thought I also detected just a hint of a pleased-with-himself smile.

I knew I should—or maybe I just *thought* I should—ask something more about them, how their date was and how soon he thought we could get something else scheduled, but right at that moment I didn't think I could bring myself to do it. Luckily, Archie spoke again before I even had the chance.

"Speaking of last night—that Du Roi dress? Good decision."

My cheeks flushed. I couldn't believe he was bringing it up again.

"Oh, well, it was just a loan," I demurred. "And it was all Harper's idea. Anyway, it'll end up going to Raya, actually."

"Oh?" he asked. "Wouldn't have thought it was quite her style."

*What, they go on one date and now he's an expert on her style?*

"She can say no, of course."

Archie didn't respond; he was too engrossed in disturbing a stack of multicolored leggings, the fox sweater folded over the crook of his arm.

"So, wait, why am I here? You seem to know what you're doing."

"Because I wanted a woman's perspective," he said. He held his arms up in the air, like, *Duh*.

"Well, I'm glad you knew not to ask Raya." I imagined the field day the press would have had catching Raya and Archie shopping at a baby store—even by celebrity standards, a relationship escalation that steep would be unprecedented.

"I'm not a complete idiot, you know," he said.

I sighed and joined him at the leggings table. "Get the red. It'll be cute with the sweater."

He held the two together and nodded.

"And then get her a toy, too. Babies themselves don't want clothes. Most *people* don't want clothes," I said. "Clothes are super boring."

Archie stepped back and eyed my outfit—a black silk shift dress and black Chelsea boots. He raised his eyebrows.

"What?" I asked, arms crossed.

"Nothing." He headed toward the cash register, and I trailed behind.

"Tell me!"

He nodded and smiled at the now four women and one man behind the counter—five people who, clearly, didn't need to be off the floor, but who were doing everything in their power to be as close as possible to Archie.

"It's just...well, maybe there's a reason you think clothes are boring," he said. He was trying *so* hard not to smile.

The young guy lurking behind the cashier giggled and I gave him my best scowl.

"Keep talking, this is good," I said. "Keep digging this hole."

He pulled a hundred-dollar bill out of his wallet, and I tried not to gape at the number of bills in its company.

"What I meant was that maybe you'd find fashion more interesting if you...branched outward. A little bit."

I scoffed. "You know, it sounds like you *think* you're making this better, but you're really not."

"You're right," he said. "I'm sorry." He paused, and I could tell he wasn't really done. I raised my eyebrows. "Basically," he went on, "if I should listen to what Harper said about, you know, *image*, maybe so should you. Because that dress looked lovely on you. And you don't have to reserve nice clothes for dates with doctors."

"I don't *have* to do anything," I felt both wounded and righteously outraged.

"You're right. One hundred percent. I'm shutting up. I will get a toy, though."

He waved a thank-you to the cashiers, and we pushed through the doors, managing to climb into his SUV just a few seconds before a small crowd of teenage girls ran down the sidewalk toward it. (*So much for no texting or tweeting*, I thought.) He waved to the fans from the car and then rolled up the windows.

"Shall we get lunch?" he asked.

We'd somehow managed to pass an hour at Fawn, and the version of me from six months ago would be rushing to get back to the office. But Joanna was always running around. In fact, most people who dealt with talent directly flitted in and out of the office so much that I could barely recognize their faces. This was my job now. Besides, it was almost 2:00 p.m. and my stomach was screaming. I checked my email—nothing urgent. I texted Harper and told her she was on her own.

"Fine," I said. "But I'm picking."

Maybe it wasn't the most glamorous venue, but Raul's felt like my own hidden gem. The taqueria was a little hole-in-the-wall spot in the East Village with scarce seating and an awning so old and faded the name was barely visible, but it was also the only place I'd found that could give the burritos back home a run for their money. Plus, they had really cheap beer.

I went to the counter and ordered (my workday usual—carnitas with extra hot sauce and a Diet Coke), then gestured for Archie to do the same. He considered the laminated menu, taped to the counter and speckled with sauce stains, and settled on "What she's having," plus some chips and guacamole. I warned him he was trying to match a pro, but he insisted, just as he insisted on paying when I awkwardly told him I could expense it. He was gracious enough to keep a straight face, given the discrepancy between our lunch total ($17.65) and the sum of bills in his pocket (no less than a cool five hundred). Probably Archie found my offer just adorable. I kind of wanted to die.

We carried our trays to one of the four tables lining the restaurant's walls and settled into our mismatched plastic chairs. For a brief moment, while watching Archie wobble in his uneven (and, honestly, uncomfortable) seat, I wondered if this—not the rogue shopping trip, and not the leveraged Du Roi dress—would be the decision that led to my undoing. Luckily for me, he reached to stuff some napkins underneath the guilty chair leg and came back up with shining eyes.

"This place is great," said Archie.

"You haven't even tried your burrito yet," I replied. My mouth was full—I was already three bites into mine, wondering how smart it was to let my client see me with sauce dripping down my chin. Archie unwrapped his and dug in.

His face was overcome with pleasure...for about three seconds. Then the heat kicked in. His cheeks went red and his eyes started tearing up, but he tried to play it cool, as if he always washed each bite down with a full glass of water. I tried and failed to stifle a laugh.

"That's not gonna work," I said.

He swallowed and gasped. "What do you mean??"

"Water doesn't help spice," I said through my own full mouth. "Milk helps."

"Do they have milk here?"

"I warned you!" I got up and walked over to the refrigerator and pulled out two Tecates. I gestured to Raul, who waved in permission, and then plopped one down in front of Archie and the other in front of me. At this point, I figured, a single workday drink wouldn't ruin me. "This will also help."

Archie took a swig and sighed in relief. "Are all burritos like this?"

"Wait," I said. "Wait. Have you...*never* had a burrito? Are you British or are you a Martian?"

"Not like this, I haven't." He lifted the burrito back up, going in for round two. I was both wary and impressed. "I went to a Taco Bell once on tour, but whatever I got was not this," he said. "So what makes you 'a pro'?"

"I grew up on this stuff, basically. San Francisco. Mexican food is a big deal out there."

"Are you from San Francisco?" Chug, bite. "I *love* San Francisco."

My stomach did a weird little flip, and I suddenly realized I couldn't take another bite. I knew this feeling—it was my nerves. I'd felt it very recently, on my date with Neil when I'd only managed to pick at my food. Archie waited for me to answer.

"I am," I said, buying myself time with a long sip of Tecate. "But I haven't been back in a while. I went to college out here."

"Far from home," he offered.

"Yes," I said, "But not as far as you."

He shrugged. "I usually get back there a couple months each year. I do miss it, but it's a bit odd to be there now."

"I can imagine," I said. "You're not just like, Archie-home-to-visit anymore."

"Not even that," he said. "I'm used to that. But the last two times I went back, it was for my mates' *weddings*. Almost all of them have gone and got families, and proper jobs. So now I'm going to visit a friend from college, and when he shows me around the house he's bought with his wife, they're painting a baby's room. They've got an herb garden, and matching dishes, and they're looking at nurseries and things. And it's just strange, because I'm still doing the same things I was five years ago." He paused, taking another bite. Either the burrito really was that irresistible (this was not out of the question), or he wanted to stop himself from whatever he'd been close to saying next. I couldn't help but think of Chloe Tan, and her pregnancy, and wonder if when Archie thought of his friends getting married and having babies, he thought of her, too.

"I thought I'd be married by the age I am now, too," I said. "But I think that's just because when you're, like, nine years old, twenty-six sounds ancient."

Archie smiled somewhat thinly and took another couple of gulps of Tecate. I had hoped, sort of, that he'd take this comment as an invitation to spill more—about Chloe in particular—but I found myself relieved when he didn't. If there had been a window, it was now closed.

"You don't have matching dishes?" I asked. He grinned, and so did I.

"I have *incredible* matching dishes," he said. "You've never seen anything like them."

I took another drink of beer, and decided I could eat a little bit more after all. Whatever weirdness I felt was purely muscle memory—me across the table from a handsome man (the understatement of the millennium), eating food, drinking beer, exchanging small talk. Maybe it was *like* a date, but only in the way the creepy wax version of Archie that stood permanently posed with a guitar in Madame Tussauds was *like* Archie himself. They looked similar, but only if you squinted.

---

I arrived at Parlor, a trendy wine bar on the Lower East Side—Neil's choice; I was impressed—twenty minutes early on purpose, so that I could reread the next date's itinerary for the fiftieth (and fifty-first, and fifty-second...) time that day.

As soon as I'd gotten back to the office after "lunch" with Archie—using that term felt like a stretch when we'd finished around 4:00 p.m.—slightly tipsy off one and a half Tecates and just as high off my own anxiety, I'd asked Archie when he thought he might be free next and he, of course, had told me to talk to Maria. So I'd thrown myself into organizer mode, contacting Maria and Pilar back and forth and back and forth, trying to get them to wrangle Archie and Raya into a date they could agree on. At one point, it looked like we couldn't line them up in the same city until six weeks later, and I began mentally writing my resignation letter. But then Maria informed me that Archie's Thursday-night plans had changed, and she knew it was late notice, but might Raya be able to meet up then? Raya had a 7:00 p.m. appearance but Pilar said she'd try to move it to 6:30, and a few minutes and chewed-off nails later, we'd settled on a time and a place: MoMA, 9:00 p.m., for a private, after-hours visit. I'd called Lucas right away, and he would be outside the museum waiting by 8:35. I read all this over and over again and then, finally, I reread the last email from Archie, sent in reply to my email to him and Maria, outlining all the details. He'd dropped her off the thread, responding only to me.

> That sounds great, Rose. Sorry to see burritos won't be involved, but as I haven't quite yet regained the sensation in my tongue, perhaps it's for the best.

Even now, on the millionth reading, I didn't quite know what to make of it. The first time I read it I smiled—just because he'd liked where I'd taken him to eat, and obviously it was cool for a cool celebrity to approve of a choice made by a mere civilian like myself. It was cool.

However, subsequent readings proved slightly more stress-inducing. Why, exactly, had he felt the need to tell me how much sensation his tongue was or was not capable of experiencing at this moment? Maybe I needed *some* updates as to the progression of his and Raya's fake relationship, but I did not need to know *all* of them.

It *was* still fake, right? *It's a* second *date*, I thought, trying to locate the source of this anxiety and tamp it down. It was a second date that I'd planned for two willing (but not apparently eager) parties. I should be happy that they got on well enough to move forward with it.

By the time I'd cycled through this now-familiar thought trajectory once more, it was 7:29. I looked up from my phone and took another sip of the $6 Pinot Grigio I'd ordered to even out my nerves prior to Neil's arrival. Another thing I'd done tipsy yesterday afternoon: reply to Neil's text, not only affirmatively but almost maniacally enthusiastic: `Neil!!!!!! I would LOVE to go out again. How's drinks, maybe tomorrow night???` Remembering it now, I sighed. I'd known better than to suggest that very evening, at least. Neil agreed (using a few exclamation points in his own text, probably in a generous effort to make me seem less crazy by comparison), and an hour later Archie and Raya's date was booked for the very same night, and I just about lost it. Harper had had to walk me through a few of her breathing exercises just to keep me from throwing up right there in our cube. "It's not the same," she kept saying. I whispered it to myself for the better part of the subway ride here. And it was true: We were meeting at different times and in vastly different parts of the city. Even as the mantra soothed me, I found there was a tiny part of me that felt oddly like remorse. I knew I wouldn't run into them, or get to see firsthand what they were like together.

Just then I felt someone lightly touch my right shoulder and I jumped, and a little bit of white wine leapt from my glass right into my lap. Mercifully, I wasn't wearing anything by Du Roi.

"I'm *so* sorry," said Neil. I smiled, waved it off, and stood to hug him. It was, as all early-stage dating hugs seem destined to be, impossibly, almost tragically awkward.

"Don't worry. There's a reason I always drink white," I said, regretting it immediately. *Great, now he'll think I'm a lush.* "I just mean, I'm prone to spilling things. Not just alcohol. Pizza sauce, spaghetti sauce. Most of the sauces." *God.*

Neil laughed.

"Don't worry, that's all better than anything that spills on me at work."

I choked on my wine. "Did you just make a really disgusting joke?"

Neil twisted his mouth into a self-conscious grin. "Yes? Unless you're offended by it, in which case, no, and *I'm* offended that you interpreted it that way."

"It's fine, I just thought bodily fluids were more of a third-date thing." The second I said it, I heard it, and Neil's wide eyes made it apparent he'd heard it, too. *Bodily fluids.* "That's not—I mean—oh God." I sank my head onto the bar. Things like this were why flirting didn't work for me. The idea of making a sexually suggestive comment was so far removed from my brain that I'd never created a filter to stop a dumb joke from coming out of my mouth and sounding like a blatant, incredibly unsexy come-on.

Neil, to his credit, bounced back with some grace. "No, you're right," he said. "The blood and guts talk should at least be reserved for after dinner."

I forced a chuckle in gratitude, and he hopped on the stool next to me. From the other end of the bar, the bartender—signaling *trendy* in his suspenders and bow tie—waved to let us know we were seen. Neil eyed my empty glass.

"Looks like you're ready for another...Chardonnay?" he guessed.

"Pinot Grigio, but um, you know what? Get me a Shiner Bock." It was a holdover from my college drinking days, and still a guilty pleasure I rewarded myself with whenever I'd had either a particularly good day *or* a particularly rough one.

"Not much for liquor, are you?" he asked.

I took this as an opportunity to launch into my by-now-well-rehearsed conspiracy theory about how anyone who says they genuinely like the taste of liquor is lying. He stiffened, and explained that I probably just hadn't tasted the right kinds of whiskey—a problem he could help me fix, since he was a member of "a really great Whiskey of the Month club." Inwardly, I made a jerk-off motion with my hands. Outwardly, I just shrugged.

"Maybe," I said. "For right now, though, I'll just stick with the beer." I excused myself and headed to the bathroom, already feeling the gears turning in my head, convincing me any hopes I had for the evening, for the doctor, were obviously misguided. I texted Harper: `The curse is real.`

The curse (or, more accurately, the second-date curse) was a theory I'd adopted after four consecutive romantic possibilities went south on date number two. By then, the flattering sheen of the first-date perspective—optimism goggles, if you will—had always faded, revealing the unfortunate political positions or unsightly habits or cringeworthy tastes underneath. And this wasn't just on their end. I, too, was susceptible to the false comfort of the second date, the kind of comfort that can convince a person it's a good idea to share that story about the time her best friend made her laugh so hard on a road trip that she'd peed her pants, or to brag about having seen every episode of *The X-Files* at least three times, or, worst of all, to tell her date she felt a real, maybe once-in-a-lifetime connection between them.

There was just no winning on a second date.

I let Harper's response go unanswered (`The curse doesn't control you. You control the curse.`) and crafted an excuse I could deliver to Neil about a work emergency that I had to tend to immediately. But when I returned to our stools, I found not one, but *two* Shiner Bocks sitting atop the counter.

"You were right," said Neil. "Beer sounds great." So I tucked the work excuse to the corner of my mind, for later use if necessary. He was trying.

We clinked our glasses and slowly settled into a groove. He told me about the stressful day he'd had at work, and my heart softened a bit more. He did have his hands literally inside another human being just hours ago, I reasoned with myself. Maybe I could give him some leeway. I told him "Raychie" was looking to be a success, and pulled my phone out to show him some of the best comments of the day. Because we were two people on a date in New York, we engaged in the obligatory exchange of apartment horror stories, and we lamented our skyrocketing rent—his, for a one-bedroom in Murray Hill, probably reaching heights I'd never even dreamed of. We laughed at the absurdity of a fancy bar charging $14 for chicken nuggets by calling them "Baked Chicken Rounds," and then ordered them anyway. As we popped the too-hot bites into our mouths, and then laughed at each other while frantically fanning our faces, I chastised myself for being so ready to give up on what was becoming—curse be damned—quite a lovely second date.

When we were both three drinks in, though, we found ourselves back on the topic of Archie.

"So what's he *really* like?" asked Neil, his words slightly slurred around the edges.

"He's fine," I said, tensing at the thought of gossiping about him. "I don't know."

"Come on, no weird secrets? He's not, like, a closet...piggy bank collector?"

I laughed. "Not really," I insisted. "He's a pretty nice, regular guy. I mean, as regular as someone who's been famous since he was nineteen can be." *Well, twenty-two*, I remembered. But that was our secret. Not that I had any good reason to be so guarded on Archie's behalf. There were plenty of harmlessly strange little tidbits I could have easily shared: his knack for baby fashion, for instance, or his burrito virginity. This wasn't a matter of client/publicist confidentiality, if such a clause even existed. But maybe I wasn't protecting Archie; maybe I was protecting this evening—my date—*from* Archie. He didn't belong here. And all of a sudden I found two sources of annoyance battling each other in my brain: Archie, for existing, and Neil, for inviting him in.

"I don't totally get it," Neil continued. "Even after seeing him in person, I don't know. He just looks like... this kind of gangly, girlie dude. Like, he could be the guy who makes my coffee."

"Mmhmm." *Maybe I'm going to the wrong coffee shops*, I thought.

"Not like I'm the kind of guy who can't admit when another guy is good-looking!" He brought the near-empty glass to his lips, tapping the few remaining drops into his mouth. "Like Thor? The guy who plays Thor? That guy is hot. I get it."

"Chris Hemsworth, yeah. He's definitely hot," I said, chewing on my straw. "Although I have to say, I'm more of a Liam girl, myself."

"Liam?"

"His brother. Now, he's someone with a good team behind him. He gives off such a strong down-to-earth vibe that even *I* buy it."

"But it's fake, yes?"

I recognized his tone. It was the voice of someone who was about to tell me what was wrong with my profession. On a clear mind, I would have shrugged it off, but working on a solid buzz? I went in.

"Well, yes and no. The public persona is always going to come from some kernel of truth. In the best cases, at least. Jennifer Lawrence is groomed to be 'the cool girl,' but the reason she's okay with being goofy in interviews and going on and on about how much she loves pizza is because she is *actually* pretty chill. Probably. She's cool—she's just also got some people telling her how best to exude that. Does that make sense?" I knew, with that last question, that I was adopting the condescending tone I expected from him. I didn't care.

"I guess so," Neil replied, though he sounded unconvinced. "I just don't get why celebrities need all of... this." He waved in my direction.

"Like, what am I, as a publicist, even good for?"

"Well, no, that's harsher than I mean it," he said. "And obviously you're really good at your job, and I don't mean to belittle it. I just don't understand, philosophically, why they can't just do their jobs like everyone else, and deal with the rest of the world like we all do—like I'm doing, right now, and I'm sorry—by just making an ass of themselves sometimes."

*Fucking Neil*, I thought. *Pick a side: Either be a jerk, or don't.*

"Oh, trust me, they still make asses of themselves," I said. "It's kind of what keeps us in business."

"Well, it must be exhausting." He tossed the last chicken nugget, now cold, I was sure, into his mouth, and asked the bartender for the check. I sighed in agreement.

"What do you think you'll do next?" he asked.

"What do you mean?"

"When you're done with celebrities—where do you go?"

*Okay, so: jerk.*

"I mean, I don't. I don't want to be 'done' with celebrities. I want to get better with them."

"You don't think you'll get bored?"

"Of course I might, and do already, sometimes. But that doesn't mean I don't also get some sense of fulfillment from it, either." I felt my voice shake, and suddenly I wanted to be anywhere in the world but at that bar. I thought of Raya. She was probably in the car with Archie right now. Was he telling her about shopping for Lark? And if he was, was I part of the story? Was he making her laugh? Probably *he* wasn't negging her about her chosen life path.

I stood up and pulled my purse over my shoulder.

"Listen, maybe we don't all save lives every day..."

Neil jumped to his feet and cut me off.

"Oh man, I'm sorry." He put his hand on my shoulder. "Really. I'm lousy with this kind of stuff. Dates. Speaking." He laughed nervously. "Did I fuck this up? I was just curious, really."

I kept his eye contact for a moment and shook my head. Maybe I could take him at his word. Maybe he was just awkward. Certainly I could empathize with that. All I knew was that this date, tonight, needed to end.

"Don't worry about it," I said. "Believe it or not, this is still one of the better dates I've been on in this city." I offered a wan smile and extended my hand. He took it, and smiled, but I could tell he was put off by this turn in the night.

"I'll see you around, Neil."

Only the tiniest part of me thought this might be true.

# 11.

I ARRIVED AT WORK EARLY the next morning, despite the dull headache that wrapped around the sides and back of my head like earmuffs. I'd woken up before my alarm went off wanting out—of whatever I was doing with Neil, of the project I'd taken on with Archie, of my bed, of my skin. Normally I'd have been too antsy to wait to get to the office before scanning the Internet for Archie/Raya news, but for whatever reason, this morning I didn't want to know just yet. I didn't want to be home when I read about it. Once I finally managed to stand up, I'd taken a brisk shower (and four ibuprofen), left my apartment just minutes after, hair wet, and got on the subway, picking up my favorite hangover breakfast (greasy egg, cheese, and avocado on a roll—the avocado for "health"—black coffee, and an orange Gatorade) from the bodega downstairs from the office. When I got to my desk, it was 7:52, and the only other person there was Ethan. He walked past the opening of my cube shortly after, apparently having heard me arrive, but quickly moved on when he saw I wasn't Harper.

I took a few minutes to swallow half my breakfast sandwich and drink my various beverages. Slowly, these (plus all the ibuprofen from earlier) began to soften my headache. They did nothing, however, for my restlessness or my irritation. I started to think about my conversation with Neil—how self-righteous he'd been, and also, considering he was a surgeon and all, how surprisingly stupid—but stopped myself. It was over. He probably wouldn't want to go out with me again, either. I'd done my dating due diligence, given the guy his second chance, and now I could stay off Tinder for at least a month without guilt.

I opened my browser and clicked through every one of my celebrity blogs, but found nothing about Archie and Raya's museum date. This was not especially surprising; it was only just 8:00 a.m.—most of the sites wouldn't start posting in earnest for another hour at least. Prime time (for non-breaking news, anyway) would be nearer to midday. Furthermore, I knew Lucas had a bit of a routine with TMZ, and would sometimes take his time handing over a set of photos. The more anxious gossip sites grew knowing the pictures existed, the more they were willing to pay for them. Once they posted the photos, of course, they'd be everywhere. But for now, I knew, I'd have to look a level deeper: fan accounts.

I went to Twitter and started my search, paging through my various bookmarked fan accounts for both Archie and Raya—accounts with names like ArchieFoxHQ and RayaRebels and even FuckMeArchieFoxxxx. At first all I saw were days-old photos, pixelated gifs accompanied by hysterical pleas—for the respective star to visit the tweeter's home country, for new photos, for tweets back, for sex—and emoji-heavy gushing. But finally, on the fifth account (ArchieFoxWorldUpdates, named as if it represented an elected, democratic office), I found something. It was grainy, and it was dark, but it was a photo. I clicked to enlarge it: it had to be from last night, because Archie was wearing an outfit I hadn't yet seen him wear in public, a light-pink polka-dot shirt under a blazer (*when did he get that?*) with the black jeans and the black heeled boots. His hair was down. Raya's bright-red hair was pulled back in a springy ponytail that set off her vintage white shift dress. Between the clothes and the hair and the piercings and tattoos, she looked like an angel gone slightly bad. But I didn't notice any of this at first because I was too busy looking at Archie's right hand. Fingers outstretched and slightly curved inward, it was pressed against the small of Raya's back.

I felt a little knot in my stomach begin to form. I looked away from the screen and back at my sandwich, now a bit deflated and sad-looking. I picked it up anyway, and bit off as much as I could fit in my mouth. Maybe I could bury the feeling in my stomach with food. Instead, I sort of choked. I started coughing, little flecks of bread and avocado dotting my desk and keyboard. My poor, poor keyboard—so often serving as an inadvertent tablecloth. I took a swig of Gatorade and cleared my throat. After a few deep breaths, another sip, and wiping off my desk and keyboard with a moist towelette, I returned to my screen.

I stared at the photo. It was taken *inside* the museum, which meant, presumably, that neither Archie nor Raya had expected they would be photographed in that moment. (Probably it had been a security guard who'd done it, one with a daughter who was such a massive Archie fan that they'd been willing to forgo the stoic, impassive standards of their profession.) This meant—this *had* to mean—that it was sincere. For some reason (and *sure*, I thought, I didn't know exactly what that reason might be), Archie had wanted to touch Raya's back while they stood in front of (I squinted) *Les Demoiselles d'Avignon*.

I felt weird. My face was hot, my jaw was clenched, and I was nauseous for reasons I knew weren't owed to the sandwich or last night's beer and wine. I should have been happy, and proud, to see that my plan—*your* plan, Rose, this whole thing was *your idea*—was working. But then, I thought, no. This was not the plan. The plan was for Archie and Raya to *pretend* to date. I had never given much thought to the possibility of them actually *liking* each other. And I was pretty sure that was because when I first started the project, it didn't matter to me at all whether they did or not. But now, clearly, it did. Because this picture did not make me feel pleasantly surprised or proud. It upset me.

I leapt up from my desk and speed-walked to the women's bathroom, where I splashed my face with cool water. Sometimes, when I was feeling angry, or hurt, or, like, oppressed by some patriarchal institution, I found it helpful to mimic the lead heroine of an emotionally stirring romantic comedy, and go to the bathroom, splash my face with water, and then lean in over the sink to look at it in the mirror. It made me feel like no matter what bullshit I was dealing with at that moment, I was still the star of this movie, and I would be okay.

This time, though, I didn't stop to look at myself, because I got this strange feeling that if I did, I would see it written all over my face, and I would no longer be able to pretend what was obviously happening was not happening. And I was afraid that what was happening was that I had gone and gotten feelings for stupid Archie Fox. And that was too ridiculous, and too embarrassing, to acknowledge.

So I patted my face dry with a paper towel and returned to my desk, and then, without really *looking* at it any more than I needed to, I downloaded the photo to my desktop. I'd need it later.

---

This Friday, like every Friday, a little before 10:00 a.m., the executives, associates, and executive assistants of Weaver-Girard gathered together in the central, glass-walled conference room and waited for Ryan to show up so we could start our weekly company-wide meeting. Sometimes we'd have to wait for Joanna, too, but not as often, and never for as long as we did for Ryan. When I'd started at the firm, I'd gone through this routine for a few weeks before asking another executive assistant named Peter why, if Ryan didn't show up until 10:15 every week, we didn't just have the meeting at 10:15, and Peter had looked at me with utter disdain, and refused to answer. I was not especially sorry when he was fired five months later.

Harper and I always got to the meeting early, mostly because I was partial to getting everywhere early, but also so that we could sit next to each other in the middle of the oval-shaped table, along the far side. (We figured it didn't look good to be near the back, but that it would seem self-important to sit near the front.) Ever since I'd gotten promoted, it was the only meeting we got to attend together, so obviously it was important to us to be as close as possible, as if we didn't spend the rest of our time at work sitting two feet away from each other. I wondered if there was an age at which one lost the elementary school reflexive panic at the prospect of *not* sitting next to one's best friend at every opportunity.

Before Harper arrived around 8:45, I'd put together the slides for my presentation. Between 8:45 and ten minutes ago, I'd caught Harper up on both my date and what I knew so far of Archie and Raya's. I showed her the photo carefully, without much comment, and when she said it looked like Project Platinum was well under way, I felt that knot in my stomach again, but I smiled and said, "I know."

Regarding my date, she'd been more wary—of Neil, of course (she was my best friend), but also of me. She knew I had a tendency to over-highlight a date's flaws, and questioned me on the details with corresponding skepticism. But we hadn't had enough time to analyze everything before having to head over to this check-in. Everyone was there apart from Ryan. When Joanna walked in a few minutes earlier I'd stared, willing her to look up and make some kind of meaningful, encouraging eye contact with me—something that would both let me know that I was doing a great job and warn me against being a fucking thirteen-year-old with an ill-advised celebrity crush. But no such luck. She walked in, sat down, and drank coffee from her travel mug all without ever taking her eyes off her phone.

Finally, at 10:14 on the dot, Ryan walked into the room.

"Great," he said. "Everyone's here." He always said something like this, as if it were a pleasant surprise that we'd all gathered here together to listen to him, and not the result of a standing calendar event organized by his newest personal assistant, Pearl (hired only days ago after Alexis quit three months into the job—the average life span for Ryan's assistants).

I was pleased to see that even Ryan's arrival did not cause Joanna to look up from her phone.

"Who wants to get started?" Ryan asked. Sam raised his

hand, and Harper lightly jabbed me with her knee under the table. *Of course.*

"Sam, go for it."

Sam was currently working with a TV actor who was widely deemed a has-been, despite the fact that he still cashed in off his crime procedural, which was critically panned but adored by octogenarians nationwide. The actor had been married to a similarly past-her-prime (but still beloved) movie star for eight years, but then they'd divorced, and were now going through a messily public custody battle. Over the course of Sam's typically over-long report, he informed us that he'd been working with the actor, his lawyers, and the actor's ex-wife, and that he thought a "sensible" solution was on the horizon. From what I knew of Sam (and the other two-thirds of the Dog), a sensible solution for a celebrity father going through a divorce was for him to grant full custody rights to his ex-wife, no matter how much he might want shared or full custody himself. They were careful not to say so explicitly, but I strongly suspected that their shared philosophy for cases like these was that a divorced dad who sent checks and presents and had the kids over for Thanksgiving was a sexier package than a single father—plus, the sooner it was settled, the sooner he could get back in the studio. Regardless, at some point, I tuned out and focused instead on my own presentation. When I could tell that Sam had wrapped up, I sat up straight in my chair.

"All right, thanks, Sam. Anyone...?" said Ryan.

I raised my hand.

"Rose," he said. "Great. Tell us all about Mr. Foxy."

I took a sip of my lukewarm coffee. I'd seen countless presentations at these meetings, and calling them "presentations" was an act of generosity. Usually it was a long ramble (on Sam's part) or a terse update (I'd once seen Keiran give a thumbs-up and say, mouth full of donut, "Smooth sailing, boss!") but I knew neither would fly for me, at least not in this instance. Maybe Ryan was lax with his guys, but that leniency wouldn't extend beyond his inner circle, and as for Joanna, I doubt she'd grant leniency to her own daughter. This would be my first solo report, and the first update I'd give on a project in which my role was slightly contentious, so I came prepared—better to be the nerd doing extra credit than the popular kid just coasting along. I opened my PowerPoint and pulled my first slide up on the big screen: a jagged line, steadily climbing, showing the increase in searches for Archie's name.

"So, as most of you know, I'm heading the Fox-Raya project, and so far it's going very smoothly. We're seeing a surge in search activity including Archie's name, but probably more significantly in mentions on Twitter, Facebook, and Tumblr."

I clicked through to my next graph, multicolored to differentiate platforms. It was the only thing my brain could focus on for the first forty minutes of my morning stupor, but honestly, it ended up pretty beautiful.

"Now, some of these mentions are from consistently updated fan accounts—which, while not significant when we're looking for evidence of audience growth, are *incredibly* significant when we're thinking about ways of achieving that growth. So let's break it down."

Next slide: a small pie graph on the left, a screenshot of Twitter analytics on the right. My mouth had gone dry, and my tongue felt scratchy along the roof of my mouth. I took the last tiny sip of coffee, but a bit too eagerly, and choked as it tickled the back of my throat. I blinked back tears and cleared my throat.

"Excuse me—wrong pipe." I looked to Harper, who gave me an encouraging smile. "Anyway, I isolated Twitter mentions—"

"Rose, excuse me, why just Twitter?"

I could identify Sam's low drawl without even turning around.

"Great question, Sam, I was just about to get to that," I said, internally repeating my calming mantra: *Kill 'em with kindness.* "I know how excited you are about Archie Fox but if you can, just sit tight for one sec." A barely audible snicker escaped Joanna, whose eyes were focused intently on the laptop in front of her. *And just a little bit of sarcasm*, I tacked on.

"As I was saying, I isolated mentions of Archie on Twitter that *didn't* come from fan accounts, since Twitter is where there would be the greatest population of diehards who might skew our numbers. Still, you'll see, proportionally, mentions are increasing. On the other side of the coin, I tracked impressions, faves, retweets of the tweets coming from those fan accounts as well as their followers, and those, too, are growing. So we're seeing more people, and my suspicion after scrolling through a few of these accounts is that it's more *young* people, joining the ranks of Fox fanatics."

I turned to the room as I clicked through to the next slide, offering Sam my best imitation of his most shit-eating grin. My stomach did a little flip-flop as I looked back up to see a row of Archie and Raya photos hovering over the conference room. I told myself, weakly, that the butter-soaked eggs were to blame.

"Lucas has been getting some great shots, which are making the usual rounds."

"Why is that one on the right so blurry?"

Sam, again.

"Oh, that one's actually an unofficial shot from their second date—after-hours visit to MoMA, I'm guessing from someone working in the museum. The fan accounts are tweeting it out."

"So you're saying we really only have paparazzi shots from one outing," Ryan added.

I looked at Joanna, who nodded at me almost imperceptibly.

"Well, yes, as of the time I made these slides, but the second date was only last night, and Lucas assures me he got clear shots. Probably TMZ bought them and is holding out until later in the day. Anyway, it's helpful, for us at least, to have fan accounts disseminate Raychie photos, because we can actually see the conversations they're sparking among the fans most likely to be unforgiving."

"Wait, I thought you said those were the accounts that would skew the numbers," said Ryan. I'd forgotten how long it had been since Ryan was actually in the trenches, before he started delegating whatever he could. Evidently, it had been long enough for him to lose track of the way young people were using the Internet.

"Yes," I continued, "but they could very well be ranting about how Raya doesn't deserve Archie, or calling for him to go back to whichever woman from his past they decided *did* deserve him. In this case, though, people are reacting fairly positively."

I clicked through to a slide of comments and tweets, pausing to allow everyone to take them in. I was pleased to see even Ryan and Keiran crack a smile.

"'Ohmyfuckinggod ADOPT ME' is a personal favorite," I said.

"And Raya fans?" Joanna asked.

"It's less clear right now—most of the reactions about Raya are just saying how good she looks, how flawless she is, et cetera."

"Well, yes, on these tweets, but what's activity looking like on her fan blogs?"

Joanna, by contrast, never lost the edge in her instincts. She was the first in the firm to suggest a client promote herself on Snapchat, and that was back when even I was certain the platform would never evolve past dick pics. Unfortunately, I hadn't been quite as on top of Raya as I could have been. I felt my chest heat up with guilt.

"You know, I haven't been watching as closely as I've been watching Archie's, but there aren't as many, and I can *definitely* scour through them this afternoon, but there are also a surprising amount of seemingly just Raya fans commenting on the gossip items, how great she looks, which is a good sign, " I said. I knew I was repeating myself, but I couldn't stop rambling.

Joanna interjected. "Just tell me you're working on a measurable way of tracking Archie Fox's infiltration of her demographic."

A headache started to settle right back in behind my eyes, and I could hear the pulse in my ears. I could handle Joanna's questions in one-on-one meetings, though they were no less scary then, and since the second date was only last night there was no time for our usual follow-ups. At least in those meetings, the questions and comments felt less like a pile-on. Here it felt like scrutiny—a betrayal, or attack, if I was feeling dramatic, and given the past twenty-four hours, I was. I swallowed.

"Yes and no."

Sam smirked.

"Raya's demo is cool teens. That's just what it is. And cool teens don't live on Twitter. They're going to be on Instagram—on Raya's Instagram—and on Tumblr. And, as you know, Tumblr is basically one giant black hole."

This brought about a scattering of groans. Tumblr, notorious for its meaningless tagging system and barely searchable database, was our white whale. It was where the most passionate fans lived, and, like Vine, was instrumental in dictating what the rest of the Internet (and then, the world) would be talking about in weeks to come. Getting some excitement brewing over Archie on Tumblr could telegraph more widespread success, but it also had to be done in the right corners of the site. One night I'd stayed late at the office trying to identify the tastemaking Tumblr elite and found myself in the dark at 10:30 p.m. lost in a mental whirlpool of terms like *aesthetic*, *vaporwave*, and *PLUR*. It was the oldest I'd felt in all of my twenty-six years. Needless to say, I'd come no closer to figuring out how best to utilize the platform.

"I suppose we could ask our data people if it's possible to track overlapping terms on Tumblr," I continued. "Maybe see who, of Raya's followers on Instagram *or* Tumblr, makes the move to follow Archie? The thing is, this demo isn't going to be showing support in buying music anyway; they're going to be buying tickets. I'll pull some numbers on ticket sales for his upcoming dates, maybe prices on StubHub and Craigslist, too."

Joanna nodded her approval. "Good. Anything else?"

"Not really. We're looking at traveling for date number three, probably Philly, since both will be in that area for a couple days for respective shows."

I looked back up at the slide, at his hand, and frowned. As if reading my mind, Keiran piped up.

"They really do look good together, I'll give you that."

"Yup," I said, minimizing the window.

"Wait, Rose." Sam, this time. "Can you pop that open again real quick?"

I sucked my teeth and reloaded the last slide.

"Okay, I'm sorry, but the photo on the right—is that a dress or a shirt?"

He pointed to Raya, whose dress was, admittedly, *very* short—the kind of thing that made her look like she'd just rolled out of bed in a hot way, but, on anyone else would quite literally resemble a pillowcase.

"Ha, ha, Sam," I said. "Any other questions?"

"You think she likes Southern men?" Sam looked to Keiran, who chuckled in agreement.

"Maybe," I said, trying to keep the rage smoke building up inside my head from blowing out my ears. "Probably not in *your* income bracket, though."

"All right," said Joanna. "Let's move on."

Sam raised his arms in defeat. "I'm just saying, she's a beautiful woman!"

Ryan, who'd been scrolling through his phone, sat up in attention. "All right, guys. Anyone have any other Fox-related thoughts to share?"

"I like his boots," Keiran said, and I smiled, pleasantly surprised.

"That's actually all Harper," I said, happy to turn the attention over to someone else.

Harper lowered her head in an exaggerated, seated bow.

"Oh yeah?" Ryan asked, swiveling in his chair to face her. "Did I miss you joining this project, Harper?" His face was smiling but his words were like ice. Harper met him with unblinking eye contact.

"Nope, Ryan, this was just your standard Sunday-night shopping trip with an international pop star."

"Ah, well, next time you decide to do some extracurriculars, maybe you could focus on some of your actual duties? Say, ones you're a little behind on?"

Harper flashed him a tight smile. Harper was a publicity assistant on the acting side, which meant she worked with Ryan a lot more frequently than I did. Theirs was not a relationship of warmth or even mutual respect, really. I tried to catch her eye to mouth an apology—I hadn't meant to throw her under the bus; if anything, I thought she'd get some brownie points—but she drew her gaze immediately back down to the notebook she was doodling in. After Ryan thanked everyone (again) for coming in, and announced the meeting officially adjourned, Harper was out the door before I'd even gathered up my things.

A few minutes later, after briefing Joanna on the plan for Philadelphia—that Raya was playing a pop-punk show on Saturday night and Archie was playing a stripped-down acoustic session hosted by a popular podcast based in Philly earlier that afternoon, and that I'd therefore planned a brunch for late Sunday morning, thinking it was about time for some paparazzi shots taken in full daylight—I walked back to my cubicle. I was on the verge of saying hi to Harper, who appeared hard at work on her computer, but when I rounded the corner of the cube, I came to an abrupt stop.

Atop my desk, to the left of my laptop, was the largest bouquet of flowers I'd ever seen in my life outside the context of a wedding or funeral: three dozen pink roses, all mixed in with—I grimaced—several sprigs of baby's breath. This was not, however, the most alarming thing sitting on the desk. That honor belonged to the even bigger stuffed teddy bear, which was *holding* the bouquet as well as a heart-shaped box of chocolates. The bear was a color I could only think to call goldenrod yellow, approximately three feet tall, and wearing a sewn-on grin that made it seem vaguely homicidal. Around his neck was a card, which read SO BEAR-Y SORRY.

"What…is…that," I said. Harper turned to look over her shoulder and I pointed at the bear, but she only shrugged and returned her gaze to her computer.

"Hello?" I said. "Are you not startled by the addition of this monster into our cubicle?"

Harper huffed a little and swiveled her chair around to face me.

"It was here when I got back, too," she said.

"Will you open the card?" I begged. "I can't." Though I could not and did not want to believe it, after the initial seconds of shock had worn off, I felt pretty sure there was only one person I knew (*sort of* knew) who could be responsible for this.

"I need to get some work done," said Harper. "As you may have heard, I'm *a little behind*."

"Ugh, yeah," I said. "That was really shitty of Ryan to do in front of everyone."

"Well, you kind of forced his hand," said Harper, and then turned her chair around, as if I was just going to sit down with my bear and move on with my afternoon.

"Are you serious?"

Harper spun back. "I mean, I kind of wish you wouldn't have brought me up," she said. "He wouldn't have said that to me otherwise. That meeting was not meant to be, like, my performance review."

"I only brought you up because Keiran complimented your work!" I exclaimed. "I thought I was hyping you up to everyone."

"Well, my job here isn't to shop for celebrities," she said. "So I don't really know why you think my boss would have been psyched to hear about it. Weaver-Girard is not a fashion consultancy."

"I know that," I said. "I just thought it might look good for you, to be taking on new responsibilities or something."

"I know you may not remember what it's like being a mere executive assistant," said Harper, "but I assure you, I have enough responsibilities as it is." She paused to glare at her lap. "Too many, apparently."

"Harper," I said. "Don't be like that. You know I'm not lording my job title over you." For a while after I'd gotten my promotion I'd wondered if it had bothered her that she hadn't, but she'd been so congratulatory, and had for so long seemed so ambivalent about Weaver-Girard, that I'd assumed it wasn't an issue. Apparently, I was wrong.

"No," said Harper with a sigh. "You're not. But just because you care so much about what Joanna and Ryan think of you doesn't mean I need to, too."

"Okay." I realized I was still standing at the edge of our cubicle, and sat down in my chair. I felt the bear lurking in my peripheral vision, so I wheeled myself closer to Harper, and farther from it. "Then why are you upset?"

"Never mind," said Harper. "I'm not."

Her delivery wasn't especially convincing, but I didn't know what else to say. Either she wanted to do better at Weaver-Girard, in which case Ryan's criticism mattered, or she didn't care, and then it didn't.

"Okay," I said. "Are you sure?"

"Positive," she replied. "Open the card."

I sighed. I knew I should probably protest, and tell her the card could wait, and say that I wanted to talk this all out now, but I was too anxious about the card (and its carrier). I had to read it immediately so that I could be done reading it, and this tiny, horrible part of my life could be over.

I pushed myself backward toward the bear and slowly, cautiously spun to face it.

"*God*," I whispered. "It's horrific." I reached forward, thinking of *Poltergeist* and feeling a little afraid that the bear would grab me by the wrist and never let go. But I plucked the card from its paw without incident, and then there was nothing left to do but open it.

The first thing I saw was the signature—a wide, scrawled attempt at cursive: *Neil.* I let out a quiet, low groan.

I took a breath and began to read aloud: "'Dear Rose, Forgive the cheesy gesture (okay—the three or four cheesy gestures; I couldn't pick just one), but I wanted to apologize for my rudeness last night and wasn't sure how else to do it.'" Here I paused to look up at Harper, and added, "Generally, the words 'I'm sorry' work pretty well, but whatever." I continued reading: "'You were nothing if not diplomatic, which is more than I deserved. I'd love to take you out again, both to make it up to you, and to show you that I'm not always such a prick. Sincerely, Neil.'"

Upon finishing the note I replaced it inside its envelope, looked over my shoulder, and tossed it behind me.

"Did it go in?" I asked.

"Almost," said Harper.

I turned to look and saw the card sitting an inch outside the garbage can that sat to the left of my desk. "*Damn.*"

"Tooooo bad," said Harper in a weird singsongy voice that made it hard for me to tell if she meant too bad about the card, or too bad about Neil, or some third option I wouldn't want to hear.

"You think I'm being too harsh?"

"I didn't say that, Rose," said Harper, throwing her hands up in exasperation.

"Well what *do* you think, then?"

"I think you have to stop asking me what I think and just decide for yourself whether you want to go out with him again or not."

My face felt flushed, the way it got when I was on the precipice of a fight I really didn't want to be in.

"I'm sorry," I said. "I didn't realize I was bothering you by valuing your opinion."

"It's not about valuing my opinion," said Harper.

"Then what is it about?"

"I don't know," said Harper. "Maybe I'm just sick of only talking about your boy problems all the time."

"*All* the time?" I felt even hotter; I was now officially pissed.

"I mean, we're not exactly passing the Bechdel test lately." Harper raised her eyebrows at me patronizingly. I hated when she did that.

"The Bechdel test is for movies. And also, I don't think it's such a bad thing to talk to your friends about your love life."

"It's about the proportion, but okay," said Harper. "Just, never mind. I barely know what I'm saying right now."

"Well I don't just want to go back to work when you're clearly upset with me."

"I'm fine," said Harper. She turned around again to face her computer, and I swallowed hard to keep myself from starting to cry. Then she looked over her shoulder. "That bear is cheesy as fuck," she said. "If you don't want to go out with him again, I think that's legit."

"Okay," I replied. "Thanks." But having her give me what I wanted only made me feel worse, because I knew she hadn't wanted to talk about it anymore, and had done it anyway. For me.

I turned to face my own computer and then, after a few moments staring blankly at the screen, I leaned over to pick Neil's card up off the floor and slid it into my purse. Then I picked up the bear, and shoved him underneath my desk, flowers and all.

# 12.

THE DAMN BEAR WOULDN'T STOP staring at me.

After a full day of squeezing my legs into the minuscule space the monstrosity had left under my desk, I decided to bite the bullet and lug the thing home. In retrospect, this may not have been the best decision. Turned out a child-size stuffed animal isn't exactly a welcome addition to a tightly packed Q train at rush hour. I learned this quickly as the object of almost every other rider's scornful glare. I spent the ride alternating between avoiding eye contact, and, when this wasn't possible, offering my most apologetic, if futile, smile.

The bear hardly felt like less of an intrusion in my own home. (Honestly, what sort of high-ceilinged, sprawling apartment did Neil think I lived in?) Maybe it was the fact that I'd been cooped up in my room since I'd gotten home four hours ago, but I could swear the bear, perched on my dresser/desk/vanity/in-desperate-times-table, was following my every movement with its beady little eyes. Not that there was much movement. I was spending my Friday night working from home, propped up in bed and surrounded by my laptop, notebook, phone, magazines, empty food wrappers, and, tonight, a half-empty bottle of Pinot Grigio. I took a long swig.

"*What?*" I said aloud to no one; to myself; to, I guess, the bear.

Beady, *judgmental* little eyes.

I stared at the ceiling and rolled out my shoulders. I needed to focus. Between the unresolved semi-fight with Harper, the tense presentation, and the apology from Neil—an apology I was refusing to acknowledge—the day had really shaken me. I'd spent most of it finalizing the details for the Philadelphia brunch. It was a deceptively simple task—Raya rejecting my first suggestion because the restaurant wouldn't disclose where they got their chickens; Archie rejecting the second because it didn't have outdoor seating—but we ultimately settled on an 11:00 a.m. meal at Tammy's, a Washington Square organic spot self-described as "high-end farmhouse." The manager, as to be expected, was thrilled.

Now, though, I was somewhat stalled. I had eleven tabs open on the laptop in front of me—Raya's Tumblr, Raya's Instagram, seven Raya fan Tumblrs, and two Twitter time lines I couldn't even remember landing on—but found little mention of Archie among them. It had started as an evening of Web meandering, and somewhere along the way I'd fallen into a deep hole of Raya stalking. True, there weren't many photos of her readily available, but plenty of evidence existed should a person want to convince herself that Raya was cool, the absolute coolest, *untouchably* cool, even. For starters: Raya's hazy Instagram shot of in-demand producer Luis Rollick sitting at a mixing board, suggesting a collaboration (*Which I should probably know about?*); the raspberry oatmeal recipe she'd shared on her

Tumblr (*so simple, but so delicious*); and, of course, all the many teens who called her "Mom." It was maddening.

*Teens could like me, too*, I thought, my face scrunching in smug indignation. *They just don't* know *me.* After all, the only reason Raya was even involved in this project was because I recognized her as someone who was worth our time. Surely, in a hierarchy of coolness, the person who discovers a cool thing (or person) was actually *cooler* than the discovered thing (or person). Right?

I was typing out my third draft of a tweet meant to prove this inherent coolness to the world (if Harper could get away with saying something was "dope," why couldn't I?) when I became overcome with frustration and closed out of Twitter entirely. I clicked back to Raya's Instagram and, in new tabs, opened the accounts of three social-media-famous teens, each of whom had more followers than many B-level actors. I pulled a notepad next to me and started jotting down the themes common among the profiles: still-life shots of succulents, close-ups of bulky sweaters, any photo with blurred edges. I focused my phone's camera on the shirt I was wearing, and was trying to fold it over on itself in a way that would scream *casual coolness* when I realized I was acting like a crazy person. It was just a theory, but maybe developing an organized system of coolness was actually antithetical to the very idea of it. I refocused my priorities, opened the Archie/Raya spreadsheet, and pressed the stuffed bear with my toe until it hit the floor.

I'd added the new photos to my ongoing PowerPoint presentation as soon as they were released. I looked through everything I had so far; objectively, this was a success. Archie's unplugged show in Philadelphia sold out in just three minutes, and tickets were currently listed on StubHub starting at $400. Granted, this was an intimate venue (read: smaller than a stadium), but Archie Fox hadn't sold out a show on this tour yet. It was good for morale. And it was good news to pass on to Joanna, which I had, the minute I'd hung up with Maria this afternoon.

Still, I couldn't kick one nagging question: Where exactly did my role end? Yes, I was coordinating dates for Archie and Raya, and then figuring out how best to present the evidence of those dates. Soon Archie would be fielding questions about the new relationship, which would mean coaching from me. And then, of course, there was the typical monitoring of public reaction: the Google alerts, the hashtags, the comments, the mentions. But this was all in service to boosting Archie's career, his image, and that went beyond his (real or fake) love life, didn't it? Wasn't it actually prudent to get to know him even better? He'd opened up a bit about home and family during our lunch—that was a gold mine. He'd have more downtime during this weekend's set; maybe he'd be well served by dropping some sentimental, personal tidbits between songs. I'd had no idea he was a godfather; that was something we could highlight, some good photo ops there. I opened my notes document and added bullet points for LARK and FAMILY. It felt strange to valorize and objectify actual parts of his life now that he was more of a real human being—possibly even a friend—to me, but I rationalized it as such: Emotional investment was (a) inevitable, and (b) just another motivation to take extra care of the project. If I had any anxiety about our closeness, it was only because I'd never experienced a relationship like this. In fact, what *felt* like jealousy over Raya was probably just a side effect of some deep-seated fear over whether or not she was the right choice for his career. It was all just part of the job. And I could believe all of this as long as I didn't look directly at the photo from the museum.

I hopped back into bed, took another sip of wine, reopened my laptop, and navigated to Facebook. Not much was happening on my newsfeed save a few bar photos automatically added from Instagram, and some quiz results from high school classmates I was friends with. A picture of my college roommate's three-month-old baby popped up, and I made a mental note to call her and check in—something the three-hour coast-to-coast time difference made it all too easy to argue was best saved for another day; to promise myself I'd do the *next* evening I had free time. But the newsfeed wasn't what I was after. Either I was going to find a reason to like him more, and then be annoyed that he'd ruined everything by being such a jerk; or I'd find a reason to like him less, and then be annoyed I'd wasted any time on him at all. It was a risk-free endeavor. I clicked onto the search bar.

*Neil*

...

*Wait*, I realized. Did I not know Neil's last name? I grabbed my phone and opened our text conversation: just Neil. I dug the card out of my purse; no luck there. I laughed. All of this nonsense over a guy I couldn't even pick out on Facebook—though I was getting tipsy enough to try. What else was I doing? I switched back to the search bar and leaned against my pillows.

*Neil + New York*

It was a start. Most Neils in New York, unsurprisingly, looked to be in the forty-to-sixty range. A lot of family photos, a couple of dogs, some yachts. New hypothesis: Neils were wealthy. By the third result page, and the last gulp of Pinot, I was annoyed. This led to hypothetical fights with Neil in my head. (*I bet Neil doesn't even have a Facebook,* I thought. *Like he's one of those people who loves saying it, even though no one asks, like, "Oh, I unplugged months ago and I feel sooooo free."*) By the fourth page, I was losing steam and interest. As I was clicking onto page five, my phone rang, muffled by my comforter. I dug around to find it, and answered right before it went to voicemail—it was Archie.

"Hi!" I said, out of breath.

"Rose? Is this a bad time?"

"No! Oh my God, nooooo, definitely not." Dammit, I was drunker than I'd realized. "I just couldn't find my phone. What's up?"

"I just wanted to check in before I left."

Archie—or, again, Big Pete—was driving to Philadelphia, since, everything accounted for, flying would actually take longer than driving, and Archie preferred to travel late at night. Fewer crowds.

"Sure, yeah, you all excited? Got your road trip planned? Pack some snacks?"

He laughed. "Um, I think I'll probably just sleep, to be quite honest."

"Mmhmm, mmhmm." I nodded my head, and my peripheral vision started blurring. I scooted off the bed, lay flat on the floor, and closed my eyes.

"So..."

"Right, sorry—you know, Friday night."

"Getting wild, Ms. Reed?"

"Oh, absolutely, if you count a night in bed as wild." He was silent for a beat, and I cringed. "No—God, no, not like that.

Like, alone in bed, with some snacks and a... truly horrific giant stuffed bear."

"Hey, listen, whatever you're into..."

I smiled, but remembered he couldn't see me. "So, you're all set for tomorrow, right? You'll check in to The Grand tonight—they know you're coming—"

"I know, Maria and I talked logistics," Archie cut in. "I wanted to talk to you about the show."

"Oh? Are you—you're not nervous, right?"

He laughed again. "Ah, no, Rose, I'm no longer nervous to play a show for two hundred fifty people."

"Oh, okay, Mr. Big Shot, but just so you know, Barbra Streisand, like, still has stage fright. *Still.* And she's Barbra fucking Streisand, so." I inched toward the corner and stretched my straight legs up against the wall. I tried to reach my toes and grunted inadvertently.

"Rose, are you doing... calisthenics right now?"

"No, I'm just stretching, Mr. Police Guard."

"*Mr. Police Guard*?" He laughed sharply and his voice rose up almost an octave. My drunk insults needed some work. "What does that even *mean*?"

I was suddenly laughing so hard my eyes were tearing. "I don't know, Archie, I'm drunk."

"I couldn't tell at all."

"So what about the show do you wanna talk about?"

"I wanted to know if you were coming."

My laughter—and my heart—froze. "What?"

"Yeah, I was just wondering if you were planning on coming."

"Oh, no, I mean, I hadn't planned on it." I hobbled to my feet and started pacing the small room. "Maria told me it wouldn't be necessary. Why?" *Why did I get so drunk?*

"Oh, well, maybe not *necessary*, I just thought you might like it." He sounded so calm. Like he had no idea he was turning my stomach into a ball of tangled knots. "And I realized this would be my first show since you took me on. Could be fun."

*Since I took him on.*

"Right. Well."

"But, ah, you can say no, if you're busy, or would just rather not." His voice was stiffened and heavier—with formality, or frustration, or maybe even something so prosaic as hurt feelings. "It's really not a big deal."

"No, of course I would love to!" I overcompensated by shouting. "I just, you know, I haven't booked anything, and I'm behind on . . . everything." I looked at the mess that was my room.

"Rose, it's Philadelphia. It's practically in New York. You don't even have to stay overnight."

I could feel my heart pounding, but couldn't find any words.

"You could invite Neil; we'll get him on the list, too."

I snorted.

"So, no Neil."

I looked over at the bear, now toppled sideways on the floor. "No Neil."

Neither of us spoke, and the silence felt so delicate I was too nervous to breathe.

"It could be a good chance for you to spend time with Raya, too; you know, she's quite keen on you."

"Really?" The skepticism in my voice was plain.

"Yes, Rose. You're easy to like."

My breath caught in my throat. I couldn't think of anything normal to say in response, so I said nothing at all.

"Okay, so, I have to go, but in sum: Get away from your weird stuffed-animal party and come to Philadelphia with the rest of the living world."

I smiled and rolled my eyes. "Maybe. Have a safe trip."

"I'll see you tomorrow, Rose."

"Good-bye, Archie."

I stared at the phone, unmoving, until the call disconnected. My face ached from smiling.

---

I arrived in Philadelphia by Amtrak around noon the next day. When Archie invited me I'd assumed I'd take the Bolt Bus, or something similarly cheap and civilian, but when I'd run my new plan by Joanna last night, she'd told me to book a round trip on the train. This conversation was over video chat, at her insistence, after I'd emailed her what I'd assumed was a sufficient update. Her response arrived almost immediately, her email chiming on my phone over the sound of the running faucet while I washed the day's residue off my face. It was brief:

`Good idea, but let's chat. Can you video call?`

My gut immediately tensed, and I did a quick internal calibration. Could I video chat my boss at just shy of 10:00 p.m., in my pajamas, while drunk? Sure. *Should* I? That was a different story. I figured it was less a request than a demand, though, and at that point I was really just tipsy. So, I downed a glass of ice-cold water, smacked my cheeks a couple times, and hoped the fear of sounding like an idiot would be enough to sober me up.

The phone rang while I settled into bed, against the bare wall. I'd had video calls with Joanna plenty of times before, whenever she was away longer than two days to see a client, but never from my home. Never looking into *her* home. I hardly had time to imagine what it would look like before her face popped up on the screen.

"Rose, thanks for calling." She was clearly on her laptop, which was settled on what appeared to be her dining room table. The lights were dim behind her, but I could see enough to know that her kitchen, which served as the backdrop, looked straight out of *Kinfolk*: raw wood shelves against a subway tile wall, holding unmarked, uniform glass jars and tins. Two candles were burning on the counter, and the corner of the fridge that I could see was covered in elementary school art. It was perfect. I tried not to drool.

"Sure thing!" I said, immediately shocked by the volume of my voice.

"So you're going to Philly."

"Um, yeah," I replied, trying to remember how I'd phrased my reasoning in the email I'd sent. "I realized, you know, it's so close. And what with Raya and Archie both being there, it seems like a great opportunity to interface with them both. Efficient. Plus, he's got that opening Q and A and I haven't really had time to prep some banter with him..."

Joanna nodded. Her face was bare, her hair was covered in a silk wrap, and she was wearing her glasses. Clearly her Friday night was no more exciting than mine, which was a comforting albeit surprising thought, given that I'd always imagined Joanna's Friday nights were spent at posh galas or backstage at concerts. Seeing her like this, settling in for the evening—the whole thing felt disarmingly intimate.

"You'll steer him away from confirming their relationship."

"Of course. He'll be coy."

"He's good at that, the whole charming thing. He's been a little out of practice, but it's there."

"Totally."

"Make sure they don't even *hint* at Chloe. We're moving on. We're past it."

"Yup, got it."

She paused and took a sip of water. "Will you be staying overnight?"

"No, of course not!" I said too emphatically, and then, seeing Joanna's confused reaction, added, "I, um, I hate sleeping in hotels. Plus, the show is early."

Joanna's eyebrow rose in slight judgment. "I didn't know that was possible. I'd sleep in a hotel bed every night if I could."

I laughed, nervous.

"You feel good about everything?" Joanna asked. "It can be overwhelming spending so much time one-on-one with a celebrity of Archie's . . . caliber."

I imagined a reality in which I could respond honestly: *Well, you know, I'm glad that you mention it, because—is it normal to start to feel attached? To maybe get a little more excited when you see him or talk to him or, I don't know, just think about him? That probably happens all the time, right, because how could it not? This is a guy who is famous for making young girls fall in love with him, for fuck's sake; it's what I'm actively selling to them* right now, *so maybe I should cut myself some slack and accept that, yeah, maybe I'll develop a little crush—so what?* And then I pictured the reaction: Joanna's dropped jaw, everything called off—the trip, the project, my job. My reputation destroyed, my career disintegrated. Harper, too embarrassed to be my friend. I'd probably get evicted. Maybe my family would disown me. Regardless: disaster.

"Yeah! Yes, absolutely." I nodded vigorously. "It's a lot, but it's good. I like it."

"Good. You're a pro; I knew you could handle it."

My stomach flip-flopped. I gave my best attempt at a smile.

"So unfortunately we're still waiting on your corporate card," she said. (The card was a nice perk that came with direct client contact, and a tangible symbol of my new, heightened status—I just hadn't received it yet.) "But go ahead and book your ticket, save your receipts, and we'll reimburse."

"No worries—the bus is like five dollars anyway."

"Rose," she sighed. "Take the train." A quiet young girl's voice sounded in the background, and Joanna turned her head toward it. "One second, baby girl—almost done!"

"I'll let you go," I said. Joanna turned back to the camera and I felt, again, like I was somehow intruding.

"Okay, yeah, we'll catch up on Monday." And suddenly, her face was gone.

So here I was, feeling almost like royalty with my ample legroom and an open seat next to me the whole ride. No matter that the ticket cost the company a mere $50—compared with my usual transportation, it felt like living large. And it was good to know that, no matter what happened today, I would be traveling back to New York around 9:00 tonight not on a bus full of giddy teens preparing to party, but on a stately train full of quiet, tired, middle-aged suits.

When I got to the Trocadero Theatre, it was just after 1:00. Archie's one-hour set would start at 3:00 p.m. sharp—unlike a typical, nighttime show, there would be no openers, and no chic dawdling. The set was being recorded for later release online, and while it could and would be edited, I knew that Archie and his band had been told to keep everything moving, and that there were at least two dozen crewmembers around to make sure it did. His show was being held in The Balcony, a smaller venue within the larger theater that sat 250 people. To get inside, I'd walked past a line, which stretched around the corner and three blocks back. Having been one of those waiting people more times than I could count—arriving for a show hours and hours early, so early I had to bring food and water and boredom-alleviating activities—it felt incredible to be able to walk right past them, show the guard outside my ID, and be told I could head not only inside, but backstage. I'd peered over my shoulder at all the girls (many of them my age, or near it) to see if they were looking, wondering who I was that I got to walk right in. Mostly, though, they were looking at their phones.

Once backstage I paused. The guard's directions for me had stopped here; Archie had told me to meet him "before the show," but hadn't said exactly when or where. I pulled out my phone to see if he'd sent any clarifying texts in the last two minutes, but no such luck. I was on the verge of turning back to ask the guard where I could find Archie or Maria (and, in so doing, inevitably reveal to him that I didn't really belong back there) when I spotted craft services, and walked toward it instead.

Spread across the eight-foot-long table was a veritable feast: there were, most important, seven types of cheese (I counted), but I also saw bruschetta, Caprese salad, chicken wings, sliced and fanned fruit, nuts, dates, brioche rounds topped with what appeared to be caviar, and a beautiful, ornate two-tiered cake. I leaned in closer to get a better look, and saw that into the bright-white fondant was screen-printed the cover of Archie's last album, *Rue*.

*Jesus.*

I looked around—the hallway was still empty—and loaded a plastic plate high with cheese, crackers, and a piece of cake. I'd been too nervous to eat much earlier; half a Clif Bar I found in the kitchen cabinet from who-knows-when for breakfast, and nothing for lunch. Now that I was here, I was starving. I took another appraising look at my plate and grabbed a small fistful of grapes, for health purposes, and then I stuffed my mouth full of habanero cheddar.

"I see you've found the snacks," said a voice behind me. A slow, deep, male, British voice. *Dammit.*

I considered attempting to swallow everything in my mouth at once, but I knew that to choke on cheese in front of Archie Fox was even more embarrassing than to be in the process of eating a month's worth of it in one go. So I turned around, pointed to my bulging cheeks, and nodded. Archie grinned, and it took every ounce of self-control I had to keep myself from smiling in return. I was sure that if I did, cheese would come spilling out.

"I'll give you a moment," said Archie. He crossed his arms in front of his chest, raised his eyes to the ceiling, and made a huge, exaggerated show of starting to whistle. My face burned, but I had no choice but to power through it. When I finally swallowed, I pushed him, and for just a moment, my hand grazed his shirt—white, short-sleeved with a pocket in front, ostensibly cotton but a class (or twenty) apart from any cotton I'd ever felt before.

"Is that new?" I asked.

"Yeah," he said. "Du Roi sent a bunch of stuff over."

"Ah," I nodded. "They saw the photos."

"Probably." Archie shrugged. Free stuff was seemingly no longer novel or particularly exciting for him. But then he asked, "Do you like it?" That he genuinely seemed to want to know if I approved took me by surprise.

"Yes," I said. "You look great." I was pretty sure I could feel myself blush. "Du Roi makes a great T-shirt. I think Harper calls them, like, carpenter chic? I don't know."

"Well, thanks," he said. "God knows I wouldn't want to muck up my first recorded show in a year by wearing something that wasn't chic-adjacent."

I laughed and, looking down, realized I was still holding my plate of cheese and cake. And grapes. Archie apparently followed my gaze, because then he said, "Come on, let's get you a place to sit."

"I don't want to get in the way," I said. "I mean, we should go over a couple things at some point before you go on, but if there's any prep you have to do first..."

"I've been prepping for ages. Come on."

I followed Archie down the hallway, all the while telling myself to *be cool*. While I'd been backstage for a couple of shows in college, for scene-y bands that probably no longer existed, I'd certainly never gone into anyone's private room. When I imagined a rock star's dressing room I pictured leather sofas, liquor, and a coffee table just *covered* in coke. While Archie had been subject to an addiction rumor or two (you couldn't be a real pop star without one, particularly if you'd experienced any weight fluctuations whatsoever), I was pretty sure his dressing room would be coke-free. *Right?* I wondered. *What is the coolest, chillest way to refuse coke from an international pop star?*

Archie pushed open an unlabeled door and I followed him inside to find a small, dark, and apparently drug-free dressing room. As he settled onto a plush, burgundy sofa, I took a look around: black fabric draped over the walls, brand-name silk handkerchiefs draped over the two lamps, a rack of freshly pressed clothing to the side of the mirror, a countertop covered in Kiehl's products. I sniffed the air.

"What's that smell?"

Archie pointed to a large, lit candle sitting on the end table at his side. "Maria believes it's soothing for me."

"Oliban by diptyque?" I thought I'd recognized the scent; I'd picked up the same candle in a department store once. I probably would have bought it, too, if it hadn't been *seventy dollars*. For a *candle*.

He lifted the candle and squinted to read its label. "... Yes."

"Well, is it?"

"Soothing?"

"Yeah."

He shrugged. "It certainly hasn't hurt." He gestured to the sofa perpendicular to his—matching, but slightly smaller. "Have a seat," he said. "Eat your cheese."

"Okay," I said, holding up a hand. "But I'll eat this cheese on my own time line, thanks."

Archie laughed. "You got it," he said. "Let's hear it, then."

"Great," I started. "Um." I'd gone over my planned spiel on the train, remembering what Joanna and I had discussed the night before. I had some fairly specific ideas of what I wanted Archie to say on stage. Now, what were they?

"I should tell them I'm newly in love, yes?" Archie's face was hard to read; his right eyebrow was lifted, but he wasn't quite smiling.

"No," I said. Too quickly. "I mean, unless you are, I guess?… Are you?"

"I'm a romantic, not a maniac."

I couldn't help but notice that—technically—he didn't answer the question.

"Okay," I said. "Great."

"It is," he said. "It's no good for anyone for me to be in love." He smiled, sort of; no dimples.

"I'm sure that's not true," I said. (*How?* How *am I sure?*)

Archie shrugged again, leaned forward, and plucked a piece of cheese off my plate. He froze. "If you can spare it," he said.

"It's all right, I have more in my purse."

Archie's eyes widened in delight. "Really?"

"*No*," I said. "God." Archie laughed, hard enough that I could see the cheese in his mouth. It wasn't *so* gross, I thought.

"Okay, for real." I turned back to the topic at hand.

Archie cleared his throat. "Yes, do be serious."

"When he asks you about your new album, I want you to say that you've been in a really good place recently, and that you've been feeling inspired in the studio."

Archie nodded. "Sure."

"He'll probably ask you why you think that is, and I want you to say something about growing up, and gaining perspective, and learning about what it is that's really important to you. And that one of those things is writing from the heart."

"Mmm," said Archie. "Subtle."

"Are you mocking me?"

"Not at all," he said, but I still couldn't tell.

"Good." I took a deep breath. "You will also be asked, in some form or another, if you're seeing someone new. Maria's told the interviewer not to mention Raya by name, but there's always a chance he'll go for it anyway. If he does, say you're 'new friends,' and you love her music. And if he asks generally, I want you to say you're single, but I want you to be as coy about it as you possibly can be. I want to see dimples."

Archie grinned in acquiescence and I looked down at my cheese plate.

"He probably won't prod, because you're a man," I continued. "But if he does, just grin and shake your head. Say 'No comment,' if you have to. People love that."

"Yes ma'am," said Archie. *Ugh. "Ma'am." Like I'm forty-five.*

I felt my stomach rumble and I took another piece of cheese.

"Is—" I said, then stopped. I wanted to know how Archie *did* feel about Raya so far, but I also felt like it was possible there was nothing I wanted to know less. Archie only looked at me, waiting. "Is it going all right, though? So far?"

"With Raya, you mean?"

"Yeah."

"Yes," he said. "She's lovely. Very bright, too."

"Oh good," I said. Cool that she was hot, hip, a talented musician, *and* super smart.

"Yeah," said Archie. "It's a nice change."

"Chloe's not the sharpest?" As soon as I'd said it I wished I hadn't; I didn't want to overestimate our level of familiarity.

"No," he said. "Chloe is *very* sharp. Lovely, on the other hand..."

I couldn't help but think of the tabloid covers. TAN'S NEW MAN. CHLOE TO ARCHIE: GET "GONE." (That one a heavy-handed reference to a song of his called—you guessed it—"Gone.") ARCHIE'S WILD BACHELOR'S NIGHT: DRINKS, DANCERS, DEBAUCHERY. Et cetera.

"Can I ask you something totally insensitive?"

"There's an offer I can't refuse."

"Is it true she broke up with you via text from her assistant?"

Archie laughed bitterly. "No," he said. "The true story was much more boring, and a bit more sad."

I tried to wait, to give him a window in case he wanted to say more or, more likely, change the topic, but I only lasted ten seconds. "I'm sorry," I said. "I know that maybe doesn't mean a lot coming from me, because I am your PR rep, and I don't know you super well, and I didn't know you at all back then, but I'm still sorry. And I think it's kind of incredible that you've done like, *anything* in public since then. Because if that happened to me I would probably take my millions and buy my way into a spot on the international space station or something."

"How much money do you think I have?"

"I truly have no idea," I responded.

"Slightly south of space station seat purchase, I'd wager."

"Well, anyway, I just wanted to say that even I know that all of this"—I gestured vaguely, but what I meant was his entire life, and now, my part in it—"is really fucking weird. And I'm not even the one living it."

Then Archie scooted over to the other end of his sofa—the

end nearer to me. He leaned forward and placed his hand—the one with the two silver rings and the spade tattoo between his thumb and forefinger—gently on top of mine. I stopped breathing altogether.

"Thank you, Rose," he said. "Sincerely."

# 13.

IN THE PEAK OF MY show-going days, I'd always wondered about the people sitting in VIP areas. Namely, who they were (if they were *really* VIPs, I'd figured, they'd be watching from backstage), and why they would opt to watch from some of the worst seats in the house. The roped-off zones—a secret second-floor balcony or a slightly elevated back corner—seemed more about exclusivity and comfort than proximity to the artist, and personally, I couldn't imagine not pushing my way right up to the stage. Now that I *was* one of those mysterious elite, sitting at one of the tall bar tables that lined the perimeter of the venue, I felt that familiar urge simmering right under my skin. From my perch, I even mapped out the route that would lead me to the stage—which couples were vulnerable from leaving too large a gap between them, who looked distracted enough to be pushed aside. The table vibrated from my foot shaking against its legs.

I sipped on an IPA (set in front of me by a very handsome, very young, topknotted waiter—a legitimate perk of the VIP area, I'd admit) and willed myself to focus. Archie was one question into his pre-performance Q&A, and already I'd caught my mind wandering. It didn't help that the host, Bill Jafari, was more interested in hearing his own voice than Archie's—he was doing roughly 70 percent of the talking. His show, *One Two One Two*, was extremely popular, and these monthly "stripped-down" shows had started gaining critical attention over the past few months, but there was no getting around the fact that he himself was insufferable. Not that it mattered; my mind was busy elsewhere replaying the conversation Archie and I had had backstage.

Well, not the entire conversation. Mostly I was reliving the moment I'd monumentally screwed everything up by pulling my arm back from his touch, and hiding my hand in my blown-out-for-the-occasion hair. After Archie had thanked me for my concern over his failed relationship, I'd gotten so flustered I abruptly changed the subject. I'd returned to the topic of space travel and gone on a mild digression about how, as much as space would be a good escape for a bad breakup, in actuality I believed that anyone who said they'd willingly go to space was lying, and that we'd all do well to show the universe the respect it deserved by leaving it alone—barring, of course, technological advancements that would allow *Star Trek*–style intergalactic travel. Archie had responded with a silent, quizzical look, and then a short burst of laughter. After we went over remaining possible interview questions (Any exciting collabs on his upcoming album? *Nothing set in stone, but definitely in the works.* Was it true he was thinking of settling down in London? *I'll always have a special place in my heart for the UK, but, for now, New York is home.*) and solidified dinner plans for after the show (I'd meet him and Raya at Azalea, the restaurant inside the The Grand Hotel, where Archie was staying),

I'd grabbed one last cube of cheddar and retreated to my VIP table. Still, though, I couldn't stop thinking of those few milliseconds before we went back to business—the brief eye contact I'd averted, the warmth I swore I could still feel where his hand had rested on my wrist.

I reached down to my bag and pulled out a pocket-size red Moleskine and pen. If I couldn't trust myself to focus, I'd have to give myself an assignment—I'd take notes. I looked up at the stage. Bill was sitting on a stool, legs crossed, and arms gesticulating widely as he continued what was apparently a long stream of thought.

"...and that's the double meaning there, right? Obviously the album comes from a deeply personal place, lamenting the catastrophic end to a relationship that—at least on the outside—looked like this kind of once-in-a-lifetime love." I squirmed in my seat, but Archie didn't even break his smile. The interviewer continued, his hands curling into fists. "But, given the restraint of this album, the pullback, *the quietude*, couldn't we also read it as sort of *ruing* that early part of your career, maybe the compromising of your creativity? A dirge, if you will, for that former pop-star self?"

Archie laughed, and I could feel all of the individual hearts breaking around me.

"You might be in the wrong line of work, mate. You've got some academia inside of you," said Archie. Quiet snickers spread throughout the audience, and he shrugged. "But honestly, it's not quite that deep. It's about love gone sour, plain and simple."

The interviewer faced the audience with an ingratiating smile. "Well, surely we can all agree that love gone sour is hardly. Simple. At all."

"This guy is such a tool." Raya had appeared as if out of thin air, leaning against the empty stool on my left. Her hair was pulled up high and tight, with new deep-purple ends that gave her ponytail the illusion of having recently been dipped in paint, and she was wearing the Du Roi dress. It looked incredible. Like it was made for her. Like, I imagined, Mr. or Ms. Du Roi had dreamed it would look when he or she designed it. I glanced down at my own outfit—a black blazer over a tank top (white, forced on me by Harper) and black jeans—and felt impossibly dull.

"Hey, that's your boyfriend you're talking about." I laughed weakly.

Raya didn't join in. She looked at me and frowned, not registering. "Not Archie. Bill."

"Oh, yeah, I was just—it was a dumb joke." Raya nodded and returned her gaze to the stage.

"He almost didn't have Arch on, can you believe that?"

This was news to me. The spot had been arranged last-minute—I'd reached out to their booking team as soon as I'd taken the project on with ideas for the more distant future, but had been surprised to get an almost-immediate return phone call from a frantic events coordinator, who explained that their August artist was dropping out and wondered if, by any chance, Archie could be ready to play in less than two weeks. What I thought would be a hard sell ended up being barely a conversation at all; Maria wrote back minutes after I sent the email, sending her and Archie's blessings. I'd been in contact with the events team since, but was surprised to hear Raya had gotten personally involved.

Because I didn't want Raya to think I didn't already know exactly what she was talking about, though, all I said was, "Oh?"

Before she could go on, a server appeared; I ordered another beer and asked Raya what she was drinking.

"Just a soda with splash of cranberry, thanks." She finished the rest of the drink she was already holding. "Doing this cleanse," she said. "Anyway, yeah, Billy and I are tight. He's a total dick, but I love the guy. Anyway, I guess when he got your email he wasn't totally sure this was the right fit for *One Two*, and, you know, he'd really only heard Archie's early stuff, I get it. But he'd seen we were 'involved'"—here she did jokey air quotes, though I couldn't exactly tell *how* jokey—"and gave me a call to, like, ask what I thought. And then when Jackson Lang bailed, I *knew* this was meant to be, that I was suddenly in the position to connect these two incredibly special men. I was like, 'B, trust me.' And, I don't know, I guess he did."

She swiveled the straw around her glass, and the ice cubes caught and reflected bits of red, yellow, blue light as they circled the bottom. So, twenty-year-old Raya had set this up. Raya had done my job for me. Excellent.

"But I got the call before you guys went out..." I said, hoping I sounded more like a publicist talking shop than a jealous girl digging for details.

"Oh, right. I guess he and I started texting pretty soon after you and I had our lunch."

I felt a lump rise up my throat. Why hadn't Archie told me any of this? Not that he was obligated to, but why didn't he want to? I thought back to Du Roi, every moment I found him smiling at his phone. Was he talking to her then? Did they have an immediate connection; were they already sharing inside jokes?

"Ah. Well. Meant to be, I guess!" I said, too loudly. A young couple sitting at the table in front of us turned around and glared at me. Raya rolled her eyes.

"Oh, come on," she whispered at them. "We're not at the fucking movies."

I gave a weak laugh. We turned our attention back to the interview, which had moved on to talk of his current love life, as was expected.

"So is there a special lady in your life these days, Archie?" asked Bill. "Maybe someone in the audience, even...?"

Some stray, high-pitched *woo*s shot out from the audience. Raya's mouth twisted into a crooked smile, and she looked down into her glass. Was she blushing?

"Ah, Bill, every lady in my life is special."

*Gross.* And not the response we'd talked about. I snuck another peek at Raya—she was still smiling, if a bit smaller than before. Her face was altogether impassive, and not for the first time, I felt jealous of performers' talent for poker faces. But then, I thought, maybe she didn't *have* anything to hide. Maybe she was so chill, so secure in being the type of woman Archie would find special, that she didn't mind the remark. I took a long gulp of beer, too much at once, and I scrunched my face.

"Want a sip?" asked Raya, holding out her glass.

I did, and took it gratefully. She was thoughtful. *Dammit.*

The crowd's giggling quieted, and Bill asked, "But surely there's one lady—or two, no judgment—who's a little *more* special than the others?"

I tried to keep my face as relaxed as Raya's, but I'd perhaps never focused on anything as intently as I focused on Archie's response. After his previous answer, he'd leaned an elbow on his chair and rested his chin in his hand; now the hand curled into a fist that covered his mouth, but not the dimples that appeared as he broke into a reluctant, closed-mouth smile. Slowly—unconvincingly—he shook his head.

"Are you refusing to comment?" said Bill. And then he grinned, like, *I feel you, my man. Guy code.*

"Oh, I think I'd call it 'politely declining,'" said Archie, and everyone laughed.

"Fair enough," Bill said, and then he moved on to ask Archie about his upcoming tour. I felt a wave of relief as well as a little bit proud. His first answer wasn't great, but he'd more than made up for it with the second. Guarded but not aloof, charming but not ingratiating. Anyone who watched the interview would come away from it feeling like all that public speculation about Raychie was as good as confirmed.

"So, how long are you staying in Philadelphia?" I turned to Raya to see her smiling earnestly. She was, really, a very nice young woman. And maybe in some alternate universe, we could even sort of be friends. But in this universe, she was six years younger than I was and en route to superstardom. If she had any normal friendships left by the time she got there, they'd dissolve soon after. And then, probably the biggest obstacle, there was the fact that I was growing increasingly resentful of her relationship—real *or* fake, though it was seeming realer by the day—which I myself had brought into existence.

"Just today, unfortunately," I said. "I need to be back in the city tomorrow morning." This was not strictly true—tomorrow was Sunday, and anything I had to do for work (surfing the Internet, mostly) I could do from anywhere.

"Oh, that's too bad," said Raya.

Applause broke out around us and the house lights turned on—the interview was over. Already roadies were running around behind the stools carrying amps and wires, as Archie brought his hands in front of his chest in a praying position and bowed slightly. When he popped back up, he waved at me (or Raya?) and winked. We both waved back, and he retreated backstage.

"He really is great," said Raya. "Like, kind of magical."

I sucked my teeth behind my lips.

"Yeah, he seems pretty cool! Things are going well then?" My voice had pitched up about half an octave.

"Oh yeah, I mean, we'd met once or twice before and I kind of thought we'd get along, but I had no idea. I can't wait for you to hear the new stuff. He played a little for me and it's sooooo great. Just really fantastic." She nodded vigorously, seemingly trying to stress the music's fantastic-ness both to me and to herself.

I forced a smile, nodding so deliberately and quickly I felt a strain in my neck. When did he have time to play his new music for her?

"Anyway, it's a bummer you're heading out tonight. I was going to tell you to come to my show."

"Oh, thanks," I said. "Yeah, I wanted to get back to the city before midnight anyway, so. I'll see you at dinner, though, right?"

Raya cocked her head. "Dinner?"

"Oh," I said. "Wait, so. You're not meeting... for dinner?"

"Not unless you count the pre-show soup and tea waiting for me at the venue. Hey, listen, I gotta run and say hi to some people before Arch starts. Great to see you!"

Raya gave me a quick hug and then was gone. My heart pounded in my chest as my mind replayed the part of the conversation when Archie had invited me to dinner: He'd asked me what I was doing after the show, I'd said probably grabbing a bite, and he'd suggested joining him ("like old people") at Azalea at 5:30. Why had I assumed Raya would be there? Was it because, if not, it would mean Archie was asking me to dinner, alone, on a Saturday night? And not at a shitty taco stand, at a swanky hotel restaurant, where they probably had dim lighting, and linen tablecloths, and (oh God) maybe even a candle on the table? And if that was the case, did it mean I'd been right (or at least not crazy) to feel what I thought I felt when he touched my wrist, something I'd been trying to push from my mind ever since?

Feeling dizzy, I flagged down one of the VIP servers with a drink tray and downed a full glass of water. It didn't help. I looked around—the stagehands in frantic preparation mode; the audience murmuring impatiently, excitedly; and Raya, standing near the edge of the stage talking to a small group of people whose grooming suggested some level of fame but whose faces I didn't recognize. YouTubers, probably. I felt faint and closed my eyes, tuning out the sounds of the room and the show happening around me. I opened them when I heard the rest of the audience begin to clap and cheer.

Archie had reemerged on stage, holding his guitar, shyly waving and winking at the front few rows of shrieking women. He sat on a stool at center stage, and the lights dimmed around him, creating a soft glow that lit up the crown of his head, his brow, his shoulders. Following his stated preference for intimate shows, the stage floor was free of mike stands; instead he wore one clipped on the lapel of his shirt. When he cleared his throat, it came through loud and clear.

"Thanks so much. It's great to be here. I know everyone says this about everywhere, but, ah, I really do love playing here. Most places I play make me incredibly nervous, but something about this one makes me feel really... at ease." He blushed, and out came the dimples. It was a great intro: charming, sincere, brief. In spite of myself, I, too, felt my nerves settle, and felt, instead of dread, a rush of gratitude—that I was here, in what was one of my own favorite music venues, in a cozy seat, watching the client I'd fought so hard for do so well.

The warmth in my chest only expanded as Archie began to play. He opened with a light, playful rendition of "Kiss Me, Kill Me," and then slowed things down with "Time Enough." Moments after I finished my beer, it was replaced with another, and I began to think I could get used to sitting in the VIP section. Between songs Archie grinned at the crowd and, once or twice—I thought, though it was hard to tell exactly from where I sat—at me. The first time it happened I attempted to look around me as slyly as possible, to see if Raya, or another likely target, was seated around me, but Raya was nowhere to be seen (most likely she stood at the side of the stage), and I saw no one else he knew. At least, no one I knew he knew.

Archie played a few more fan favorites, talking a bit between each song as I'd encouraged him to do beforehand. As I downed the last gulp of my third beer, he cleared his throat again.

"If it's okay with you, I'd like to play something new."

The crowd whooped and clapped in agreement, and Archie grinned nervously.

"Now, this isn't a new single, at least not yet. I'm still… working things out, so to speak, but, this is just something I've been working on for a while and… yeah. We'll see how it sounds outside of the shower."

*God*, I thought, grinning a big, goofy grin along with every other damn woman in the audience. What must it be like to just ooze with such sexy, easy charm?

And then he started playing, the sudden loudness and aggressiveness of the guitar sending a jolt through the audience. The song was much more rock-oriented than what he'd played thus far, and angrier, too. When he began to sing his expression changed entirely—his features were harder, his eyes closed. He growled the lyrics, and the effect was not *unpleasant*, per se, but harsh and surprising. I was so stunned that I couldn't focus on the lyrics, until he came to the chorus, which was repeated enough that I couldn't ignore it:

*The highs are high and the lows so low*
*I want you to stay and I want you to go*
*But baby I never loved you more*
*than when you walked out of my door*

By the end of the song Archie's forehead glistened with sweat, and a pall had fallen over the crowd. I looked at their faces, hoping for evidence that my opinion was an outlier, honestly wanting to be wrong. But though they were rapt, and though they clapped loudly and enthusiastically when Archie finished and ran his hand through his hair, I knew that the prevailing feeling about the song mirrored my own, and it wasn't a good one. The song... kind of... sucked.

As Archie thanked the crowd and took a few bows, and the house lights came back on, I swallowed hard, all of my previous anxiety returning, prickling at my skin. *Maybe it's fine*, I thought. Even he said it wasn't a single—or had he only said that it wasn't *yet*? I watched Archie leave the stage, and once he had, I flagged down a server holding a tray of water. I downed a glass in two gulps, set it on the table along with a few bills, and sped down the stairs of the VIP section onto the main floor.

I had never eavesdropped harder in my life than I did at that moment, making my way toward the exit among the crush of fans. I was still hoping to hear something contradictory; if I heard even one girl telling her friend how much she adored the new song (had he even told us its name?), I would feel mollified. But all I heard were girls talking about how much they liked that version of "Kiss Me, Kill Me," and that moment halfway through when he'd bit his lip, and how funny he was, how gorgeous. Nobody I could hear said anything bad about the new song. Worse, nobody said anything about it at all.

# 14.

I'D BEEN SITTING IN THE lobby of The Grand for long enough that I was pretty sure the concierge thought I was a stalker. When I sat down a few minutes before 5:00 he'd asked how he could help, and I'd told him I was waiting for my "friend," who had a reservation at the restaurant for 5:30. And while I could sense his suspicion (and possible distaste) for my continued presence, I knew there wasn't much he would do unless it became clear my "friend" wasn't really coming. Which (I looked at my phone; it was 5:42) I was starting to think might actually happen.

For the fiftieth time I took what I hoped was an extremely casual look around me: the cool, warehouse-like gray floor; the cozy sitting area where a pair of businessmen sat on black leather sofas, drinking whiskey and intermittently asking each other something about the weather or the agenda of the conference they were both here to attend; the art deco light fixture hanging directly above my head. I still couldn't decide whether the overall feel was cold or elegant, and I felt less sure than I had before I came in that the two were mutually exclusive.

I unlocked my phone and reread my text conversation with

Harper. I hadn't been able to keep myself from texting her about Archie, despite our argument the day before. I thought she still seemed a bit short, but maybe I was reading too much into it.

UGGHHHH I'd written, around 4:15, just after leaving the Trocadero.

???, she'd written back.

I just left Archie's show

And...

I don't know how to say this

OMG what???

He played a new song and it was...

...

JUST SAY IT

Bad.

Oh god. Really???

Really. I mean, I think so. Idk. Maybe it's just me??

I mean, you aren't his BIGGEST fan...

I like his music!!

That's a new development

I guess

Well, it's just one song, right?

Yeah. That's true.

Then I'd given up and called her, recapping the show from the beginning. And as soon as I'd told her the part about Archie saying that "every lady" in his life was special, I stopped worrying about whether or not she was still mad at me, because she screamed into the speaker.

"*You like him*," she said.

"No?" I said, unconvincingly.

"Why are you even trying to lie to me?"

"I don't know," I said. "I just want it on the record that I resisted."

"The feelings, or telling me?"

"Both."

I'd talked to Harper while I walked the 0.8-mile route I Google Mapped from the theater to the hotel, and then I'd sat outside until we were done. She'd screamed several more times—at the arm touch, at the post-interview wink toward an unknown target, at the fact that we were meeting for dinner without Raya, and that we'd be doing so at the place where (I hadn't thought of this until she said it) he'd be sleeping later tonight. Throughout our conversation I'd only gotten more and more anxious, eventually deciding that I couldn't hang up, and would have to keep her on the line throughout dinner. I was about to tell her more about Archie's new song—not that I knew how to describe, exactly, what was wrong with it—but then she told me she had to go get ready for a date. So after requesting one last thirty-second pep-talk-slash-reminder that it was natural for me to have a smallish crush on someone widely considered to be the sexiest man alive (*Society*, 2014 & 2015) but that I was meeting Archie for dinner as his employed publicist and not his love interest ("Though he should *be* so lucky," she said), I let her go and walked inside to the lobby. For the first thirty minutes that I sat there, I remained as nervous as before, but then 5:30 came and went without word from Archie, and now I was pissed.

I turned to look at the concierge, who quickly looked back at his computer.

"Excuse me," I said. "What's the time?" I wanted him to know I was still thinking of my dinner, and that I was just as concerned about our tardiness as he was, but I also wanted to make sure there hadn't been some global phone data error that caused my phone to say it was 5:52 when it was really only, say, 5:22.

"It's five fifty-two," he said, his tone a bit pitying.

"Thanks."

His phone rang, and I eavesdropped. When he picked up the receiver, he said, "You've reached The Grand, this is Charlie, how may I help?" *I feel like he should go by Charles*, I thought. "Yes," he said. "There is, yes. Mmm. She does." At this I looked up to see Charlie looking back at me. I looked away. "Yes, sir. Of course. You're welcome." He hung up the phone.

"Miss Reed?" he asked.

"Yes?" I said.

"Your host has asked me to direct you to his suite in lieu of the Azalea."

"My host."

"Yes," he said. It was clear he was trying to avoid saying Archie's name out loud.

"Which suite?"

Charlie looked at me like I was the biggest idiot who'd ever lived. "The penthouse suite."

"Okay," I said. "I mean, I didn't want to assume."

"Of course."

I gathered up my purse, gave what I hoped was a courteous but slightly snotty nod to Charlie, and headed upstairs. *Archie could have just texted me*, I thought. But then, maybe Charlie would have had security tackle me before I made it to the elevator.

Archie needed to vouch for me in order for my presence to make sense. I got in the elevator behind another woman near my age, and when I got to lean forward and press PH after she pressed the extremely boring 9, I felt a tiny thrill of undeserved superiority. It was only between levels 9 and PH that I realized where I was going: Archie's room. Archie's *room.* Not a restaurant in the same building where he'd be sleeping. The *actual room* where he'd be sleeping. Or, at least, the room next to that room. Just the two of us.

So I forgot all about the song.

The elevator opened and I closed my eyes, because I accidentally imagined the doors opening right onto Archie's bed with him in it. But when I opened them I saw that I was in a tiny hallway, and the penthouse door in front of me was closed. I knocked twice, and waited.

Archie opened the door with one hand and held up a large paper grocery bag with the other. "Sorry I'm late. I bought food!" he said. "Well, I should say, I had food bought."

"Ah," I said. "Big Pete?"

"Sent him in with a little list," he grinned. "The man knows how to pick good produce." He stood back for me to enter, and I walked inside and looked around. The room—a living room and kitchen—had the same minimalist chic decor as the lobby: a stark white carpet; three angular sofas in a dusky gray; curtains, also gray. Silver fixtures, geometric art.

"Fairly prison-y, isn't it?" asked Archie. He'd set the groceries on a kitchen island and was watching me survey the room.

I laughed. "A little. But in a cool way."

"Good," he said. "Now, everything I've got here is vegan. I hope that's all right?"

"You're kidding."

He broke out in a grin and lifted two packages of salmon from the bag. "I *have* cut out red meat, though," he said.

"I read this article once that said fish are actually much worse to eat, environment-wise," I said. "Everyone thinks it's not as, like, morally unsound as eating beef, but that's just because humans don't think fish are as cute as cows."

Archie let his hands, still holding the packaged fish, fall onto the countertop. "Well, now I feel awful."

"Oh my God, don't," I said. "I mean, I read this article, but it's not like I've eaten any less fish. I just repeat this fact at parties and stuff."

"I bet you are just a hit," he said, and the dimples appeared. *Dammit.* He lifted the fish back up and looked from one to the other. "*I* think you're cute."

I laughed, and watched him slice open the packages with a knife. "You're going to help, right?" he asked, looking up.

"Oh," I said. "I was hoping you would help *me*."

Archie's eyebrows rose halfway up his forehead.

"It's just, I'm a really good cook, and I don't exactly get to employ that talent in my closet-size kitchen," I said.

"Fair," he replied.

I tried desperately not to smile. "...and there's nothing worse than mediocre salmon."

"Mediocre?"

"Yeah," I said. "I just think it'd be safer for both of us if—"

"*Safer*?" he said.

"No offense."

"*Lots* of offense!" he said, and I laughed. He blinked at me, eyes wide, as if trying to decide how much of what I'd said was serious.

"I'm sorry," I offered. "This is your kitchen, sort of. I'm sure you know what you're doing and neither of us will get parasites."

"Oh my *God*," said Archie. He rolled his eyes, but when they returned to me he broke into a smile. "Rose Reed, I've known since that meeting you were cheeky, but this..." He trailed off and just shook his head, looking from me to the fish now lying on the counter. "Can you believe this?" he asked them. Turning to me again, he said, "All right, you take the salmon, and I'll take the rice and veg. Can you trust me with rice and veg?"

"Mm." I considered. "I think so."

"Are you *sure*?"

"I'm not sure," I said. "But you're the only other person available in this suite."

Archie laughed, but then he leaned in closer to me and I stopped smiling. He looked at me for a moment or two (it was impossible to tell how long) and then I saw, in my peripheral vision, the package of fish rising up between us.

"*Rose*," he croaked, holding the fish in front of his face. "*Please. Don't mess this up. My friend and I shan't have died in vain.*"

I laughed, and swatted the fish away. "I think that's my cue to open a bottle of wine." I pointed to a smaller paper bag on the counter. It was a complete (and not unpleasant) surprise to find that Archie Fox, international rock star, tabloid-rumored lothario and bad boy, was kind of... a dork.

While Archie prepared the pot of rice and set it on the stovetop to cook, I pulled out the bottle of wine and tried not to exclaim when I read the label. I didn't know a *ton* about wine, but I knew enough to know that a French Bordeaux from 2009 had to have cost upward of $100. I poured us each a glass and held his out for him to take.

"Well, cheers," I said. "To . . . your new record."

"Cheers," said Archie. "That's sweet."

I watched him take a sip, waiting for him to exclaim, having recognized that this bottle of wine was not meant for us, not for *this* occasion, but for something much more important. But all he did was make a little satisfied noise and nod, and so I closed my eyes and took a sip from my own glass, expecting my life to change. I peered into the glass once I was ready to open my eyes. It was good, obviously. But I wasn't sure I could say it was definitely, without qualification, better than the boxed wine I bought from Trader Joe's.

I took my glass with me to the opposite counter, turned the oven to 350 degrees, and began preparing the fish.

"Do you have spices in here?" I asked, opening the cabinets to find a surprisingly full stock.

"They know I like to cook," Archie said, shrugging.

"Jeez." I took out the cayenne pepper, black pepper, mustard seed, garlic powder, and onion powder. I found a small mixing bowl, mixed the spices together, and set it aside. I dug around until I located a glass baking dish, which I lined with parchment paper. ("You even have *parchment paper* in here?" I asked. Archie only laughed.) I laid the fish in the pan and coated them with extra-virgin olive oil, and then I shook the spice mix over the top, spreading it across the slimy surface with my hands until it was evenly seasoned.

"Can I use this lemon?" I asked, turning to face Archie, who jumped, then hunched his body over the cutting board and vegetables. "Are you trying to keep your dish a secret? You already told me the gist."

"But not the details!" he said. "Don't look!" He looked at me over his shoulder. "And yes, I got the lemon for the fish. Not that I know *anything* about cooking salmon," he added.

"Clearly not," I replied. I cut the lemon into thin slices and laid them over the top of the salmon, and then I wrapped the extra parchment paper tightly over the top and rolled the ends so it was secure. I slid the dish into the oven and set the timer for twenty minutes.

"Okay," I said. "I'm warning you, I'm about to turn around."

"You're safe," he said. "I've concealed the evidence." I turned to look and saw a mixing bowl on the counter, covered with a dish towel. Archie was leaning against the counter, and he smiled at me over his wineglass and then took a sip. I met his eyes for no more than a second and then moved my gaze to my glass, as if I were reading our future in my wine.

"So, how'd I do today?" he asked, his voice echoing against the walls of the cabinet his head and shoulders were currently hidden in. He emerged with pot in hand and turned the front burner on. The coils glowed red. "I hate cooking on electric, but apparently hotels find an open flame unsafe," he added, before I could answer.

He poured water into the pot, covered it up, and then took another swig from his glass.

"Can you imagine—a respectable gentleman such as myself not being trusted with some measly fire?"

I hopped up onto the island and hoped it looked smoother than it felt. I could sense Archie's eyes on me as I readjusted my tank top, which had slipped precariously low on my chest—a fact confirmed when I looked up and he immediately spun around to face the stove—and I crossed my legs in front of me. If pressed, I'd deny any flirtation with Archie until I was blue in the face, but I couldn't deny being pleased by the look I thought I'd seen him giving me.

"Right," I said. "I mean, it's not as if you've ever—oh, I don't know—had to have the fire department called in to break up a night of debauchery."

In the first year of Archie's fame explosion, he'd done what most young men did when given sudden access to unconscionable amounts of money and little supervision: gotten himself into some trouble. Nothing too damning—no peeing off balconies or egging neighbors' houses, à la Justin Bieber; mostly public intoxication and all-night penthouse parties—but it wasn't a great look, and it culminated in a PR tour (pre-Weaver-Girard) of repentance after a forgotten joint ("a friend's," he'd insisted) set off a fire alarm at the New Orleans Hilton he and his then-manager were staying at.

"Okay, that's not fair," he said, stirring rice into the now-boiling water. "It was *hardly* debauchery."

"That's not what I heard..." My voice lilted in a singsong.

"I was twenty-two! It was New Orleans!"

I shrugged.

"It wasn't even my joint, it was—"

"*My friend's*," we said in unison, and then burst into laughter.

"Okay, fine," he said. "It was my joint. But don't you dare tell a soul."

I mimed zipping up my lips.

"See, this isn't fair, though," he said. "This relationship"—he waved his hand in the air between us, and my skin tingled—"is all off kilter. You already know all my sins."

"The whole world knows them," I agreed.

"Exactly! It's only right that we level the playing field." He refilled his glass and topped off mine. "What sort of trouble did twenty-one-year-old Rose Reed get into?"

I took a long sip to buy some time. In truth, there wasn't much trouble to report. There never had been, at least, not by the standards of my high school, and then NYU, peers. Their trouble involved MDMA-fueled all-nighters at sweaty clubs or vacated apartments. I'd been to my share of parties at some rich kid's condo while his parents were away, but the worst that ever happened there was consuming one too many beers or getting caught up in a regrettable make-out session. My kind of trouble was more about sneaking into shows or talking my way backstage, but even those minor adventures fell by the wayside as college progressed and I became more serious about school, and then internships, and then work.

I had, for the most part, grown out of the particularly teenage fear of uncoolness, but a familiar pang of insecurity continued to pop up every now and then, mostly when a social event turned into a competition over whose lawless youth was more exciting. In those moments, when I'd realize I had nothing of import to contribute, but still felt the pressure to do so, I felt as much of an outsider as I had ten years prior, when it seemed everyone was making those stories without me. I didn't think Archie would judge me or deem me Uncool for never having broken a law or stolen some booze from my parents' liquor cabinet, but I was suddenly struck with doubt over how well I knew him, and how well I wanted him to really know me.

"I'm afraid the answer will disappoint you," I said finally.

"Try me."

"There just isn't very much," I paused, but Archie stayed quiet, watching me intently. "I wasn't cool or popular in high school, and I spent most of my time studying. Or hanging out with my boyfriend. Dave."

Archie's eyes lit up. "Oooh, and what was Dave like?"

"He was fine."

"Ouch."

I laughed. "No, really, he was cool. For a while." Archie wagged his eyebrow, and I reached out to gently shove him. "And we were both music nerds. Went to a lot of shows. Sometimes we'd smoke clove cigarettes...?"

"No, you didn't," Archie gasped, and closed the gap between us, leaning against the island I was still perched on. He was *loving* this. I decided to double down.

"Oh yeah, big time." I shifted to face him and leaned forward, lowering my voice to a hush. He smelled amazing. "And there was this one time, right before graduation, we wanted an epic kind of send-off. So we scheduled what we called a night of rebellion."

"Because *that* is the key to anarchy," said Archie. "Proper planning."

"Right, advance notice is very important."

He nodded. "Sync those calendars up."

"So, *anyway*," I continued. "We figured we'd do it end of June, right after finals but before graduation."

"Of course."

"Dave had an older brother who kind of looked like him, so we snagged his ID, but when we went to the liquor store, we just couldn't decide. I hated any booze I'd ever tried, and I wanted to pick something we'd actually like. We were taking forever looking at all of these fruity liqueurs, so this guy who's working there comes up to ask if we need help, and I just panic and grab this bottle with a picture of a martini glass on its label, filled with some kind of orange concoction. Looked delicious. The guy gives us a weird look—one hundred percent knew we were underage, I'm sure now—but he rings us up and we leave and walk to a park."

He looked at me expectantly, and I smiled.

"And then we spend the rest of the night pretending to enjoy straight triple sec."

Archie threw back his head and let out a howl of laughter. "You're kidding me," he said.

"I wish I was."

"That is exceedingly lame."

I threw my hands up in admission. "I warned you."

"Endearing, though." He grinned.

"I like to think so."

Archie walked back to the stove and poured some oil into a saucepan over a different burner. I tried to bite my tongue when I saw him lift the wooden spoon, but failed.

"Don't stir the rice!"

Archie whirled back to face me. "Rose, you said you *trusted* me."

"I do, it's just—it's a common mistake. Impatience. Everyone always wants to stir the rice and then, boom, you've got a pan of mush."

Archie raised his eyebrow and then took three emphatic steps to the side. Without saying a word or breaking eye contact, he lifted the cloth from his bowl of vegetables, dumped them in the saucepan, and stirred.

"Okay, okay, I'm sorry," I said. "I won't say another word."

"So what else did you and Dave get into?" he asked, his back to me. "Steal some cars? Forge some checks?"

"Not so much," I said, hoping to let the topic fizzle out. "We both went to college in New York, and then... that was kind of just it."

"Ah, the let's-stay-together-in-uni relationship that lasts until about two days after uni starts? I don't know it personally, of course, but I know of it."

*Oh, right*, I remembered. *Because instead of going to college you became internationally famous.*

"Well, sort of," I said. "Just, you know, add a couple years on there."

Archie turned around, licking whatever mysterious sauce he'd concocted off the spoon. I tried not to stare.

"Oh, so that was quite serious!"

"I guess." I shrugged. Talking about Dave somehow reminded me of the song Archie had played only an hour or two earlier, and suddenly, uncharacteristically, I found it impossible to elaborate.

The timer on the salmon went off, and I hopped down from the countertop and nudged Archie away from the oven.

"I'm sorry," he said. "I get pushy sometimes. You don't have to talk about it if you'd rather not."

"No, it's fine," I said, pulling the pan out and peeling the parchment paper back. "It wasn't a big deal. We dated a while, we started growing apart, college life, he cheated on me, it happens."

"Oh, Rose." Archie set his wineglass down and placed his hand on my shoulder. My entire body pulsed, but I inched away and poured all of my focus into searching through the cabinets for a platter.

"Really, it's fine, it feels like forever ago. And like, I wasn't really... I don't know."

"What?"

"I wasn't in love with him by then, so it feels sort of silly now to even dwell on the fact that he cheated. It makes it sound more dramatic than it really was. And in a way I should be glad, because if he hadn't done it, I don't really know how long I would have just kept on because I didn't know that it was over. I just got so sucked into the life we had that I forgot about everything else that was supposed to matter."

"You should be glad he cheated on you?"

"Well, you know what I mean."

"Rose Reed, were you raised Catholic?"

I laughed. "Yes, but I don't see what that has to do with anything," I said, and he laughed, too.

"I know what you mean about getting sucked into...a particular life," he said. "And there's nothing silly about it. It's a loss not only of another person, but a part of you as well."

He looked at me intently, and I blinked what I feared might be the early stages of tears back from my eyes. Archie turned around then, reached up into a cabinet above the stove, and pulled down a black ceramic plate. He handed it to me and I sighed.

"You're right," I said. "It fucking sucked."

"Damn right it did!" He clinked my glass and killed the wine in his own. "To hell with the lot of them." He lowered the heat on his vegetables and started fluffing the rice. "Besides, I can tell that Dave never deserved you."

"He really didn't," I said, splitting the last of the wine between our two glasses. "He was the kind of guy who'd be like, 'Oh, *actually*, the song is called "Baba O'Riley." ' Like, come on, dude."

Archie howled again. Making him laugh was quickly becoming a favorite activity.

"No! I *hate* that guy. Just let the person call it Teenage Wasteland, we all know what they're talking about."

"Right?"

"Can I tell you a secret?" he asked. I nodded, and then remembered he couldn't see me. The two of us were working back-to-back—me, plating the salmon with the care and diligence of every *Master Chef* episode I'd ever watched; Archie, tossing spices and herbs into his mystery sauce; both of us keeping up with this game of needing to surprise each other with our dishes.

"Please," I said.

"Chloe recorded a single, but her manager wouldn't let her release it. It was that bad."

My hand flew to my mouth. "No!" I gasped.

"It's true. She was beyond even the help of Auto-Tune."

"Amazing."

"Well, we can't all have *the gift*," he said, his voice deepening and trilling on the last words. I could hear his mouth cracking into a smile.

"Oh my God, are you ready yet?" I asked. The smell of garlic wafted past him and made my mouth water, and I turned to try to peer over his shoulder. "I'm starving."

He swatted me away without looking back. "Now who's being impatient?"

"Me! It's me."

"Okay, yes, go set the salmon down and uh…get some glasses of water. By the time you do, I'll be ready."

I dragged out a long and dramatic sigh. "This better be the best damn rice I've ever had."

"It will be," Archie insisted.

I pulled some glasses down from the cabinet, plopped some ice in, and filled them up, hoping tap would be fine. The table—a narrow rectangle with six chairs around it—was already set for a three-course feast, with stacks of two plates in decreasing size and one tiny bowl. Everything was jet black, with the occasional gold filigree, and the napkin rings were in the shape of little birds—the perfect junction of morbid and twee.

I set the salmon down in the center of the table, and placed our glasses across from each other. I turned around, ready to loudly clear my throat, but was distracted by the view. Archie was hunched over the serving bowl, stray strands of hair having fallen free from his bun and against his face. His sleeves were rolled up near his shoulders, and I felt like I was getting a glimpse of what domestic life with Archie Fox would be like.

*How am I here right now?*

Suddenly he raised his arms in triumph, knocking me back into reality. He looked at me with pure joy in his eyes. "It's done."

I applauded slowly as he walked over, and he bowed, presenting what he called Cajun rice and beans. It looked spectacular, all deep reds and rich browns. He ignored my place setting, and instead pulled out the chair at the head of the table, gestured for me to sit, and then took the seat next to me. I couldn't help but notice how close our hands were.

"You never answered my question," he said, offering up the rice and beans.

"Which question?" I asked, dropping a hefty scoop onto my plate.

"How'd I do today?"

"You were great," I said. And then, in my best British drawl, "*Every lady in my life is special.*"

"That's me, then?"

"It is."

"Look, I clammed up."

"It's okay," I said. "It went over fine." I was relieved at the diversion in subject, as I hadn't yet figured out how I'd get around revealing my actual feelings about his new song. I decided to focus on the interview portion and hope the rest would go unnoticed. "Just as we planned; you hardly gave me any heart attacks."

I dropped a piece of salmon on my plate and passed the platter to him.

"Right, but that's the boring bit. What'd you think of the set?"

I felt my heart start to race, pounding in my chest the way it did whenever I was presented with an opportunity to lie and was seriously considering taking it.

"You sounded great," I said, and that much, at least, was true. "The acoustics there are just fantastic. And the crowd was so into it, you really had them."

"Good... that's good to hear," Archie drawled. He waited, clearly expecting more.

"I thought 'Kiss Me, Kill Me' sounded nice slowed down, which honestly surprised me," I said. "I almost never like stripped-down pop. It always ends up so twee."

Archie laughed. "Do go on, please."

Calmed by his good-natured smile and emboldened by the wine, I did.

"I think you should consider 'Find You' for the encore on your next tour. Every woman in the audience was like, losing her mind when the beat dropped. Or, when the beat would drop with the band there. And even without them, it's just such a powerhouse song."

"Noted," said Archie. "And thank you."

"You're welcome," I blushed. "I had a really nice time." And I had. Watching him play in person, up close, interacting with the audience and so clearly passionate about his music—and thoughtful, too, more than I ever would have suspected from someone I'd previously dismissed as manufactured, cookie-cutter, and worst of all high on his star power and deeply uninterested in the music itself—that afternoon, I had turned into a genuine fan.

"Okay, but what about 'Highest Low'?"

I tried my hardest not to wince. "Is that the name? Of the new song you played?"

Archie nodded, his eyes bright and eager. He *loved* that song, I realized.

"It was... different," I started. Archie tilted his head, a little like a dog whose owner was talking to him as though he were a person.

"Different good, or...?"

"Different, ah... different."

Archie lifted his hands and pressed them into a fist he held in front of his mouth. And he waited.

"I..." I stopped, sighed, played with the rim of my wineglass. "I didn't love it."

Archie dropped his hands—not lightly—on the table, and leaned back in his chair. Moving farther away from me.

"Okayyyy," he said slowly. "Was it just—what about it didn't you like? Because normally it'd have a backing band, obviously, and with this one that might make more of a difference—"

"It wouldn't," I said. Then I clapped my hand over my mouth.

Archie laughed—a single "*ha!*"—and ran his hand through his hair, shaking his head. "Right," he said.

"I'm sorry, that was—"

"No, I mean, you're allowed your opinion—"

"I...know..."

"It's just a bit of a surprise, that's all," said Archie. "Raya *loves* that song."

*I don't see how* that's *possible*, I thought. But what I said was: "Oh, well *then*. See? Ignore me. I'm just PR."

"No, see, now I have to know *why* you didn't like it," said Archie. He was attempting to smile but his tone was clear: He was annoyed as hell. And that—the thin-skinned-ness of it, the inability to take (mild!) criticism, so typically male, the childishness of pointing out that *Raya loved it*—made *me* annoyed. And unfortunately for me, when I get annoyed, I get even more honest. (Well, honest *or* ruthless, depending who you asked.)

"I thought it was kind of derivative."

"Of what?"

"Well, how much Whitesnake were you listening to when you wrote it?"

Archie rolled his eyes, shook his head. But he didn't say anything.

"Okay, doesn't matter. My point is, it sounded like...I guess, to me, it sounded like the first song a pop star makes when he's trying to make it clear he no longer wants to be seen as a pop star."

"Meaning?"

"Meaning, it sounded a little... empty. There was so much less heart in that song than the others. And the lyrics are kind of basic. And the melody doesn't do your voice justice at all."

Archie huffed in apparent disbelief, and crossed his arms in front of his chest. "Anything else? My guitar playing was shit? My jokes were bad?"

"The guitar sounded fine," I said.

He nodded. "Well, that's something."

We were quiet for a moment, and the magnitude of the critiques I'd just rambled off settled into the space between us. And though I was still a bit angry and hurt—at what, exactly, I was too drunk to articulate—there was also a small knot of guilt gaining weight in my chest.

"And you were funny and charming," I said. "As usual."

"I know you think I ought to feel complimented right now," said Archie. "But I don't."

"I wasn't trying to insult you," I said. "You have such great stage presence that—"

"—Oh, don't patronize me," Archie groaned. "You wouldn't know—you just... Ugh. Never mind."

Whether it was justified or not, whether it was only a way to stifle my regret or not, I felt a welcome resurgence of anger just then. "Look, you asked me what I thought," I said. "Did you want my opinion, or did you just want me to fawn? Because if it's the latter, maybe you can wink or something when you ask me what I think, and that way I'll know I should just blow smoke up your ass."

I glared at Archie and he glared back at me, and I became aware, all at once, that under the table, our knees were touching.

Just slightly—nothing more than could have been explained away as the unintentional by-product of relatively close quarters—but unmistakably nonetheless. I looked away and lifted my wineglass. Then, thinking better of it, I set it down and took a big gulp of water instead.

"You're right," he said. I raised my eyes to meet his, hoping the next thing out of his mouth would be *I'm sorry, or I do want to know what you think or I had a feeling it wasn't my best work.* Instead, what he said was, "I should have known better than to ask you."

My face burned. "Ah," I said. I folded up the napkin in my lap and placed it gently on the table. "Well, I apologize for answering. It's not my place."

"That's not what I meant," he said. But when I looked at him, I couldn't tell if Archie meant what he said, and suddenly I was too confused and too tired to be there even five minutes longer. I stood up from my chair and slipped my phone from the back pocket of my jeans. It was 8:22. I had until 9:00 before I *needed* to leave to make my train, but Archie didn't have to know that.

"What time is your train again?"

"Nine fifteen," I said. The truth was 9:45.

"Ah," he said. I watched his face soften; he opened his mouth to speak then closed it. And then he said, "Shame you can't stay."

Unless I was very much mistaken, Archie Fox blushed a little just then.

"Raya's show later, I mean," he added. "Should be great."

"I'm sure," I said. I got up from my chair and took both our plates to the sink. I went to wash them but Archie said, "Leave them. I love washing up." I was too annoyed and uneasy to find this cute. I stood there for a moment behind the sink, awkwardly looking around for something else I might clean up or move around or busy myself with so I wasn't just *standing* there, wanting both to stay and to leave as fast as I possibly could. But then Archie got up from the table and carried our wineglasses to the sink, and then we were *both* just standing there. And before I knew what was happening, or how he'd gotten so close to me without me realizing, Archie's hand was in my hair. I inhaled sharply, and he leaned in a bit closer. I felt myself close my eyes, seemingly without any direction whatsoever from my brain, and then I heard him say, "I think... you have a piece of rice in your hair."

I flung my hands to my face, muttering "*Oh my God*" and swatting his hand away, all in an attempt to distract him from the fact that I'd closed my eyes. He laughed, but not unkindly, and instead of letting himself be pushed away, he grabbed hold of my right wrist in the same hand that I'd *thought* was caressing me but was actually scavenging for food.

"Stop," he said. "Let me." I froze. Still holding my wrist in his left hand, his right reached over and pulled gently at a strand of hair. Embarrassingly, he held out his palm so that I could see the single, horrible piece of Cajun rice in its center. No, "embarrassing" was the wrong descriptor. I was livid.

"Thank you *so much*," I said.

"Hey!" he said, still laughing, still standing so close. I was no longer into the dimples. I hated them now. "Come now, Rose."

"I've gotta go," I told him. "I'm going to miss my train."

"Big Pete will drive you to the station."

"No, thank you," I said. "I'll get a cab."

"I insist," said Archie.

"You can't have *everything* just how you want it." At that,

Archie stopped smiling, and I felt that knot of regret—about what I'd just said, about what I'd said earlier, about signing up for this whole thing in the first place. I felt like I should tell him I was sorry, but I wasn't sure what I'd be saying it for, nor did I want to admit to having done anything that required an apology. Archie stepped back and leaned against the counter behind him.

"Right you are," he said. He paused, watching me again. I said nothing. "Well, Rose," he continued. "It was my pleasure. Phenomenal salmon, truly."

"Thank you," I said. "Thanks for dinner. And wine."

"Like I said, my pleasure."

He was looking at me so intently I had to look away, so I adjusted my bag on my shoulder and once again took out my phone: 8:31. "I should—" I gestured vaguely at the door behind me. Archie nodded.

"I'll, uh, email you soon. About next steps," I said, walking backward down the hallway.

Archie gave me two thumbs up (*ugh*) and said, "Sounds like a plan, Ms. Reed."

With that I gave a dumb little wave, turned my back on him, and walked out the door.

---

I woke up for probably the eighth, and ultimately the last, time around 6:52 a.m. I'd only gotten home a little after midnight thanks to Amtrak delays followed by subway delays, but I hadn't been able to sleep. Shortly after getting on the train I'd sent Archie a text: `Hey. Sorry if I was harsh earlier. Thanks again for dinner.` I regretted sending it a little more the farther I got from Philadelphia and the more my wine buzz wore off, and by the time I got home, I was in a full-on panic. I started sending texts to other people, as if pushing my message to Archie farther down in my message box could eventually erase it from his phone, too. I texted Harper a rough summary of everything I'd said to Archie about his new song. (Her response: `Lol, yikes.` Then, after I'd sent back a string of crying emojis, `Hey, if it sucked, better he knows now than later.`) I texted Chelsey to ask if she could pick up toilet paper when she came home the next morning. And then, because I'd run out of people I could think of to text, and because the wine buzz wasn't *all* the way gone, I texted Neil: `Hi.`

I managed to fall asleep around 1:00, but I woke up each hour afterward, almost exactly on the hour, and instinctively reached for my phone to check for texts. Chelsey wrote back (`u got it`) at 2:47 a.m., but otherwise, my phone remained resolutely inactive. So when I woke up a little before 7:00, squinting into the bright light now streaming in through my window and slightly sweaty under my ratty old WHAM! T-shirt, I gave up the ruse. I threw off my sheets, got up, and set my phone on my dresser. I crossed my arms and stared it down, willing it to produce results by the time I got back from the shower. Though I took my time, even going so far as to use actual shaving cream on my legs, I came back to my room nine minutes later, holding my breath, to find nothing.

After downing two Advils with a full glass of water, I climbed back into bed, still in my towel, and picked up my laptop from its position on the pillow next to mine. My plan was to watch *The X-Files* until an hour at which I could call Harper without her murdering me for it, and by doing so pretend not to be pathetically waiting by my phone. I started an episode, but I couldn't focus on the screen, and instead my eyes glazed over somewhere just above it. I could not *believe* this was how I was spending my Sunday morning. I should have been sleeping. I should have had brunch plans. I should, at the very least, have been on my way to an expensive fad workout class where a muscular person would scream at me about how I should believe in myself.

I should have been waking up next to a person, not my laptop.

What *shouldn't* have happened was my text to Neil. In the rush of post-teddy-bear mortification and Philadelphia preparation anxiety, I'd forgotten to text him to say thank you for the gift. Maybe I'd chosen not to. I wasn't totally sure. I knew it was rude not to acknowledge his apology, however overblown it may have been, but I hadn't been sure how to accept it without making it seem like I was still interested, because I wasn't sure I was. Now, though, I had not only missed the window for gracious (or at least civil) acceptance of his gesture, but I'd sent what could only be described as an incredibly mixed (and very lame) message. How could he even respond? My only comfort was in the fact that he probably wouldn't want to.

That I was (possibly) being ignored for my own apology did not escape me. I replayed the previous night's conversation in my head—the details a bit fuzzy in places—and groaned, sinking deeper into my pillows. Just how crazy (or drunk) had I been to think that Archie had been leaning in to, what, *kiss* me? Had I invented the way he'd looked at me completely, or was there something there that suggested motives other than Cajun rice retrieval? I closed my eyes and tried to remember the way his hand felt in my hair, and then I tried to remember another time in my life when anyone had touched my head so softly.

Still, I didn't need to be so curt, or leave so abruptly. I was just embarrassed, and confused, and hurt in a way that I couldn't even explain. In my head I tried to replay the night over and over, but the only thing I could remember perfectly was calling his new song "derivative." Why had I thought that was something he wanted, much less needed, to hear? I was the PR girl, not his producer. Why had I risked ruining our professional rapport—to prove to him I knew something about music, to show that even though he was the mega-famous, mega-rich pop star, someone like me could still take him down a peg? Archie was my client, and my work with him wasn't done, and we needed to be on good terms until it was. *And then?* I thought. But there probably wouldn't *be* a then.

I decided to check Archie's social media, trying to prepare myself for the fact that if he'd tweeted or posted an Instagram picture since I left his suite, it would mean that he'd definitely already seen my text, and chosen to ignore it. (I'd been hoping, I guess, that he'd gone *straight* to Raya's show and then *straight* back to his hotel, to bed, all without checking his phone, and that when he woke up around 8:00 or, fine, 9:00, he'd see it and respond. It could start off something like, *OMG, so sorry, I was asleep.*) First I checked Twitter, but saw nothing. When the same was true for Instagram, I breathed a sigh of relief.

Then, though, I got this feeling. I wasn't expecting to see any Archie/Raya photos until Monday, after Lucas had had time to negotiate a deal for the brunch date photos he'd be taking later this morning. But something—a hot, insistent pressure in my chest—was telling me to look anyway, and so I typed *Raychie* into the search bar on Twitter and hit ENTER.

It popped up right away—the same photo set, over and over again, tweeted by a dozen or more Archie Fox fan accounts, and a couple of Raya ones, too: On the left, the unmistakable back of Archie Fox's body walking into the hotel; and on the right, in very nearly the same back-to-camera position, someone who looked an awful lot like Raya, going through the same set of gold-edged doors. She was wearing loose jogger-style sweatpants, a white crop tee, and her hair stuffed under a baseball cap: post-concert loungewear. Archie was wearing a jean jacket over a T-shirt (ridiculous, considering the heat) and the jeans he'd been wearing at our dinner; it was strange, I thought, to see the back of his bun in this photo, knowing that I'd seen him pull it back myself. Slung over his shoulder was an electric purple T-shirt a particularly observant Raya fan had zoomed in on and identified as her official tour tee.

I could see the magazine profile now: *Though the demands on a famous musician on tour are many—and, to be clear, not just any kind of famous, but the kind of famous five years in the making, the kind of famous that requires changing hotel arrangements in the middle of the night because a teenager has tweeted your whereabouts to tens of thousands of other teenagers—and though speculation about his romantic life has largely been kept at bay since his much-publicized split with Chloe Tan, make no mistake: Archie Fox has the shining, slightly manic look of someone freshly, optimistically in love. Asked about his rumored relationship with the rainbow-haired rising indie princess Raya, Archie smiles and says only: "We're each other's number one fan."*

I forced myself out of my reverie and reexamined the photos.

They weren't time-stamped, but the texts above the photos in each of the tweets were variations on the same theme: `omfg archie going into his hotel at midnight...and 30 mins later...[like 17 cry-laughing emojis].` I clicked on each tweet I could find, scrolling through all the replies to each. There were so many of them. The teens were losing their shit. I read through their exclamation points and monkey-covering-its-mouth emojis and *YASSSSSS*'s, unblinking, until my eyes teared up and I lost focus.

I gave myself thirty seconds, and then I saved the photos to my desktop. I added them, along with screenshots of the best fan response tweets, to my PowerPoint.

It was perfect, really—most of Archie's fans seemed to have warmed to Raya, and those who hadn't were only holding back because she was a woman who wasn't them. Raya's fans, too, seemed excited by the photos, convinced they demonstrated Archie's genuine support of Raya's music. And because a fan had taken them, not a paparazzo—and because their backs were turned, and they were arriving separately, late at night—the photos seemed romantic and spontaneous rather than sleazy. So much for the brunch photos; we didn't need them. These pictures made Archie and Raya's relationship appear organic rather than organized.

They made it seem real.

I picked up my phone and, with only the briefest inward acknowledgment that it was not yet 8:00 a.m. and therefore much too early to be texting anyone, started typing a message anyway: `Hi again. Sorry for last night's message. That was dumb. What I should have said, and` probably sooner, was thank you. I'd like to see you again, if you're up for it.

And then, before I could reconsider, I pressed SEND, and dropped my phone on the bed.

Not five minutes' worth of blankly staring at the wall later, my phone buzzed with a response.

Really glad you texted again. Do you have dinner plans tonight?

I texted back that I did not, and that was that. I'd made my third date with Neil.

# 15.

I PROMISED MYSELF I WOULDN'T spend my date thinking about Archie—not the pictures, not the show, not anything from the night before—but that was proving difficult, especially given the fact that the date was, per Neil's suggestion, "a home-cooked dinner in." This time, however, the phrase "home-cooked" was very loosely applied, which I learned upon entering Neil's Murray Hill third-floor walk-up at 8:30 p.m. on the dot.

"Ah, you're early," he said when he answered the door, sheepishly eyeing the plastic Seamless bags that were set on the counter behind him. He looked at his watch. "Or, well, you're punctual, but, let's be real, in New York, that's the same thing as being early."

I hovered in the doorway, my own plastic bags filled with salad ingredients in hand. "I could go back down if you'd like, do a couple loops around the block," I offered.

Neil's face scrunched in confusion, his head cocked to the side.

"Neil. I'm kidding. Can I...?" I nodded inside, toward an apartment that appeared to be more spacious than any I'd seen in my seven years in the city.

His hand flew to his forehead. "Oh, yes, of course! Please." He took the bags from my hand and turned to place them next to the takeout. I watched him closely; I'd forgotten how attractive he was. Maybe his looks had been overshadowed by his irritating behavior, but tonight's circumstances allowed me—encouraged me, even—to savor it: the dark-rinse jeans slung low on his hips, the pale-pink button-up shirt cuffed to his elbows, the perfectly coiffed hair, the early-onset salt-and-pepper scruff. Our chemistry wasn't exactly off the charts, but there was no getting around the fact that he was objectively very attractive. At least he was a grown-up. His shirt was ironed, for God's sake.

"I don't know who I'm kidding," he said, unpacking plastic quart containers filled with maroon and green concoctions. "It's not like I was going to be able to pull this kind of meal off as my own. I hope Indian is okay?"

"Indian is great!" I said. "I brought over some veggies—if you have yogurt, I could maybe pull a decent cucumber salad together?"

Neil winced. "You can check the fridge, but I wouldn't advise it."

I decided to brave it, and pulled open the stainless-steel door to find a beautiful, multishelved expanse mostly empty save for ketchup, a half-empty bottle of white wine, a half-empty six-pack of beer, and two Tupperware containers I'd wager were homes to thriving microbial ecosystems. I slammed the door shut.

"Come on, man," I groaned, half-jokingly. "Do you know how many people would kill to have this piece of equipment in their kitchen?"

Neil held up his arms in defeat. "I know, I know—every year

my resolution is to learn how to cook, and then every year I remember how much better the people making my takeout are at it. You know how it goes, if it ain't broke..."

"Okay," I said, throwing my best side-eye. "I *guess*."

He laughed. "Well listen, I was going to grab some wine anyway, so let me pick up some yogurt for you? I'd hate to miss out on what I'm assuming is one of your famous dishes."

I smiled. He was trying.

"You could say that. I mean, it's pretty much just cucumbers and yogurt, but I mix them together very well."

Neil raised an eyebrow. "Sounds great," he said. "Is plain good?"

I nodded, and he dashed out the door, leaving me to inspect my surroundings. The fact that Neil was so comfortable leaving a date alone in his apartment wasn't lost on me. It wasn't like I had anything too incriminating at my own place, but still—I'd be nervous to leave someone unsupervised in my room for more than five minutes. There were some bits of information whose big reveal a person might want to control: like, say, that a person has not one but *two* I WANT TO BELIEVE *X-Files* shirts in their closet; or that a person sleeps with a retainer; or that a person may have all of her ticket stubs from concerts—including those from her brief emo phase—stashed in a decorated shoe box.

Looking around, Neil's lack of concern made more sense: stainless-steel pots and pans hung from a wire grid along the ceiling; benign pieces of abstract art reminiscent of a dentist's office waiting room dotted the wall; a fringed white throw blanket draped across the back of a brown leather couch; a flat-screen TV hung over a small fireplace and mantel; issues of *The New Yorker* and *The Economist* sat neatly stacked on the coffee table in front of it. Everything was just so *normal.* The apartment looked almost-but-not-quite lived in, like one of those model homes used to sell units in a suburban development. I pulled out my phone, planning to take a picture to text Harper, but found that my phone had died. I did some brief snooping in the usual places (kitchen drawers, coffee table) before finding a useless (to me) Android charger plugged into his living room wall. *Of course he'd be an Android guy.*

But maybe I was being too hard on him. Just because his apartment lacked character—and even that wasn't necessarily true; it just lacked the certain kind of character I was prone to looking for—it didn't mean he was boring. And even if he was boring, there were worse things a person could be. Like: infuriatingly charming, or misleadingly flirtatious, or internationally famous. I willed myself to shove my judgment aside, found a cutting board and knife, and got to work.

When Neil returned with yogurt and a bottle of nice-but-not-too-nice Pinot Grigio, I'd all but rewritten him in my mind in an effort to start fresh. He poured me a glass of wine and watched intently as I diced the cucumber, then asked me to teach him how to do it so quickly without chopping off his fingertips. He told me about his past week (a couple of sixteen-hour shifts, a risky surgery gone smoothly) and I told him about mine (a work trip to Philadelphia, definitely no embarrassing breakdowns). He tested the celebrity gossip waters, asking my thoughts on the most recent starlet scandal—an obvious, but sweet, gesture. Clearly he'd been reading up on the goings-on in my world.

"I was looking up your guy Archie last night," he called

from across the kitchen, transferring curries into serving bowls. "Seems like that project with what's-her-name is going well!"

"He's not my guy," I said, too quickly.

"Oh, I thought—is that not the singer you're working with?"

My heart raced. "I mean, duh, yes, of course. Yup!" I spun around, almost grazing Neil, who was suddenly standing much closer.

"Whoa, killer!" he said, pulling the knife from my hand. "If you didn't wanna talk about work, you could've just said so."

I laughed, hoping it didn't sound as manic to him as it did to me. "Yeah, let's skip it. Work is a drag."

"Fine by me." Neil smiled, and rested his hand on the small of my back. The sudden pressure felt heavy, awkward. I gently twisted away and lifted the bowl up between us.

"Shall we?" I asked.

Neil directed me not toward the dining room table—though in the open layout of his apartment, each "room" was more of a corner in one giant space—but instead toward the oval coffee table sitting low in front of the couch. He'd set tan cushions around the table and two place settings close to each other.

"Do you mind?" asked Neil, gesturing to the cushions. "I almost never use the dining room table. It's basically for show."

"No, this is great," I said, and it was. Across from the table was a fireplace that, though technically non-functioning, was outfitted with four candles of various heights. The overhead light was dimmed, and the cushion beneath me so plush it enveloped my entire bottom half. The whole thing was like an indoor picnic, so romantic I'd have to be actively *un*attracted to Neil to not feel butterfly-ish toward him in this moment. I was considering whether or not the magic was working when he switched on the TV.

"Do you wanna watch something?"

Neil leaned back against the sofa, arms resting on its seat, while he scrolled through the shows on his DVR—*Louie*, *Archer*, a variety of *CSI*s, and, somewhat surprisingly, *The Good Wife*.

"Oh, um. Sure!" It didn't exactly match the ambience of our surroundings, but who was I to deny some television? Television was one of my all-time favorite things.

"Great," said Neil, still scrolling. "I feel like I never have a chance to clear out my DVR. Do you watch *Sons of Anarchy*?"

"I don't, but I hear it's great! I keep meaning to start."

He leaned forward to scoop some saag paneer onto his plate. "Oh it's *sooo* good. Wanna check it out?"

I tried to hide the bemusement that was surely spreading across my face.

"I mean, I won't really know what's going on, right?"

"No, no, it's totally fine!" said Neil, clicking the latest episode. "You'll catch on, and I can fill you in. You're gonna love it, I promise, and if you don't we can change it."

He pressed PLAY before waiting for a response, and sidled closer to me, his arm now draped over my shoulder. I felt transported to the many aborted dates I'd experienced in my last year of college, sitting in common lounges or dorm rooms, waiting for unimpressive crushes to make a move, but finding them ultimately more interested in whatever gross-out comedy we'd agreed to watch. I tried to pay attention to the show in front of me but, after fifteen minutes of failing to keep up, abandoned the effort. I asked Neil to point me to the bathroom and once there, I stared at my reflection in the mirror. What was I doing?

The awkwardness between Neil and me was palpable, and I couldn't *not* compare it with the previous night with Archie—the effortless rapport, the cheesy jokes, the meaningful glances.

*Except, last night wasn't what I thought it was.*

That's what I had to keep reminding myself. Everything I'd thought was special about that night was just Archie being Archie. How many times had I seen him in action? How many interviews had I watched of him charming each late-night host, each red-carpet reporter? How many quips did he have on hand, how much cheeky flattery? He was a universal chemistry kit—works with any warm-blooded human, just add British pop star.

I flushed the toilet, though I hadn't even used it, and headed out, mulling over how I would say my early good night. It still wasn't even 10:00 p.m., but I certainly didn't have another forty-five minutes of biker family drama in me. When I arrived back at the table, though, I found the TV turned off and Neil sitting on the couch.

"I can watch another time," he said, holding his hand out for mine. "I, uh. I don't really date very much. Which is why I'm not very good at it."

I sighed and took his hand, falling next to him. "I mean, I'm not exactly a seasoned pro, myself," I said as Neil, cupping my chin in his hand, turned my face gently toward him. "But even I can tell you it's not the best idea to ignore your date for a bunch of fictional bikers."

He chuckled, his face coming so close to mine I could feel the breath of his next words on my lips.

"Let me make it up to you?"

With countless excuses ready to go, I felt my mind, to my surprise, say yes. This wasn't exactly my dream date, and Neil was far from my dream man, but he was here. And he was really very cute. And he was interested. I couldn't remember the last time a man had been this close to my face, and goddammit, I deserved to be kissed, so why not have that kiss come from a hot, if a little clueless, doctor? Why *not* let Neil make it up to me? And not only for this kind of rocky date, but for all of it—my embarrassing dinner with Archie, my fight with Harper, my work anxiety, the creepy teddy bear we still hadn't even acknowledged? Why not fuck him for the sake of being out of my own head for even just an hour?

I leaned in and discovered, happily, that Neil was a far better kisser than he was a conversationalist. He pulled me toward him, his arms stronger than I'd imagined. I was surprised at how quickly I was able to forget about all of the wrongs he'd committed, but they slipped away with every kiss on my neck, or nibble on my bottom lip, or tease of the tip of his tongue. His hands traveled up my shirt and I tried not to obsess over sucking in my stomach. Whatever he thought about what he felt, he acted happy with it, and he shifted our weight to lay me on my back. I looked up at his face and felt a dull throb deep in my chest—a sense of sadness I tried to wipe away by fumbling with the buttons of his shirt. He tossed his shirt across the room and I did the same, but the sadness returned, and more acutely this time.

I squeezed my eyes shut and pulled him down toward me, kissing him wildly, telling myself it was good. But when he brushed his hand through my hair, I couldn't escape the memory of Archie doing the same the night before, and the well of regret erupted in my chest. I stifled a sob and pulled back from Neil, breathing heavily. He hovered over me.

"Is everything okay?"

It wasn't, but I wanted it to be, so I nodded and reached my arms around his neck. But the damage was done. All I could think about now was Archie—what it would be like to feel *his* weight on top of me, *his* hair between my fingers, *his* hands on my hips. Why couldn't it be him? Why couldn't I get the guy I wanted? All I could feel was Archie's absence, and it wasn't fair to Neil, and it wasn't good for me. I sat up, and hoped Neil couldn't see the tears welling in the corners of my eyes.

"Actually, um, it's not okay," I said, my arms crossed over my nearly bare chest. "I'm sorry. I shouldn't have come."

Neil took my hand in his and used the other to brush the hair from his face.

"What's going on? Is it me? Was uh, was that not working for you?"

"No, oh my God, no—you're, um. That was good." I laughed weakly. "I just... ah, fuck."

I covered my face in my hands to hide the flow of tears that refused to be held back any longer.

"Hey, hey," said Neil, his voice low and gentle. He enveloped me in a hug; it was, ironically, the closest I'd felt to him yet. After a few seconds of sniffling into his chest, I pulled back.

"So is this the worst date you've ever been on? Girl bursts into tears in the middle of making out?"

He laughed. "No. Well, maybe."

"Hey!" I shoved him lightly.

"I'm kidding, I'm kidding."

"You have to be nice to me right now. I'm crying."

"Do you want to... talk about it?"

I met his eyes and saw behind them the fear that I would say yes. Poor, sweet, clueless Neil.

"No, but thank you," I said, standing to gather my shirt and things. "I should go."

"Okay, yeah. Do you want me to call you a cab?"

"No, no, it's fine, really. Maybe you could direct me to a tissue though?"

"Oh, of course!" Neil hopped off the couch and ran down the hall, a hall he probably thought he'd be walking me down later that evening, to a room I guessed I'd never see. He came back with tissue box in hand. I pulled out a couple and stuffed them in my pocket.

"Thanks."

He nodded, and then held out his hand. "Well, it was great to meet you, Rose. And if you ever... change your mind, about this..." He trailed off, and shrugged the rest.

I gave him an awkward hug, feeling briefly embarrassed at how weird it felt before remembering that I'd just burst into tears, topless, in front of this near stranger. "It was great to meet you, too, Neil. Maybe I'll send you an apology bear for this sometime."

He looked at me quizzically, the same way he'd greeted me just a couple hours ago. I leaned up and gave him a quick kiss on the cheek, and wished him good night.

# 16.

THE NEXT MORNING, RUNNING THROUGH Union Square with a coffee in each hand, my hair a frizzy, half-wet mess from rushing out the door before I could blow it dry, I wondered why I was in this position *again*. I was usually so strict with my morning routine, never allowing myself more than a single, six-minute sleep delay beyond my original alarm, which I set deliberately too early, so that if I *did* press SNOOZE, I would actually be getting up when I was supposed to. But when I got home I'd realized my phone charger was at the office, and while I lay in my bed wondering if I should force myself to get up and buy another one from a bodega I'd fallen asleep in my clothes. It was purely a miracle that my body had woken me up in time for work. So there I was, trotting up Broadway as fast as I could manage without spilling the coffee. Well, *more* of the coffee—I had doused my left breast shortly after buying it. Thankfully it was my coffee, not Joanna's, and thankfully, as per usual, I was wearing black. I was, however, increasingly certain that the stiff scratching at my throat meant that my sweater was on backward.

When I got to the office, Joanna was nowhere to be found,

so I left her coffee on her desk, writing a neat Post-it note with today's date, and swept the four almost-empty others still sprawled across her desk into my arms. I dumped them out in the bathroom sink, and then I sped over to my cubicle, staring at my feet and so deeply enveloped in the muck of my thoughts that I very nearly collided with Harper.

"Where the fuck have you been??"

"Am I late?" I looked around—at least a few of the cubicles were still empty. I'd been sure I was on time, if not a few minutes early.

"Not that," said Harper. "Why is your phone off?"

"It died during my date with Neil, and I left my stupid charger here," I said.

Her eyes widened. "Did you . . . are you coming right from—"

"Ha, *no*," I said. Not even close. "I just fell asleep, but then I didn't have my alarm, so I woke up late . . ." I reached into my purse for my phone to plug it in, and Harper yanked my arm, pulling us both into our cube. She waited for me to charge my phone, still gripping my arm, and then inhaled dramatically.

"Archie *called me*."

"What? Why?" I felt panicky and jealous and angry and excited all at once.

"Because he couldn't get through to *you*."

She raised her eyebrows at me, waiting for me to react. Harper was a big fan of the dramatic pause.

"Tell me what he said, obviously! What's wrong with you?"

"Okay, okay. *Wellllll*, so this was around, like, eleven thirty. And I don't have him in my contacts, so I was like, 'Who the fuck is calling me at this hour?' Plus it was a New York number, so I was kind of worried it was a girl I took out of my phone or something. So I actually let it go to voicemail."

"Oh my God, Harper."

"I know. But you honestly cannot blame me."

"Whatever. Continue."

"Okay, so about a minute later, I have a voicemail. Normally I would not listen to it, because anyone who needs to get in touch with me that badly should text me like a normal person. Like, it's 2016."

"Harper!"

"Okay! I decide to listen to it anyway, because now I'm curious as to which girl is still so in love with me. But then it's not a girl. It's Archie. And he goes, 'Harper, it's Archie Fox. Rose's client.' As if I would be like, 'Huh, *which* Archie Fox?' "

"Can I just listen to it? Please?"

"I deleted it."

"*Harper.*" I sank into my chair, covering my face with my hands. Harper sat down, too, and scooted her chair close.

"Okay, I know. But normally I hate having messages I've already heard just sitting there. I was on autopilot, okay? I wasn't thinking!"

"It's *Archie Fox*," I said. "You had a voicemail from Archie Fox." Even as I said it, though, I felt strange. He remained a world-famous celebrity, of course, but reminding Harper (and myself) of his status as such—and the inherent coolness value of having a voicemail message from him—felt icky.

"I *know*," said Harper. "Think how many parties I would have been the heroine of."

"But anyway..."

"Anyway, he was like, 'I haven't been able to get in touch with her, so I thought I'd try you. I guess I got worried, though now I realize it's fairly late on a Sunday night, and I feel a bit silly. Anyway. I'm sure I'll talk to her tomorrow, though do let me know if something's gone wrong. Cheers.'" At that, Harper, having performed the entire message in a very bad British accent, mimed tipping a top hat.

"That's it?"

"Yup."

"He didn't say what he wanted to talk about?"

"No."

I looked at my phone, which had come to life partway through Harper's recap. All that had come through was a handful of work emails, a couple of late-night frantic texts from Harper, and (I groaned) one from Neil. (`Hope you're feeling all right. It's too bad the spark wasn't there, but I'll remember you every time I make cucumber salad poorly.` So *nice.*) I had no voicemails of my own.

"Are you sure there wasn't like, a second message?"

"I'm sure."

"He can't have tried *that* hard to get in touch with me," I said. "He didn't even text me, much less leave *me* a voicemail."

"Maybe he was too nervous? Plus, missed calls don't show up when your phone is off."

"Nervous about *what*?" My tone was purposefully incredulous, but my heart betrayed me, seemingly skipping five or six beats in a row. Could he have been calling me to talk about the night before? Could I have been wrong about where he stood? Or, in other words, could my original assessment—my original hope, anyway—have been right? I had filled Harper in about the night's events, in painstakingly texted detail, on Sunday. Did she now see reason to read feelings where she'd been neutral, at best, before?

"I don't know," said Harper. "Maybe... he felt something on Saturday, too."

It was clear from her face that Harper was hesitant to encourage me; she presented herself as someone who approached romance straightforwardly, cautiously, held at arm's reach between the forefinger and thumb of a hand wearing a protective glove. Of course, as her best friend, I knew this was mostly bullshit. She was a romantic through and through. She wanted to find love, and she wanted me to find it, too. But she also knew, as did I, that this was not an especially likely place to find it.

"No way," I said, shaking my head firmly. "It wouldn't have ended like that. Or he would have at least texted me back after I left. I don't buy it."

"Well, you could call him and ask."

I pretended to consider this. "I have too much to do this morning," I said. "If he needs to get in touch with me, he will."

"Too much to do... with Archie... to call Archie?" Harper was trying, and failing, to suppress a snarky grin.

"Yes," I said. "I'm extremely busy. Leave me alone." I spun around to face my desk, and looked over my shoulder at Harper until she did the same.

"Fine," said Harper. "Want to get stupid salads at one?"

"Duh."

---

At 2:52 that afternoon—after our check-in meeting, in which I shared the "Raychie hotel photos" (both the more popular fan-taken shots and the TMZ shots that had been published early that morning, but well after the fan photos had made the rounds a few times over) and earned the conservative praise of Joanna, as well as the slightest nod of approval from Ryan; a lunch with Harper during which I stayed mostly silent, anxiety wrapped tightly around my brain like a straitjacket, and tried my hardest to listen to her thoughts about a recent runway show; and an hour (or two) spent searching for any other detail I could find about when Archie and Raya left the hotel—I got an email from Archie himself:

Rose,

Maria may have told you, but just in case she hasn't, I'll be back in New York Friday afternoon, instead of Thursday night as originally planned–decided to add a second show at Fenway. I leave for London on Saturday–bit of a rush–so I wanted to check in now and make sure we're on the same page.

–A

I read the message three times through, whispering it aloud on the last go. Incidentally, I *had* gotten an email from Maria, early this morning, but she hadn't mentioned the change in schedule. Instead, she'd merely gushed about the hotel photos, and asked if we could "circle back" next week to set up the next date. I hadn't yet replied because I hadn't been able to bring myself to do so; it was the weirdest thing, but my finger clicked out of the REPLY box each time I tried. Strange, though, that she hadn't mentioned this update, and that I'd only found out from Archie himself. At first, I was mildly indignant—did she not think I needed to know this information?—but as I reread, and reconsidered, I only grew more confused. Why *did* it matter for me to know that Archie was getting back to the city fifteen or twenty hours later than originally planned? We had no meetings booked, and no social outings yet on the calendar. In an earlier meeting—well, just ten days ago or so, I realized; it felt much longer—we'd tentatively agreed that it didn't make sense with Raya's schedule to arrange anything during this leg of Archie's tour, and that we would set something up soon after he finished. Especially now, I thought, this early on, another photo op would read as too whirlwind-y, too starry-eyed and young, too codependent. Fans liked seeing evidence of romantic overtures and infatuated inseparability, and soon, but after something so major as those hotel shots, it was best to let the dust settle just a bit. Too much too soon would raise red flags more than it would tug on heartstrings. People would probably start saying Raya was pregnant.

I snapped out of my strategy reverie and returned to the issue at hand: this incredibly confusing, infuriating, *stupid* email. "Make sure we're on the same page"? About *what*?

Surely he couldn't mean...feelings. That could not possibly be the page he was talking about. He was probably talking about a different book altogether. All he'd wanted to accomplish with this email, probably, was making sure that I didn't need anything more from him before he set off for London. He just wanted to clear his plate before his time off.

But if that's all it was, why had he (allegedly) spent last night trying to get in touch with me? All of that, for this?

Anxious, I started tapping a pen against my desk. That lasted about a minute before Harper hissed "*Stop it!*" over her shoulder.

"Sorry," I whispered.

I stared at Archie's email until my eyes started to lose focus, and then I sat up, set down the pen, and opened a reply.

Archie—

Thanks for the update. Good luck with your remaining shows. Please let me know if there's anything you need—

Here I paused, and then tapped furiously at the DELETE button. Even though I couldn't really conceive of a world in which Archie's email (and calls) meant more than what this message plainly stated, something in me—perhaps just the length of time it had been since I'd felt this way about someone, or a sort of exhaustion with my own reluctance, and closed-off-ness, and unwillingness to do or say the scary, vulnerable thing—made me want to give just the smallest opening, or the smallest hint that even if there wasn't more there for him, there was for me. I rewrote:

Archie—

Thanks for the update. Sorry to hear New York will get less time with you than planned. Enjoy your remaining shows and, more important, your trip home.

Rose

It wasn't the *most* forward email in the world, but in the extremely narrow Rose Reed scale of romantic boldness, it was above-average, and that was the best I could do given how uncertain I felt. Immediately, as quickly as I could move my fingers—before my heart burst right through my chest, or I vomited into my recycling bin, or my fight-or-flight response kicked in and forced me to delete the message altogether—I pressed SEND.

About ten minutes later, my phone began to buzz violently, and I was torn from a glazed-over daydream in which I envisioned running up the stairs of Archie's apartment building—which, not having been there, I imagined in all grays and brushed metals, cold and futuristic—reaching his door, and knocking on it. Then he'd open the door, and I'd collect my breath, and say...

"Hello?" The number on my phone was unknown to me, but had a New York area code. As soon as it occurred to me that I should have answered more professionally, I realized I needn't have worried.

"Hey girrrrrrlllllll," said Raya. "What's going on?"

"Oh, hello, Raya," I replied. Out of my periphery I could see Harper whip around in her chair. "Um, I'm just...at the office. Did you get a new phone?"

"Nah, I'm using the landline, l-o-l. My ancient studio still has one."

"Ah," I said. She was, of course, referring to Features, one of the city's most famous and most storied recording studios, where I knew she'd been working with a number of producers (including Marty Freeman and EDM up-and-comer Neutrino, no less) and songwriters on her upcoming LP. "How's...it going?" I asked, cringing a little at how lame I sounded. *Why is Raya calling me?* I thought.

"Amazing," she sighed. "I'm really feeling it today."

"That's great."

"Totally. So, yeah, I thought you might come by." The way she presented it made it clear that it had not occurred to Raya that I might say no.

"Oh!" I said. "Now?" I looked at the clock on my computer—6:03. I could be on my way home. I could be taking off my heels in thirty-five minutes.

"Yeah, dude! Have you ever been?"

"No, I haven't," I said, annoyed that she'd managed to identify my weak spot. I'd wanted to see the inside—like, the *real* inside, not the tourist-approved inside—for ages, and had always hoped to be invited along on one of Joanna's client visits.

"Then come on! I wanna play something for you," said Raya. "I, like, *really* need your opinion on this." Coming from her, this was as baffling as it was flattering. How did she know I knew anything about music beyond PR?

"Plus, we can talk about Archie stuff," she added. My stomach dropped; I could almost hear her winking through the phone.

"Okay," I conceded. "I'll be there in twenty."

I gave her ten seconds to squeal her approval, and then I hung up. On my way out of the building I passed Joanna's office, but it appeared she'd already gone home. I pulled out my phone and typed up a quick email:

Joanna—Raya just called and asked if I could stop by Features, so I'm headed there now. Just wanted to let you know. Will talk through hotel photos with her while there. I can update you tomorrow.

Before I could even get my phone back in my purse it vibrated, alerting me to a reply from Joanna.

Features. Big deal. She doesn't have any interviews on the books, but let's prep her in case. Chat tomorrow.–J

I read the email three times, mouthing the words as I went. What did it mean? Did she mean "big deal" as in, like, Features is a big-deal studio? Or did she mean it more like, "Features... big *fucking* deal"? The latter seemed a bit out of step with Joanna's typical lexicon, but her emails had a way of making me question everything I thought I knew about reading tone.

Seventeen minutes later I got out of a cab on 45th Street in Hell's Kitchen, smoothed down the flyaways from my ponytail, and pushed open Features' wide glass doors. I tried to remain cool as I gave the security desk my name, posed for a temporary badge photo, and followed the burly, heavily tatted guard's directions, taking the elevator to the fourth floor and turning left down the hall for the E studio.

Once outside the door (marked with a large plated E—not sure what I'd been expecting), I hesitated, unsure if knocking on it would violate some recording studio protocol I wasn't insider-y enough to know about. Soon enough, though, I realized there wasn't really any other way to alert people on the other side of a door to my presence, and rapped lightly with my knuckles. After a minute without answer, I knocked harder.

The door swung open to reveal a young, handsome guy with what I could only describe as a bob—and eyebrows to match—dyed hot pink. The hair color was new; in the last photos I'd seen, published by Pitchfork, his hair (pulled up into two tiny Leia buns) and brows were the soft pastel-green color of after-dinner mints.

"What up," said Neutrino, waving me inside.

"Hi," I said. "I'm Rose, I'm here for—"

"I know," he said. "It's cool." He pointed to his left, where I saw Raya, headphones on, seated on a stool on the other side of the glass. She was wearing an oversize silk blazer on top of what I had to assume was meant to be a slip, her hair pulled up into a messy, curly red topknot. When she saw me she leapt up, burst through the door, and pulled me into a tight hug.

"Thank you *so* much for coming," she cooed. She released me and looked at me. "I just really needed someone outside the machine, you know?" Neutrino nodded sympathetically, and Marty continued messing with the dials, ignoring her. I looked around the room, but Pilar was absent. As if sensing my question, Raya added, "I sent Pilar to pick up a prescription and candy for me. She was driving me insane."

I wasn't sure whether "candy" meant actual candy or some kind of youth drug I was too old to know about, but I was afraid to ask. Instead I said, "Ah. Well, it's my pleasure." I looked around the room and got goose bumps—the walls were adorned with platinum records ranging from Leonard Bernstein to No Doubt. "I've always wanted to see this place," I confessed, too excited to play it cool any longer.

"Aww. It really is magic, isn't it? I came here first when I was, what... eighteen? God." She laughed, as if that were such a very long time ago.

"Ray, sorry—can I grab you for just a sec?" Neutrino interjected, now hovering over the soundboard next to Marty.

"Just a sec," said Raya. She squeezed my arm and turned, joining the huddle with her producers. "Oh!" She pointed to a mini fridge alongside a set of leather couches built into the wall. "Help yourself to whatever—the Revive Juice is one hundred percent organic and, I swear, will make your skin just *glow*," she said, throwing her hands up to her face as if to prove the claim. I wondered how the candy fit into the clean and conscious eating regimen.

"Sweet!" I chirped (*Kill me*, I thought). I crossed the room, dropping my purse on the couch and sitting next to it. I watched them, trying to eavesdrop—wanting to hear the music specifics they were discussing even though I probably wouldn't understand them—but Neutrino spoke in a whisper, and the others followed suit.

For a few minutes I made myself busy scanning the records hanging around the room, but the longer I sat, the more my thrill at being there was replaced by wondering why I was. I got up and (as quietly as I could) examined the fridge, taking a small bottle of Pellegrino. Still, nobody turned around. I stared at the back of Raya's head, wanting desperately to ask her about Archie, and the hotel, but struggling to think of a normal, casual way to do so.

"Okay!" Raya exclaimed. She smiled and waved me over. "It'll sound better the closer you are." She pushed open the booth door, and I walked over and stood a few feet back from

Neutrino and Marty. She resumed her perch on the stool and, looking up, waved me even closer.

"Okay, just talk," said Marty, still pushing switches up and down across the board.

Raya looked at me and said, "This is what Archie and I were doing the other night."

My heart stopped. *What other night?* I thought. The hotel night? Was it really possible that they had stayed there all night just to chastely, platonically make music?

"...Mostly," she added. And then she winked at me.

Neutrino laughed softly. My face burned, twisting into what I could only hope would be read as a smile.

Before I could spiral too deeply, though, Marty started the track, and I was pulled back into the room. A twinkly synth danced over pulsing, heartbeat bass, and I pictured, one after another, the earnest, innocent, hopeful, romantic dance-floor scene of every teen movie I'd ever watched—the song that comes on as the lights dim, and the camera pans over sparkling disco balls and streamers and twenty-somethings playing kids wearing too-trendy dresses and suits, and the boy looks at the girl, and suddenly it doesn't matter that anyone else is there.

Then Raya started singing—not lyrics, but notes, hummed and sung along to a melody that did not yet, apparently, have words to go with it. Still, her voice was gorgeous: strong and clear in a way that soared above the breathy, strained, stretched-vowel style so popular with her peers. Behind her voice, cymbals wavered, growing louder, building along with her voice toward a soaring chorus.

I remained frozen in place through the last lingering note, which Raya faded out by leaning away from the mike. When it was done she waited a moment before opening just one eye to gauge our reactions, and it was then that I realized my mouth was open.

Neutrino and Marty started clapping, and I joined them. Raya grinned and emerged from the booth. "Well?" She looked around at each of us, but I knew the question was directed at me.

"Holy shit," I said.

"Yeah?"

"Yeah. Wow. That was incredible," I said.

"You really think so?"

"Yes. Absolutely."

"Thanks," she said. "I kinda feel like it's still missing something, but... whatever, we have time."

"Well, lyrics would be great," I said.

Raya giggled. "Well, besides that," she said. "God, you *are* funny. But yeah, Archie's writing the lyrics."

"Oh!" I said. "That's wonderful."

"I hope! I mean, he's great, I'm *sure* they'll be great. As long as he, you know, sticks to his roots—"

"Yeah," I said. "That's my hope, too."

"Like, I do not want some 'Highest Low' situation, you know?" She stuck her finger in her mouth, and I wondered if saying "gag me" was in again. "At least I know my melody is good."

"I thought you loved that song," I said, trying to recall her wording at the show. Something with a lot of *so*'s. *So so so* good. SO good.

Raya leaned her head back and laughed. "Ha! No. God, no."

"Oh."

"I mean, don't tell him I said that—I, like, *never* want to be that person who blocks another artist's shine, you know? I just don't think that was shine. It was more like...suburban dad music." She shuddered. I didn't necessarily disagree, but I found this surprising coming from Raya, given what she'd said about it last time I saw her.

"Well, I'm excited to hear it in full," I offered, changing the subject back. "I can't wait to know what it's called."

Raya cringed again. "Ugh, titles."

"What?"

"I just hate labels, you know? I'm, like, not about labels. If it were up to me I wouldn't name my songs at all. How do you even give something like *music* a *name*?"

*Pretty easily?* I thought. *All the time?*

"Yeah," I said. "Good point."

"Okay, well, I better get back to it," said Raya. "Thank you *so* much for coming, Rose. I'm really glad you like the track. I feel so much more, like, *centered* about it now."

"I'm glad," I said. "I really think you guys have a hit here."

Raya nodded. "My psychic said the same thing the other day. Well, she said that one of my creative endeavors was going to be a success, so. More or less."

I nodded.

"Okay!" Raya smiled and opened her arms, and I hugged her. "Talk to you soon!" She leaned behind me and opened the studio door, and suddenly I understood that I was being kicked out. She'd squealed for me, and hugged me (twice!), and offered me fancy water, and now it was time for me to go. I remembered Joanna's email, and held my hand against the door to prevent her from closing it on me.

"Um," I said. "By the way, has anyone gotten in touch for an interview?"

"Oh!" said Raya. "Like, about...?"

"The, uh. Hotel photos."

"Oh, ha. Not that I know of. You could ask Pilar."

I tried to read her face, looking for clues as to what might have happened that night, but all I saw there was her impatience for me to retreat so she could close the door. *This is your chance*, I thought. *Her producers aren't listening, Pilar isn't here, and neither is Archie.* Maybe she wouldn't think it was weird. Maybe she'd think it was just girl talk. But I couldn't bring myself to ask her, and it wasn't just because I knew it was too nosy. I just wasn't sure if I wanted to know the answer.

"I will," I said. "I'm sure you'll be fine, but if anyone—a blogger, a photographer, hotel concierge, whoever—asks about those photos in particular, ignore them. Keep walking."

Raya sighed, but nodded.

"So if someone shouts at you, like, 'Have you seen the pictures of you leaving Archie's hotel in the morning—'" Here I paused to swallow and read her face (again, infuriatingly impenetrable). "—you just keep walking."

Raya raised three fingers in the Girl Scout salute. "You got it."

From the other side of the door, no longer in my sight, I heard Marty call, "Raya!"

"Okay, see you later," I said. "Call me if you need anything."

"Thanks, girl." She gave me a little wave and closed the door.

I was left alone in the hallway, and I walked through it slowly, savoring my first time inside Features in case it was also my last. I replayed the song in my head, wanting nothing more than to text Archie and tell him how much I loved it. But when I pulled out my phone, I saw that it was almost 8:00, which meant Archie would be getting ready to go on stage in Boston. I'd already emailed him, anyway, and he hadn't replied yet. I was sliding my phone back into my pocket when I came upon the door to the men's restroom and ground to a halt, my mouth falling open. Inside, I knew, was the graffiti-and-magazine-clipping-covered backdrop to an *Alternative Press* cover featuring Everyday Tragedy that had hung above my childhood bed since I was fourteen years old. On another day, I would have kept walking, too afraid of somehow getting in trouble or being seen as unserious, unprofessional. I'd have gone home and felt sorry about what I didn't do for days until I found some other untaken risk to regret. And for some reason I couldn't totally explain, I decided I didn't want this to be one of those times. So I hovered for thirty seconds to make sure nobody was inside, and then I pressed the door open slowly, pausing to listen again, and when I heard nothing, I went in.

The bathroom was poorly lit, unlike the cover, and apparently dingier than it had looked fifteen years earlier, but there was no mistaking it, and I ran my fingers over the spray paint and clippings with barely contained glee. I bent over to double-check for feet below the stalls, and then opened them one by one until I found, painted above the toilet, the giant yellow smiley face from the magazine cover. I squealed (quietly), and took about a hundred photos. I posed in front of it, too, sticking my tongue out just like Everyday Tragedy's bassist, my favorite. When I was done, I ran out of there as quickly and non-suspiciously as I could. On the train home I scrolled through the photos feeling thoroughly impressed with myself, thinking the only way they could have been better was if someone else had been there to take them for me.

# 17.

When I woke up on Friday morning, and realized that it was, indeed, Friday morning, I was mildly stunned. The days that had apparently passed between sending that email to Archie and now felt like a single, sustained haze. Archie had not replied, and, *completely* unrelatedly, I had submerged myself in work, getting into the office early (so early, in fact, that Joanna had complained that her coffee was cold by the time she got in), and staying until 8:00 or 9:00 each night. A little of that time was devoted to Project Platinum—keeping an eye on fan accounts, saving the most popular tweets and blog posts in a document for later presentation—but with Archie out of town doing shows up and down the eastern seaboard, there wasn't as much to be done. So, to fill the rest of the time, I volunteered to take on extra work from Joanna and Ryan. I spent much of my Tuesday through Thursday facilitating interviews, radio spots, and social media Q&As on behalf of some of the firm's lesser clients (the star of a terrible new teen drama about merpeople called *Fin*; a Vine star hoping to break into television; a member of a late-1990s ska band debuting a solo album). I'd also spent the better part of one day at former child-star Casey Lake's photo shoot for the cover of her new memoir, *Underwater*, providing moral support as well as a bridge between Casey and the mini fridge stocked with coconut water and low-fat string cheese.

At the morning meeting, I gave progress reports on all of the above. I'd prepared my notes the night before, and delivered my presentation largely on autopilot, surfacing only when Sam or Ryan asked a question. Joanna, meanwhile, was silent until the very end when she said, "Thank you, Rose." And then, to the rest of the room, "Rose has taken on an enormous amount of work in the small amount of downtime she has on her main project, which I would hope serves as an example to everyone else." Her tone was somehow pleasant and threatening in equal measure, and I swallowed my surprise and my pride, trying hard not to blush.

After the meeting, walking back to my desk, I heard, "Rose?" and turned to see Joanna standing in the doorway of her office. "Do you have a minute?"

Once I'd entered her office, I moved to sit in the chair across from her own, but Joanna stopped me. "No need," she said. "This will only take a moment."

I thought my stomach was going to drop right out of my body. My mouth went dry, so instead of replying I just nodded manically.

"I wanted to talk to you about something, but this isn't really the place. I've got to head to the airport—sort of last-minute, but I'm going to the LA office to handle some loose ends—but I'm back late Sunday, and I'd like for us to get breakfast at Elsie's on Monday. Around, let's say, 8:00." Joanna always presented plans in this way: as foregone conclusions, the time and place already picked out, an event already in progress; the implication being that if you were, for some unimaginable reason, to decline, it would go on without you.

"Y...es," I said. "I mean, of course." *What could she possibly need to talk to me about alone? And outside the office?*

"Great," said Joanna as she opened the door and gestured for me to leave.

Harper and I spent the better part of lunch trying to decipher what Joanna had said to me, and at least half of *that* time was taken up by Harper dismissing my repeated concerns that maybe she was going to fire me. ("She wouldn't *take you to breakfast* to fire you," she said. "Especially not such a, like, farm-to-table artisan-French-toast-and-hipster-bullshit breakfast." I argued that it could be a sort of spoonful-of-sugar approach, literally, and Harper groaned so loudly the people at the next table stopped eating to stare.) By the end of it, I felt mildly more confident that my job was not on the line, but no more certain of what we *could* be meeting about. Harper asked why I didn't just "email Joanna and ask her" what it was about, as if that were a remotely plausible suggestion. I told myself that Harper didn't know Joanna as well as I did; she certainly didn't value (or fear) Joanna's opinion of her the way I did. Mine was a problem without a solution, apart from simply waiting to see what happened. So instead of protesting, I just said, "Yeah, maybe," and resolved to suffer the entire weekend in silence, though when Harper ducked out of the office at 5:30 (for a 6:00 happy-hour date in Williamsburg) she told me to call her in the event of a nervous breakdown.

It was only a few minutes after she left that I heard my phone buzzing. When I looked at the screen, I saw that it was Archie, and reflexively, I pushed it across my desk. I watched it slide from my area to Harper's and knock into her keyboard, and then I finally leapt out of my chair to pick it up. I took a deep breath and pressed ACCEPT.

"Rose Reed," I said. (I was pretending I didn't know who it was.)

"Rose," he said. *Whyyyy* did he have to say my *name* in that *accent*? "It's Archie."

"Archie!" I chirped. "How are you?"

"Good. Just got back in town, actually."

"Oh, great," I said. There was a pause so long I had time to imagine Archie, and what he was wearing, on the other end of the phone. (A white T-shirt; a denim jacket; the kind of celebrity sweatpants that hardly classified as sweatpants; some kind of ridiculous boot.) "Um, how were the shows? Everything I've seen online looks positive." This was not strictly true; he'd been a little flat in Montreal, and a small subset of people on Twitter had noticed. Most fans, though, chalked his slightly strained vocals up to the emotions he was feeling for Raya. ("omg that crack at 1:28 tho. you can *literally* see it in his face. raychie is my otp," read one YouTube comment I remembered with crystalline clarity, for some unknown reason.) His last show of the tour, in Boston, had been excellent, and that was what really mattered.

"They were all right," said Archie. "I'm keen to get to work on new stuff. I'm at the point, singing the same lyrics for the fifty thousandth time, where I start thinking, *Christ, what rubbish.*"

"Hey now," I said. "I happen to think 'Make Your Mark' is a classic for the ages."

"Why thank you, Rose," he said. "Not a fan favorite, that."

"It's ahead of its time," I replied. It was true, I was sure of it; this time next year, *all* the chart leaders would feature flute riffs.

There was another pause; I heard Archie clear his throat.

"Anyway, I swear I had a point in calling."

"Yes?"

"I was wondering if you might meet me for a drink. Maybe a bit of food," he said.

"Oh, um," I stammered dumbly.

"Unless you have a date, of course," he said.

"No, I—um. I do not."

"Can I persuade you to join me, then? It'd, ah. It'd be great to see you."

I inhaled sharply. *Don't* say *shit like that to me*, I wanted to say. *Not if you don't mean it the way I want you to.*

"Roooose? Rosie?"

"Ew, *never* Rosie," I said.

"Noted," he said, laughing.

"And yes, where were you thinking?

"I know a spot," he said. "Can I pick you up? Are you still at the office?"

"Yeah," I started. "But I—"

"Great. We're downstairs."

"What?"

"I took a gamble."

I wanted to be angry at the presumptuousness of this, but I couldn't help but laugh. "All right," I said. "Give me five minutes to finish up here."

"Not a problem."

"I'm just in work clothes, obviously," I blurted out. I

immediately closed my eyes and punched myself lightly in the forehead. *Why did I just warn him about my clothes.* "I just mean, I hope we're not going anywhere too fancy? Um. Just, casual Friday, you know."

"I do," he said. "I am certain you won't be underdressed."

When I got downstairs, after leaping out of my chair with purse and blazer in hand and running to the bathroom to pull pointlessly at different parts of my blouse and skirt and to attempt to fix up my not-as-clean-as-I'd-like-for-Archie-Fox hair, I saw the black SUV sitting about twenty yards up the street. I approached it cautiously (in the event that it was a *different* celebrity waiting to pick up another employee in my building), but when I was five feet away, the door slid open and Archie peeked his head just slightly out to smile at me. He was wearing a baseball cap, sunglasses, a white T-shirt, and a jean jacket. Incognito wear, and, incidentally, exactly what I'd imagined him in.

"Cheers!"

"Hi," I said. Archie slid over and I climbed in next to him. "Hi, Big Pete."

"Good evening, Ms. Reed," said Big Pete. He smiled at me through the rearview window, and once my seat belt was fastened he pulled out into traffic.

"I hope you don't mind," said Archie, "but I've got a few things I need to finish up on the way over." He lifted his phone, and I nodded. *Cool*, I thought. *I will just ride with him to an unknown destination in silence, then.* I pulled my own phone from my purse and refreshed both my work and personal emails. As I'd checked them both six minutes earlier, there was nothing new. I scrolled through Twitter as we cut across Houston and headed south on West Street. The next time I looked up, we were heading into the Battery Tunnel.

"Brooklyn?" I asked.

"You seem surprised," said Archie.

"That's because I am."

"I've heard of it, too, you know."

"All right. Easy," I said. He grinned and shifted in his seat, and my eyes were drawn to his phone, now faceup atop his legs.

"You're playing *Neko Atsume*? That's the thing you needed to 'finish up'?"

Archie glanced at his phone, saw that he'd been caught red-handed, and then looked back at me, ever so slightly sheepish.

"Before we picked you up I got this new cat that's wearing this little suit, and I needed to take some photos," he explained. He was trying to remain straight-faced, but his eyes sparkled.

"Mmm," I said. "That *does* sound urgent."

"It's *extremely* cute," he said, and held up the phone for me to see the little cat who was, indeed, wearing a tiny red coat with yellow piping, a red top hat, and a mustache.

"I understand," I said. "When Kim Kardashian's game first came out I lost a month of my life and about forty-five dollars."

Archie looked solemn. "I had to make Maria take that one off my phone." I couldn't tell if he was kidding or not, but either way, I couldn't stop laughing, and then, neither could he.

Ten minutes later we pulled up behind the restaurant. I'd read something about it on Grub Street a month or two earlier, a bit before it opened—about the flagship location in Portland that had apparently drawn nationwide interest and culinary acclaim over the past year, and the planned expansion to Red

Hook—but, as with most of the cool-sounding restaurants whose openings I read about online, I'd never been.

Archie pulled his cap down toward his brow, the brim shadowing his face, and then hopped out of the car ahead of me. He held out his hand to help guide me out of the SUV, and as his fingers grasped mine I felt my legs go weak. I turned to say good-bye to Pete, who'd sunk into his now-reclined seat with a well-worn paperback thriller already open in his hand, and he waved in response. I leaned into Archie's ear once we'd shut the door behind us. "Will he just... wait here?" I whispered.

"Who, Pete?" asked Archie, guiding me toward the entrance. "He loves it, are you kidding? He's getting paid to lie down and read."

"It does kind of seem like a dream job when you put it that way," I conceded. Archie sidled up to the host stand with a little wave; the young host, clearly frazzled on this hectic Friday night, held up a hand to ask for us to wait before looking up and seeing who was standing in front of her. Her eyes widened roughly to the size of dinner plates, and she quickly ushered us to a small table tucked in the back corner.

"Right, especially when one has twin four-year-olds at home," continued Archie, motioning for me to take the booth as he settled into his chair.

As our host scurried back to her post to deal with the line of people we'd blown right past, I looked around to assess our surroundings. The dining room was long and narrow and, like all dining rooms in hip Brooklyn restaurants, lit a shade too dimly. This darkness was made worse by the fact that the menu in front of me was covered so fully in a font so small it was like the owner had needed to cram five pages' worth of dishes onto a single-page cheat sheet. Our table was nestled up against the wall on one side, and much too close to our neighbors' table on the other, but if our fellow diners recognized Archie, they were hiding it very well. A few servers and busboys were huddled in front of the computer at the edge of the bar, looking around at our table conspiratorially every now and then, so I was glad it was me facing them, not Archie. As for Archie, he was currently hunched over the menu, using his phone as a flashlight to illuminate it.

"Christ, they're really not making it easy to decipher this thing, huh?" said Archie.

"They really aren't." I laughed. "It doesn't help that I recognize maybe three things on here."

He was nodding in agreement, his eyebrows furrowed, when our server—a bright-eyed, wide-smiled, and bespectacled thirty-something—appeared as if from thin air. The other servers were watching intently from across the room; clearly he was savoring his good fortune.

"Hey guys! My name is Ted! Welcome to Kao!" He looked back and forth between us; I tried my best to match his enthusiasm with my smile. "Have you been here before?"

Archie and I shook our heads, and Ted's eyes lit up.

"Oh, excellent. I *love* first-timers! Let me explain to you how it works."

Archie's eyes locked on mine and his face spread into a dimpled smile. "There are special instructions!" he stage-whispered, and I choked back a laugh.

"Well, not really *instructions* per se," said Ted, clasping his hands together under his chin. "It's just that a Kao dining experience isn't like other dining experiences."

Ted went on to explain how our next hour or so would look: Everything would be shared, "family-style," and he suggested we order at least four plates between the two of us—plates that he helped us select based on dietary restrictions (none), spice tolerance (high for me, mild for Archie), and hunger level (very). After settling on two salads, one curry, the tilapia special, and a directive to never let ourselves run out of sticky rice, Archie and I found ourselves quietly, somewhat awkwardly, looking at each other, the momentum that had driven the previous hour slowing to a halt, the tension of last week's events creeping back in. Suddenly, I remembered: I was kind of *annoyed* with him.

"So, how've you been?" I asked.

"Good, good."

Ted returned with two glasses of Prosecco—"on the house"—and a wink. Archie nodded in thanks.

"Does that always happen?" I asked.

"Usually," he said. We clinked our glasses, and I gulped down a large sip.

"How's Neil?"

I choked on the bubbles caught in the back of my throat.

"Excuse me?"

"Neil. Hot Doctor." Archie stared into his glass, twirling it in his hand. "How's he doing?"

"He's fine." My pulse quickened. I couldn't help feeling like I was being put on the defensive, and it wasn't a position I particularly enjoyed—especially when, of the two of us, I was not the one who'd let a text go unanswered for days. But because I am who I am, I added, "Probably."

Archie looked at me, eyebrow arched, when a young server appeared with a salad in one slightly shaking hand, some baskets of sticky rice balancing on his other. He placed them down on the limited real estate between us, knocking into a water glass hard enough for a few splashes to leap out and land in Archie's lap.

"Oh my gosh," the boy squeaked, his hand flying to his forehead. "I'm so sorry, Arch—sir. Mr. Fox. Oh my God."

Archie smiled and placed his hand on the boy's shoulder. The muscle in his forearm rippled as he squeezed in reassurance. *Do not get sucked in*, I thought.

"No worries, mate," he said. "Just a bit of water, right?"

The boy smiled weakly, most of the color drained from his face, and then dashed away.

"So . . . 'probably,' " he said.

"Is there a question in there?"

"Are you, ah, no longer in touch?"

"Why do you ask?" That Archie wanted apparent confirmation of my romantic failure was both aggravating and irresistible. *Why does he care?*

He gulped down some water, his eyes tearing up from the heat of the salad.

"Just making conversation."

I closed my eyes and dropped my arms on the table. I refused to dance around it. "Why didn't you text me back?"

Archie's eyes flew up to meet mine, just as Ted returned with two plates in hand.

"All right folks, we've got the chicken curry, *very* spicy, so the gentleman should approach with caution." He looked to Archie for a laugh, but Archie's gaze didn't falter. "Oookay, and then over here, we've got some ribs—chef's specialty, our treat."

I made up for Archie's silence by offering an emphatic thank-you, and then ordered another glass of Prosecco.

"You know, it's not, like, normal to get a bunch of free shit when you go out to eat," I said through a half-full mouth. "Maybe you've forgotten that. But it's polite to at least thank them for it."

Archie leaned across the table, his voice lowered. "Why did you run out of that hotel room like you'd just seen a ghost?"

"I would *never* run away from a ghost sighting. It is my dream to see a ghost," I hissed.

The corner of Archie's mouth crept into a smile, which he swiftly wiped away.

"Rose."

I sighed. "You embarrassed me! Or, I embarrassed myself… or maybe it was both! Everything was embarrassing!"

"*I* embarrassed *you*?" Archie practically guffawed. "You told me you hated my music."

"I didn't say I *hated*—"

But then Ted was back, again, with the Prosecco and a large plate holding a full tilapia—head and eyes and all. He shuffled some plates around to make room, a process that couldn't have taken longer than ten seconds but felt like it lasted about ten minutes. Holding a stack of cleared plates, he looked at us with a satisfied smile.

"Anything else I can—"

"We're great Ted, thanks!" I said, feeling immediately guilty as he turned on his heel, his smile dimmed. *This is how it happens*, I thought. *This is how you become the asshole who doesn't thank the staff for free ribs.*

I looked back at Archie. "I didn't say I hated your music. I said I didn't like *one* song." *Raya didn't like it, either*, I thought. But then, I realized, he probably still didn't know that.

"It wasn't just any song, though."

"I know. I'm sorry." And I was. It didn't matter, I realized, that I'd meant every word I'd said. It mattered that saying them had hurt him.

"It's all right," said Archie. He shrugged. "After that I took a bit of a team poll and it turned out nearly *everyone* thought it was total crap. Even Maria. It was just that she hadn't wanted to say."

"Wow," I said, as much at the fact that the unshakable Maria had apparently been too nervous to tell Archie the truth as at the relief I felt in no longer being the only one to have told him so.

"I know," said Archie. "So, I scrapped it."

"Oh." I had the urge to say *I'm sorry* again, but I fought it, because I wasn't. I also had the urge to say *THANK GOD*, but I tamped that down, too.

"Better off. I think—well, I hope that the new stuff I've been working on is much better."

"Well, I loved what I've heard so far," I said. "Like, really loved."

"I'm glad to hear that," said Archie. "Raya told me after your visit, of course, but, ah, she's been known to . . . exaggerate."

From the way he looked at me I wondered if maybe he *did* know she'd hated "Highest Low" after all. I wondered whether it was wise for me to agree with him, but before I could, Archie said "Right!" and moved to serve us both some tilapia. I took a drink, hoping we'd moved on from what I'd said earlier. But after I'd taken a couple of very delicious bites, I looked back at Archie's face, and I could tell that he hadn't.

"Why did you say I embarrassed you?"

"Never mind."

"I do mind," said Archie, and he put down his knife and fork, leaning back and making a big show of folding his hands behind his head as if to indicate that his food would get cold if I didn't speak up soon. I took a deep breath and blew it out resignedly.

"You made me believe..." I drifted off, shaking my head.

Archie reached across the table and rested his hand on mine. "I made you believe what?"

It felt like my heart had leapt into my throat. The last two plates that Ted had dropped were still untouched on the table.

"Do you have feelings for her?" I asked. I felt shaky, but my voice was even.

"Rose."

I covered my face in my hands, feeling my eyes tearing. *Goddamn trigger-happy tear ducts.*

"I need to know, Archie. And I know this is wildly unprofessional, and I'm sorry, but then again this has been kind of outside the Weaver-Girard handbook since Du Roi."

He looked at me, his face entirely unreadable.

"She's a lovely girl..."

"Oh my God. Oh my *God.*" Everything in my peripheral vision blurred into shadows, and the surrounding chatter muffled into an increasingly overwhelming static. I knew that tone. It was the same adopted by any guy who had ever needed to let me down easy. Of course he had feelings for her. How could I have done this? What was I thinking? The past weeks flashed through my mind, followed swiftly by my entire, brief career. I was going to have to quit. What would I tell Joanna? What would I tell Harper? How could I have misread Archie's feelings for me—or, as it now appeared, the lack thereof—so completely? I was suddenly very conscious of the closeness of every table around us, the narrow path to the exit, and my breath felt short and shallow. I stood up on shaky legs.

"Rose, wait." Archie looked up at me but his voice sounded far away.

"Don't," I said. I took a breath. "I need to get some air."

I grabbed my bag and beelined to the front door, brushing past servers and diners, a stream of *excuse me*'s and *I'm sorry*'s following me out. I had no real plan; I just needed to leave, and I kept walking until I reached the alley between the building housing Kao and the bar next door. I pulled my phone out to call Harper—for advice, for a rescue mission, I didn't know—but was startled when I felt a strong, soft hand on my wrist. I looked up, and just as my mind registered that it was Archie's face looking down at me, his lips were on mine.

I threw my bag to the ground and wrapped my arms around his neck as he pushed me up against the wall. His lips were soft; he tasted sweet; and we kissed like we were running out of time—until I realized where we were, and who he was, and pushed him away from me.

"Archie," I said, out of breath. "We can't."

His face fell.

"I mean, we can! We should. Just, not here." The alley was dark, but we were still close enough to other people to hear their conversations.

He closed the gap between us and ran his hand through my hair.

"Let them watch."

"It's not that simple, and you know it."

He sighed and backed up next to me against the wall.

"I told you from the beginning that this—me and Raya—it was always just business," he said slowly.

"But the hotel photos—"

"We were working on the song!" he said. "You know, the one she played for you?"

"I know, but I wasn't sure that was *all*—"

"It was."

"But that night... and then after... you ignored me!"

"I was trying to woo my publicist and I thought I had failed miserably!"

I turned to face him and poked him playfully in the chest.

"Are you *pouting* right now?"

He glanced down at me from the corner of his eye. "Maybe."

For a moment we just watched each other. Then Archie grabbed my hand. "Can I kiss you again?"

"Absolutely not."

I breathed in a deep sigh, trying to make sense of the last five minutes, trying to return to publicist mode.

"Okay, here's what's going to happen. You need to go back inside. Maybe order a drink. Start eating some of that damn fish. If we leave abruptly, they'll assume you didn't like it, or that something's amiss. We don't want to give them such a blow to their reputation."

"I don't think Ted could handle it."

"Ted needs this, Archie."

He laughed.

"I'll follow like five minutes behind you," I assured him.

He nodded and walked away—with the quick interruption of him running back to me, giving me a quick peck on the forehead, and me pushing him away—and I killed my five minutes by muffling a scream into my sleeve and then sending Harper a text guaranteed to infuriate her:

`I can't say anything more about it and I'm so sorry but ummmmmmm Archie just kissed me OK TALK LATER BYE`

(She responded immediately: `ARE YOU FUCKING KIDDING ME CALL ME OMFG`)

When I returned to our table, Archie was digging into some ribs, poker face on.

"So, everything settled?" he asked, louder than necessary.

"Yup," I said. "Everything's... clear."

We spent the rest of the meal alternating between taking bites of food and stealing furtive, smiling glances. Ted returned with another set of cocktails, this time from "the ladies at the bar"—my jealousy curtailed by the fact that they'd sent two drinks over, not one. We waved in thanks and drank them quickly. Another fan—this time a young girl, maybe twelve years old—approached our table to tell Archie how much she loved him, looking back frequently at her mother, who was offering her two thumbs up from the table. Archie was gracious, asked her name, and then went up for a high five, feigning injury from the girl's strength, much to her glee. Soon after, Ted returned with dessert menus ready.

"Would you like to hear about our special sweets for the evening?" he asked.

I looked at Archie and shrugged. "I'm okay, do you...?"

I felt his hand crawl up my skirt and squeeze my thigh. I cleared my throat, and told Ted we'd just take the check.

Archie's fingers didn't stray from my skin—not as we walked out to the car, his hand on my lower back, the tip of his thumb hooked over my waistband; not as we sat in the backseat, his index and middle fingers tracing along the back of my neck. I knew that going to his place was far too risky, and so directed Pete to my place. It wasn't until we walked the four floors up to my apartment, out of breath more from the workout and less from the heat of the moment, that the reality of the situation started to sink in: Archie was coming back to my place. *My place.* My prewar, four-hundred-square-foot apartment, with shitty air-conditioning, 1990s-era appliances, and a crappy couch we bought for $30 from the tenants who'd lived there before us.

"So, um." I stopped at the front door, my hand hovering in front of the lock. "You know you're about to see how people actually live in New York. Or, at least, how the other ninety-nine percent live in New York."

Archie brushed his hand through my hair.

"I'm serious," I said. "Like, my entire apartment is probably the size of your bathroom."

He pulled back, placed one hand on each of my shoulders, and looked me in the eyes. "You know, I'm not an asshole," he said.

"I know, I know." I turned away from him and struggled to get the key in the lock. Perhaps those free drinks were catching up with me.

"And it's not like I was born in a palace, to kings and queens," he continued. I felt the lock click open, and shoved the door in. "Plus, again, you overestimate my wealth."

I looked back at him skeptically. Maybe Archie wasn't traveling-to-space rich, but he was certainly penthouse wealthy. I wasn't buying it, and was opening my mouth to call him out on it when a voice behind me piped up.

"Whoa, are you that guy?"

I spun around again to face the apartment—essentially my living room, dining room, and kitchen in one space—and saw Chelsey's boyfriend, Jay, pop his head up over the top of the couch, his eyes red from the weed I could still smell. I slinked out of my coat and grabbed Archie's from him.

"Archie, Jay; Jay, Archie," I muttered, draping our coats over the many already hanging on the back of our front door. "Jay is my roommate's boyfriend. Where *is* Chelsey?"

"Hey," Chelsey drawled, her voice almost entirely disembodied, save for the arm that waved weakly from the side of the couch. I walked over to the fridge and saw a scene from *Sherlock* frozen on the screen of the laptop in front of her.

Archie bent down to shake her hand and hovered awkwardly over the stoned couple. It was oddly comforting. I didn't know he was capable of awkward.

"Wait, no, really dude, I know you," said Jay, jumping up to rest on his knees.

"Jay, stop being a spaz," Chelsey said. I couldn't tell if she was extremely adept at playing it cool, or if she actually hadn't looked away from the screen yet. "You've probably just seen him around the neighborhood. Put the show back on."

"No, man, you're that singer!"

I could feel my face reddening, but Archie just laughed, prompting Chelsey to tilt her head up toward him with eyes that squinted and then widened with recognition.

"Holy shit, you *are* that singer," she said.

Archie raised his arms up in mock defeat. "Guilty," he said, and I could hear the smile in his voice.

I pulled out a bottle of (miraculously unopened) white wine from the fridge, two glasses, and a half-eaten sleeve of cookies from the cabinet, and sidled up behind him. I couldn't gauge his level of discomfort, if there even was any. Surely this was something he must be used to. Maybe it seemed unconscionably awkward to me—the celebrity equivalent of bringing a guy back to your parents' house only to find your mother still awake and ready to exclaim, *Oh, I've heard so much* about *you!*—but as far as sightings go, this was pretty mild. If a little mood killing.

"Archie Fox, I fucking *knew* it," said Jay, his face glued to his phone.

Chelsey eyed me with a look that appeared to signal approval, maybe even a bit of admiration, but either way it was one I'd never seen from her before. For my part, I, for the first time in our knowing each other, tried some wordless communication with her, transmitting a desperate plea for her to stop the flow of questioning and clear the space before Archie decided there was a reason he only ever went home with other famous people.

Jay did not get the message. To my surprise, he transformed into a gushing fangirl, digging out a ziplock bag filled with weed and a bowl from beneath a cushion with a look of frantic glee on his face.

"Dude, you have to smoke with me. Do you smoke?"

Archie and I locked eyes, trying desperately to hold back

our laughter. Chelsey—bless her—closed the laptop, shoved it under her arm, and placed the other arm around Jay.

"Oh my God, you are so embarrassing," she said. "That guy did not come over here to smoke with you. Come to bed."

Jay rose from the couch with puppy-dog eyes, and Archie extended a hand to shake his.

"Good to meet you, mate, and thanks for the offer," he said.

Jay disappeared into Chelsey's dark room, and Chelsey turned to close the door, but not before throwing me an almost-imperceptible wink. The door closed, I looked at Archie, and I was suddenly very aware of the fact that there was nothing—*finally*, nothing—keeping us apart.

"Well," said Archie.

"Well." I held up the wineglasses in one hand, the bottle of wine and sleeve of cookies in the other. Archie looked at them, and then at me, and then he took everything out of my hands and set it all down on the counter.

"Go," he said, in a low whisper, nodding toward my bedroom. Slightly startled, I nodded and turned toward my room. I pushed the door open slowly, nervously, but breathed in relief when I saw my impeccably made bed, my nightstand clean of embarrassing toiletries, my regularly dusted windowsill, my small shelf of books arranged by cover color. The only offender was a raggedy hot-pink "RUSH FALL 2010" pajama T-shirt, still strewn across the pillow. (I hadn't gotten a bid from the house widely considered to be the best one on campus, and so I'd decided not to rush at all. But that was after they gave us all T-shirts.) I swiped the shirt off the bed and tossed it into my hamper in one swift motion, and then I turned back to face Archie, who was in my room, closing the door behind him.

For a moment we just stared at each other, and then we heard a cackle from across the apartment. Chelsey.

"It's not the *most* soundproof apartment," I said.

"I can be quiet. Can you?"

My mouth was too dry to speak, so I gave another nod, and then the two or three feet of space between us was closed and we were kissing. Archie's hands gripped the back of my neck, my back, then my ass. My hands grazed his chest, his stomach, the hem of his T-shirt. I slid my hands underneath it and lifted up. He took his hands off my body at the last possible second, raising his arms so I could pull his shirt up over his head. I watched his tangled hair fall back to his broad shoulders and then, looking at his chest and stomach, I froze, remembering all the times I'd paged past pictures of this same torso in a gossip magazine—muscular, marked and delineated with tattoos of various flora and fauna; most famously, a pair of birds across his chest. It was so much different in person: gentler, more human. Archie took my stillness as an opportunity to begin unbuttoning my blouse, which he did so quickly and frantically that he missed two separate buttons and had to go back. We both started giggling, but then my shirt was open, then off, and then we stopped.

Archie edged backward until he reached the bed, and sat down on it. He pulled me in by the waist until I stood between his legs, his eyes on my own chest and stomach. He reached his hands up, tracing the top of my bra, the cups of it, my back under the strap, twisting it gently until it came apart and together we slid it off my arms. I felt, if not *un*self-conscious, less self-conscious than I would have expected. Archie's eyes were so steady, and his touch so soft that I felt like someone he felt lucky to be this close to. I stepped in nearer to him, and he kissed the tops of my breasts. His breath was hot on my chest, and between that and the warmth of my small, un-air-conditioned room, I felt almost faint.

"Take off my skirt," I whispered. Archie looked up at me, eyes widening slightly. With one of his hands, he reached around to the zipper on the back of my skirt, and with the other he reached up my skirt, between my legs and up. When he touched me, I inhaled sharply.

I slid my hands down to help him help me wriggle out of my skirt, and then I was standing in front of him, in nothing but my underwear. (Plain cotton, unfortunately, but black, *thank God.*)

"Rose."

I put one knee on the bed and then the other, straddling him.

"Yes?" I said.

But he didn't answer, instead leaning back and pulling me down on top of him. He kissed my mouth and neck and I reached down to feel him, hard, beneath me; this time it was him who sucked in his breath. I unzipped his jeans, but before I could do anything else, he secured an arm around me and flipped me over onto my back.

Archie watched me as he moved down my body, grasping my breasts, my waist, and finally the waistband of my underwear. He moved to pull it down and I winced just slightly, thinking about the grooming situation he'd find there.

"Is this okay?"

"Yes," I said. "I mean, *yes*. I just…I didn't know this was going to happen, so—"

Archie slid a hand beneath my underwear and I tried to be still. "I like it," he said. "I like *you*."

"I like you, too."

Then his mouth was on me, soft but firm. He squeezed the top of my thigh with one hand and moved the other down my leg until his fingers were inside me. I dug my heels into the mattress and moaned, and right away Archie leaned forward and cupped his free hand over my mouth.

"Remember," he said, and grinned. "*Quiet.*"

I nodded, breathing against his palm, and then he lifted it. He lowered his face back onto me, increasing the pressure of his tongue, thrusting inside me with his fingers. When I came, I bit the flesh of my upper arm to keep from crying out.

Archie lifted his head to look at me.

"Wow," he said.

"Yeah," I said. He lunged forward toward me, kissing me, fumbling around with his back pocket and then his wallet. He stopped to lean back and remove a condom from it, and I pulled his jeans down to his knees. As soon as it was on, he was on top of me, inside me. He grasped my hair and my neck and I dug my hands into his lower back and then his ass. If the bed creaked I didn't care enough to hear it.

When he came he rolled over to my side, and we both lay there, breathing heavily and looking at each other, waiting for the other to say something first. I pushed my now-damp hair off my face, and he grabbed a tissue off my nightstand to clean up. When he came back he leaned over me and snaked an arm around my waist. I ran my fingers up and down his arm, tracing his tattoos.

"How many are there altogether?"

"Thirty-nine," he said.

"Wow." I paused, wondering if it was okay to ask what I

wanted to ask, and deciding I was going to either way. "How many do you regret?"

"Two," he admitted. He made no move to indicate which, but I wondered if one was the small black heart on his shoulder, which rumors held he got for Chloe.

"That's not bad," I said.

"Not at all."

It got quiet again. Archie placed his other hand across my upper chest and moved it down—between my breasts, across my stomach, coming to rest between my hipbones. He looked at me, and the dimples reemerged.

"Do you want more?" he asked.

It was perhaps the easiest yes I'd ever given.

# 18.

On Monday morning I got to Elsie's twenty minutes early on purpose. I wanted to get there before Joanna to make sure she didn't have to wait for a table (or a glass of ice water), true, but I also wanted time to fantasize. Since Friday night, I'd been carving little windows of fantasy time out of my daily routines—brushing my teeth a little more slowly, forgoing a book on the subway, picking up bodega groceries with headphones in, but nothing playing—in order to dedicate myself to picturing Archie and me in my bed. Or, more accurately, *on* it. Already I was nervous that I would forget some essential part of it—his eyes on me as he slid down my body, the coolness of his silver rings on my mouth when he covered it, the way his hair smelled when he buried his face in my neck. I hoped that by replaying it, and replaying it, I could preserve it in my memory—one I could recall, on command, for the rest of my life.

After all, I wasn't sure when (or if) it would happen again.

I'd half woken around 5:30 the morning after to Archie gathering his things to go, and when he noticed I was up, he leaned over the bed and kissed me on the forehead. We'd exchanged brief, groggy good-byes, and then he'd headed for the airport, and then on to London. Once he'd landed he sent me a text that was short, but otherwise perfect: `Just landed. Wish I was spending the night with you.` There had been about a million things I'd wanted to write back, but what I sent was: `Me too. Enjoy London.` In the one and a half (radio-silent) days that had passed since, I'd spent much of the time wondering if I should have said more, cringing at the travel-agent-like command "Enjoy London." I kept calm by reminding myself I would certainly hear from him; it was only a matter of when. Sitting at the little corner table in the café, I quickly checked Archie's Twitter and Instagram accounts—much to my relief, there were no new posts to either. *Remember: He's on vacation. And he* did *text you. And you* know *that he likes you, because he told you so.*

Then again, I thought, surely I was far from the first non-famous woman Archie Fox had slept with; nor could I be the first non-famous woman to believe that Archie Fox thought she was special, that he *really liked* her.

I cleared my throat, took a sip of coffee, and grimaced; I added another creamer, stirred in a second packet of sugar. The host reappeared, hovering over the table.

"Everything still all right?" he said with a glance toward the empty seat. Since I'd arrived, Elsie's had filled up, and I knew the wait for a table was probably now hovering around twenty-five minutes. *Which is why I got here early,* I said, telepathically, to the server.

"Yes, thank you," I said. "My boss—oh, actually, there she is." Joanna had just pushed through the front door, and I watched as she maneuvered gracefully through the throngs of people hoping to offset their Monday-morning gloom with large stacks of buckwheat pancakes.

"Wonderful," said the host. "I'll alert your server."

Joanna arrived tableside with sunglasses on and her lips pursed. She didn't seem to be in especially good spirits, but, then again, she never exactly radiated exuberance. She dropped her bag to the floor, wrapped her (completely unnecessary, weather-wise) neon-pink blazer around the chair's back, sank into her seat, and slid a folded sheet of paper across the table before even responding to my greeting.

My smile shrank.

Staring up at me from the table were three printed photographs—dark and grainy from having been zoomed in too close on their subjects, but clear enough. It was us. Me and Archie—here, his hand on my cheek; here, wrapped up in a kiss; here, my head resting on his shoulder. Moments ago I'd been wishing for a way to immortalize a night that, in many ways, had seemed too good to be true, and here was my wish, granted. Better to have stuck with the memory.

"Joanna," I began, not entirely sure yet how I would finish. She held up a hand to stop me and looked me straight in the eyes.

"Your client, Rose? *Our* client?"

I could feel a lump rising in my throat. I opened my mouth to speak, but Joanna shushed me again.

"Do you know what it's like to wake up to this?"

"Joanna, I'm so sorry." *Don't cry*, I thought. *Do not. Cry.*

"Sorry doesn't matter," said Joanna, pulling the sheet back and jamming it in her purse. "I don't care about sorry."

I'd never experienced this feeling before: the shameful certainty that I'd disappointed a superior. Chalk it up to my tendency toward overachieving, but the result—apart from earning, until now at least, consistent recognition for my work ethic, in school and at my job—was a complete unpreparedness for handling this kind of confrontation. I'd done something wrong, and I was caught. Joanna could fire me right at this moment, and no one would question her decision. The fact of it sank in my stomach like a rock: I'd fucked up, and I couldn't pretend that I hadn't, on some level, understood so when I did it. I'd been able to push that aside for the fantasy, a fantasy that had just come to a crashing halt. Had kissing Archie—and everything that followed—been worth it? I eyed my phone, perched at the edge of the table, quiet and textless, and realized I wasn't sure.

A petite middle-aged woman with a ponytail sprouting from the top of her head approached the table. Joanna rattled off an order she'd clearly made many times before (a three-egg [two whites] garden veggie omelet with greens instead of toast; coffee, black) and my barely functioning brain settled on the simplest thing I could find (two eggs, scrambled, with bacon and toast)—though I doubted I would be able to get anything down.

As the server walked away, I returned my gaze to Joanna to find her eyes had softened ever so slightly. I pounced.

"Joanna, listen, I know this looks bad." Joanna let out one sharp, high-pitched laugh, but I had no choice but to press on. "But I can fix this. You know I can."

She looked at me for a dragged-out moment, and then released a long, defeated sigh.

"How long have you two been fucking?" I choked on my water, but Joanna continued. "Please, Rose. We're all adults here. The photos are pretty clear. I need to know exactly what we're dealing with."

I took this as a good sign—that the conversation was actually continuing, that the revelation of the photos wasn't the start and finish.

"Well, um," I said. This wasn't exactly how I wanted my first one-on-one bonding opportunity with Joanna to go. "We aren't, or, we weren't. Until Friday."

Joanna nodded but didn't say a word.

"I swear, that"—I gestured to her bag—"was the first time. And it could be the last time, too."

The second I said the words, I felt my heart go heavy—not only because I didn't want to say them, but because I meant them. I hadn't thought about it in exactly those terms until just this moment, but if it came down to choosing between Archie and my job, my gut told me to go with my job. It was safer. Smarter.

"Is that what you want?" asked Joanna.

Our coffees arrived; I used the opportunity to stall my answer.

"No," I finally admitted. "Of course it's not."

"And what he wants...?"

"I don't know."

Joanna paused again, considering what I'd just laid out in front of her. I—her quasi-protégée, with whom she'd entrusted one of her biggest clients after I'd failed to listen to her first directive, keeping my mouth shut—had possibly destroyed our professional relationship with that client because I'd been utterly incapable of experiencing a feeling and not expressing it. A feeling that he just happened to reciprocate, or so he'd told me.

"They're running the photos at two," said Joanna.

The strangeness of the circumstances dawned on me suddenly. Why, two days later, did Joanna have the photos on some shitty printout? Why weren't they spreading across fan accounts and blogs like wildfire? Until now, the world outside of this restaurant—and its reaction to this news—remained a hypothetical problem.

Joanna sensed my confusion. "They're Lucas's," she said, and I felt my jaw tighten. *That little shit.*

"Some friend," I spat, garnering an icy glare from Joanna.

"He's not a friend, he's a contact," said Joanna. "And he'd be an idiot to sit on these."

I dropped my eyes to my lap.

"Anyway, he says he didn't realize it was you until he'd already sold them. You can believe him or not; regardless, he gave us a heads-up, which is more than he owed us."

I sank back into my chair. "Shit."

Joanna nodded.

"You know, I'd actually invited you to breakfast because I wanted to run a new opportunity by you," said Joanna. "Of course, now..."

She left the sentence open-ended, echoing the sentiment that had colored everything that had happened to me since Friday night. It wasn't lost on me that us sleeping together shifted the tone of this project, and with Archie in another country and mostly out of reach, I'd spent the weekend vacillating between fluttery excitement and uncertainty about our relationship—working or otherwise. But here was another thing I'd quickly forgotten in my panic: Joanna had scheduled this breakfast *before* that dinner with Archie. Before the kiss. Before the pictures. *Goddammit, Lucas.* He and I had become somewhat friendly in my time working with Joanna, but I couldn't say I was surprised. I'd never known a paparazzo who wouldn't sell out his own mother for a buck.

"And now...do I, um. Am I still in a position that would allow me to pursue a new opportunity?" I asked.

"I'm not sure yet," she said.

I'd asked the question anticipating that very answer (or worse), but it still gutted me to hear it.

"Weaver-Girard Public Relations is going to lose the Girard," Joanna continued. I tried not to let my jaw drop. "They don't know it yet, but it won't be long. There have been too many... philosophical differences, for too long."

I was surprised, but I also couldn't blame her. Ryan wasn't just a jerk—though he was that—but also tone-deaf and often regressive in a way that was becoming increasingly disruptive to the firm's success. One could only ignore the opinions and desires of young women for so long in an industry dependent on those women's whims (album purchases and box-office numbers) before being written out of said industry. It was young women, after all, who made up the lion's share of large, social-media-active, money-spending fandoms. If Joanna had asked me—though technically she hadn't—Ryan's days as an influential, respected publicity exec were numbered.

"So you're...?" I began.

"Going solo, yes," she said. "That's why I was out in LA—spreading the word, gathering clients. Quietly, of course. And I asked you to meet with me today because I wanted you to come with me." Hearing the past tense, I swallowed hard. But she went on. "I am not yet closing that door altogether, Rose. Despite . . . this, you have been instrumental to the firm. You're savvy. And I believe you have good instincts. But you messed up."

I nodded, forcing myself not to look down at my plate, like I wanted, and to maintain eye contact with her. Something she had told me to do early on.

"Professionally, this was a mistake," she continued. "I'm not talking about the rest of your life. I will not tell you what to do with the rest of your life. Do you understand me?"

I decided to be honest. "I'm not sure."

"I would never ask you to give up your life for this job. I don't think that's what makes someone successful. Or, at least, it's not the *only* way to be successful. Ryan might think so, and I might have thought so when I was your age, but now, I don't know. I don't buy it. There is more to be done in one's life. So what I want you to understand is this: While it is my job, as your boss, to inform you that you fucked up here, it is not my job to tell you that you did the wrong thing. Okay?"

I nodded slowly. "Okay."

Joanna clenched her jaw slightly, and her face, having softened in a way I'd never seen before, resumed its resting sternness. "And I understand this to be a complicated, unique situation, yes? So, because it is complicated, and unique, I expect it to stay that way. I expect that, if we were to continue to work together, nothing like this would happen again."

"No," I said. "It would not."

"So here's what I'm going to do," said Joanna. "I'm going to give you a week. And I'm going to watch how you spin this."

"Thank you," I said.

"Don't thank me," said Joanna, sharply. I snapped my mouth shut and, much to my shock, she laughed. "Rose," she continued. "If you are going to work with me, you need to be less grateful. You are not *lucky*."

I nodded yet again. "I know," I said. "I assure you, I will make this...development...work. My primary concern is the successful launch of Archie—Mr. Fox's album release."

Just then, the server returned with our food and slid each of our dishes in front of us. She smiled, opened her mouth to ask us something, and then, seeming to sense the seriousness of our discussion, said only "Enjoy!" and quickly walked away.

"Save it for Ryan," said Joanna. *Is she holding back a smile?* I thought. "He is going to pop an artery over this, and you're going to have to sit through it. No matter what happens, I am not announcing my departure—or any other staffing decisions I might make—until Friday. Understood?"

"Yes," I said.

"Good," she replied, and stabbed her fork into her omelet.

---

We'd eaten quickly, and largely in silence. I'd half expected Joanna to rebuke me further, or to remind me at the end of the meal that I needed to impress her, but I wasn't sure why. I had never known Joanna to repeat herself, much less to handhold. If what she said didn't sink in the first time, that was the listener's problem, not hers. We were therefore early to the office. As soon as I'd sat down at my desk, I sank my head into my hands and did my best (and much-practiced) silent cry. I felt completely overwhelmed and—in the still-dark office, without my best friend, an ocean between me and the person at the root of all this, the person who'd landed in my life like a meteor—utterly alone. *Shit*, I remembered. *Archie.* I had to let him know about the pictures, and warn him that, come 2:00 p.m. (EST) today, everything we'd worked for over these past few weeks could very well implode. Because while I'd assured Joanna that I would spin this, the truth was that there was only so much I could control. A week was not very much time to make repairs, especially when it came to broken hearts—not those of the celebrities in question, but those of their public, for whom a sin like this (kissing a woman other than the woman with whom you have been officially shipped) constituted a violation of trust. In his songs Archie told girls that he loved them, that they were perfect, and special, and unforgettable; that it was *he himself* who always seemed to get his heart broken. How could that kind of romantic hero jump from one girl to the next within the span of a few days? How could anyone believe anything he said after it?

That's when it came to me—just the start of a sketch of an outline, but a start nonetheless. While I wasn't certain I could make this better, I knew I had no choice but to move forward. I had lost control of the project, and I was the only person who could regain it. So I sat up straight in my chair, wiped the leaky mascara from underneath my eyes, and took a few deep breaths. In a small, strange way (and one I would never have asked for), the impending release of the photos came as something of a relief: Our future was no longer open-ended, hazy, with an indeterminate amount of time left in which I might, as in the handful of brief and pseudo-romantic sexual encounters I'd had previously, wait passively, wondering what (if anything) would happen next. Something *was* going to happen, because I was going to make it happen, and I was going to make it happen by the end of the week. And right now, I didn't have the time or mental energy to care if that conclusion had anything to do with Archie and me, the human beings. All that mattered, for right now, was Archie, the Superstar, and me, the PR specialist, who wanted to keep her job.

I looked at the clock. It was just around 2:00 p.m. in London. A text would do nothing but inspire panic. An email felt too cold. I knew I didn't exactly have a lot of time to talk through the nuances of the situation with Archie (oh God, and Raya—I'd have to let Raya know, too), but it was the best possible solution, especially given that my plan was still forming in real time.

Archie answered after the first ring—"Good morning, Rose!"—and for a moment I was tempted to ignore the reason for my call, to pretend this was nothing more than a girl snagging a quick hello from her boyfriend before the drudgery of the week set in, imagining an alternate reality in which such a relationship for me and Archie could exist.

Instead, I cleared my throat.

"So, something's happened. In any other scenario I'd be calling to yell at you about something like this, but given the circumstances..."

"Is this a riddle?"

A quiet chuckle escaped my throat. "Please don't make me laugh."

"Okay, well, now you're worrying me."

I let in a deep breath and sank my head into my free hand. "Someone got a photo of us."

A beat of silence passed.

"Outside of Kao."

Still nothing.

"In . . . a compromising position?"

". . . Huh," said Archie. An utterly anticlimactic response that irritated me for reasons I couldn't pinpoint.

"Which is an issue, since, as I'm sure you're aware, we've sort of been spending this past month building up your public romance with someone else," I continued. I knew I was being condescending but I couldn't help myself. "Raya being someone the people buying your music have become very keen on."

"Well." He paused. Suddenly I was dying to know where, exactly, he was taking the call. "So they'll become keen on you. Shouldn't be too hard."

In an alternate world, this—a quasi-commitment to us in the face of adversity, a subtle reminder of Archie's own fondness for me—could have come across as a romantic gesture. But here, now, it struck me primarily as the blasé, endearing-if-it-weren't-so-infuriating artlessness of a guy who'd always had a team of professionals dealing with his scandals before he even knew those scandals existed. Why *wouldn't* this breeze over, at least in his mind? He'd probably forgotten just how much was riding on him and Raya to begin with. Or maybe he really did view us as interchangeable.

I swallowed my own feelings and tried to keep my publicist hat on. "It's not exactly that simple," I said.

"Why not?" asked Archie, a bit livelier now. "It's not as if Raya and I ever confirmed we were together. And even if people thought we were, well, couples break up all the time. The fans can be adults about it."

"Except they're not adults, Archie. They're fourteen-year-olds."

"Even more evidence that they shouldn't be dictating my life!"

"It's not just your life, Archie!" I was suddenly filled with the urge to bang my head against my desk. "And I'm sorry to be the one to break this to you, but the approval of those fourteen-year-olds is non-negotiably essential if the life you want involves real commercial success. There's a reason we met in the first place, and it was your failure to cooperate with how this whole machine works."

"Ouch."

I sighed. This was so much harder from across an ocean.

"I'm sorry, it's just... You're being awfully cavalier about something that affects my career, too. Just because my name isn't in the tabloids—yet—doesn't mean it isn't on the line."

"You're right," said Archie, his voice softened. "I'm sorry. You're right."

"This is going to blow up, Archie." My voice cracked. "It's going to be bad."

We sat in silence for a moment.

"Okay, so what do we do?" Archie asked.

"Damage control, mostly," I said, letting my mind open up to all the possible (and maybe probable) disaster scenarios. This would be so much easier if I were looking at his face. "We set aside whatever ideas we had about... this."

"Rose—"

"It's fine, Archie." It wasn't fine, not for me, but Archie and I hadn't exactly committed to each other. The chances of this become a bona fide *thing* were looking slimmer and slimmer, and if it was going to be squashed I'd rather it be on my terms than on his or, worse, the media's. This was the smart thing to do.

"Is that what you want?" asked Archie.

"It's what we need to do," I said. My heart ached. "That night was fun. But it would be silly to pretend it could've been more than it was."

Archie paused. "Right."

"Listen, I've got a lot more calls to make. I'll email soon with action items." I winced at the coldness of the corporate-speak. "Just. Try not to let this ruin your trip home, Archie. And *please* try not to comment on it."

"Roger that," he said. "No tweets, no grams, no carrier pigeons."

I smiled, said good-bye, and immediately missed him. Luckily I had plenty of work to keep my mind busy.

# 19.

WHEN 2:00 (EST) ARRIVED, I noted the time, but did not go looking for the photos. Part of me hoped that if I didn't actually *see* them online, they weren't there, but I was only able to maintain the delusion until 2:17, when a chat box appeared at the bottom of my screen. It was Ryan.

`Can you come to my office?`

Even though I'd known it was coming, and had had nearly six hours to prepare, I still felt like I might throw up. I took a few deep breaths and typed back: `Be right there.`

When I opened Ryan's door, I saw that Joanna was already inside, sitting in one of the two chairs that faced his desk. It was a relief, at least, to do this in closed quarters, without the rest of the firm there to witness it, though surely they'd find out soon, if they hadn't already. Still, that relief was pretty small and forgotten as soon as Ryan turned his computer monitor around so Joanna and I could see it.

There they were again, this time in bright, over-saturated color, with little zoomed-in insets presented for their damning, grainy detail. As my eyes ran over the shot of us kissing, my arms broke out in goose bumps. Above the trio of pictures, a headline blazed in red capital letters—ARCHIE FOX: CHEATING ON GIRLFRIEND RAYA WITH MYSTERY BRUNETTE? I glanced at Joanna, who stared back at me, unblinking.

"I would ask you to explain," said Ryan, "but I suppose it's self-explanatory. He's Archie Fox and you're a twenty-four-year-old woman. Which, frankly, was my main objection to your handling this in the first place."

"I'm twenty-six," I said. I knew it wouldn't help my standing in Ryan's eyes to correct him, but I didn't like the implication he'd made: that I was nothing more than a silly girl, and a slutty one to boot.

"Two years' less excuse, then," he said.

"Ryan," interjected Joanna. "Let's not make this about something it isn't."

"I'm sorry," said Ryan. "I thought this was about one of our publicists fucking her client. Is that not what it's about?"

"Yes and no," Joanna replied as I looked down at my lap, wanting to evaporate into the air. "What matters most are those photos. And what people think of those photos."

"So it doesn't matter if she fucked a client if Archie's fans think they're cute together?"

"It matters," said Joanna. "Rose's actions were grievously unprofessional, and far out of step from the otherwise top-grade work she's done for this project."

"Oh, well, since she did such a *great job* before she got down on her knees like a groupie, everything's totally cool."

"That's not—" I started, but Joanna held up her hand, silencing me.

"Don't respond to that," she said. To Ryan, she said, "Let's drop the Howard Stern act, shall we?"

"I'm just stating the obvious."

"What you're doing is brushing up against a line you don't want to cross."

For a moment they just glowered at each other. I was sure I'd never felt so tense in all my life.

"Rose?" said Ryan. "Do you have anything to say?"

I paused to think, unsure how much I should grovel, and unwilling to say the words "I'm sorry" aloud to Ryan. "This is not something I set out to do, and it's not representative of my work ethic, or my determination to do this job well," I finally said.

"You don't really get to decide whether it's representative or not," said Ryan. I swallowed hard; he might be an asshole, but he was right about that.

"I will fix this," I said. "I'm not going to let this undo what I've done for this project so far."

Ryan laughed bitterly. "You think you're staying on this project? After this?"

"Ryan," said Joanna, "we discussed this." It was only then I realized, *duh*, they'd been sitting in this office talking about me (and my fate) before I came in.

"And I still don't agree with you."

"Well, it doesn't really matter if you don't," said Joanna. "Maria still wants her."

"What?" said Ryan and I, in unison. I'd emailed Maria this morning, immediately after seeing the photos, but she hadn't responded to me; between the stress of talking to Archie himself and waiting for the photos' release, I'd forgotten that I still hadn't heard from her. Apparently she *had* gotten my email, but had talked to Joanna about it instead of me. Not that I could really blame her.

"I talked to her this morning," said Joanna, "I told her I thought that the only person who could possibly get Archie out of this mess was the person who got him in it, and she agreed."

I stared at Joanna, trying to read her face for further information; there was *no way* it could have been that simple a conversation. Maria Bird wasn't exactly known for being eager to forgive. I desperately wanted to have heard their conversation, to have heard Joanna make the case for me. Of course, I would sooner die than ask her for more information right now.

"Really," said Ryan, but it wasn't a question. "And I suppose I'm meant to just take your word on that."

"Unless you'd like to bother one of our most prestigious clients' managers by calling her up and explaining to her why my word wasn't good enough for you, yes, I do." Joanna's eyes were so narrow you could barely see anything but the black of her pupils. Even though I wasn't the one on the receiving end of her stare, I was close enough to feel its intensity secondhand. Ryan's jaw twitched.

"Fine," he said. Eventually, he looked at me. "You get one week. I don't give a shit what Maria says. If you haven't turned this into roses and fucking rainbows by next Monday, I'm putting Keiran on it, and Maria will deal with it."

Under normal circumstances, I was certain Joanna would have argued with him. To say Maria's preference didn't matter was simply ludicrous; it was she, more than anyone, who could make or break the firm's relationship with Archie. But then, what any given client thought of Weaver-Girard wouldn't matter so much to Joanna after Friday. And that's when I realized it: *She's planning to take Archie with her.* With—I hoped, I prayed—*us.*

So, by way of reply, Joanna simply looked at me. I looked at her, and then at Ryan, and then back at her. "Thank you for giving me a second shot," I said. "You won't regret it." She nodded curtly, and Ryan cleared his throat.

"All right," he said. "Better get to it, then."

With that, I got up and walked out of Ryan's office. As soon as I was outside the door I rushed down the hall to the bathroom, and once I'd established it was empty, I threw up.

When I reentered the cubicle, Harper whirled around in her chair to face me.

"I wasn't even doing anything," she said. "I was too nervous to work. I've just been typing gibberish into a Word document."

"Well, I still have my job," I said. "At least for one more week."

"What does that mean?"

"Ryan gave me an ultimatum, basically," I said. "But the only reason I'm even getting that week is Joanna."

"So he doesn't know?" she whispered. I had, of course, told her about Joanna's plans as soon as she got into the office. She'd listened to my entire recap of our clandestine breakfast with a hand clamped over her mouth.

"No."

"Wow. He's going to lose his mind."

"I know."

"*Sooo* glad I get to be here for that." Harper rolled her eyes, but there was an ounce of something beyond sarcasm in her tone—sadness, or anger maybe. I was ashamed to admit it, but I hadn't thought about the fact that leaving the company would also mean leaving Harper behind until I'd told her Joanna's plan. And the truth was, if our situation had been reversed, I would have been devastated, and more than a little resentful. Harper, always the less selfish and more Zen between us, had responded with nothing other than shock and support. If she were wounded by this (potential) turn of events, she was keeping it to herself. "Anyway," she continued. "What are you going to do?"

"Well, the first thing I have to do is talk to Raya." Immediately after contacting Maria, I'd emailed Pilar, who'd responded in a way that was somehow polite and hysterical at once. She'd gotten in touch with Raya, who agreed they could take a brief break from her vocal lessons to take a Skype call with me this afternoon. I looked at the clock—I had to call her in eleven minutes.

"God," said Harper. "Good luck with that."

"Harper!"

"I mean, it'll be *fine*. What's she gonna do to you over Skype?"

"I don't know," I said. "She's very intimidating for a twenty-year-old."

"She has her entire career ahead of her," offered Harper. "This is just an extremely exciting start for her."

"You're right," I said. "Actually—okay, that gives me an idea. Thank you." I leapt out of my chair and picked up my laptop to take into the conference room.

"What is it? What did I say?"

"I'll let you know after if it's gonna work," I said. "I gotta go call her!"

Harper groaned, and for the second time that day I found myself legitimately running down the hall.

I set up quickly and took the remaining four minutes to write a few notes out on a legal pad. At 4:00 p.m. exactly, I pressed CALL.

The computer chimed, teasing me with its bubbly tones while I indulged a faint hope that Raya just wouldn't answer, that I could avoid actually facing the consequences, that, miraculously, the whole debacle would just dissolve. But then her face popped up.

"Hi, Raya!" I said with too much energy. Raya appeared unmoved. Her hair—now more purple than red—was tangled and askew, but somehow it appeared intentionally so. Her eyes were heavily lined, and her lips painted black. She held a glass travel mug in front of her, tea tag hanging out, so that her now-manicured nails were on display, the dark maroon accenting the black and blue stars tattooed between her knuckles.

"Hey, Rose," she said, her voice slightly husky, as if just coming back from a cold. "Gimme one sec, P's calling in."

I jammed my shaky hands under my thighs. Pilar hadn't explicitly mentioned she'd be in on the call, though it wasn't surprising news. I just hated group calls—everyone talking over everyone else, one person's connection lagging after another. It was an added stress to an already-awkward situation.

Pilar's tiny face appeared and froze in the corner of my screen. "Hey, girls," she said, her mouth failing to keep up with her words. "Don't mind me, just here to keep track of everything. Rose, Ray is up to date on . . . the situation."

My eyes shot to Raya, but she made no move to speak. *The "situation"?* That made it seem like more than what it was—three completely contextless photos and a tornado of conjecture surrounding them. Anyone who'd opened a laptop, flipped on a TV, or turned on their phone was technically up to date.

"Right," I said, not sure if it would be polite or presumptuous to apologize. To say I was sorry would be to assume Raya had developed feelings for Archie, despite the fact that she'd adamantly denied her interest in doing so, and to suggest I had the power to *hurt* her. It was a suggestion that, from my vantage point, seemed somehow absurd. Part of Raya's whole thing was an appearance of invulnerability. I knew this was branding, but it was a brand well packaged and sold. I went in with baby steps. "So, how are you... feeling about everything?"

Raya lifted her eyebrows as she raised her tea to her lips. She took a long sip. "You mean about the fact that you made out with my boyfriend?"

I felt my chest tighten and my mouth go dry. *Okay. Everything's fine. I'm probably just having a heart attack.*

"Raya, I—"

But Raya interrupted me with a burst of laughter. "I'm kidding, dumb-ass!"

"Raya." Now it was Pilar's turn to interrupt.

Raya held up her hand in defeat. "I'm sorry, I'm sorry. Mom hates it when I swear."

I made out a tiny eye roll in the corner of my screen. My pulse returned to normal, and Raya's eyes were smiling behind her mug.

"Shit, Rose, your face though," she said, drawing in another sip. "I think you became a ghost for a sec."

I tried not to be angry. It wasn't the most professional move on her part, but then again she wasn't technically my client, she was six years my junior, and also, I *had* made out with her boyfriend. Sort of.

"So... you're not upset," I said, more of a statement than a question.

"Oh my God, no," said Raya. "I mean, it would've been nice to know before the rest of the world, but to be honest, I sort of did." Her face went serious, her eyes narrowed. "I'm incredibly intuitive about these things; I'm always the one who knows people are into each other before they actually know it, and then they tell me, and I'm like, *Uh, yeah, duh.*"

I, miraculously, held back my own eye roll.

"You guys just have an energy," she continued. "Plus, he was always talking about you."

I bit down on my lip to try to contain my smile, but the effort was unsuccessful.

"Shut up, you guys are too gross," said Raya, her smile belying her irony. "Anyway, the way I see it, this does me more good than harm—now I can write a bunch of nasty breakup songs and people will assume they're about how good-boy Archie brutally betrayed me. I've been looking for an excuse to record some angry tracks."

My brain recalibrated—it was a lot to go through in a span of about two minutes—and I fell back into publicist mode.

"That's actually what I wanted to talk about."

I launched into what I envisioned for the following week: First, both Raya and Archie would indirectly comment on the photos via some vague tweets (*Don't believe everything you read*, et cetera). Since the pair had never officially confirmed being together, a formal-sounding statement about the possibility of their *not* being together would read too clearly as damage control, even though that was exactly what it was. (No one ever wanted to be told *exactly* what was going on. If they did, I wouldn't have a job.) Instead, they would tease the relationship while throwing in clues designed to complicate the assumption that it was a romantic one. Raya would #tbt a photo of Archie from the hotel room where they'd been working on music together (luckily, being twenty, she was already in the habit of documenting *everything*), with a playful caption telling fans to stay tuned. Archie would retweet video clips from Raya's show with words of encouragement. Then, days later, he would "leak" a ten-second raw clip of the track, no vocals, no elaboration. Most important, we'd divert the attention from me.

This would leave no question in the fan base's mind that the two remained on positive terms, and while some would maintain that the pair were still a couple, many would make the leap to perceiving their relationship as more of a collaborative, professional friendship. As we intended. Then, while working up enough mystery to keep everyone furiously guessing, we'd schedule an appearance for both of them on Kimmel on Friday, where they would announce their collaboration and play an acoustic version.

Pilar was in the corner furiously jotting down notes. It was a lot to throw at them, and it was all dependent on Archie going along with it—I'd emailed him the defensive part of the plan, but not the offense: the collaboration, the leak, the performance—but I didn't have time to even entertain the possibility of this plan not working. He'd go along with it. He'd have to.

"Did you get all that?" I asked, letting out a deep breath. "How do you feel about it?"

Raya nodded slowly. "I like it. I mean, the song is still a little unfinished at the moment, but we can pull it off unplugged for sure. Archie on guitar, I could do a standing drum. Although, I wonder if Rick would be available for keys..."

I could see Raya getting away from me, but I needed one more confirmation before she signed off completely.

"Okay, so Pilar, I'll email you with details on Friday, just keep it clear on her schedule. And Raya, one more thing—it's going to have to become very clear on Friday that you guys were never romantically involved, that you feel more like brother and sister, and that the very idea of it borders on disgusting for you. Okay? So, no revenge fantasy songs. At least not in the near future."

"Ugh, fine. No euphemistic fox-hunting imagery. Got it." She paused. "So are you guys, like, a thing now? When do you go public?"

I winced. "Um, I don't know. *We* don't know. It's hard. I'm a 'mysterious brunette,' you know? It's a tough sell to a bunch of fans who are already notoriously judgmental." I paused briefly, wondering why I'd said all that to her. And finally, the dread I'd felt underlying this roller coaster of a morning began to sink in: This kind of thing—someone like Archie with someone like me—just didn't happen. "Anyway, it's not the priority right now."

Raya's face went solemn. "But that isn't your truth, Rose. Leave it behind. You have to follow *your truth*." She looked deeply into my eyes—at least, as deeply as possible over Skype—and I nodded in a way that I hoped suggested deep consideration. I thanked her and Pilar and signed off.

It was a sweet, vaguely meaningless sentiment, the kind of honeyed affirmation that populated Raya's Instagram and Tumblr, usually spelled out in looped fonts over images of mountains, or bouquets in pristine vases, or a perfectly disarrayed bed filled with old books. I believed that she believed it, that she thought something could be as simple as two people wanting to be together and then just *being together*, but I knew better than to believe it myself. I opened up my calendar and booked the conference room for the rest of the day. I had a lot of work ahead of me, and I needed to do it alone.

# 20.

I SPENT THE FOLLOWING FOUR days in a work-fueled blackout. Each morning I arrived at the office no later than 8:00 a.m. and left no earlier than 8:00 at night. It wasn't so much there was *that* much more work to do, though I certainly had a lot. In the past I might have been able to pretend otherwise, but no longer could I trick myself into thinking my workaholism was coincidental; I knew it was all I could do to push aside thoughts of Archie. I'd even made Harper do a SoulCycle class with me, just to force myself outside my own brain for an hour and a half (the class itself, plus half an hour for Harper to complain about the overly peppy teacher). After the photos spread into the wild, theories about my identity ran rampant. *People* found a "close friend of Raya" who IDed me as Archie's personal trainer (which literally made me laugh out loud) and insisted Raya was "absolutely heartbroken," while TMZ's source claimed I was just one of many groupies Archie was cycling through on the side. I thought I was in the clear for a miraculous forty-eight hours—until a C-list, one-man gossip blog called Jimmy Kartrashian ran my name on Wednesday morning.

EXCLUSIVE! ARCHIE FOX GETTING PRIVATE WITH HIS PUBLICIST?

Well, this is disappointing.

Rumors have been flying since Monday about the mystery woman seen swapping saliva with Archie Fox in New York City, but Jimmy Kartrashian's anonymous tipster confirms she's no one to get excited about. The woman is one Rose Reed, a lowly associate at PR firm Weaver-Girard, and apparently, she's been trying to make this happen for months.

"Rose practically forced herself into this role, since she's basically an assistant," says a colleague who requested anonymity. "*Everyone* has noticed the way she just lusts after him. It's sad, honestly."

Sad indeed, especially since it doesn't look to have changed anything with Raya—the two have been swapping flirty tweets and gramming intimate photos. Maybe all's forgiven? Either way, Archie, if you're into regulars now, give me a call.

I read the story—and then again, and again—before even leaving my bed. I opened up a text to Harper, then changed my mind and scrolled up to Archie, then gave up and threw my phone across the room. I was so angry I couldn't think straight. I had a fair idea of who this "anonymous tipster" was—"Basically an assistant"? "*It's sad*"? The whole pathetic pile of garbage had Sam's name written all over it, and I was certain everyone else in the office would recognize it, too—but I also knew the blame would still land solely on me. Even though Sam would've known all too well that he was blemishing the firm's name while dragging me through the mud, the scoop itself wasn't a lie.

Luckily, the blog was small enough for its post to go relatively unnoticed—especially because no follow-up photos had emerged, Raya and Archie were getting along swimmingly, and bigger rags were still churning out bad tips, anyway. There were plenty of sexier fabrications out there than Archie sleeping with a nobody—including the utterly absurd fan favorite: that I was Chloe Tan's less hot younger sister—and those were the stories that were selling, regardless of how improbable they were. Still, it was only a matter of time before my name was confirmed, especially if Archie and I wanted to see each other again (*Would we?* I wondered, and then pushed the question to the deep recesses of my brain). I, more than most people, knew what that meant—paparazzi photos, tireless scrutiny, ruthless dissection of every bit of my public persona.

So I distracted myself, and the rest of the Raychie fandom, by preserving the relationship I'd worked so hard to build. By Thursday, all of the necessary social media posts were up, and fans were eating it up; Raya's Instagram photo of Archie in the hotel room was shared so widely and swiftly that I'd abandoned any attempt at tracking it in real time. When Archie flew to LA on Thursday afternoon to prepare for Friday's appearance, the paps knew exactly where to find him and Raya rehearsing. Then, the coup de grâce: at 12:01 a.m. Friday, a commentary-less tweet from Archie's account, linking to a ten-second tease of a SoundCloud clip, followed by radio silence. By the time I arrived at the office that morning, it had already been covered—with tempered to overwhelming excitement—by Pitchfork, Vulture, MTV, and a smattering of blogs.

At this point, there wasn't much left to do but wait. Which wasn't especially easy, since our communication had been minimal after I first told Archie of the plan. This was partly because of my own slightly masochistic, forced emotional distance, but then, when I'd texted him after my name came out and received back a polite but terse, `Sorry to hear that, hope you're hanging in there`, I couldn't tell if he was pulling back of his own volition or just following my lead. I responded by pulling back even more, and had dealt primarily with Maria ever since. If there was one thing I hated, it was a lack of control. And now, with the plan set up and out of my hands, every aspect of my future felt alarmingly precarious.

From a professional standpoint, it appeared the situation was successfully spun. Which was great, except for the fact that such a success would tear down a significant barrier between me and Archie, only to lead to a new one. If the fans welcomed and believed in Raychie-as-collaborators (even if some still shipped them), then the door was open to introduce a different relationship. And that new woman—no matter how much Archie actually cared about her, or not—would have to be packaged flawlessly. And how could any amount of PR savvy get me to Archie-worthy flawless? How much did it matter if *he* thought of me that way, and I thought of myself that way, if, every day on the Internet, hundreds of thousands of strangers wrote Tumblr posts wondering what he could possibly see in me, and posted unflattering pictures of me on Instagram with hilariously cruel captions, and tweeted *kill yourself u ugly bitch* at me? I cycled through well-known examples of fans turning on their idols' significant others—Lorde and her photographer boyfriend, Robert Pattinson and FKA Twigs, and so on—and tortured myself by consuming as many vicious comments as I could stomach. How could it possibly be worth it?

For what felt like the six hundredth time that week, I picked up my phone and held my thumb over Archie's name. It was a little after 6:00, which meant that it was 3:00 in Los Angeles. I knew he'd finished filming about an hour ago, when Jacob—a rep from our LA office who'd been assigned to attend the show with Archie, as I had been deemed *unfit*—emailed Joanna and me a photo of him and Raya on stage with a thumbs-up emoji. There was a decent chance Archie was still at dinner with a friend, or celebratory drinks with Raya, but I was so worked up, and so upset, and so sick of *not* calling him when I wanted to call him, that I decided I didn't care what he was doing. Maybe I was a "regular," but he could take the time to talk to me about my stupid regular-person feelings. I pressed his name and held the phone to my ear, and then I waited. But his phone didn't even ring, instead going straight to voicemail. It was automated (obviously Archie Fox couldn't identify himself and thus confirm his telephone number), so I didn't even get the comfort of hearing his voice. When the beep came I realized I had no idea what to say; certainly nothing that could be effectively summarized in a thirty-second voicemail. So I hung up.

*Why is his phone off?* I wondered. Or was it actually on, but he silenced it so fast upon seeing my name that I only *thought* it was off? He hadn't tried to get in touch with me since the texts on Tuesday; suddenly my decision to maintain a cool, professional distance in the time between then and now seemed completely idiotic. I knew he was still alive as of an hour ago, but now? What if he had died? Or worse—what if he was still alive but had completely lost interest in me, both professionally and... otherwise?

I took a deep breath, closed my eyes, and told myself: *Archie is not dead, and you are thinking like a crazy person.* Probably he was out to dinner and turned off his phone to be polite. Maybe he was asleep, because he got up at 5:00 a.m. to rehearse with Raya before the taping. Maybe he was fucking somebody else. *No!* I scolded myself. *You stop that right now. Breathe. Inhale, exhale. Inhale—*

"What...are you doing?" Harper's voice broke through my thoughts, and I turned to face her. "You sound like my dog right before he throws up."

"Sorry," I said. "I was trying to calm myself with deep-breathing techniques."

"Did it work?"

"No."

"What is it?"

"I just tried to call him and his phone was off. Apparently."

"That doesn't mean anything," said Harper.

"Well. Maybe."

"It doesn't. Don't go off on some spiral over this, okay?"

"It is much too late for that," I said, feeling annoyed. Admittedly, I'd been a nervous wreck for much of the week, and yes, Harper had borne the brunt of my anxious energy. And yes, she'd been pretty patient during my many apocalyptic lunchtime predictions of how badly the week might turn out, and how I would be fired, and how I would have to leave New York, and how when I moved back home to San Francisco my parents would be too ashamed of me to let me stay with them while I looked for a new job, and how I would be forced to sleep on the living room couch of Dave and the new wife he'd have met and married within six months, because I didn't have any friends left who lived there, and I would be so badly off that even his wife would take pity on me, and would love him all the more for being so charitable. But still.

"Rose," she said. "Everything is going to be okay." She was trying to be patient, I knew, but she also said it in a tone that very much meant *I have said this sentence to you fifty or so times already this week.*

"You don't *know* that!" I snapped.

Harper looked at her watch and sighed. "You're right," she said. "I don't. Probably better to assume the worst." She got up from her chair and started packing up her things.

"Wait," I said, but it was a halfhearted protest. Still, she paused at the door.

"You know, you haven't asked me anything about *my* life in, like, two weeks."

My face burned. "I'm really sorry, Harper," I said. She was right; I'd fallen into a deep, deep well of self-involvement and pity.

She shrugged. "It's close enough to six for me. I'm going home. And you should, too."

"I'll leave soon," I replied, and she nodded and walked away.

On my way out twenty or so minutes later, I stopped by Joanna's office to see if she was still in. Her door was closed, but I could see the light from her desk lamp shining out from beneath it. I hesitated, not sure what, if anything, I wanted to say to her. Until tonight's show aired, and until we could analyze how the public's response unfolded over the weekend, I knew there was nothing she could say to reassure me. Either my plan would work well enough to satisfy her, or it wouldn't. I could be sure, though, that if the results weren't good enough for Joanna, they wouldn't be good enough for Ryan. It was obvious he was champing at the bit to get rid of me. If I didn't have a job with Joanna by next Tuesday, I didn't have a job at all.

Just when I'd made the decision to head for the doors, Sam rounded the corner. Seeing me, he came to a stop.

"Rose," he said. He seemed startled, but quickly recovered his default smirk. "Heading out so soon?" Sam stuck his hands into his pockets and leaned up against the wall on the other side of Joanna's door. I couldn't help but feel that he'd wanted her to hear him—to note that I was leaving the office only a few minutes after hours and question my dedication.

"We can't *all* have your work ethic, Sam," I said, affecting a simpering tone.

He chuckled; my sarcasm had gone completely unregistered. "Well," he said. "You've had a rough week."

"Oh, I don't know about that," I said. "I'm *basically* just an assistant."

Sam just stared at me for a moment, and I stared right back. Finally, he cleared his throat. "Well," he said. "Have a good weekend."

"You too, Sam!" I chirped. I shifted my purse to head out, and when I walked past, I patted him—hard—on the arm.

# 21.

THE SECOND I GOT ON the train, I collapsed into a corner seat, letting weeks of built-up tears pour out. *How did I end up here?* A few weeks ago I was thriving, tasked with the biggest—and most promising—undertaking of my life; today, my best friendship was strained, my career was in jeopardy, and the guy I'd risked it all for was currently MIA. I let my mind wander into exercises of magical thinking, bargaining with some vague, omniscient entity. What would I give for a RESET button? And if I were miraculously granted such a thing, how would I undo whatever had gotten me into this mess?

I jumped back to that morning in the conference room, the first time I'd seen Archie in person, remembered the electric charge I'd felt instantaneously. I dulled its edges in memory and traveled forward. The clothes shopping—I wouldn't have lingered on that first time I made him laugh; when he'd asked me to lunch after Fawn, I would've respectfully declined. I'd have suggested an alternative setting for my and Neil's first date; I would've never taken a call late at night, on my floor, feeling hopeful; I would've left Philadelphia right after his show. I would've kept up a wall; I would've talked myself down; I would've reminded myself I was one of millions who'd fallen under his spell. I wouldn't have envisioned a future with a person who practically lived in another reality.

But then, Kao. No matter how many iterations of this mind game I played, each time I got to Kao my efforts were stymied. I could fool myself to an extent, but not once I got to that kiss, or later to my apartment. I could try to pretend I'd go back and change everything to avoid how terrible I felt right now, crying in public, not sure of anything, but all I had to do was place myself back in that bed, in his arms, and I knew I was full of shit. Some mistakes were worth making. And if this whole situation did indeed turn out to be a mistake, I thought, it would be one of them.

I jolted to attention when I heard the conductor announce Seventh Avenue, wiped the tears and smudged mascara from my cheeks, and dashed out. I ducked into my favorite sushi spot and turned my mind to other, pleasant, non-Archie topics: the name of my future hypothetical dog, the spicy tuna that would soon be in my mouth, my planned Coney Island excursion with Harper next weekend. Shit. Harper. The image of her face in our last conversation—not even anger, but a resigned disappointment—leapt to the forefront of my mind, and my stomach tensed. I hated when we disagreed about where to get lunch; this was almost unbearable. As I walked in the front door of my apartment, I pulled out my phone.

Harper. I'm so sorry. I've been a terrible friend, but it's just been this, like, double whammy with Archie affecting work AND my love life, plus you know I'm just a mess with my love life in general.

I read it back before sending and held down the DELETE button. *Too many excuses.*

```
Harper. I'm so sorry. I've been a terrible
friend, and there's no excuse. I don't know
what else to say.
```

Sent. I threw my phone on the couch and then decided to do something I hadn't done since my last big heartbreak: I drew up a bath and tossed in some bubbles. I dragged one of the cheap side tables from the living room into the bathroom, set it next to the tub, and placed my sushi and a glass of wine on top of it. I tried—not entirely successfully—to avoid spilling either while I ate, but the bubbles quickly swallowed up the stray piece of rice or drop of wine. I tried to think of absolutely nothing. When I'd soaked to a sufficient level of wrinkliness, I let the water drain around me, and only when I was sitting naked in an empty tub did I actually get up. I tossed my slightly oily (but delightfully scented) hair up into a bun, threw my favorite sweatshirt (TURKEY TROT 2004, the collar and sleeves frayed) over some leggings, and posted up in front of the TV. I checked my phone—still no response. I flipped between a rerun of *Friends* and a real estate reality show, but I could just barely follow the saga of whichever couple was deciding whether or not low ceilings were a deal-breaker. My body was counting down the minutes to 11:35, regardless of what my mind wanted. And when the time came, my hand—clammy, slightly shaking—changed the channel as if by instinct.

I realized then that it'd be the first time I'd seen Archie—*really* seen him, talking, and smiling, and laughing—since our night together, and my stomach fluttered. I didn't feel ready. When Chelsey walked in halfway through the monologue and saw my face, she asked who'd died. I forced a laugh in response, but the confused look Chelsey threw me suggested it hadn't come out sounding quite as breezy as I'd hoped. I topped off my glass of wine, Chelsey disappeared into her room, and Jimmy Kimmel welcomed his first guest.

Under any other circumstance I would've been engrossed in the interview with Emma Watson; I would've probably gone out of my way to record it. It wasn't her fault I couldn't focus on one goddamn word. It seemed to have been a very charming interview, eliciting audience laughter that pierced my anxiety here and there. Then there was nothing but a bunch of commercials for toilet paper, and vitamins, and new jeans at Old Navy separating me from what I'd been waiting for. That's when it hit me: I wasn't just anxious about seeing Archie because of what it would do to me; I was nervous *for* him, because I knew what he had on the line. I wanted him to succeed, not because he was my client, but because he was Archie, someone whose emotions felt perilously close to my own.

When he strolled into view of the camera, I held my breath. He looked good. He looked happy. And when he walked across the stage, waving at the audience, it was hard not to feel like he was smiling straight at me. His hair was down and perfectly askew, and he was wearing a sheer black button-down (nearly halfway unbuttoned) over distressed, ripped-up black jeans and his now-famous sparkling ankle boots. He was alone for the interview portion, and he did everything right. When Jimmy asked about his rumored relationship with Raya he laughed readily—*Good*, I thought. *Doesn't seem defensive; clear he has a sense of humor about himself*—but also plainly denied it, and then he diverted the conversation to their collaboration. I hadn't been able to coach Archie in person, but it was clear he'd read and taken to heart the notes I'd emailed him: Plug the upcoming album (*check*), drop the word "sister" at least once when talking about Raya (*check*), thank the fans for their support (*check*), say that album name one more time for good measure (*check*), and when the photos of us inevitably came up, assert your bachelor status. I was still waiting on that one. I'd emphasized to Archie that this wasn't the time to announce a new development (I'd written and deleted *relationship* twice, ultimately deciding it was too presumptuous), and that baby steps here were key.

"Okay, dude, listen, I have to ask," Jimmy began, a sheepish grin spreading across his face as he held up the photo of us kissing in front of him. "Who's the mystery babe?"

Archie shifted in his seat, a crooked smile on his face. I inched toward the edge of the couch.

"Jimmy, you know I'm not going to answer that," said Archie. It wasn't exactly what I'd call an assertion, but it was enough to strike a little bit of fear into Jimmy.

"I'm sorry, I get it, but you know, had to ask." He chuckled.

"No worries. It's just, some things you want to keep for yourself, you know?"

My breath quickened.

"Well it sounds special, man, and I'm happy for you," said Jimmy, tossing the photo under the desk. Archie nodded and then, almost imperceptibly, winked at the camera. It felt like a punch to the gut. *What is he doing?*

"So, let's cut to the chase," continued Jimmy. "You've got a new song, and I gotta say, I listened to it at sound check and it's just—ah, man, it's *sick*."

"Oh, thank you." Archie shook his hair loose and then pushed it away from his face. It was a tell that I'd only recently figured out meant he was feeling uncomfortable—his infuriatingly sexy version of a nervous tic. "That's really kind."

"It's the truth! So you're gonna play for us—it's the first track off the upcoming album, yeah?"

"Yup." Again, the hair. "Just something Raya and I have been working on. Slightly different than each of our individual sounds, but it's just been a blast to put together."

"And a blast to hear. So you're gonna play—what's it called?"

" 'By Any Other Name.' "

I felt a lump rise in my throat. *Not that that title* means *anything*, I thought as Raya walked out on stage wearing a cropped white polo and high-waisted shorts, which, together with her hair and tattoos, created an image of the coolest bad girl at Wimbledon. Archie and Raya hugged, and the crowd applauded wildly. *It could be a reference to literally anything*, I thought, watching them move into place behind their mikes, which, as instructed, were positioned close together but not *too* close. The only reason my heart was pounding was definitely because I wanted him to do well for his own sake.

But then, the guitarist started playing—we'd decided to use the show's band, leaving Archie free to full-on croon at the mike. It was the song Raya had played me in her studio, only brought more fully to life, the soft heartbeat of it murmuring throughout the show's set. It sounded even more amazing than

I remembered. Then Archie started to sing. I watched his face so intently that his verse was over before I could absorb any of it, and then Raya came in. When she sang, she sang to the crowd, and when the camera panned to him, he was watching her—smilingly, but not adoringly. Soon she stopped, and the guitar led into the bridge, and I refocused, listening carefully as Archie sang:

*By any other name*
*we might be sweet but not the same*
*No other smile I need*
*No other voice I crave*

*By any other name*
*it might be simpler, but then again*
*I wouldn't have it any other way*
*My rose, I hope you stay*

My phone rang immediately, and Harper's face lit up the screen. I answered to high-pitched screaming ("OH MY GOD OH MY GOD OH MY GOD"), which I overlapped with shouting of my own ("I KNOW I KNOW I KNOW") until the instrumental interlude ended and we went silent in anticipation of the next verse.

"What's going on?" Chelsey emerged from her room, following my gaze to the TV. "Oh hey! It's your dude!" She watched, listened. I was frozen doing the same. Then Archie sang the chorus again. "Ha!" Chelsey laughed. "'My rose'! Like you!" She looked at me, then stopped. "Wait," she said. "... Wait."

"It might not be—"

"*Holyyyy shit!*" Harper resumed her shrieking from somewhere across town. I put her on speaker and placed the phone on the table.

"It's not exactly an uncommon metaphor," I said, trying to dissuade myself as much as I was her. Our eyes remained glued to the screen, watching as Archie and Raya sang the final harmony. As the audience started clapping, and Archie and Raya each nodded their thanks, Jimmy joined them on stage.

"That was fantastic," he said. "That was 'By Any Other Name,' the lead single off *Back to You*, out October fifth. Archie, Raya, thank you both!" They shook Jimmy's hand and murmured their appreciation, and then, just before the show cut to commercial, Archie looked directly into the camera. I knew it was a little silly to think so, given the fact that he was on TV—and across the country, no less—but I felt certain, in that moment, that he was looking at me. And I decided to stop telling myself that everything I'd felt until that moment couldn't be true, or amount to anything more than that one night; I wasn't crazy to think that when he sang the words "my rose," he meant me.

"Damn," said Chelsey. "He is hot as fuck."

"He really is," Harper chimed in, reminding me she was still, sort of, in the room. At this point, my brain couldn't keep up. I grabbed the phone. Chelsey's eyes remained glued on the screen as Archie charmed the crowd while the credits rolled.

"Harper, you got my text, right? Are we... okay?"

"Jesus, Rose, of course we're okay. I mean, yes, you were being totally self-absorbed, and yes, you're lucky I'm the most gracious best friend in the world, but we can deal with that later and celebrate the fact that a pop star just proclaimed his love for you on national television."

I tried, unsuccessfully, to hold back a smile. "No, he didn't."

"Yes, he did."

It struck me then what I had to do.

"Harper, I don't deserve you. I have to go."

"Good, because I'm actually on a date."

"Harper!"

She laughed and hung up. I dropped the phone on the couch and opened an email to Archie on my laptop, typing out frantically:

> Archie—just saw the show. The song was incredible. You were incredible. The night we had was incredible. I'm sure I knew other adjectives at some point in my life but I don't remember them right now. I just wanted to say that I want you. There is so much else that's up in the air but this is what I am sure of. I'm sorry for emailing this to you in the middle of the night but it feels like I've been waiting ages to say it and I couldn't wait any longer.
>
> It's true what you said: I'm yours.
>
> —Rose

Just as I hit SEND, the apartment buzzer went off.

"Chelsey," I said. She'd just gone back into her room, and now poked her head around the open doorway.

"What?"

"Your boyfriend's here."

"Oh!" She got up and walked into the living room, but stopped next to the refrigerator. "Wait," she said. "Jay's not coming over, I just left *his* place."

"Oh. Huh." We both paused, and then the buzzer went off again.

She walked the rest of the way to it and pressed UNLOCK without picking up the phone.

"Chelsey!"

"What?"

"You don't think you should ask who's there that wants to come into our building at one a.m.? You probably just let in a murderer."

"Oh my God." She pressed her hands to her cheeks. "What if it's the Zodiac? They never caught him."

"Are you high?"

"Yes! I'm sorry! I didn't mean to get us killed!"

I couldn't help but laugh at her deeply concerned expression. "It's okay," I said. "Someone's booty call probably just pressed the wrong apartment number. And our door is locked."

"Should we make a barricade?"

"I think it's okay." I settled back onto the couch, but Chelsey remained still, hovering by the door. "Chelsey. Really."

Just then we heard footsteps coming up the stairs, and Chelsey whipped around to look at me, her red-rimmed eyes wide. "*It's him*," she whispered.

"There are eight apartments on this floor," I whispered back. Still, though, I felt slightly uneasy. And then whoever it was stopped walking.

And then our doorbell rang. Chelsey screamed and sprinted

to her room, pulling her door closed hard behind her, and I leapt up from the couch.

"*Are you serious?*" I hissed. I tried to pretend I was more annoyed with Chelsey for abandoning me than I was afraid; I thought, *If it's Jay standing out there, I am going to throw a fit.* I tiptoed over to the door and, as slowly and silently as possible, looked through the peephole and gasped.

It was not Jay who stood on the other side, nor was it (presumably) the Zodiac Killer, but Archie Fox, leaning toward the peephole as if he, too, could see through to the other side.

"I can see the shadows from your little feet," he said.

I unhooked the chain and swung open the door.

"Who is it?" came Chelsey's muffled scream.

"It's...Archie," I said. He stood still in the doorway, and I stood still holding the doorknob, staring at him, as incapable of coming up with a lie that wouldn't draw Chelsey out of her room as I was at believing that it was really him. "Hi," I said.

"Hi."

Our silence was broken by Chelsey flinging open her door. "Hiiiii," she said. "We just watched you on TV!"

"Did you?" said Archie, and though he spoke to Chelsey, he didn't take his eyes off me.

"Sick song," she said.

"Thank you very much," said Archie.

Suddenly becoming aware that he was still standing in the doorway, I pulled it all the way open.

"I'm so sorry," I said. "Uh. Come in."

"Thanks." As he walked past me I shot a desperate look to Chelsey. Immediately, she grabbed a tote bag off the back of her door.

"Ahhh, okay," she said. "I think I'm actually gonna sleep at Jay's."

"You're sure?" I wanted her to go, of course, but I also knew she'd just come back from there, and I didn't want to be a bad roommate just because a pop superstar I was possibly in love with was in our living room.

"Yeah. My, uh, hairbrush is there. So."

"Would you like a ride?" asked Archie. "My driver's downstairs."

"Whoa," said Chelsey. "Um. Yeah, that would be awesome. Thank you."

"It's no problem, I'll let him know." Archie pulled out his phone and I inhaled sharply. Surely if he hadn't already seen my email, he would see it now. He looked at the screen for a moment, and then typed out a text. "You'll see him."

"Thanks!" She threw her bag over her shoulder and went to shake Archie's hand. "You're a good dude." He laughed. On her way out the door, after making sure Archie wasn't looking, she winked at me, and I said a silent thank-you to Craigslist, for finding me a roommate so noble as she was.

I locked the door behind her, and when I turned around Archie was there, standing in front of me, pressing me against the door, his breath warm on my face, and then his mouth on mine. I felt like my whole body sighed in relief, and I tightened my grasp around his back, trying to pull him even closer. But then I remembered what day it was, and where we were, and *who* we were, and I stopped.

"How?" I asked. His eyes didn't leave my mouth.

"How…?"

"How are you *here* when you were just... there?" I pointed at the TV. He raised an eyebrow and looked from my hand to the TV, and when he looked back, I saw dimples. I laughed. "You know what I mean."

"We taped early, and as soon as we were done, I jumped on a flight," he said.

"What about the rest of your vacation?"

"I'll have it here."

"What about Jacob?"

Archie broke out into a full-on grin. "I imagine he's learnt I'm not really using the toilets."

"Ohhhhh my *God*." I couldn't help but grin as well. I lifted my hands and pressed them against the soft T-shirt covering his chest, where I fixed my gaze, feeling in that moment that it was safer than looking at his face. "Okay, but, um. *Why* are you here?"

"Is that not rather obvious?"

"Maybe. I'm not sure," I said. "I want you to tell me, just in case."

Archie looked away and cleared his throat, then ran a hand through his hair. *He's nervous*, I realized. "I'm here," he said, "because I didn't want to wait another day to see you, much less four of them. I'm here because I had to know right away what you thought of the song, because you're brilliant, but also because your opinion of my music is probably the only one around me that I can really, truly trust. And I'm here because I wanted to tell you in person, as soon as possible, that that song was for you, because I knew that you'd be here, on your settee, finding some ludicrous reason to tell yourself that it wasn't, even though it so obviously was."

I laughed. I felt goose bumps on my arms and crossed them in front of me, but then Archie laughed, too, and unhooked them. I couldn't look away.

"I know this isn't what you had planned. And I know this makes things complicated, to put it mildly, at your job. The last thing I want to do is fuck that up. I think what you do is amazing. I wouldn't even be getting the kinds of calls I'm getting now without you. You've changed my life, Rose," he said. He paused. Still holding my hands, he placed them around his back and slid his own up from my wrists, to my shoulders, and finally to my face. "I don't know exactly how being together might change yours," he continued. "But if you feel the same way about me as I do you, then I think it's worth taking that risk. I don't know what people are going to say about any of this tomorrow, or the day after that, but I know that I want to be with you tonight, and tomorrow, and the day after that."

I put my hands around the back of his neck and then in his hair, and pulled his face to mine. "I want to be with you, too," I said. I looked into his eyes and saw the same thing I'd seen when watching him sing on TV. I hadn't imagined any of it. And while it was definitely crazy, and nearly impossible to believe, that didn't mean it wasn't all—amazingly—true.

---

ARCHIE AND HIS "ROSE": WE'RE DATING!!!!!

A rep from Archie Fox's team has confirmed that the British heartthrob is officially TAKEN. (Cue the sound of a million hearts breaking.) The lucky lady? Publicist Rose Reed—first identified by yours truly, ahem. The couple have been flaunting their new love all over town, and according to a close friend of Archie's, the singer has never been so happy.

"He's over the moon," the friend told us. "At his heart he's just such a real guy, a family man, wants to settle down—honestly, I'm so happy he's done messing around with the other drama queens."

Ouch!

As for his former rumored fling? A Raya contact insists she was burned by the blatant love song to another woman: "It was so cold, and Raya had no idea it was coming. She's trying to put on a brave face, but those of us who are close to her know how much it hurt."

Well, it certainly isn't showing—considering Raya was seen swapping saliva with model/DJ Kadia days later.

Ah, young love. We here at JK just hope these crazy kids find what they're looking for!!

# Epilogue

I TRIED NOT TO STARE at the clock. At 1:00 p.m., it had already been a long day—actually, it'd been six weeks of long days; it turns out starting up a new firm requires a lot of overtime—and I hadn't even had lunch yet. I glanced at the to-do list tucked away in the top corner of my monitor: email the agent at WME looking to sell Trevor James's life story, confirm Archie and Raya's appearance on *SNL*, call Mom. I tackled the quickest task (email, almost on autopilot) and then opened a new tab to browse what people were saying about Archie on Twitter.

Fan response had been pretty stellar since the performance, for the most part, and the subsequent release of the single resulted in it being the number one streaming song for six weeks. The past week, he'd done a stealth midnight drop of two more singles, both to overwhelmingly positive reviews.

While making the usual Internet rounds, I noticed a particularly amazing headline popping up a few times on my time line—WOULD EVERYONE STOP BEING A BUNCH OF IDIOTS AND JUST ADMIT ARCHIE FOX IS REALLY FUCKING GOOD?—and clicked through. It was a recent article, published just an hour prior on an indie music site called Tuner. I scanned through it, quickly realizing that it was the kind of article that, while *great* for us (new demographics!), was also mildly infuriating: *Oh, we can finally take this artist seriously now that a white male critic approves?* Still, the review had some stellar lines, and I grabbed a screenshot of one—"Archie's voice on the folk-pop anthem 'Brightest Light' is whiskey-tinged and gleeful and will make you believe, for three and a half glorious minutes, not that everything will be okay, but that everything *is already okay.*"—and tweeted it out with a link.

If the original goal of the entire Raya/Archie endeavor was to revamp Archie's fan base, there was no denying it had been a success, which was why I was even sitting in this expansive DUMBO office. Forever loyal to her word, Joanna had, with little ceremony, offered me the position she'd suggested at the morning meeting that felt so long ago now. The Monday after Archie's Kimmel performance, I'd found in my personal inbox a contract for my new role as junior media coordinator at the brand-new JG Publicity. The few times I ran into her that day we shared knowing smiles and furtive nods, and it felt exhilarating—even for such a brief period—to be two people in on a huge, life-changing secret.

Once that secret was out (by end of that same day), Joanna's departure wasn't nearly as messy as I'd feared it would be. Most of the conversations happened behind closed doors, and Ryan, who was essentially losing half of his clients, was way too proud to admit someone else, a woman no less, could damage his business. Both Joanna and I gave two weeks' notice to "ease the transition," but Ryan threw a fit at the prospect of my staying around, and neither of us thought it worthwhile to fight him on it. Joanna was another story; though he'd never admit it, he needed her, and, from what I heard, used those two weeks to fit in as much antagonistic favor-requesting as he could manage and she would allow. I was excited at the prospect of having a forced vacation, until my phone buzzed Tuesday morning with an email from Joanna giving me a list of current and potential clients to reach out to. My heart dropped when I noticed Archie's name was missing from the list until Joanna, after forwarding me an email from Maria congratulating her on the move, asked if I wanted to remain his publicist.

It was the very definition of mixing business and pleasure, the very thing adults universally warn against, and yet—who else would know the client better? Who else should reap the benefits of the work I'd done? And who, besides Joanna herself, could I trust to present *my* relationship without manipulating it? When I considered all that, it wasn't even a question. For better and for worse, this was the path I'd headed down the moment we first kissed. Maybe even earlier than that. So I'd been doing both in tandem, exploring a new relationship while engineering its reception by the fans. The hardest part thus far had been figuring out how to stay true to our own pace—how to move forward comfortably when millions of young girls were begging either for full-blown True Love (especially now that the people were running with the "settling down" theme) or a nasty breakup. It was more the former than the latter—apparently, seeing Archie Fox date a commoner had inspired a lot of hope that one day they, too, could meet a similar fate—but I was still thickening my skin against such soul-crushing criticisms as "she looks old as hell" and "her hair is so boring." There were worse things.

I looked at my phone—nearly 1:30, and my stomach felt like it was eating itself. I forced myself to shut my laptop, threw on a light jacket, and grabbed my bag. In the move, I'd upgraded to my own office (albeit an itty-bitty one), and though the view of the bridge from my window was pretty spectacular, I still found myself making excuses to work out in the trenches, mostly because that's where Harper was.

The morning after Archie surprised me at my door, I surprised him in turn by leaving him alone in my bed for an hour while I met up with Harper. I'd woken up at 7:00 on the dot, restless, exhilarated, incapable of holding back the goofiest of smiles every time I closed my eyes and reopened them to see Archie, asleep, lying next to me. I'd pulled my phone into bed and texted Harper on the off chance she'd be awake, too.

`Harper. I can't sleep. Archie is passed out next to me. Please tell me you're awake and down to grab some coffee.`

Her response came seconds later: `Hungry Ghost in 30?`

I slid out of bed, threw on jeans and a tee, and—when he stirred, half asleep—assured Archie that I'd be back in a bit. It felt a little crazy to leave my bed while he was in it, but in some ways his being there already felt comfortable, almost obvious. We'd spent most of the night fighting sleep with sex and conversation, and I woke up realizing the tension in the pit of my stomach wasn't about him anymore—it was about Harper. I knew our brief détente the night before wasn't enough to make the weeks of my ignoring her right, and I was desperate to just see her and talk.

We met at the café, equidistant from our apartments, and Harper managed to both beat me there *and* not look like she'd just rolled out of bed. I joined her at our usual table, in the far back corner where employees would be less inclined to kick us out or mean-mug us into buying a refill. Harper's eyebrows shot up to her forehead the second I sat down.

"So?"

I grinned. "So . . . it was a really good night."

She threw her head back and shrieked, causing the few other patrons, all serious and stern in front of their laptops, to turn and glare in our direction.

"Is he, like, your *boyfriend*?"

"I don't know!" I laughed. "I guess? Yeah. Yes. Archie Fox is my boyfriend."

Harper shook her head and took a sip from her latte. "Unreal."

My heart thumped in my chest—Harper was like a sister to me, but that fact didn't make uncomfortable conversations with her any less nerve racking.

"So, listen." I took in a deep breath. "I know I've been a jerk these past few weeks . . ."

I looked up at her; she didn't disagree.

"And I know you said we were fine last night, but it was kind of a chaotic moment and I wanted to make sure we were *really* fine."

She paused before answering. "We're always going to be fine, Rose. It's just—I'm not just your sidekick, you know?"

"Of course! I know."

"It doesn't really feel like you do, though. Not always."

"I'm so sorry, Harp," I said, tears welling up in my eyes. It didn't feel like enough, but I didn't know what else to say.

Harper grabbed my hand and smiled. "It's okay. This is a pretty unprecedentedly batshit-crazy situation you've found yourself in. And I'm so excited for you. Just don't forget to ask me about my little plebeian life, too."

So she filled me in for the next forty-five minutes—about the girl she'd been sort of seeing but who, she feared, was becoming a little too clingy; about the new unsolved mystery documentary on Netflix she was currently obsessed with; and about the fact that she'd been pumping up her résumé to send out for a job in her actual field.

"I just figured it's never going to be the exact right time," she said, "so why not just do it now?"

I told her to forward me a copy ("just in case anything comes up"), and when I emailed Joanna to formally respond to her job offer, I attached Harper's résumé. I suggested that hiring Harper as her in-house image consultant would set us apart from every other PR firm in the city, and insisted that if my work with Archie had earned me this offer, Harper was equally deserving of one, too, and I couldn't respond to my own until I knew Joanna agreed. Joanna's response was characteristically frightening ("You sure you want to put conditions on this offer, Rose? From the position you're in?"), but I stood by it, and no more than fifteen minutes later Harper called me, squealing about the email Joanna's assistant had just sent her.

---

I stopped by Harper's desk to see if she wanted anything while I was out. She was currently working on a red-carpet look for one of our newer clients, a sixteen-year-old country sweetheart, and images of off-white gauzy gowns were layered over each other on her monitor. She spun around in her chair before I'd even stopped walking.

"She booked a flight!" Harper squealed. I didn't have to ask who "she" was. Two weeks earlier, Raya—who, no, wasn't heartbroken or blindsided by the song she had co-written, and who'd since stopped kissing her DJ friend—had dropped by the new office to check in, and on her way out had bumped into Harper. I made the introduction, they'd promptly followed each other's various social media, and they'd been flirty-texting ever since. Last I'd checked, Harper was pleading for Raya to fly out and let Harper take her on a proper date; apparently, she'd finally conceded.

"Oh my God," I said. "When?"

"Next week!" Her eyes went wide. "Oh my God. I need to deliver on this. It has to be the best date she's literally ever been on. Should we go to Basile?" She laughed somewhat manically. "Is that crazy? That's crazy. Right?"

It was the first time I'd ever seen Harper as the nervous one in a courtship, and I took it as a good (and slightly comforting) sign. And the idea of double-dating with the two of them was almost too cute (weird, but cute) for me to handle. The press would have a field day.

My phone buzzed: `Downstairs.`

"I have to go," I said to Harper. "But, yes—do not go to Basile. That's super weird."

"You're right, you're right," she mumbled, spinning back to face her computer.

I opened a response to Archie.

`On my way down. How bad is it?`

`Eh. Worse than Roberta's, better than my place.`

Archie and I had taken to rating the sea of paparazzi and fans that often surround us by locale; so far, no crowd had been more persistent than the one that met us the morning after my first overnight stay at his apartment.

`Noted. How do you feel about sushi?`

I put on my sunglasses and stepped into the elevator.

`Mmmm...what about that new vegan spot we keep talking about?`
`Yesssssss.`

The elevator opened into the bright, marble lobby, and then I saw him—wearing a black Members Only jacket, skinny black jeans, and a gray beanie with spirals of hair peeking out. Seeing him still gave me butterflies. The feeling made me almost nauseous, but I hoped it would never stop. Beyond him, pushed up against the tall glass doors, waited about twenty fans and photographers, all of them eager for a selfie, or a comment, or that one big-money shot. I came up beside him and linked my arm in his.

He pushed the door open, and the chaos was immediate. I knew the drill—head down, small wave as the requests flooded in.

"Archie! Archie! Over here!"

"Is it true you've got a baby on the way?"

"Rose! Do you think Raya's new single 'The Other Girl' is about you?"

"Give us a kiss!"

I totally wasn't used to it yet (would I ever be?) and there had been times when I wondered if it was worth it. But then I'd catch his quick smile from the corner of my eye, or feel the tiniest squeeze on my arm, and I'd be grounded. After all, the flashing lights weren't so blinding as long as we kept our eyes on each other.

# Acknowledgments

Many thanks to our brilliant agent, Allison Hunter, for her endless enthusiasm, support, and guidance. Thank you to our editor, Maddie Caldwell, for turning a fantasy romance into something that feels real and messy and tangible, as well as the rest of the Grand Central Publishing team. Special thanks, too, to Kristin Dwyer.

Thanks to the forever-1DAF, for never tiring of gushing about what the boys are up to—especially Mackenzie Kruvant, Logan Sachon, Alana Massey, Abby Armada, Matt Bellassai, and Jackie DeStefano. Thank you to Erin Chack, for always knowing when a walk (and talk) is needed. Thank you to the BuzzFeed editors who let us basically write fan fic on the site: Summer Anne Burton, Isaac Fitzgerald, Jack Shepherd, you guys get it. And, of course, big thanks to the boys who've had us creating fan fic in our heads since before we knew what fan fic was: Harry, Justin, Orlando, et. al.; our fake relationships have been magnificent.

**Arianna wants to thank:**

Her real boyfriend, Brendan Newell: Thank you for turning our home into a space of encouragement, love, and creativity;

for humoring my excessive fangirling; and for showing me that real relationships are so much better than the fantasy. You are the ultimate hunk.

Her first partner in boy band obsession, Emily Roberts: You taught me how fun it could be.

Her family: Mom, Dad, Nenns, Jordan, Dylan. You are at the core of everything I do, you make it all possible.

And finally, Katie Heaney, a million times: Thank you, thank you, for being the best friend and creative partner a woman could dream of. You make me a better writer and thinker and person, and every day I'm grateful that four years ago I didn't care how creepy it might look to email you and tell you we should be friends. Look at us now!!! I can't wait for everything that comes next.

**Katie wants to thank:**

Arianna Rebolini, the Rose to her Harper (even though we both know Arianna is the stylish one). Writing this book was a joy from start to finish, in large part thanks to your friendship, support, and talent. I am so glad we thought up Rose on that hike, and even gladder that we met in the first place. I can't wait to do this 500 more times!!

Her family: Mom, Dad, Joe, and Dan. Thank you for your continual support and love.

Her girlfriend, Lydia. Thanks for listening patiently, and enthusiastically, while Arianna and I performed scenes from the book out loud. Thanks also for sending me gifs of Harry Styles and pictures of you in which you look like Harry Styles. You're a dreamboat.

# About the Authors

**Katie Heaney** is a senior editor at BuzzFeed whose writing has appeared in *Cosmopolitan*, Vulture, The Hairpin, The Awl, and Pacific Standard, among other places. She is the author of the memoir *Never Have I Ever* and the novel *Dear Emma*. She lives in Brooklyn.

**Arianna Rebolini** is a writer and editor whose work has been published in *The Guardian*, The Hairpin, and at BuzzFeed. She lives in Brooklyn.